Praise for *A Maiden's Grave*

"Outstanding, gripping, brilliant, spectacular . . . a plot with double-whammy twists . . . a great thriller."
—*Publishers Weekly*

"Wonderful, riveting, vivid . . . rings with an atmosphere of haunting realism."
—Steve Martini, author of *The Judge*

"A stunner. . . . Deaver ignites diabolical new fireworks that will leave you agog."
—*Kirkus Reviews*

"Hits hard and keeps hitting . . . readers who bite their fingernails might lose some fingers."
—John Lutz, author of *Single White Female*

"A gripping page-turner that deserves to be read in a single sitting."
—*Denver Post*

"A violent and especially well done thriller. . . . Deaver gets it all right."
—*St. Louis Post-Dispatch*

More Praise . . .

"Deaver does a great job of methodically building the tension while dribbling bits of his main characters' histories and skillfully orchestrating their clashes. Grabs the reader right up front and delivers a tension-filled ride that doesn't stop until the last page is turned. Definitely a stay-up all-night read."

—*Houston Chronicle*

"*A Maiden's Grave* is an effective hostage thriller, as dramatically entertaining as any you will read this year. A first-rate thriller that grabs readers and holds them until the final page. Readers will be absorbed."

—*The Observer*

"A winner. Thoroughly recommended."

—*Mystery Lover's Bookshop Newsletter*

"A powerhouse novel that will not only chill to the bone with a sense of menace and evil, but also echo through the mind on many other levels."

—*Arizona Daily Star*

"A gripping page-turner that deserves to be read in one sitting."

—*Purloined Letter*

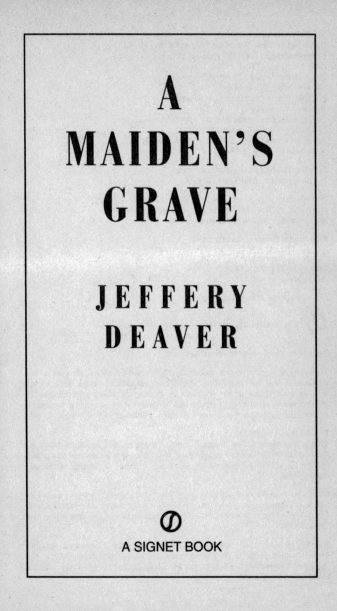

A
MAIDEN'S
GRAVE

JEFFERY
DEAVER

A SIGNET BOOK

SIGNET
Published by New American Library, a division of
Penguin Putnam Inc., 375 Hudson Street,
New York, New York 10014, U.S.A.
Penguin Books Ltd, 27 Wrights Lane,
London W8 5TZ, England
Penguin Books Australia Ltd, Ringwood,
Victoria, Australia
Penguin Books Canada Ltd, 10 Alcorn Avenue,
Toronto, Ontario, Canada M4V 3B2
Penguin Books (N.Z.) Ltd, 182–190 Wairau Road,
Auckland 10, New Zealand

Penguin Books Ltd, Registered Offices:
Harmondsworth, Middlesex, England

Published by Signet, an imprint of New American Library,
a division of Penguin Putnam Inc. This book previously
appeared in a Viking hardcover edition.

First Signet Printing, October 1996
20 19 18 17 16

Map design by Jeffrey L. Ward

Ⓟ REGISTERED TRADEMARK—MARCA REGISTRADA

Printed in the United States of America

PUBLISHER'S NOTE
This is a work of fiction. Names, characters, places, and incidents either are
the product of the author's imagination or are used fictitiously, and any resem-
blance to actual persons, living or dead, events, or locales is entirely
coincidental.

*To Diana Keene, for being
an inspiration, a discerning critic,
a part of my books, a part of my life,
with all my love.*

ACKNOWLEDGMENTS

I'd like to give special thanks to Pamela Dorman at Viking, an editor with the persistence and patience (not to mention just plain guts) to keep authors striving for the same level of excellence she achieves in her craft. My deepest appreciation too to Deborah Schneider, dear friend and the best agent in the world. And to the entire Viking/NAL crew, especially Barbara Grossman, Elaine Koster, Michaela Hamilton, Joe Pittman, Cathy Hemming, Matthew Bradley (who's earned the title Combat Publicist a hundred times over), and Susan Hans O'Connor. No mention of gratitude would be complete without acknowledging the fine folks at Curtis Brown in London, especially Diana Mackay and Vivienne Schuster, and at my top-notch British publisher, Hodder-Headline, notably my editor, Carolyn Mays, and Sue Fletcher and Peter Lavery. Thanks to Cathy Gleason at Gelfman-Schneider, and thanks and a "hey" to my grandmother Ethel Rider and my sister and fellow author, Julie Reece Deaver, and to Tracey, Kerry, David, Taylor, Lisa (Ms. X-Man), Casey, Chris, and Bryan Big and Bryan Little.

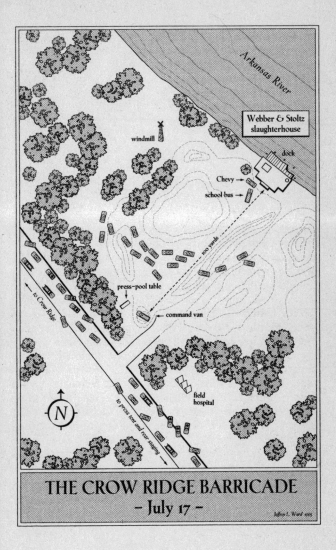

Arkansas River

Webber & Stoltz
slaughterhouse

dock

windmill

Chevy →

school bus →

100 yards

press-pool table

to Crow Ridge

← command van

field hospital

N

to press tent and Icon staging →

THE CROW RIDGE BARRICADE
- July 17 -

Jeffrey L. Ward 1995

I

THE KILLING
ROOM

8:30 A.M.

"Eight gray birds, sitting in dark.
    Cold wind blows, it isn't kind."

The small yellow school bus crested an abrupt rise on the highway and for a moment all she could see was a huge quilt of pale wheat, a thousand miles wide, waving, waving under the gray sky. Then they dipped down once again and the horizon was gone.

"Sitting on wire, they lift their wings
    and sail off into billowy clouds."

When she paused she looked at the girls, who nodded approvingly. She realized that she'd been staring at the thick pelt of wheat and ignoring her audience.

"Are you nervous?" Shannon asked.

"Don't ask her that," Beverly warned. "Bad luck."

No, Melanie explained, she wasn't nervous. She looked out again at the fields that streamed past.

Three of the girls were drowsing but the other five were wide awake and waiting for her to continue. Melanie began again but was interrupted before she'd recited the first line of the poem.

"Wait—what kind of birds are they?" Kielle frowned.

"Don't interrupt." From seventeen-year-old Susan. "People who interrupt are Philistines."

"Am not!" Kielle shot back. "What is that?"

"Crass dummy," Susan explained.

"What's 'crass'?" Kielle demanded.

"Let her finish!"

Melanie continued:

"Eight little birds high in sky,
They fly all night till they find sun."

"Time out." Susan laughed. "It was *five* birds yesterday."

"Now *you're* interrupting," lean tomboy Shannon pointed out. "You Philadelphian."

"Philistine," Susan corrected.

Chubby Jocylyn nodded emphatically as if she also had caught the slip but was too timid to point it out. Jocylyn was too timid to do very much at all.

"But there are eight of you so I changed it."

"Can you do that?" wondered Beverly. At fourteen, she was the second-oldest student.

"It's *my* poem," Melanie responded. "I can make it as many birds as I want."

"How many people will be there? At recital?"

"One hundred thousand." Melanie looked quite sincere.

"No! Really?" offered enthusiastic eight-year-old Shannon, as a much older eight-year-old Kielle rolled her eyes.

Melanie's gaze was again drawn to the bleak scenery of south-central Kansas. The only color was the occasional blue Harvestore prefab silo. It was July but the weather was cold and heavily overcast; rain threatened. They passed huge combines and buses filled with migrant workers, their Porta-Pottis wheeling along behind. They saw landowners and sharecroppers, piloting their huge Deeres, Masseys, and IHs. Melanie imagined them glancing nervously at the sky; this was harvest time for the winter wheat, and a storm now could ruin eight months of arduous work.

Melanie turned away from the window and self-consciously examined her fingernails, which she trimmed and filed religiously every night. They were coated with faint polish and looked like perfect flakes of pearl. She lifted her hands and recited several poems again, signing the words elegantly. Now all the girls were awake, four looking out the windows, three watching Melanie's fingers, and round Jocylyn Weiderman watching her teacher's every move.

These fields go on forever, Melanie thought. Susan's gaze followed Melanie's. "They're blackbirds," the teenager signed. "Crows."

Yes, they were. Not five or eight, but a thousand, a flock of them. The birds watched the ground, the yellow bus, and the overcast sky, gray and purple.

Melanie looked at her watch. They weren't even to the highway yet. It would be three hours before they got to Topeka.

The bus descended into another canyon of wheat.

She sensed the trouble before a single clue registered in her conscious thoughts. Later she would conclude that it was no psychic message or premonition; it was Mrs. Harstrawn's big, ruddy fingers flexing anxiously on the steering wheel.

Hands, in motion.

Then the older woman's eyes narrowed slightly. Her shoulders shifted. Her head tilted a millimeter. The small things a body does that reveal what the mind is thinking.

"Are girls asleep?" The question was blunt and the fingers returned immediately to the wheel. Melanie scooted forward and signed that they weren't.

Now the twins, Anna and Suzie, delicate as feathers, were sitting up, leaning forward, breathing on the older teacher's broad shoulders, looking ahead. Mrs. Harstrawn waved them back. "Don't look. Sit back and look out opposite window. Do it. Now! The left window."

Then Melanie saw the car. And the blood. There was a lot of it. She shepherded the girls back to their seats.

"Don't look," Melanie instructed. Her heart pounded fiercely, her arms suddenly weighed a thousand pounds. "And put seatbelts on." She had trouble making the words.

Jocylyn, Beverly, and ten-year-old Emily did as instructed immediately. Shannon grimaced and peeked, Kielle blatantly ignored Melanie. Susan got to look, she pointed out. Why couldn't *she?*

Of the twins, it was Anna who'd gone still, hands in her lap and her face paler than usual, in sharp contrast to her sister's nut-brown tan. Melanie stroked the girl's hair.

She pointed out the window on the left side of the bus. "Look at wheat," she instructed.

"Totally interesting," Shannon replied sarcastically.

"Those poor people." Twelve-year-old Jocylyn wiped copious tears from her fat cheeks.

The burgundy Cadillac had run hard into a metal irrigation gate. Steam rose from its front end. The driver was an elderly man. He lay sprawled half out of the car, his head on the asphalt. Melanie could now see a second car as well, a gray Chevy. The collision had happened at an intersection. It looked like the Cadillac had had the right of way and had slammed into the gray car, which must have run a stop sign. The Chevy had skidded off the road into the tall wheat. There was no one inside; its hood was twisted and steam plumed from the radiator.

Mrs. Harstrawn brought the bus to a stop, reached for the worn chrome handle of the door.

No! thought Melanie. Keep going! Go to a grocery store, a 7-Eleven, a house. They hadn't passed anything for miles but surely there was something up ahead. Don't stop. Keep going. She'd been thinking those words but her hands must have been moving because Susan responded, "No, we have to. He is hurt."

But the blood, Melanie thought. They shouldn't get his blood on them. There was AIDS, there were other diseases.

These people needed help but they needed *official* help. *Eight gray birds, sitting in dark . . .*

Susan, eight years younger than Melanie, was the first one out of the school bus, running toward the injured man, her long, black hair dancing around her in the gusting wind.

Then Mrs. Harstrawn.

Melanie hung back, staring. The driver lay like a sawdust doll, one leg bent at a terrible angle. Head floppy, hands fat and pale.

She had never before seen a dead body.

But he isn't dead, of course. No, no, just a cut. It's nothing. He's just fainted.

One by one the little girls turned to gaze at the accident; Kielle and Shannon first, naturally—the Dynamic Duo, the

Power Rangers, the X-Men. Then fragile Emily, whose hands were glued together in prayer. (Her parents insisted that she pray every night for her hearing to return. She had told this to Melanie but no one else.) Beverly clutched her chest, an instinctive gesture. She wasn't having an attack just yet.

Melanie climbed out and walked toward the Cadillac. Halfway there she slowed. In contrast to the gray sky, the gray wheat, and the pale highway, the blood was so very red; it was on everything—the man's bald head, his chest, the car door, the yellow leather seat.

The roller coaster of fear sent her heart plummeting toward the ground.

Mrs. Harstrawn was the mother of two teenage boys, a humorless woman, smart, dependable, solid as vulcanized rubber. She reached under her colorful sweater, untucked her blouse and tore off a strip, making an impromptu bandage, which she wrapped around a deep gash in the man's torn head. She bent down and whispered into his ear, pressed on his chest and breathed into his mouth.

And then she listened.

I can't hear, Melanie thought, so I can't help. There's nothing I can do. I'll go back to the bus. Keep an eye on the girls. The roller coaster of her fear leveled out. Good, good.

Susan crouched too, stanching a wound on his neck. Frowning, the student looked up at Mrs. Harstrawn. With bloody fingers she signed, "Why bleeding so much? Look at neck."

Mrs. Harstrawn examined it. She too frowned, shaking her head.

"There's hole in his neck," the teacher signed in astonishment. "Like a bullet hole."

Melanie gasped at this message. The flimsy car of the roller coaster dropped again, leaving Melanie's stomach somewhere else—way, way above her. She stopped walking altogether.

Then she saw the purse.

Ten feet away.

Thankful for any distraction to keep her eyes off the injured man, she walked over to the bag and examined it.

The chain pattern on the cloth was some designer's. Melanie Charrol—a farm girl who made sixteen thousand, five hundred dollars a year as an apprentice teacher of the deaf—had never in her twenty-five years touched a designer accessory. Because the purse was small it seemed precious. Like a radiant jewel. It was the sort of purse that a woman would sling over her shoulder when she walked into an office high above downtown Kansas City or even Manhattan or Los Angeles. The sort of purse she'd drop onto a desk and from which she'd pull a silver pen to write a few words that would set assistants and secretaries in motion.

But as Melanie stared at the purse a tiny thought formed in her mind, growing, growing until it blossomed: Where was the woman who owned it?

That was when the shadow fell on her.

He wasn't a tall man, or fat, but he seemed very solid: muscled the way horses have muscle, close to the skin, rippled and defined. Melanie gasped, staring at his smooth young face. He wore a glossy crewcut and clothes gray as the clouds speeding by overhead. The grin was broad and showed white teeth and she didn't believe the smile for a second.

Melanie's first impression was that he resembled a fox. No, she concluded, a weasel or a stoat. There was a pistol in the waistband of his baggy slacks. She gasped and lifted her hands. Not to her face but to her chest. "Please, don't hurt me," she signed without thinking. He glanced at her moving hands and laughed.

From the corner of her eye she saw Susan and Mrs. Harstrawn stand uneasily. A second man was striding up to them; he was huge. Fat and tall. Also dressed in overwashed gray. Shaggy hair. He was missing a tooth and his grin was hungry. A bear, she thought automatically.

"Go," Melanie signed to Susan. "Let's go. Now." Eyes on the yellow skin of the bus, she started walking toward the seven unhappy young faces staggered in the windows.

Stoat grabbed her by the collar. She batted at his hand, but cautiously, afraid to hit him, afraid of his anger.

He shouted something she didn't understand and shook her. The grin became what the grin really was—a cold glare. His face went dark. Melanie sagged in terror and dropped her hand.

"What's ... this?" Bear said. "I'm thinking we ... about that."

Melanie was postlingually deaf. She began losing her hearing at age eight, after her language skills were honed. She was a better lipreader than most of the girls. But lipreading is a very iffy skill, far more complicated than merely watching lips. The process involves interpreting movements of the mouth, tongue, teeth, eyes, and other parts of the body. It is truly effective only if you know the person whose words you are trying to decipher. Bear existed in a different universe from Melanie's life of Old English decor, Celestial Seasonings tea and small-town, midwestern schools. And she had no idea what he was saying.

The big man laughed and spit in a white stream. His eyes coursed over her body—her breasts beneath the high-necked burgundy blouse, her long charcoal-gray skirt, black tights. She awkwardly crossed her arms. Bear turned his attention back to Mrs. Harstrawn and Susan.

Stoat was leaning forward, speaking—probably shouting, as people often did with the Deaf (which was all right because they spoke more slowly and their lip motion was more pronounced when they shouted). He was asking who was in the bus. Melanie didn't move. She couldn't. Her sweaty fingers gripped her biceps.

Bear looked down at the injured man's battered face and tapped his booted foot lethargically against the head, watching it loll back and forth. Melanie gasped; the casualness of the kick, its gratuitousness, was horrifying. She started to cry. Bear pushed Susan and Mrs. Harstrawn ahead of him toward the bus.

Melanie glanced at Susan and shot her hands into the air. "No, don't!"

But Susan was already moving.

Her perfect figure and runner's body.

Her one hundred and twelve muscular pounds.

Her strong hands.

As the girl's palm swung toward Bear's face he jerked his head back in surprise and caught her hand inches from his eyes. The surprise became amusement and he bent her arm downward until she dropped to her knees then he shoved her to the ground, filthying her black jeans and white blouse with dust and mud. Bear turned to Stoat and called out something.

"Susan, don't!" Melanie signed.

The teenager was on her feet again. But Bear was prepared this time and turned to meet her. When he grabbed her his hand found her breasts and lingered there for a moment. Suddenly, he grew tired of the game. He hit her solidly in the stomach and she dropped to her knees, clutching herself and struggling for breath.

"No!" Melanie signed to her. "Don't fight."

Stoat called to Bear, "Where . . . he?"

Bear motioned toward a wall of wheat. He had a curious expression on his face—as if he didn't approve of something but was afraid to be too critical. "Don't . . . time . . . this bullshit," he muttered. Melanie followed his eyes and looked into the shafts of wheat. She couldn't see clearly but from the shadows and dim outlines it appeared to be a man, bending down. He was small and wiry. It seemed that his arm was raised, like in one of those Nazi salutes. It remained poised there for a long moment. Beneath him, she thought, was the form of a person, dressed in dark green.

The woman who owned the purse, Melanie understood in a terrible flash.

No, please, no . . .

The man's arm descended leisurely. Through the undulating wheat she saw the dull glint of metal in his hand.

Stoat's head bent slightly; he'd heard a sudden noise. He winced. Bear's face broke into a smile. Mrs. Harstrawn's hands rose to her ears, covering them. Horrified. Mrs. Harstrawn could hear perfectly.

Melanie stared into the wheat, crying. She saw: The shadowy figure crouching lower, over the woman. The elegant movement of the tall wheat, swaying in the intemperate July wind. The motion of the man's arm rising and falling slowly, once, twice. His face studying the body lying in front of him.

Mrs. Harstrawn fixed Stoat with a stoic gaze. ". . . us go and . . . won't bother you. We won't . . ."

Melanie was comforted to see the woman's defiance, her anger. The sturdy set of her jaw.

Stoat and Bear ignored her. They herded Susan, Mrs. Harstrawn, and Melanie toward the bus.

Inside, the younger girls huddled in the back. Bear pushed Mrs. Harstrawn and Susan inside and gestured toward his belt, where his gun bulged. Melanie was the last person inside before Stoat, who shoved her into the back. She tripped and fell on top of the sobbing twins. She hugged them hard then gathered Emily and Shannon into her arms.

The Outside . . . Caught in the terrible Outside.

Melanie glanced at Stoat and saw him say, "Deaf as . . . all of them." Bear squeezed his fat torso into the driver's seat and started the bus. He looked in the rearview mirror and frowned then spun around.

In the distance, at the end of the ribbon of asphalt, was a dot of flashing lights. Bear pressed the pad on the steering wheel and Melanie felt the vibrations of the horn in her chest.

Bear said, "Man, what the fuck's . . . think we . . ." Then he turned his head and the words were lost.

Stoat shouted toward the wheat. He nodded when, apparently, the man answered. A moment later the gray Chevy sped out of the field. Badly damaged but still drivable, it rolled onto the shoulder, paused. Melanie tried to glance into the front seat for a glimpse of the man behind the wheat but there was too much glare. It appeared there was no driver at all.

Then the car accelerated fast, fishtailing onto the asphalt. The bus followed, easing forward into the faint clouds of blue tire smoke. Bear slapped the steering wheel, turned for a moment and barked some words to Melanie—angry words, vicious words. But she had no idea what they might be.

The brilliant flashing lights grew closer, red and blue and white. Like the Fourth of July fireworks over the park in Hebron two weeks ago, when she'd watched the streamers of color crisscross the sky, felt the explosions of the white-hot bangs against her skin.

She looked back at the police car and knew what would happen. There'd be a hundred squad cars all converging up ahead. They'd pull the bus over and these men would get out. They'd put their hands up and be led off. The students and teachers would go down to a stationhouse somewhere and make statements. She'd miss the Theater of the Deaf performance in Topeka this time—even if they still had time to make it—but there was no way she'd get up on stage and recite poetry after all of this.

And the other reason for her trip?

Maybe it was a sign that she shouldn't go, shouldn't have made those plans. It was an omen.

All she wanted to do now was go home. Back to her rented house, where she could lock the door and have a cup of tea. Okay, a hit of blackberry brandy. Fax her brother in the hospital in St. Louis, tell him and her parents the story. Melanie fell into a nervous habit, twining her blond hair around her bent middle finger, the other digits extended. This hand shape was the symbol for "shine."

Then there was a sudden jolt. Bear had turned off the asphalt and was following the gray car down a dirt road. Stoat was frowning. He asked Bear something Melanie didn't see. The big man didn't answer but just spit out the window. Another turn and another, into hillier country. Getting close to the river.

They passed under an electric wire covered with a hundred birds. Big ones. Crows.

She looked at the car ahead of them. She still couldn't see him clearly—the driver, the man from the wheat field. At first Melanie thought he had long hair, then a moment later he seemed bald or crew-cut, then appeared to be wearing a hat.

With a skidding turn the gray car spun to the right and bounded down a narrow weed-filled driveway. Melanie guessed that he'd seen the dozens of police cars up ahead—the cars racing toward them to save them. She squinted and looked. No, nothing ahead of them. The bus turned and followed the Chevy. Bear was muttering, Stoat was looking back at the police car.

Then Melanie turned and saw where they were headed.

No! she thought.

Oh, please no.

For she knew her hope about the men surrendering to the trooper who was fast approaching was just a fantasy. She understood where they were going.

The worst place in the world.

The gray car suddenly broke into a large, weed-filled field. At the end of the field, on the river, squatted a red-brick industrial building, long abandoned. Dark and solid as a medieval fort. The acreage in front of the plant still held a few of the fences and posts from the animal pens that had subdivided the area long ago but mostly the field had been reclaimed by the Kansas prairie of mid-high grass, sedge, bluestem, and buffalo grass.

The Chevy raced right for the front of the building, the bus following. Both skidded to a stop just to the left of the door.

Melanie peered at the ruddy brick.

When she was eighteen, and a student herself at the Laurent Clerc School, a boy had brought her here, supposedly for a picnic but of course to do what boys of eighteen will do—and what Melanie too wanted, she believed at the time. But once they'd snuck inside, carting a blanket with them, she'd looked at the gloomy rooms and panicked. She'd fled and had never seen the perplexed boy, or the building, again.

But she remembered it. An abandoned slaughterhouse, a place of death. A place that was hard and sharp and dangerous.

And dark. How Melanie hated the dark. (Twenty-five years old and she had five night-lights in a six-room house.)

Stoat flung open the bus door, dragged Susan and Mrs. Harstrawn out after him.

The police car—a single trooper inside—paused at the entrance to the field. He leapt out, pistol in his hand, but he stopped short when Bear grabbed Shannon and put a gun to her head. The eight-year-old surprised him by spinning around, kicking his knee hard. He flinched in pain then shook her until she stopped squirming. Bear looked across the field at the trooper, who made a show of putting his gun back into his holster and returning to his car.

Bear and Stoat pushed the girls toward the slaughter-house door. Bear slammed a rock into the chain that bound the door closed and snapped the rusted links. Stoat grabbed several large bags from the trunk of the gray car, where the driver continued to sit, staring up at the building. The glare still prevented Melanie from seeing clearly but he seemed relaxed, gazing with curiosity at the turrets and black windows.

Bear yanked open the front door and he and Stoat pushed the girls inside. The place stank of cave more than building. Dirt and shit and mold and some sweet-sickly decay, rancid animal fat. The interior was a maze of walkways and pens and ramps and rusted machinery. Pits surrounded by railings and parts of old machines. There were rows and rows of rusted meat hooks overhead. And it was just as dark as Melanie remembered.

Bear herded the students and their teachers into a semi-circular, tiled room, windowless and damp. The walls and cement floors were stained dark brown. A worn wooden ramp led to the left side of the room. An overhead conveyor holding meat hooks led away from the right side. In the center was a drain for the blood.

This was the room where the animals had been killed.

Cold wind blows, it isn't kind.

Kielle grabbed Melanie's arm and pressed against her. Mrs. Harstrawn and Susan embraced the other girls, Susan gazing with raw hatred at whichever of the men happened to catch her eye. Jocylyn sobbed, the twins too. Beverly struggled for breath.

Eight gray birds with nowhere to go.

They huddled in a cluster on the cold, damp floor. A rat scurried away, his fur dull, like a piece of old meat. Then the door opened again. Melanie shielded her eyes against the glare.

He stood in the cold light of the doorway.

Short and thin.

Neither bald nor long-haired but with shaggy, dirty-blond strands framing a gaunt face. Unlike the others he wore only a T-shirt, on which was stenciled the name L. Handy. But to her he wasn't a Handy at all—and definitely not a Larry or a Lou. She thought immediately of the actor in the Kansas State Theater of the Deaf who had played Brutus in a recent production of *Julius Caesar*.

He pushed inside and carefully placed two heavy canvas bags on the floor. The door swung shut and once the ashen light vanished she could see his pale eyes and thin mouth.

Melanie saw Bear say, "Why . . . here, man? No fucking way out."

Then, as if she could hear perfectly, Brutus's words sounded clearly in her mind, the phantom voice that deaf people hear sometimes—a human voice yet with no real human sound. "It don't matter," he said slowly. "Nope. Don't matter at all."

Melanie was the one he looked at when he said this and it was to her that he offered a faint smile before he pointed to several rusty iron bars and ordered the other two men to wedge the doors tightly shut.

9:10 A.M.

He'd never forgotten an anniversary in twenty-three years.

Here's a husband for you.

Arthur Potter folded back the paper surrounding the roses—effervescent flowers, orange and yellow—mostly open, the petals perfect, floppy, billowing. He smelled them. Marian's favorite. Vibrant colors. Never white or red.

The stoplight changed. He set the bouquet carefully on the seat beside him and accelerated through the intersection. His hand strayed to his belly, which pressed hard against his waistband. He screwed up his face. His belt

was a barometer; it was hooked through the second-
to-the-last hole in the worn leather. Diet on Monday, he
told himself cheerfully. He'd be back in D.C. then, his
cousin's fine cooking long digested, and could concentrate on counting grams of fat once more.

It was Linden's fault. Let's see . . . last night she'd made
corned beef, buttered potatoes, buttered cabbage, soda
bread (butter optional, and he'd opted), lima beans, grilled
tomatoes, chocolate cake with vanilla ice cream. Linden
was Marian's cousin, in the lineage of the McGillis fore-
bear Sean, whose two sons, Eamon and Hardy, came over
in steerage, married within the same year and whose wives
gave birth to daughters, ten and eleven months, respec-
tively, after the vows.

Arthur Potter, an only child orphaned at thirteen, son of
only children, had enthusiastically adopted his wife's
family and had spent years plotting the genealogy of the
McGillises. Through elaborate correspondence (handwritten on fine stationery; he did not own a word processor) Potter kept up religiously, almost superstitiously,
with the meanderings of the clan.

Congress Expressway west. Then south. Hands at ten to
two, hunched forward, glasses perched on his pale fleshy
nose, Potter cruised through working-class Chicago, the
tenements and flats and two-family row houses lit by the
midwestern summer light, pale in the overcast.

The quality of light in different cities, he thought.
Arthur Potter had been around the world many times and
had a huge stockpile of ideas for travel articles he would
never write. Genealogy notes and memos for his job, from
which he was soon to retire, would probably be the only
Potter literary legacy.

Turn here, turn there. He drove automatically and
somewhat carelessly. He was by nature impatient but had
long ago overcome that vice, if a vice it was, and he never
strayed above the posted limit.

Turning the rented Ford onto Austin Avenue, he
glanced in his rearview mirror and noticed the car.

The men were in a blue-gray sedan, as nonde-
script as could be. Two clean-shaven, clean-living, clean-
conscienced young men, and they were tailing him.

They had Federal Agent printed on their foreheads.

Potter's heart thudded. "Damn," he muttered in his low baritone. Furious, he tugged at a jowl and then wrapped the green paper tighter around the flowers as if anticipating a high-speed chase. When he found the street he sought, however, and made the turn, he was doing seven cautious miles per hour. His wife's bouquet rolled against his ample thigh.

No, he didn't speed. His strategy was to decide that he was mistaken, that the car contained two businessmen on their way to sell computers or printing services and that it would turn off on its own route soon.

And leave me in peace.

But the car didn't do any such thing. The men maintained an innocuous distance, traveling at the identical, irritatingly slow speed of Potter's Ford.

He pulled into the familiar driveway and continued a lengthy distance, then rolled to a stop. Potter climbed out of his car quickly, cradling the flowers to his chest and waddling up the walk—defiantly, he hoped, daring the agents to stop him here.

How had they found him?

He'd been so clever. Parking the car three blocks from Linden's apartment. Asking her not to answer the phone and to leave her machine off. The fifty-one-year-old woman, who'd be a Gypsy if she could have rearranged her genes (so different from Marian, despite their common blood), excitedly accepted his instructions. She was used to the inexplicable ways of her cousin-in-law. She believed his manner was somewhat dangerous, if not sinister, and he could hardly dissuade her of that, for so it was.

The agents parked their car behind Potter's and climbed out. He heard their footsteps on the gravel behind him.

They didn't hurry; they could find him anywhere, and they knew it. He could never get away.

I'm yours, you self-confident sons of bitches.

"Mr. Potter."

No, no, go away! Not today. Today is special. It's my wedding anniversary. Twenty-three years. When you're as old as I am you'll understand.

Leave. Me. Alone.

"Mr. Potter?"

The young men were interchangeable. He ignored one and thus he ignored both.

He walked over the lawn toward his wife. Marian, he thought, I'm sorry for this. I've brought trouble with me. I am sorry.

"Leave me alone," he whispered. And suddenly, as if they'd heard, both men stopped, these two somber men, in dark suits, with pale complexions. Potter knelt and laid the flowers on the grave. He began to peel back the green paper but he could still see the young men in the corner of his eye and he paused, squeezing his eyes closed and pressing his hands to his face.

He wasn't praying. Arthur Potter never prayed. He used to. Occasionally. Although his livelihood entitled him to some secret, personal superstitions he'd stopped praying thirteen years ago, the day Marian the living became Marian the dead, passing away in front of his joined fingertips as he happened to be in the middle of an elaborate negotiation with the God he had, all his life, more or less believed existed. The address he'd been sending his offers to turned out to be empty as a rusted can. He was neither surprised nor disillusioned. Still, he gave up praying.

Now, eyes closed, he lifted those same fingertips and gave a backhanded wave, warding off the indistinguishable men.

And federal agents, yes, but God-fearing agents perhaps (many of them were), they kept their distance.

No prayers, but he spoke some words to his bride, lying in the same place where she had lain for these long years. His lips moved. He received responses only because he knew her mind as well as his own. But the presence of the men in the matching suits kept intruding. Finally he rose slowly and looked at the marble flower etched into the granite above her tombstone. He'd ordered a rose but the flower looked like a chrysanthemum. Perhaps the stonecarver had been Japanese.

There was no point in delaying any longer.

"Mr. Potter?"

He sighed and turned away from the grave.

"I'm Special Agent McGovern. This is Special Agent Crowley."

"Yes."

"Sorry to trouble you, sir. Mind if we have a word?"

McGovern added, "Maybe we could step to the car."

"What do you want?"

"The car? Please." No one says "please" quite the way an FBI agent does.

Potter walked with them—he was flanked—to their vehicle. He realized only when he was standing beside it that the wind was steady and ridiculously cold for July. He glanced at the grave and saw the green paper of the flowers roll in the steady breeze.

"All right." He stopped abruptly, deciding to walk no further.

"We're sorry to interrupt your vacation, sir. We tried to call the number where you're staying. There was no answer."

"Did you send somebody over there?" Potter was worried that Linden would be upset if agents came calling.

"Yessir, but when we found you we radioed them."

Potter nodded. He looked at his watch. They were going to have shepherd's pie tonight. Green salad. He was supposed to pick up something to drink. Samuel Smith Nut Brown Ale for him, oatmeal stout for them. Then, after dinner, cards with the Holbergs next door. Hearts or spades.

"How bad is it?" Potter asked.

"A situation in Kansas," McGovern said.

"It's bad, sir. He's asked you to put together a threat management team. There's a DomTran jet waiting for you at Glenview. Particulars are in here."

Potter took the sealed envelope from the young man, looking down, seeing to his surprise a dot of blood on his own thumb—from, he supposed, a latent thorn somewhere on the stem of a rose with petals like a woman's floppy-brimmed summer hat.

He opened the envelope and read through the fax. It bore the speedy signature of the director of the Federal Bureau of Investigation.

"How long since he went barricade?"

"First report was around eight forty-five."

"Any communication from him?"

"None yet."

"Contained?"

"Completely. Kansas state troopers and a half-dozen agents from our Wichita office. They're not getting out."

Potter buttoned then unbuttoned his sports coat. He realized that the agents were looking at him with too much reverence and it set his teeth on edge. "I'll want Henry LeBow as my intelligence officer and Tobe Geller for communications. Spelled with an *e* but you pronounce it Toby."

"Yessir. If they're unavailable—"

"Only them. Find them. Wherever they are. I want them at the barricade in a half-hour. And see if Angie Scapello is available. She'd be at headquarters or Quantico. Behavioral Science. Jet her out too."

"Yessir."

"What's the status of HRT?"

The Bureau's Hostage Rescue Team, consisting of forty-eight agents, was the largest tactical barricade force in the country.

Crowley let McGovern deliver the unfortunate news.

"That's a problem, sir. One team's deployed to Miami. A DEA raid. Twenty-two agents there. And the second's in Seattle. A bank robbery that went barricade last night. Nineteen there. We can scramble a third team but we'll have to pull some agents off the other two. It'll be a while before they're assembled on site."

"Call Quantico, put it together. I'll call Frank from the plane. Where is he?"

"The Seattle incident," the agent told him. "If you want us to meet you at the apartment so you can pack a bag, sir . . ."

"No, I'll go right to Glenview. Do you have a siren and light?"

"Yessir. But your cousin's apartment's only fifteen minutes from here—"

"Say, if one of you could take the paper off those flowers, there on that grave, I'd appreciate it. Maybe arrange them a little, make sure the wind doesn't blow them away."

"Yessir, I'll do that," Crowley said quickly. So there *was* a difference between them; McGovern, Potter realized, was not a flower arranger.

"Thank you so much."

Potter started down the path again, following McGovern. The one thing he'd have to stop for was chewing gum. Those military jets climbed so fast his ears filled up like pressure cookers if he didn't chew a whole pack of Wrigley's as soon as the wheels left the asphalt. How he hated to fly.

Oh, I'm tired, he thought. So damn tired.

"I'll be back, Marian," he whispered, not looking toward the grave. "I'll be back."

II

THE RULES OF
ENGAGEMENT

10:35 A.M.

As always, an element of circus.

Arthur Potter stood beside the FBI resident agency's best car, a Ford Taurus, and surveyed the scene. Police cars drawn into a circle like pioneers' wagons, press minivans, the reporters holding their chunky cameras like rocket launchers. There were fire trucks everywhere (Waco was on everyone's mind).

Three more government-issue sedans arrived in caravan, bringing the total FBI count to eleven. Half the men were in navy-blue tactical outfits, the rest in their pseudo Brooks Brothers.

The military jet bearing Potter, reserved for civilian government transport, had touched down in Wichita twenty minutes before and he'd transferred to a helicopter for the eighty-mile flight northwest to the tiny town of Crow Ridge.

Kansas was just as flat as he'd expected, though the chopper's route took them along a wide river surrounded by trees, and much of the ground here was hilly. This, the pilot told him, was where the mid-high-grass and short-grass prairies met. To the west had been buffalo country. He pointed toward a dot that was Larned, where a hundred years ago a herd of four million had been sighted. The pilot reported this fact with unmistakable pride.

They'd sped over huge farms, one- and two-thousand-acre spreads. July seemed early for harvest but hundreds of red and green-and-yellow combines were shaving the countryside of the wheat crop.

Now, standing in the chill wind beneath a dense overcast sky, Potter was struck by the relentless bleakness of this place, which he would have traded in an instant to be back amid the Windy City tenements he'd left not long before. A hundred yards away was a red brick industrial building, like a castle, probably a hundred years old. In front of it sat a small school bus and a battered gray car.

"What's the building?" Potter asked Henderson, special agent in charge of the FBI's Wichita resident agency.

"An old slaughterhouse," the SAC responded. "They'd drive herds from western Kansas and Texas up here, slaughter 'em, then barge the carcasses down to Wichita."

The wind slapped them hard, a one-two punch. Potter wasn't expecting it and stepped back to keep his balance.

"They've lent us that, the state boys." The large, handsome man was nodding at a van that resembled a UPS delivery truck, painted olive drab. It was on a rise overlooking the plant. "For a command post." They walked toward it.

"Too much of a target," Potter objected. Even an amateur sportsman could easily make the hundred-yard rifle shot.

"No," Henderson explained. "It's armored. Windows're an inch thick."

"That a fact?"

With another fast look at the grim slaughterhouse he pulled open the door of the command post and stepped inside. The darkened van was spacious. Lit with the glow from faint yellow overhead lights, video monitors, and LED indicators. Potter shook the hand of a young state trooper, who'd stood to attention before the agent was all the way inside.

"Your name?"

"Derek Elb, sir. Sergeant." The red-haired trooper, in a perfectly pressed uniform, explained that he was a mobile command post technician. He knew SAC Henderson and had volunteered to remain here and help if he could. Potter looked helplessly over the elaborate panels and screens and banks of switches and thanked him earnestly.

In the center of the van was a large desk, surrounded by four chairs. Potter sat in one while Derek, like a salesman, enthusiastically pointed out the surveillance and communications features. "We also have a small arms locker."

"Let's hope we won't be needing it," said Arthur Potter, who in thirty years as a federal agent had never fired his pistol in the line of duty.

"You can receive satellite transmissions?"

"Yessir, we have a dish. Any analog, digitized or microwaved signal."

Potter wrote a series of numbers on a card and handed it to Derek. "Call that number, ask for Jim Kwo. Tell him you're calling for me and give him that code right there."

"There?"

"That one. Tell him we want a SatSurv scan fed into—" he waved his hand at the bank of monitors—"one of those. He'll coordinate the tech stuff with you. All that loses me, frankly. Give him the longitude and latitude of the slaughterhouse."

"Yessir," Derek said, jotting notes excitedly. In seventh heaven, techie that he was. "What is that, exactly? SatSurv?"

"The CIA's satellite surveillance system. It'll give us a visual and infrared scan of the grounds."

"Hey, I heard about that. *Popular Science*, I think." Derek turned away to make the call.

Potter bent down and trained his Leica field glasses through the thick windows. He studied the slaughterhouse. A skull of a building. Stark against the sunbleached grass, like dried blood on yellow bone. That was the assessment of Arthur Potter English lit major. Then, in an instant, he was Arthur Potter the Federal Bureau of Investigation's senior hostage negotiator and assistant director of the Bureau's Special Operations and Research Unit, whose quick eyes noted relevant details: thick brick wall, small windows, the location of the power lines, the absence of telephone lines, the cleared land around the building, and stands of trees, clusters of grass, and hills that might provide cover for snipers—both friend and foe.

The rear of the slaughterhouse backed right onto the river. The river, Potter mused. Can we use it somehow?

Can *they?*

The roof was studded with parapets, a medieval castle. There was a tall, thin smokestack and a bulky elevator hut that would make a helicopter landing difficult, at least in this choppy wind. Still, a copter could hover and a dozen tactical officers could rappel onto the building with little difficulty. He could make out no skylights.

The long-defunct Webber & Stoltz Processing Company, Inc., he decided, resembled nothing so much as a crematorium.

"Pete, you have a bullhorn?"

"Sure." Henderson stepped outside and, crouching, jogged to his car to get it.

"Say, you wouldn't have a bathroom here, would you?" Potter asked Derek.

" 'Deed we do, sir," said Derek, immensely proud of Kansas technology. The trooper pointed to a small door. Potter stepped inside and put on an armor vest beneath his dress shirt, which he then replaced. He knotted his tie carefully and pulled on his navy-blue sports coat once again. He noted that there was very little slack on the draw strap of the Second Chance vest but in his present state of mind his weight had virtually ceased to trouble him.

Stepping outside into the cool afternoon, he took the black megaphone from Henderson and, crouching, hurried through a winding path between hills and squad cars, telling the troopers, eager and young most of them, to holster their pistols and stay under cover. When he was about sixty yards from the slaughterhouse he lay on a hilltop and peered at it through the Leica glasses. There was no motion from inside. No lights in the windows. Nothing. He noted that the glass was missing from the front-facing windows but he didn't know if the men inside had knocked it out for better aim or if local schoolboys had been practicing with rocks and .22s.

He turned on the bullhorn and, reminding himself not to shout and thus distort the message, said, "This is Arthur Potter. I'm with the Federal Bureau of Investigation. I'd like to talk to you men in there. I'm having a cellular telephone brought up. I'll be getting it to you in about ten or fifteen minutes. We are not planning an assault. You're in no danger. I repeat: We are not planning an assault."

He expected no response and received none. In a crouch he hurried back to the van and asked Henderson, "Who's in charge locally? I want to talk to them."

"Him, there."

Crouching beside a tree was a tall, sandy-haired man in a pale blue suit. His posture was perfect.

"Who is he?" Potter asked, polishing his glasses on his lapel.

"Charles Budd. State police captain. He's got investigative and tactical experience. No negotiating. Spit-shined record."

"How long on the force?" To Potter, Budd looked young and callow. You expected to see him ambling over the linoleum in the Sears appliance department to shyly pitch an extended warranty.

"Eight years. Flew upstream fast to get the ribbons."

Potter called, "Captain?"

The man turned his blue eyes to Potter and walked behind the van. They shook firm hands and made introductions.

"Hey, Peter," Budd said.

"Charlie."

To Potter he said, "So you're the big gun from Washington, that right? Pleasure to meet you, sir. Real honor."

Potter smiled.

"Okay, sir, near as I can tell, here's the situation." He pointed to the slaughterhouse. "There's been movement in those two windows there. A glint, maybe a gun barrel. Or a scope. I'm not sure. Then they—"

"We'll get to that, Captain Budd."

"Oh, hey, call me Charlie, why don't you?"

"Okay, Charlie. How many people you have here?"

"Thirty-seven troopers, five local deputies. Plus Pete's boys. Yours, I mean."

Potter recorded this in a small black notebook.

"Any of your men or women have hostage experience?"

"The troopers? A few of them probably've been involved in your typical bank robbery or convenience store situations. The local cops, I'm sure they never have. Most of the work round here's DWI and farm workers playing mumbledypeg on each other Saturday night."

"What's the chain of command?"

"I'm supervisor. I've got four commanders—three lieutenants and one sergeant waiting for rank—overseeing those thirty-seven, pretty evenly split. Two squads of ten, one nine, one eight. You're writing all this down, huh?"

Potter smiled again. "Where are they deployed?"

Like the civil war general Budd would one day resemble he pointed out the clusters of troopers in the field.

"Weapons? Yours, I mean."

"We issue Glocks here, sir, as sidearms. We've got about fifteen riot guns between us. Twelve-gauge, eighteen-inch barrels. I've got six men and a woman with M-16s, in those trees there and over there. Scopes on all of 'em."

"Night scopes?"

He chuckled. "Not round here."

"Who's in charge of the local men?"

"That'd be the sheriff of Crow Ridge. Dean Stillwell. He's over yonder."

He pointed to a lanky, mop-haired man, whose head was down as he talked to one of his deputies.

Another car pulled up and braked to a quick stop. Potter was greatly pleased to see who was behind the wheel.

Short Henry LeBow climbed from the car and immediately pulled on a rumpled tweed businessman's hat; his bald crown had offered a glistening target more than once during the two hundred hostage negotiations he and Potter had worked together. LeBow trudged forward, a pudgy, shy man, and the one hostage-incident intelligence officer Potter would rather work with than anyone else in the world.

LeBow listed under the weight of two huge shoulder bags.

The men shook hands warmly and Potter introduced him to Henderson and Budd.

"Look what we have here, Henry. An Airstream trailer to call our very own."

"My. And a river to catch fish in. What is that?"

"The river? The Arkansas," Budd said, with the emphasis on the second syllable.

"Takes me back to my youth," LeBow offered.

At Potter's request Henderson returned to his car to radio the FBI resident agency in Wichita and find out when Tobe Geller and Angie Scapello would arrive. Potter,

LeBow, and Budd climbed into the van. LeBow shook Derek's hand then opened his satchels, extracting two laptop computers. He turned them on, plugged them into a wall socket, and then connected a small laser printer.

"Dedicated line?" LeBow asked Derek.

"Right there."

LeBow plugged in and no sooner had he gotten all his equipment on line than the printer started to groan.

"Goodies already?" Potter asked.

LeBow read the incoming fax, saying, "Prison department profiles, probation reports, yellow sheets and indictments. Very preliminary, Arthur. Very *raw*." Potter handed him the material delivered by the agents in Chicago and the voluminous notes he'd begun jotting on the plane. In terse words they described the escape of Lou Handy and two other inmates from a federal prison in southern Kansas, their murder of a couple in a wheat field several miles from the slaughterhouse and the taking of the hostages. The intelligence officer looked over the hard copies and then began typing the data into one of his computers.

The door opened and Peter Henderson entered. He announced that Tobe Geller would be here momentarily and Angie Scapello would be arriving within the hour. Tobe had been flown in via Air Force F-16 from Boston, where he'd been teaching a course in computer-programming profiling as a way to establish the identity of criminal hackers. He should arrive any minute. Angie was taking a Marine DomTran jet from Quantico.

"Angie?" LeBow said. "I'm pleased about that. Very pleased."

Agent Scapello resembled Geena Davis and had huge, brown eyes that no amount of failing to wear makeup could make less seductive. Still, LeBow's excitement had nothing to do with her appearance and everything to do with her specialty—hostage psychology.

En route to the barricade Angie would stop at the Laurent Clerc School and gather as much information about the hostages as she could. If Potter knew her at all he guessed she was already on the horn to the school, writing up profiles of the girls.

LeBow taped a large sheet of blank paper on the wall

above the desk and hung a black marker by a string from it. The sheet was divided in half. The left was headed "Promises," the right, "Deceptions." On it LeBow would record everything Potter offered to Handy and every lie he told the man. This was standard procedure in hostage negotiations. The use of the crib sheet could be explained best by Mark Twain, who'd said that a man needs a good memory to be an effective liar.

Surprised, Budd asked, "You really going to lie to him?" LeBow smiled.

"But what exactly is a lie, Charlie?" Potter asked. "The truth's a pretty slippery thing. Are any words ever one hundred percent honest?" He tore pages from his notebook and handed them to LeBow, who took the small sheets, along with the faxes that were spewing from the printer, and began typing on the keyboard of the computer that was labeled "Profiles," the word written long ago on a piece of now dirty masking tape. The label on the second computer read "Chronology." The latter screen contained only two entries:

0840 hours. Hostages taken.

1050 hours. Threat Management Team—Potter, Le-Bow—in place.

The backlit liquid-crystal screens poured eerie blue light onto the man's round face; he looked like an Arthur Rackham rendering of the man in the moon. Charlie Budd gazed at the man's fingers, flying invisibly over the keys. "Lookit that. He's worn off half the letters."

LeBow grumbled to Potter, "Saw the building. Lousy situation. Too well shielded for SatSurv and not enough windows for infrared or mikes. The wind's a problem too."

As in most barricades the bulk of information here would have to come from traditional sources—released or escaped hostages and the troopers who took food and drinks to the HTs and stole a glance inside.

LeBow tapped computer buttons and created a small window on the chronology computer. Two digital stopwatches appeared. One was headed "Elapsed"; the other, "Deadline."

LeBow set the elapsed time clock to two hours, ten minutes and pushed a button. It began moving. He glanced at Potter with a raised eyebrow.

"I know, Henry." If you don't contact the hostage taker

soon after the taking they get nervous and begin to wonder if you're planning an assault. The negotiator added,
"We'll give Tobe a few minutes then have the briefing."
He looked out over the fields behind them, the tall pale
blanket of grass waving in the chill breeze. A half-mile
away the combines moved in gentle, symmetrical patterns, cropping the wheat fields like a new recruit's scalp.

Potter examined a map of the area. "All these roads
sealed off?"

"Yessir," Budd said. "And they're the only way in."

"Set up a rear staging area there, Charlie." He pointed
to the bend in the road a mile south of the slaughterhouse.
"I want a press tent set up near there. Out of sight of the
barricade. Do you have a press officer?"

"Nup," Budd said. "I usually give statements 'bout incidents around here if somebody's got to. Suppose I'll
have to here."

"No. I want you with me. Delegate it. Find a low-rank-
ing officer."

Henderson interrupted. "This is a federal operation,
Arthur. I think I should make any statements."

"No, I want somebody state and without much rank.
That way we'll keep the press in the tent, waiting. They'll
be expecting somebody with the answers to show up. And
they'll be less likely to go poking around where they
shouldn't."

"Well, I don't exactly know who'd be good at it," Budd
said uncertainly, looking out the window, as if a trooper
resembling Dan Rather might just wander past.

"They won't have to be good," Potter muttered. "All
they have to do is say that I'll make a statement later. Period. Nothing else. Pick somebody who's not afraid to say
'No comment.' "

"They won't like that. The press boys and gals. I mean,
there's a fender-bender over on Route 14 and reporters
here're all over the scene. Something like this, I'll bet
they'll be coming in from Kansas City even."

SAC Henderson, who'd served a stint in the District,
laughed.

"Charlie—" Potter controlled his own smile—"CNN
and ABC networks are already here. So's the *New York*

Times, the *Washington Post,* and the *L.A. Times.* Sky TV from Europe, the BBC, and Reuters. The rest of the big boys're on their way. We're sitting in the middle of the week's media big bang."

"No kidding. Brokaw, too, you think? Man, I'd like to meet him."

"And set up a press-free perimeter one mile around the slaughterhouse, both sides of the river."

"What?"

"Put five or six officers in four-by-fours and start cruising. You find any reporter in that zone—anybody with a camera—you arrest them and confiscate the camera."

"Arrest a reporter? We can't do that. Can we? I mean, look at 'em all out there now. Look at 'em."

"Really, Arthur," Henderson began, "we don't want to do that, do we? Remember Waco."

Potter smiled blandly at the SAC. He was thinking of a hundred other matters, sorting, calculating. "And no press choppers. Pete, could you get a couple Hueys down here from McConnell in Wichita? Set up a no-fly zone for a three-mile radius."

"Are you serious, Arthur?"

LeBow said, "Time's awasting. Inside for two hours, seventeen."

Potter said to Budd, "Oh, and we need a block of rooms at the nearest hotel. What'd that be?"

"Days Inn. It's up the road four miles. In Crow Ridge. Downtown, as much as they've got a downtown. How many?"

"Ten."

"Okay. What's the rooms for?"

"The parents of the hostages. Get a priest and a doctor over there too."

"Maybe they should be closer. If we need them to talk to their kids, or—"

"No, they shouldn't be. And station four or five troopers there. The families are not to be disturbed by reporters. I want anybody harassing them—"

"Arrested," Budd muttered. "Oh, brother."

"What's the matter, Trooper?" LeBow asked brightly.

"Well, sir, the Kansas state song is 'Home on the Range.' "

"Is that a fact?" Henderson asked. "And?"

"I know reporters, and you're gonna be hearing some pretty discouraging words 'fore this thing's over."

Potter laughed. Then he pointed to the fields. "Look there, Charlie—those troopers're all exposed. I *told* them to stay down. They're not paying attention. Keep them down behind the cars. Tell them Handy's killed officers before. What's his relationship with weapons, Henry?"

LeBow typed and read the screen. He said, "All indictments have involved at least one firearms count. He's shot four individuals, killed two of them. Fort Dix, M-16 training, he consistently shot low nineties on the range. No record of sidearm scores."

"There you have it," Potter told Budd. "Tell them to keep their heads *down*."

A light flashed toward them. Potter blinked and saw, in the distance, a combine had just turned on its lights. It was early of course but the overcast was oppressive. He gazed at the line of trees to the right and left of the slaughterhouse.

"One other thing, Charlie—I want you to leave the snipers in position but give them orders not to shoot unless the HTs make a break."

"HTs—that's the hostage takers, right?"

"Even if they have a clear shot. Those troopers you were telling me about, with the rifles, are they SWAT?"

"No," he said, "just damn fine shots. Even the girl. She started practicing on squirrels when she was—"

"And I want them and everybody else to unchamber their weapons. Everybody."

"What?"

"Loaded but not chambered."

"Oh, I don't know 'bout that, sir."

Potter turned to him with an inquiring look.

"I just mean," Budd said quickly, "not the snipers too?"

"You can pull the bolt of an M-16 and shoot in under one second."

"Not and steady a scope you can't. An HT could get off three shots in a second." The initials sat awkwardly in his mouth, as if he were trying raw oysters for the first time.

He's so eager and talented and correct, Potter mused.

What a day this is going to be.

"The takers aren't going to come out and shoot a hostage in front of us before we can react. If it comes to that, the whole thing'll turn into a firefight anyway."

"But—"

"Unchambered," Potter said firmly. "Appreciate it, Charlie."

Budd nodded reluctantly and reiterated his assignment: "Okay, I'm gonna send somebody down to give a statement to the press—or not to give a statement to the press, I should say. I'll round up reporters and push 'em back a mile or so, I'll get us a block of rooms, and tell everybody to keep their heads down. And deliver your message about not loading and locking."

"Good."

"Brother." Budd ducked out of the van. Potter watched him crouching and running down to a cluster of troopers. They listened, laughed, and then started herding the reporters out of the area.

In five minutes the captain returned to the command van. "That's done. Those reporters're about as unhappy as I thought they'd be. I told 'em a Feebie'd ordered it. You don't mind me calling you that, I hope." There was an edge to his voice.

"You can call me whatever you like, Charlie. Now, I want a field hospital set up here."

"Medevac?"

"No, not evacuation. Trauma-team medics and triage specialists. Just out of clear range of the slaughterhouse. No more than sixty seconds away. Prepped for everything from third-degree burns to gunshot wounds to pepper spray. Full operating suites."

"Yessir. But, you know, there's a big hospital not but fifteen miles from here."

"That may be, but I don't want the HTs to even hear the sound of a medevac chopper. Same reason I want the press copters and our Hueys out of earshot."

"Why?"

"Because I don't want to remind them of something they might not think of themselves. And even if they do ask for a chopper I want the option to tell them that it's too windy to fly one in."

"Will do."

"Then come back here with your commanders. Sheriff Stillwell too. I'm going to hold a briefing."

Just then the door opened and a tanned, handsome young man with black curly hair bounded inside.

Before he greeted anyone he looked at the control panels and muttered, "Excellent."

"Tobe, welcome."

Tobe Geller said to Potter, "Boston girls are beautiful and they all have pointy tits, Arthur. This better be important."

Potter shook his hand, noting that the dot of earring hole was particularly prominent today. He recalled that Tobe had explained the earring to his superiors in the Bureau by saying he'd done undercover work as a cop. He never had; he simply liked earrings and had quite a collection of them. The MIT graduate and adjunct professor of computer science at American University and Georgetown shook everyone's hand. He then looked down at LeBow's laptops, sneered, and muttered something about their being antiquated. Then he dropped into the chair of the communications control panel. He and Derek introduced themselves and were immediately submerged in a world of shielded analog signals, subnets, packet driver NDIS shims, digital tripartite scrambling, and oscillation detection systems in multiple landline chains.

"Just about to brief, Tobe," Potter told him and sent Budd to run his errands. To LeBow he said, "Let me see what you've got so far."

LeBow turned the profile computer to Potter.

The intelligence officer said, "We don't have much time."

But Potter continued to read, lost in the glowing type of the blue screen.

11:02 A.M.

The jackrabbit—not a rabbit at all but a hare—is nature's least likely fighter.

This is an animal made for defense—with a camouflaging coat (gray and buff in the warm months, white in the winter), ears that rotate like antennae to home in on threatening sounds, and eyes that afford a three-hundred-and-sixty-degree view of the terrain. It has a herbivore's chiseling teeth and its claws are intended for tugging at leafy plants and—in males—gripping the shoulders of its mate when creating future generations of jackrabbits.

But when it's cornered, when there's no chance for flight, it will attack its adversary with a shocking ferocity. Hunters have found the bodies of blinded or gutted foxes and wildcats that had the bad judgment to trap a jackrabbit in a cave and attack it with the overconfidence of sassy predators.

Confinement is our worst fear, Arthur Potter continues during his lectures on barricades, and hostage takers are the most deadly and determined of adversaries.

Today, in the command van at the Crow Ridge barricade, he dispensed with his *Wild Kingdom* introduction and told his audience simply, "Above all, you have to appreciate how dangerous those men in there are."

Potter looked over the group: Henderson, LeBow, and Tobe were the federal officers. On the state side there was Budd and his second-in-command, Philip Molto, a short, taciturn officer in the state police, who seemed no older than a high-school student. He was one of the tactical unit commanders. The others—two men and a woman—were solemn, with humorless eyes. They wore full combat gear and were eager for a fight.

Dean Stillwell, the sheriff of Crow Ridge, looked pure hayseed. His lengthy arms stretched from suit coat sleeves far too short and his mop of hair could have been styled from the early Beatles.

When they had assembled, Charlie Budd had introduced Potter. "I'd like you to meet Arthur Potter of the Federal Bureau of Investigation. He's a famous hostage negotiator and we're pretty lucky to have him with us today."

"Thank you, Captain," Potter had jumped in, worried that Budd was going to begin a round of applause.

"Just one more thing," the young captain had continued. He glanced at Potter. "I forgot to say this before. I've been in touch with the attorney general. And he's mobilizing the state Hostage Rescue Unit. So it's our job—"

Keeping an equable face, Potter had stepped forward. "Actually, Charlie, if you don't mind . . ." He'd nodded toward the assembled officers. Budd had fallen silent and grinned. "There'll be no state HRT involvement here. A federal rescue team is being assembled now and should be here later this afternoon or early this evening."

"Oh," Budd began. "But I think the attorney general—"

Potter glanced at him with a firm smile. "I've already spoken to him and the governor on the plane here."

Budd nodded, still grinning, and the negotiator proceeded with the briefing.

Early that morning, he explained, three men had murdered a guard and escaped from Callana maximum-security federal penitentiary outside Winfield, Kansas, near the Oklahoma border. Louis Jeremiah Handy, Shepard Wilcox, and Ray "Sonny" Bonner. As they drove north their car was struck by a Cadillac. Handy and the escapees murdered the couple inside and got as far as the slaughterhouse before a state trooper caught up with them.

"Handy, thirty-five, was serving a life sentence for robbery, arson, and murder. Seven months ago he, Wilcox, Handy's girlfriend, and another perp robbed the Farmers & Merchants S&L in Wichita. Handy locked two tellers in the cash cage and set the place on fire. It burned to the ground, killing them both. During the getaway the fourth robber was killed, Handy's girlfriend escaped, and Handy and Wilcox were arrested. Visual aids, Henry?"

With an optical scanner LeBow had digitized mug shots of the three HTs and assembled them onto a single sheet of paper, showing front, side, and three-quarter views, highlighting distinguishing scars and characteristics. These were now spewing out of his laser printer. He distributed stacks to the people assembled in the van.

"Keep one of those and pass them out to the officers under you," Potter said. "I want everybody in the field to get one and memorize those pictures. If it comes down to a surrender things may get confusing and we've got too many plainclothesmen here to risk misidentification of the HTs. I want everybody to know exactly what the bad guys look like.

"That's Handy on top. The second one is Shep Wilcox. He's the closest thing Handy has to a friend. They've worked together on three or four jobs. The last fellow, the fat one with the beard, is Bonner. Handy apparently's known him for some time but they've never worked together. Bonner's got armed robbery on his sheet but he was in Callana for interstate flight. He's a suspected serial rapist though they only got him for his last assault. Stabbed the victim repeatedly—while he was in flagrante. She lived. She was seventeen years old and had to change her eleventh plastic surgery appointment to testify against him. Henry, what can you tell us about the hostages?"

LeBow said, "Very sketchy so far. Inside we have a total of ten hostages. Eight students, two teachers from the Laurent Clerc School for the Deaf in Hebron, Kansas, about fifteen miles west of here. They were on their way to a Theater of the Deaf performance in Topeka. They're all female. The students range in age from seven to seventeen. I'll be receiving more data soon. We do know that they're all deaf except the older teacher, who can speak and hear normally."

Potter had arranged for a sign language interpreter but even so he knew the problems they could anticipate; he'd negotiated in foreign countries many times and negotiated with many foreigners in the United States. He knew the danger—and the frustration—of having to translate information precisely and quickly when lives hung in the balance.

He said, "Now, we've established a threat management team, consisting of myself; Henry LeBow, my intelligence officer and record keeper; Tobe Geller, my communications officer, and Captain Budd, who'll serve as a state liaison and my right-hand man. I'm the incident commander. There'll also be a containment officer, who I haven't picked yet.

"The TMT has two jobs. The primary one is to effect the surrender of the HTs and the release of the hostages. The secondary job is to assist in a tactical resolution if an assault is called for. This includes gathering intelligence for the hostage rescue team, distracting the HTs, manipulating them however we can to keep casualties to an acceptable level."

In barricade incidents everybody wants to be the hero and talk the bad guys out with their hands up. But even the most peace-loving negotiator has to keep in mind that sometimes the only solution is to go in shooting. When he

taught the FBI's course in hostage negotiation one of the
first things Potter told the class was, "Every hostage situation is essentially a homicide in progress."

He saw the looks in the eyes of the men and women in
the van, and recalled that "cold fish" was among the
kinder terms that had been used to describe him.

"Any information you learn about the takers, the hostages,
the premises, anything, is to be delivered immediately to
Agent LeBow. Before me if necessary. I mean *any* information. If you find out one of the HTs has a runny nose, don't
assume it isn't important." Potter glanced at two hip young
troopers rolling their eyes at one another. Looking directly at
them, the agent said, "It might mean, for instance, that we
could slip knockout drops in cold medicine. Or it might indi-
cate a cocaine addiction we could use to our advantage."

The young men were above contrition but they reined
in their sarcasm.

"Now I need that containment officer. Lieutenant Budd
here thought that perhaps some of you have had hostage
experience." He looked out over the group of cocky
young law enforcers. "Who has?"

The woman state trooper spoke up quickly. "Yessir, I
have. I took the NLEA hostage rescue course. And I've
had negotiating skills training."

"Have you negotiated a release?"

"No. But I backed up the negotiator in a convenience
store robbery a few months ago."

"That's right," Budd said. "Sally led the tactical team.
Did a fine job too."

She continued, "We got a sniper inside the store, up in the
acoustic tile. He had all of the perps acquired in his sights.
They surrendered before we had to drop any of them."

"I've had some experience too," a trooper of about thirty-
five offered, his hand on the butt of his service automatic.
"And I was part of the team that rescued the teller in the
Midwest S&L robbery last year in Topeka. We iced the
perps, nailed 'em cold, not an injury to a single hostage."

One other trooper had trained in the army and had been
part of two successful hostage rescue assault teams.
"Saved them without a single shot being fired."

Peter Henderson had been listening with some dismay.

He piped up. "Maybe I better take that job, Art. I've had the standard course and the refresher." He grinned. "And I read your book. Couple times. Should've been a best-seller. Like Tom Clancy." His face went somber and he added softly, "I think I really ought to. Being federal and all."

Dean Stillwell lifted his head then glanced at the troopers, decked out in flak jackets and dark gray ammunition belts. The movement of his moplike hair gave Potter the chance to avoid answering Henderson and he asked Stillwell, "You going to say something, Sheriff?"

"Naw, I wasn't really."

"Go ahead," Potter encouraged.

"Well, I never took any courses, or never shot any—what do you call them?—hostage takers. HTs, heh. But I guess we have had us a coupla situations down here in Crow Ridge."

Two of the troopers smiled.

"Tell me," Potter said.

"Well, there was that thing a couple months ago, with Abe Whitman and his wife. Emma. Out on Patchin Lane? Just past Badger Hollow Road?"

The smiles became soft laughter.

Stillwell laughed good-naturedly. "I guess that does sound funny. Not like the terrorists you all are used to."

Budd glanced at the troopers and they went straight-lipped again.

"What happened?" Potter asked.

Stillwell, looking down, said, "What it was, Abe's a farmer, pig farmer born and bred, and none better."

Now Peter Henderson, SAC though he was, struggled to stifle his own smile. Budd was silent. Potter gestured for Stillwell to continue and, as always, Henry LeBow listened, listened, listened.

"He took a bad hit when the pork belly market went to heck and gone last spring."

"Pork belly?" the woman trooper asked incredulously.

"Just tumbled." Stillwell missed, or ignored, the mockery. "So what happens but the bank calls his loans and he kind of cracks up. Always been a little bit of a nut case but this time he goes off the deep end and holes up in his barn with a shotgun and the knife he used for dressing the pigs he kept for his own table."

"Cooked up that pork belly, did he?" a trooper asked.

"Oh, not just bacon," Stillwell explained earnestly. "That's the thing about pigs. You know that expression, don't you? 'You can use everything but the squeal.' "

Two troopers lost it at this point. The negotiator smiled encouragingly.

"Anyway, I get a call that something's going on out at his farm and go out there and find Emma in front of the barn. His wife of ten years. He'd slit her from groin to breastbone with that knife and cut her hands off. Abe had his two sons in there, saying he was going to do the same to them. That'd be Brian, age eight, and Stuart, age four. Sweet youngsters, both of 'em."

The troopers' smiles were gone.

"Was about to cut off little Stu's fingers one by one just as I got there."

"Jesus," the woman trooper whispered.

"What'd you do, Sheriff?"

The lanky shoulders shrugged. "Nothing fancy. In fact, I didn't really know *what* to do. I just talked him up. I got close but not too close 'cause I've been hunting with Abe and he's a heck of a shot. Hunkered down behind a slop trough. And we just talked. Saw him inside of the barn there, not but fifty feet in front of me. Just sitting there, holding the knife and his boy."

"How long did you talk for?"

"A spell."

"How long a spell?"

"Must've been close to eighteen, twenty hours. We both got hoarse from shouting, so I had one of my boys go out and get a couple of those cellular phones." He laughed. "I had to read the instructions to figure out mine. See, I didn't want to drive the cruiser up and use the radio or a bullhorn. I figured the less he saw of cops, the better."

"You stayed with it the whole time?"

"Sure. In for a penny, in for a pound, is what I say. Well, twice I stepped away for, you know, natural functions. And once to fetch a cup of coffee. Always kept my head down."

"What happened?"

Another shrug. "He came out. Gave himself up."

Potter asked, "The boys?"

"They were okay. Aside from seeing their mother that way, course. But there wasn't much we could do about that."

"Let me ask you one question, Sheriff. Did you ever think of exchanging yourself for the boys?"

Stillwell looked perplexed. "Nope. Never did."

"Why not?"

"Seemed to me that'd draw his attention to the young-sters. I wanted him to forget about them and concentrate just on him and me."

"And you never tried to shoot him? Didn't you have a clear target?"

"Sure I did. Dozens of times. But, I don't know, I just felt that was the last thing I wanted to have happen—any-body to get hurt. Him, or me, or the boys."

"Correct answers, Sheriff. You're my containment offi-cer. Is that all right with you?"

"Well, yessir, whatever I can do to help, I'd be proud to."

Potter glanced at the displeased state commanders. "You and your officers will report to the sheriff here."

"Say, hold up here, sir," Budd began, but didn't quite know where to take it from there. "The sheriff's a fine man. We're friends and everything. *We've* gone hunting too. But . . . well, it's like a technical thing. See, he's lo-cal, municipal, you know. These're mostly state troopers. You can't put them under his command. That'd need, I don't know, authorization or something."

"Well, I'm authorizing it. You can consider Sheriff Stillwell federal now," Potter said reasonably. "He's been deputized."

LeBow looked quizzically at Potter, who shrugged. There was no procedure that either of them knew about for field-deputizing federal agents.

Peter Henderson's face, alone among the crowd at the briefing, was still smiling. Potter said to him, "You too, Pete. I want any agents not involved in intelligence gath-ering, forensics, or liaising with HRT under Sheriff Still-well's direction."

Henderson nodded slowly, then said, "Could I talk to you for a minute, Art?"

"We don't have much time."

"Just take a minute."

Potter knew what was coming and understood that it was important for it not to happen in front of the other commanders. He said, "Let's step outside, what do you say?"

In the shadow of the van Henderson said in a harsh whisper, "I'm sorry, Arthur. I know your reputation but I'm not putting my people under some hick."

"Well, Pete, my reputation's irrelevant. What counts is my authority."

Again Henderson nodded reasonably, this man in a white shirt immaculately starched and a gray suit that would gain him entrance into any restaurant within a mile of Capitol Hill.

"Arthur, I ought to be more involved in this thing. I mean, I *know* Handy. I—"

"How do you know him?" Potter interrupted. This was news to him.

"I had agents on the scene at apprehension. At the S&L. I interviewed him after the collar. I helped the U.S. Attorney make the case. It was our forensics that put him away."

Since Handy'd been caught in the act and there were direct eyewitnesses, forensics would be a mere technicality. On the DomTran flight Potter had read the interview conducted by, apparently, Henderson. The prisoner had said virtually nothing except "Fuck you."

"Anything you can tell us about him would be appreciated," Potter said. "But you don't have the sort of experience we need for containment."

"And Stillwell does?"

"He has a containment officer's temperament. And judgment. He's not a cowboy."

Or, thought Potter, a bureaucrat, which was just as bad, if not worse.

Finally Henderson looked down at the muddy ground. He growled, "No fucking way, Potter. I've been stuck in this hellhole plenty long enough. Not a damn thing happens down here except copping applesauce and Dictaphones from the Air Force base. And Indians pissing into fucking Minuteman silos. I want a piece of this."

"You don't have any barricade experience, Pete. I read your sheet on the way here."

"I have more law enforcement experience than that Gomer Pyle you've picked. For chrissake, I've got a law degree from Georgetown."

"I'm putting you in charge of the rear staging area. Co-ordinating medical, press liaison, the facilities for the hostages' families, and supplies for the containment troopers and hostage rescue when they get here."

There was a pause as Henderson gazed at his fellow agent—only a few years older—with shocked amusement then, suddenly, pure contempt, which was sealed with an abrupt nod and a chill grin. "Fuck you, Potter. I know the other part of your reputation. Grandstanding."

"It's an important job, rear staging," Potter continued, as if Henderson hadn't spoken. "It's where you'll be the most valuable."

"Fucking holier than thou . . . You've gotta have the limelight, don't you? Afraid somebody a little showier, with a little more class might play better on camera?"

"I think you know that's not my motive."

"Know? What do I know? Except that you breeze into town with the Admiral's blessing, send us off to get your fucking coffee. After the shootout—where, who knows, a dozen troopers and a hostage or two're killed—you give your press conference, take credit for the good stuff, blame us for the fuckups. And then you're gone. Who's left to deal with the shit you leave behind? Me, that's who."

"If there's nothing else—"

Henderson buttoned his suit jacket. "Oh, there'll be something else. Don't you worry." He stalked off, ignoring Potter's matter-of-fact suggestion not to present too much of a target to snipers in the slaughterhouse.

11:31 A.M.

Arthur Potter stepped back into the van, the eyes of the assembled troopers following him cautiously. He wondered if they'd overheard the exchange between him and Henderson.

"Now," the agent continued, "the rules of engagement."

Potter dug a fax from his jacket pocket.

On the jet from Glenview, Potter had spoken via conference call with the Bureau's director, its assistant director of criminal investigations, and Frank D'Angelo, commander of the Bureau's HRT, and had written the rules of engagement for the Crow Ridge barricade. This had taken much of the flight and the result was a single-spaced two-page document that covered every eventuality and gave Potter specific orders about handling the situation. It had been written with much circumspection. Alcohol, Tobacco and Firearms and the FBI had taken serious flak for the handling of the Koresh standoff in Waco and the Bureau itself had been vilified for the Randall Weaver barricade in '92, in which the rules of engagement had been written so broadly that sharpshooters believed that they had orders to shoot any armed adults if they had clear shots. Weaver's wife was mistakenly killed by an FBI sniper.

Potter was looking mostly at Stillwell when he said, "Your job is to contain the HTs. Containment is a tactical function but it's purely passive. There'll be no rescue attempts whatsoever."

"Yessir."

"You'll keep the takers inside whatever perimeter I decide is active. It might be the building itself, it might be a line a hundred yards around the building. Whatever it is, they are not to cross that boundary alive. If any one of them does, whether or not they have a hostage with them, your troops're green-lighted. You know what that means?"

"They're cleared to shoot."

"That's correct. And you shoot to kill. No attempts to wound. No threats. No warning shots. Lethal fire or no fire at all."

"Yessir."

"There are to be no shots through open windows or doorways, even if you see a hostage threatened, without express authorization from someone on the threat management team."

Potter noticed that Budd's face grew dark when he heard this.

"Understood," Stillwell said. The commanders nodded reluctantly.

"If you're fired upon, you'll take defensive positions and wait until you have the okay to return fire. If at any time you or another officer are actually threatened with deadly force, you may use deadly force to protect yourself or that person. But only if you're convinced that there is a true present danger."

"A present danger," a trooper muttered sarcastically.

They're hoping for a turkey shoot, Potter thought. He glanced at the clock on LeBow's computer. "We're going to establish contact in about five minutes. I'm going to warn the takers about the perimeter and I'll let you know, Sheriff, that they've been so notified. From that moment on you're instructed to contain them as I've outlined."

"Yessir," the sheriff answered calmly, and brushed his mop of hair, mussing it further.

"For the time being, the kill zone will be any area outside the building itself. After they send somebody out to get the phone nobody comes outside unless it's under a flag of truce."

Stillwell nodded.

Potter continued. "Henry here will be feeding you data that's tactically relevant. Types of weapons, location of hostage takers and hostages, possible exits, and so on. There's to be no contact directly between you and the HTs. And don't listen in on my conversations with Handy."

"Right. Why not?"

"Because I'm going to be establishing rapport with him and trying to be reasonable. You can't afford to have any sympathy for him. You have to be able to green-light him instantly."

"Fine by me."

"Now, I don't want any accidents," Potter said. "Lieutenant Budd has already told all the troopers to unchamber weapons. That correct? Snipers included?"

Budd nodded. His mouth tightened. Potter wondered just how angry the captain was. Thinking: He'll be angrier yet before this is over.

"My men," one of the troopers said stiffly, "don't have itchy trigger fingers."

"Not now they don't. But they will. In ten hours you'll be drawing down on your own shadow. Now, Dean, you might see reflections from inside. You'll be thinking rifle scopes. But they'll probably just be mirrors, like periscopes. Takers who've done time learned that trick inside prison. So tell your people not to panic if they see a flash."

"Yessir," Stillwell said slowly, the way he seemed to say everything.

Potter said, "Now a few final words. Generally, criminal hostage takers are the easiest to deal with. They're not like terrorists. Their purpose isn't to kill anyone. It's to escape. Given enough time they're going to realize that the hostages are more of a liability than anything and dead hostages mean nothing but trouble. But the psychology of what's going on now is that they're not thinking rationally. They're pumped up on adrenaline. They're scared and confused.

"We have to defuse the situation. Make Handy believe that he'll survive the incident through rational action. Time works in our favor. We don't establish any deadlines. We want to stretch this out longer than any of us can stand. And then longer. And then longer still.

"When HRT gets here we'll prepare for a tactical resolution but that'll still be our last resort. As long as Handy is still talking to us there won't be any rescue attempt. We'll call it the pork belly approach to hostage rescue." Potter smiled toward Stillwell, then continued, "Delay is the name of the game. It wears down the HTs, makes them bored, brings them and the hostages closer together."

"Stockholm syndrome," one of the commanders said.

"Exactly."

"What's that?" another one asked.

Potter nodded to LeBow, who said, "It's the psychoanalytic process of transference as applied to a hostage taking. The term comes from a bank robbery in Stockholm about twenty years ago. The robber forced four employees into the bank vault. They were later joined by a former prison-mate of the taker. They all stayed together for over five days and when they finally gave up, several of the hostages were madly in love with their captors.

They'd come to feel that it was the police who were the
bad guys. The robber and his cellmate had formed strong
feelings of affection for the hostages too and wouldn't
think of hurting them."

"Time to get to work," Potter announced. "Sheriff,
you'll proceed with containment. I'll make initial contact
with the takers."

Bashful Dean Stillwell motioned to the commanders.
"If you all'd come outside, maybe we'll move some of
those troopers of yours around a bit. If that's all right with
you. What do you say?"

"Pork belly" was the only response, but it was said very
softly. Potter believed he was the only one who heard.

The water poured like a shower, a silver stream falling
through gaps in the ceiling high above them, probably
from rank pools of old rainwater on the roof.

It dripped onto rusting meat hooks and chains and rubber conveyor belts and disintegrating machinery, just outside the killing room, where Melanie Charrol sat, looking
over the girls. The seven-year-old twins, Anna and Suzie,
huddled against her. Beverly Klemper brushed her short
blond hair from her face—round with baby fat still, though
she was fourteen—and struggled to breathe. The others
were clustered together at the far side of the killing room.
Ten-year-old Emily Stoddard rubbed frantically at a rust
stain on her white tights, tears running down her face.

Melanie glanced at Mrs. Harstrawn and Susan Phillips,
crouching together, speaking in abrupt sign. The teenage
girl's pale face, framed by her stark hair, was still filled
with anger. Her dark eyes were the eyes of a resistance
fighter, Melanie thought suddenly. Their conversation
had to do with the students.

"I'm worried they'll panic," Susan said to the older
teacher. "Have to keep them together. If somebody runs,
those assholes will hurt them."

With the audacity of an eight-year-old, Kielle Stone
signed, "We *have* to run! There're more of us than them.
We can get away!"

Susan and Mrs. Harstrawn ignored her, and the little
girl's gray eyes flashed with anger.

All the while Melanie agonized: I don't know what to do. I don't *know*.

The men weren't paying much attention to the girls at the moment. Melanie rose and walked to the doorway. She watched them pull clothes out of canvas bags. Brutus stripped off his T-shirt and with a glance at her walked under the stream of water, letting it cascade over him as he gazed up at the murky ceiling, eyes closed. She saw his sinewy muscles, his hairless body, marred by a dozen pink scars. The other two men looked at him uncertainly and continued to change clothes. When they pulled off their workshirts she could read the names stenciled on their T-shirts. Stoat's said *S. Wilcox*. Bear's, *R. Bonner*. But still, seeing Bear's fat, hairy body and Stoat's lean one, his slippery eyes, she thought of them only by the animal names that had instinctively occurred to her.

And, seeing the look of amused malice on his face as he stood under the cascading water, arms outstretched like Christ's, she understood that Brutus was a far better name for him than *L. Handy*.

He now stepped from the stream of water, dried off with his old shirt, and pulled on a new one, dark green flannel. He picked the pistol up from the oil drum and gazed at his captives, that curious smile on his face. He joined the other men. They looked cautiously out one of the front windows.

This can't be happening, Melanie said to herself. It's impossible. People were expecting her. Her parents. Danny, going into surgery tomorrow. She'd been in her brother's recovery rooms after every one of his half-dozen operations in the past year. She felt the absurd urge to tell these men that they *had* to let them go; she couldn't disappoint her brother.

Then there was her performance in Topeka.

And of course her plans afterwards.

Go say something to him. Now. Plead with him to release the little girls. The twins, at least. Or Kielle and Shannon. Emily.

Beverly, racked with asthma.

Go. Do it.

Melanie started forward then looked back. The others

in the killing room—all nine of them—were staring at her.

Susan held her eyes for a moment then gestured for her to return. She did.

"Don't worry," Susan signed to the girls, then pulled the tiny, chestnut-haired twins to her. Smiling. "They're going to leave soon, let us out. We'll be in Topeka late, that's all. What do you want to do after Melanie's recital? Everybody tell me. Come on!"

Is she crazy? Melanie thought. We're not going to . . . Then realized that Susan was saying this to put them at ease. The girl was right. The truth didn't matter. Keeping the younger girls comforted did. Making sure there was no excuse for the men to get close to them; the memory of Bear gripping Susan's breasts, holding Shannon tight to his fat body came starkly to mind.

But no one wanted to play the game. Until Melanie signed, "Go out for dinner?"

"Arcade!" Shannon signed suddenly. "Mortal Kombat!"

Kielle sat up. "I want to go to real restaurant. I want steak medium rare and potatoes and pie—"

"Whole pie?" Susan asked, mock astonishment on her face.

Choking back tears, Melanie couldn't think of anything to say. Feebly she signed, "Yes. Whole pies for everyone!"

The girls glanced at her but their eyes returned immediately to Susan.

"Might get bellyaches." Mrs. Harstrawn gave an exaggerated frown.

"No," Kielle responded. "Whole pie would be *crass*." She gave an indignant glance to Susan. "Only Philistines eat whole pies. We'll order one piece each. And I'm going to have coffee."

"They don't let us drink coffee," Jocylyn stopped rubbing her tearful eyes long enough to sign.

"*I'm* having coffee. Black coffee," Shannon the knee-kicker signed.

"With cream," Kielle continued. "When my mother makes coffee she puts it in glass cup and pours cream in.

It swirls like cloud. I'm going to have coffee in real restaurant."

"Coffee ice cream maybe." Beverly struggled to suck air into her lungs.

"With sprinkles," Suzie offered.

"With sprinkles *and* Reese's Pieces," echoed Anna, her junior by thirty-some seconds. "Like at Friendly's!"

And, once again, Melanie could think of nothing to say.

"Not *that* kind of restaurant. I mean *fancy* restaurant." Kielle didn't understand why nobody else was excited at the prospect.

A huge smile on Susan's face. "We're all decided. Fancy restaurant. Steak, pie, and coffee for everybody. No Philistines allowed!"

Suddenly twelve-year-old Jocylyn broke into hysterical tears and leapt to her feet. Mrs. Harstrawn was up in an instant, cradling the rotund girl, pulling her close. Slowly she calmed down. Melanie lifted her hands to say something comforting and witty. Finally she signed, "Whipped cream on everyone's pie."

Susan turned to Melanie. "You still ready to go on stage?"

The young teacher stared back at her student for a moment then smiled, nodding.

Mrs. Harstrawn, eyes flitting nervously to the main room of the slaughterhouse, where the men stood talking, their heads down, signed, "Maybe Melanie can recite her poems again."

Melanie nodded and her mind went blank. She had a repertoire of two dozen poems she'd been planning on performing. Now she could remember nothing but the first stanza of her "Birds on a Wire." Melanie lifted her hands, signed:

"Eight gray birds, sitting in dark.
Cold wind blows, it isn't kind.
Sitting on wire, they lift their wings
and sail off into billowy clouds."

"Pretty, isn't it?" Susan asked, looking directly at Jocylyn. The girl wiped her face on the sleeve of her bulky blouse and nodded.

"*I* wrote some poems," Kielle signed emphatically.

"Fifty of them. No, more. They're about Wonder Woman and Spider-Man. And X-Men too. Jean Grey and Cyclops. Shannon's read them!"

Shannon nodded. On the girl's left forearm was a faux tattoo of another X-Man, Gambit, which she'd drawn with Pentel marker.

"Why don't you tell us one?" Susan asked her.

Kielle thought for a minute then confessed that her poems still needed some work.

"Why are birds gray in your poem?" Beverly asked Melanie. Her signing was abrupt, as if she had to finish every conversation before one of her wrenching asthma attacks.

"Because we all have a little gray in us," Melanie answered, amazed that the girls were actually rallying, distracted from the horror unfolding around them.

"If it's about us I'd rather be pretty bird," Suzie said, and her twin nodded.

"You could have made us red," suggested Emily, who was dressed in a Laura Ashley floral. She was more feminine than all the rest of the students combined.

Then Susan—who knew facts that even Melanie did not; Susan, who was going to attend Gallaudet College next year with straight A's—explained to the other girls' fascination that only male cardinals were red. The females were brownish gray.

"So, they're cardinals?" Kielle asked.

When Melanie didn't respond the little girl tapped her shoulder and repeated the question.

"Yes," Melanie answered. "Sure. It's about cardinals. You're all flock of pretty cardinals."

"Not archbishops?" Mrs. Harstrawn signed, and rolled her eyes. Susan laughed. Jocylyn nodded but seemed stymied that someone had once again beaten her to a punch line.

Tomboy Shannon, devourer of Christopher Pike books, asked why Melanie didn't make the birds hawks, with long silver beaks and claws that dripped blood.

"It is about us then?" Kielle asked. "The poem?"

"Maybe."

"But there are nine, including you," Susan pointed out

to her teacher with the logic of a teenager. "And ten with Mrs. Harstrawn."

"So there are," Melanie responded. "I can change it." Then thought to herself: Do something. Whipped cream on pie? Bullshit. Take charge!

Do something!

Go talk to Brutus.

Melanie rose suddenly, walked to the doorway. Looked out. Then back at Susan, who signed, "What are you doing?"

Melanie's eyes returned to the men. Thinking: Oh, don't rely on me, girls. That's a mistake. I'm not the one to do it. Mrs. Harstrawn's older. Susan's stronger. When she says something, people—hearing or deaf—always listen.

I can't. . . .

Yes, you can.

Melanie took a step into the main room, feeling the spatter of water that dripped from the ceiling. She dodged a swinging meat hook, walked closer to the men. Just the twins. And Beverly. Who wouldn't let seven-year-old girls go? Who wouldn't have compassion for a teenager racked by asthma?

Bear looked up and saw her, grinned. Crew-cut Stoat was slipping batteries into a portable TV and paid no attention. Brutus, who had wandered away from the other two, was gazing out the window.

Melanie paused, looked back into the killing room. Susan was frowning. Again she signed, "What are you doing?" Melanie sensed criticism in her expression; she felt like a high-school student herself.

Just ask him. Write the words out. *Please let little ones go.*

Her hands were shaking, her heart was a huge, raw lump. She felt the vibrations as Bear called something. Slowly Brutus turned.

He looked at her, tossed his wet hair.

Melanie froze, feeling his eyes on her. She pantomimed writing something. He walked up to her. She was frozen. He took her hand, looked at her nails, a small silver ring on her right index finger. Released it. Looked into her face and laughed. Then he walked back to the other two men, leaving her alone, his back to her, as if she posed no threat whatsoever, as if she were younger than the youngest of her students, as if she were not there at all.

She felt more devastated than if he'd slapped her.

Too frightened to approach him again, too ashamed to return to the killing room, Melanie remained where she was, gazing out the window at the row of police cars, the crouching forms of the policemen, and the scruffy grass bending in the wind.

Potter gazed at the slaughterhouse through the bulletproof window in the truck.

They'd have to talk soon. Already Lou Handy was looming too large in his mind. There were two dangers inherent in negotiating. First, making the hostage taker bigger than life before you begin and therefore starting out on the defensive—what Potter was beginning to feel now. (The other—his own Stockholming—would come later. He'd deal with it then. And he knew he would have to.)

"Throw phone ready?"

"Just about." Tobe was programming numbers into a scanner on the console. "Should I put an omni in it?"

Throw phones were lightweight, rugged cellular phones containing a duplicate transmitting circuit that sent to the command post any conversations on the phone and a readout of the numbers called. Usually the HTs spoke only to the negotiators but sometimes they called accomplices or friends. These conversations sometimes helped the threat management team in bargaining or getting a tactical advantage.

Occasionally a tiny omnidirectional microphone was hidden in the phone. It'd pick up conversations even when the phone wasn't being used by the HTs. It was every negotiator's dream to know exactly what was said inside a barricade. But if the microphone was found, it might mean reprisals and would certainly damage the negotiator's credibility—his only real asset at this stage of the situation.

"Henry?" Potter asked. "Your opinion. Could he find it?"

Henry LeBow tapped computer keys and called up Handy's rapidly growing file. He scrolled through it. "Never went to college, got A's in science and math in high school. Wait, here we go. . . . Studied electronics in the service for a while. He didn't last long in the army. He knifed his sergeant. That's neither here nor there. . . . No, I'd say don't put the mike in. He could spot it. He excelled in engineering."

Potter sighed. "Leave it out, Tobe."

"Hurts."

"Does."

The phone buzzed and Potter took the call. Special Agent Angie Scapello had arrived in Wichita and was being choppered directly to the Laurent Clerc School in Hebron. She and the Hebron PD officer who'd be acting as interpreter would be arriving in a half-hour.

He relayed this information to LeBow, who typed it in. The intelligence officer added, "I'll have CAD schematics of the interior in ten minutes." LeBow had sent a field agent to dig up architectural or engineering drawings of the slaughterhouse. These would be transmitted to the command post and printed out through computer-assisted drafting software.

Potter said to Budd, "Charlie, I'm thinking we've got to consolidate them. The hostages. The takers're going to want power in there but I don't want to do that. I want to get them a single electric lantern. Battery powered. Weak. So they'll all have to be in the same room."

"Why?"

LeBow spoke. "Keep the takers and the hostages together. Let Handy talk to them, get to know them."

"I don't know, sir," the captain said. "Those girls're deaf. That's gonna be a spooky place. If they're in a room that's lit with just one lantern, they'll . . . well, the way my daughter'd say, they'll freak."

"We can't be worried much about their feelings," Potter said absently, watching LeBow transcribe notes into his electronic tablet of stone.

"I don't really agree with you there, sir," Budd said.

Silence.

Tobe was assembling the cellular phone, while he

simultaneously gazed at six TV stations on a single monitor, the screen split miraculously by Derek Elb. All the local news was about the incident. CBS was doing a special report, as was CNN. Sprayed-haired beauties, men and women, held microphones like ice cream cones and spoke into them fervently. Potter noticed that Tobe'd taken to the control panel of the command van as if he'd designed it himself, and then reflected that perhaps he had. He and red-haired Derek had become fast friends.

"Think about it, though," Budd persisted. "That's a scary place at high noon. At night? Brother, it'll be awful."

"Whatever happens," Potter replied, "these next twenty-four hours aren't going to be very pleasant for those girls. They'll just have to live with it. We need to bunch them up. A single lantern'll do that."

Budd grimaced in frustration. "There's a practical matter too. I'm thinking if it's too dark they might panic. Try to run. And get hurt."

Potter looked at the brick walls of the old processing plant, as dark as dried blood.

"You don't *want* them to get shot, do you?" Budd asked in exasperation, drawing LeBow's glance, though not Potter's.

"But if we turn the power on," the agent said, "they'll have the whole slaughterhouse to hide themselves in. Handy could put them in ten different rooms." Potter pressed his cupped hands together absently as if making a snowball. "We *have* to keep them together."

Budd said, "What we could do is get a generator truck here. Feed in a line. Four or five auto repair lights—you know, those caged lights on hooks. Just enough current to light up the main room. And that way if you ordered an assault we could shut down the juice any time we wanted. Which you couldn't do with a battery unit. And, look, at some point we're gonna have to communicate with those girls. Remember, they're deaf. If it's dark, how're we gonna do that?"

That was a good point, one that Potter hadn't considered. In an assault someone would have to issue sign language evacuation instructions to the girls.

Potter nodded. "Okay."

"I'll get on it."

"Delegate it, Charlie."

"I aim to."

Tobe pushed buttons. A hiss of static filled the van. "Shit," he muttered. He added to LeBow, "Got two men with Big Ears closer than they ought to be," referring to small parabolic microphones that under good conditions could pick up a whisper at a hundred yards. Today they were useless.

"Damn wind," LeBow muttered.

"Throw phone's ready," Tobe announced, pushing a small olive-drab backpack toward Potter. "Both downlink circuits're ready to receive."

"We'll—"

A phone buzzed. Potter grabbed it.

"Potter here."

"Agent Potter? We haven't met." A pleasant baritone boomed out of the speaker. "I'm Roland Marks, the assistant attorney general of the state."

"Yes?" Potter asked coolly.

"I'd like to share some thoughts with you, sir."

Potter's impatience surged. There's no time for this, he thought to himself.

"I'm very busy right now."

"Some thoughts about state involvement. Just my two cents' worth."

Potter had Charlie Budd, he had his containment troops, he had his command van. He needed nothing else from the state of Kansas.

"This isn't a good time, I'm afraid."

"Is it true that they've kidnaped eight young girls?"

Potter sighed. "And two teachers. From the deaf school in Hebron. Yes, that's right. We're just about to establish contact and we're on a very tight schedule. I don't—"

"How many takers are there?"

"I'm afraid I don't have time to discuss the situation with you. The governor's been briefed and you can call our special agent in charge, Peter Henderson. I assume you know him."

"I know Pete. Sure." The hesitant voice suggested he

had little confidence in the man. "This could be a real tragedy, sir."

"Well, Mr. Marks, my job is to make sure it doesn't turn out that way. I hope you'll let me get on with it."

"I was thinking, maybe a counselor or priest could help out. In Topeka we've got ourselves this state employee assistance department. Some top-notch—"

"I'm hanging up now," Potter said rather cheerfully. "Pete Henderson can keep you informed of our progress."

"Wait a minute—"

Click.

"Henry, pull some files. Roland Marks's. Assistant AG. Find out if he can make trouble. See if he's filed to run in any elections, got his eye on any appointments."

"Just sounds like some do-good, knee-jerk, bleeding-heart liberal to me," scowled Henry LeBow, who'd voted Democratic all his life, Eugene McCarthy included.

"All right," Potter said, forgetting immediately about the attorney general's call, "let's get a volunteer with a good arm. Oh, one more thing." Potter buttoned his navy jacket and lifted a finger to Budd. He motioned to the door. "Step out here, would you please, Charlie?"

Outside they stood in the faint shadow of the van. "Captain," Potter said, "you better tell me what's eating you. That I stepped on your toes back there?"

"Nope," came the chilly response. "You're federal. I'm state. It's in the Constitution. Preeminence, they call it."

"Listen," Potter said firmly, "we don't have time for delicacies. Get it off your chest now. Or live with it, whatever it is."

"What're we doing? Taking off our insignias and going at it?" Budd laughed without much humor.

Potter said nothing but lifted an eyebrow.

"All right, how's this? What's eating me is I know you're supposed to be good at this and I've never done a negotiation before. I hear you barking orders right and left like you know exactly what you're doing but don't you think there's one thing you neglected to mention?"

"What?"

"You didn't say hardly three words about those girls in there."

"What about them?"

"I just thought you should've reminded everybody that our number-one priority is getting those girls out alive."

"Oh," Potter said, his mind elsewhere as he scanned the battlefield. "But that's not our number-one priority at all, Charlie. The rules of engagement are real clear. I'm here to get the takers to surrender and, if they don't, to help Hostage Rescue engage and neutralize them. I'll do everything in my power to save the people inside. That's why it's me, not HRT, running the show. But those men in there aren't leaving Crow Ridge except in body bags or handcuffs. And if that means those hostages have to die, then they're going to die. Now if you could find me that volunteer—a fellow with a good arm to pitch the phone. And hand me that bullhorn too, if you'd be so kind."

NOON

As he walked through a shallow gully that eventually ran into the south side of the slaughterhouse, Arthur Potter said to Henry LeBow, "We'll want engineer reports on any modifications to the building. EPA too. I want to know if there're any tunnels."

The intelligence officer nodded. "It's being done. And I'm checking on easements too."

"Tunnels?" Budd asked.

Potter told him about the terrorist barricade at the Vanderbilt mansion in Newport, Rhode Island, three years before. The Hostage Rescue Team had completely surprised the HTs by sneaking through a steam tunnel into the basement of the building. The tycoon had ordered the furnace installed away from the house so the noise and smoke wouldn't disturb his guests, never knowing that his sense of social decorum would save the lives of fifteen Israeli tourists a hundred years later.

The agent noticed that Dean Stillwell had reorganized troopers and agents in good defensive positions around the building. Halfway to the slaughterhouse Potter paused suddenly and looked toward the glint of water in the distance.

To Budd, Potter said, "I want all river traffic stopped."

"Well, um, that's the Arkansas River."

"So you told us."

"I mean, it's a big river."

"I can see."

"Well, why? You thinking they'll have accomplices floating in on rafts?"

"No." In the ensuing silence Potter challenged Budd to figure it out. He wanted the man to start *thinking*.

"You're not afraid they'd try and swim out to a barge? They'd drown for sure. It's a mean current here."

"Ah, but they might want to try. I want to make sure they don't even think of it. Just like keeping the choppers away."

Budd said, "Okay. I'll do it. Only who should I call? The coast guard? I don't think there's any such thing as a coast guard on rivers here." His frustration was evident. "I mean, who should I call?"

"I don't know, Charlie. You'll have to find out."

On his cellular phone Budd placed a call to his office and ordered them to find out who had jurisdiction over river traffic. He ended the conversation by saying, "I don't know. You'll have to find out."

SAC Peter Henderson was at the rear staging area, setting up the medical unit and coordinating with other troopers and agents coming into the area, particularly the BATF agents and U.S. marshals, on site because there'd been firearm violations and an escape from a federal prison. The SAC's bitter parting words still echoed in Potter's mind. *Oh, there'll be something else. Don't you worry.*

He said to LeBow, "Henry, while you're looking up our friend Roland Marks, check out Henderson too."

"*Our* Henderson?"

"Yep. I don't want it to interfere with working the incident but I need to know if he's got an agenda."

"Sure."

"Arthur," Budd said, "I was thinking, maybe we should

get this fellow's mother here. Handy's, I mean. Or his father or brother or somebody."

It was LeBow who shook his head.

"What? I ask something stupid?" Budd asked.

The intelligence officer said, "Just watching too many movies, Captain. A priest or family member's the last person you want here."

"Why's that?"

Potter explained, "Nine times out of ten their family's part of the reason they're in trouble in the first place. And I've never known a priest to do anything more than rile up a taker." He was pleased to notice that Budd took this not as a chastisement but as information; he seemed to store it somewhere in his enthusiastic brain.

"Sir." Sheriff Dean Stillwell's voice floated to them on the breeze. He trooped up and mussed his moppish hair with his fingers. "Got one of my boys gonna make the run with that phone. Come over here, Stevie."

"Officer," Potter said, nodding, "what's your name?"

"Stephen Oates. I go by Stevie mostly." The officer was lanky and tall and would look right at home in white pinstripes, working on a chaw of tobacco out on the pitcher's mound.

"All right, Stevie. Put on that body armor and helmet. I'm going to tell them you're coming. You crawl up to that rise there. See it? By that old livestock pen. I want you to stay down and pitch the knapsack as far as you can toward the front door."

Tobe handed him the small olive-drab satchel.

"What if I hit those rocks there, sir?"

"It's a special phone and the bag's padded," Potter said. "Besides, if you hit those rocks, you should get out of law enforcement and try out for the Royals. All right," he announced, "let's get this show on the road."

Potter gripped the bullhorn and crawled to the top of the rise where he'd hailed Handy last time, sixty yards from the black windows of the slaughterhouse. He dropped onto his belly, caught his breath. Lifted the bullhorn to his lips. "This is Agent Potter again. We're sending a telephone in to you. One of our men is going to throw it as close to you as he can. This is not a trick. It's simply a cellular phone. Will you let our man approach?"

Nothing.

"You men inside, can you hear me? We want to talk to you. Will you let our man approach?"

After an interminable pause a piece of yellow cloth waved in one window. It was probably a positive response; a "no" would presumably have been a bullet.

"When you come out to get the phone we will not shoot at you. You have my word on that."

Again the yellow scrap.

Potter nodded to Oates. "Go on."

The trooper started toward the grassy rise, staying low. Still, Potter noted, a rifleman inside could easily hit him. The helmet was Kevlar but the transparent face mask was not.

Of the eighty people now surrounding the slaughterhouse, not a soul spoke. There was the hiss of the wind, a far-off truck horn. Occasionally the sound of the chugging engines of the big John Deere and Massey-Ferguson combines swam through the thick wheat. It was pleasant and it was unsettling. Oates scrabbled toward the rise. He made it and lay prone, looking up quickly, then down again. Until recently, throw phones were bulky and hardwired to the negotiator's phone. Even the strongest officer could pitch them only thirty feet or so and often the cords got tangled. Cellular technology had revamped hostage negotiation.

Oates rolled from one clump of tall bluestem to another like a seasoned stuntman. He paused in a bunch of buffalo grass and goldenrod. Then kept going.

Okay, thought Potter. Throw it.

But the trooper didn't throw it.

Oates looked once more at the slaughterhouse then crawled over the knoll, past rotting posts and rails of livestock pens, and continued on, a good twenty yards. Even a bad marksman would have his pick of body parts from that range.

"What's he doing?" Potter whispered, irritated.

"I don't know, sir," Stillwell said. "I was real clear

about what to do. I know he's pretty worried about those girls and wants to do everything right."

"Getting himself shot isn't doing anything right."

Oates continued toward the slaughterhouse.

Don't be a hero, Stevie, Potter thought. Though his concern was more than the man's getting killed or wounded. Unlike special forces and intelligence officers, cops aren't trained in anti-interrogation techniques. In the hands of somebody like Lou Handy, armed with only a knife or a safety pin, Oates'd spill everything he knew in two minutes, telling the location of every officer on the field, the fact that HRT wasn't expected for some hours, what types of guns the troopers had, anything else Handy might be curious to know.

Throw the damn phone!

Oates made it to a second rise and quickly looked up at the slaughterhouse door again then ducked. When there was no fire he squinted, drew back, and launched the phone in a low arc. It passed well over the rocks he'd been worried about and rolled to a stop only thirty feet from the arched brick doorway of the Webber & Stoltz plant.

"Excellent," Budd muttered, clapping Stillwell on the back. The sheriff smiled with cautious pride.

"Maybe it's a good omen," LeBow suggested.

Oates refused to present his back to the darkened windows of the slaughterhouse and eased backward into the grass until he was lost to sight.

"Now let's see who's the brave one," Potter mumbled.

"What do you mean?" Budd asked.

"I want to know who's the gutsiest and most impulsive of the three in there."

"Maybe they're drawing straws."

"No. My guess is that two of them wouldn't go out there for any money and the third can't wait. I want to see who that third one is. That's why I didn't ask for Handy specifically."

"I bet it's him, though," Budd said.

But it wasn't. The door opened and Shepard Wilcox walked out.

Potter studied him through the binoculars.

Taking a casual stroll. Looking around the field.
Wilcox sauntered toward the phone. A pistol butt pro-
truded from the middle of his belt. "Looks like a Glock,"
Potter said of the gun.

LeBow wrote down the information in a small notebook, the data to be transcribed when he returned to the
command post. He then whispered, "Thinks he's the
Marlboro man."

"Looks pretty confident," Budd said. "But I suppose
he's got all the cards."

"He's got *none* of the cards," the negotiator said softly.
"But either one'll give you all the confidence in the
world."

Wilcox snagged the strap of the phone's backpack and
gazed again at the line of police cars. He was grinning.

Budd laughed. "It's like—"

The crack of the gunshot echoed through the field and
with a soft *phump* the bullet slapped into the ground ten
feet from Wilcox. In an instant he had the pistol in his
hand and was firing toward the trees where the shot had
come from.

"No!" cried Potter, who leapt up and raced into the
field. Through the bullhorn he turned to the cops behind
the squad cars, all of whom had drawn their pistols or
lifted shotguns and chambered rounds. "Hold your fire!"
He waved his hands madly. Wilcox fired twice at Potter.
The first shot vanished into the cloudy sky. The second
split a rock a yard from Potter's feet.

Stillwell was shouting into his throat mike, "No return
fire! All unit commanders, no return fire!"

But there was return fire.

Dirt kicked up around Wilcox as he flung himself to the
ground and with carefully placed shots shattered three police car windshields before reloading. Even under these
frantic conditions Wilcox was a fine marksman. From a
window of the slaughterhouse came the repeated explosions of a semiautomatic shotgun; pellets hissed through
the air.

Potter remained standing, in plain view, waving his
hands. "Stop your firing!"

Then, suddenly, complete silence fell over the field.

The wind vanished for a moment and stillness descended. The hollow cry of a bird filled the gray afternoon; the sound was heartbreaking. The sweet smell of gunpowder and fulminate of mercury, from primers, was thick.

Gripping the phone, Wilcox backed toward the slaughter-house.

To Stillwell, Potter called, "Find out who fired. Who-ever fired the first shot—I want to see him in the van. The ones who fired afterwards—I want them off the field and I want everybody to know why they're being dismissed."

"Yessir." The sheriff nodded and hurried off.

Potter, still standing, turned the binoculars onto the slaughterhouse, hoping to catch a glimpse of the inside when Wilcox entered. He was scanning the ground floor when he observed a young woman looking through the window to the right of the slaughterhouse door. She was blond and seemed to be in her mid-twenties. Looking right at him. She was distracted for a moment, glanced into the bowels of the slaughterhouse then back to the field, terror in her eyes. Her mouth moved in a curious way—very broadly. She was saying something to him. He watched her lips. He couldn't figure out the message.

Potter turned aside and handed LeBow the binoculars. "Henry, fast. Who's that? You have any idea?"

LeBow had been inputting the identities of those hostages they had information about. But by the time he looked, the woman was gone. Potter described her.

"The oldest student's seventeen. It was probably one of the two teachers. I'd guess the younger one. Melanie Charrol. She's twenty-five. No other information on her yet."

Wilcox backed into the slaughterhouse. Potter saw nothing inside except blackness. The door slammed shut. Potter scanned the windows again, hoping to catch an-other glimpse of the young woman. But he saw nothing. He was silently duplicating the motion of her mouth. Lips pursed together, lower teeth touching the upper lips; lips pursed again, though differently, like in a kiss.

"We should make the call." LeBow touched Potter's el-bow.

Potter nodded and the men hurried back to the van in

silence, Budd behind them, glaring at one of the troopers who'd returned fire at Wilcox. Stillwell was reading the man the riot act.

Lips, teeth, lips. What were you trying to say? he wondered.

"Henry," Potter said. "Mark down: 'First contact with a hostage.' "

"Contact?"

"With Melanie Charrol."

"What was the communication?"

"I don't know yet. I just saw her lips move."

"Well—"

"Write it down. 'Message unknown.' "

"Okay."

"And add, 'Subject was removed from view before the threat management team leader could respond.' "

"Will do," replied meticulous Henry LeBow.

Inside the van Derek asked what happened but Potter ignored him. He snatched the phone from Tobe Geller and set it on the desk in front of him, cradled it between his hands.

He looked out through the thick window over the field, where the flurry of activity after the shooting had stopped completely. The front was now quiet; the errant officers— three of them—had been led off by Dean Stillwell, and on the field the remaining troopers and agents stood with dense anticipation and fear and joy at the prospect of battle—a joy possible because there're thirty of you for each of them, because you're standing behind a half-ton Detroit picket line and wearing an Owens-Corning body vest, a heavy gun at your side, and because your spouse awaits you in a cozy bungalow with a beer and hot casserole.

Arthur Potter looked out over this cool and windy afternoon, an afternoon with the taste of Halloween in the air despite the midsummer month.

It was about to begin.

He turned away from the window, pushed a rapid-dial button on the phone. Tobe flipped a switch and began the recording. He hit another button and the sound of the ringing crackled through a speaker above their heads.

The phone rang five times, ten, twenty.

Potter felt LeBow's head turn toward him.

Tobe crossed his fingers.

Then: *Click.*

"We've got an uplink," Tobe whispered.

"Yeah?" The voice rang through the speaker.

Potter took a deep breath.

"Lou Handy?"

"Yeah."

"This is Arthur Potter. I'm with the FBI. I'd like to talk to you."

"Lou, that shot, it was a mistake."

"Was it now?"

Potter listened carefully to the voice, laced with a slight accent, mountain, West Virginian. He heard self-confidence, derision, weariness. All three combined to scare him considerably.

"We had a man in a tree. He slipped. His weapon discharged accidentally. He'll be disciplined."

"You gonna shoot him?"

"It was purely an accident."

"Accidents're funny things." Handy chuckled. "I was in Leavenworth a few years back and this asshole worked in the laundry room choked to death on a half-dozen socks. Had to've been a accident. He wouldn't go chewing on socks on purpose. Who'd do that?"

Cool as ice, Potter thought.

"Maybe this was that kinda accident."

"This was a run-of-the-mill, U.S.-certified accident, Lou."

"Don't much care what it was. I'm shooting one of 'em. Eenie meenie miney . . ."

"Listen to me, Lou. . . ."

No answer.

"Can I call you Lou?"

"You got us surrounded, don'tcha? You got assholes in the trees with guns even if they can't sit on branches without falling. Guess you can call me what you fucking well like."

"Listen to me, Lou. This's a real tense situation here."

"Not for me it ain't. I ain't tense at all. Here's a pretty little blond one. No tits to speak of. Think I'll pick her."

He's playing with us. Eighty percent he's bluffing.

"Lou, Wilcox was in clear view. Our man was only eighty yards away, M-16 with a scope. Those troopers can drop a man at a thousand yards if they have to."

"But it's awful windy out there. Maybe your boy didn't compensate."

"If we'd've wanted your man dead he'd be dead."

"That don't matter. I keep telling you. Accident or not," he snarled, "gotta teach you people some manners."

The bluff factor dropped to sixty percent.

Stay calm, Potter warned himself. Out of the corner of his eye he watched young Derek Elb wipe his palms on his pants and stuff a piece of gum into his mouth. Budd paced irritatingly, looking out the window.

"Let's just put it down to a mishap, Lou, and get on with what we have to talk about."

"Talk about?" He sounded surprised. "Whatta we gotta talk about?"

"Oh, lots," Potter said cheerfully. "First of all, is everybody doing okay in there? You have any injuries? Anybody hurt?"

His instinct was to ask specifically about the girls but negotiators try never to talk about the hostages if possible. You have to make the HT think that the captives have no bargaining value.

"Shep's a little bent outta shape, as you'd imagine, but otherwise everybody's right as rain. Course, ask again in five minutes. One of 'em ain't gonna be feeling so good."

Potter wondered: What did she say to me? He pictured Melanie's face again. Lips, teeth, lips . . .

"You need any first-aid supplies?"

"Yeah."

"What?"

"A medevac chopper."

"That's kind of a tall order, Lou. I was thinking more bandages or morphine, something like that. Antiseptic."

"Morphine? That wouldn't be to make us all dopey, would it? You'd like that, bet."

"Oh, we wouldn't give you enough to dope you up, Lou. You need anything at all?"

"Yeah, I need to shoot somebody's what I need. Little blondie here. Put a bullet 'tween the tits she don't have."

"That wouldn't do anybody any good now, would it?"

Potter was thinking: He likes to talk. He's unstable but he likes to talk. That's always the first hurdle, sometimes insurmountable. The quiet ones are the most dangerous. The agent cocked his head and prepared to listen carefully. He had to get into Handy's mind. Fall into his speech patterns, guess what the man is going to say, how he's going to say it. Potter would play this game all night until, by the time things were resolved one way or another, part of him would *be* Louis Jeremiah Handy.

"What's your name again?" Handy asked.

"Arthur Potter."

"You go by Art?"

"Arthur, actually."

"Ain't you got the info on me?"

"Some. Not much."

Potter thought spontaneously: *I killed a guard escaping.*

"I killed me a guard when we were escaping. Didn't you know that?"

"Yes, I did."

Potter thought: *So the girl without any tits don't mean shit to me.*

"So killing this girl, little blondie here, it don't mean nothing to me."

Potter pushed a mute button—a special device on the phone, which cut off his voice without a click on the other end. "Who's he talking about?" he asked LeBow. "Which hostage? Blond, twelve or under?"

"I don't know yet," the intelligence officer responded. "We can't get a clear look inside and don't have enough information."

Into the phone he said, "Why d'you want to hurt anybody, Lou?"

He'll change the subject, Potter guessed.

But Handy said, "Why not?"

Theoretically Potter knew he should be talking about

frivolous things, stretching out the conversation, winning the man over, making him laugh. Food, sports, the weather, conditions inside the slaughterhouse, soft drinks. You never talked to the HTs about the incident itself at first. But he was assessing the risk that Handy was about to kill the girl and the bluff ratio was down to thirty percent; he couldn't afford to chat about hamburgers and the White Sox.

"Lou, I don't think you want to kill anybody."

"How d'you figure?"

Potter managed a chuckle. "Well, if you start killing hostages I'll have to conclude that you're planning to kill them all anyway. That's when I send in our hostage rescue team to take you all out."

Handy was laughing softly. "*If* them boys was there."

Potter and LeBow frowned at each other. "Oh, they're here," Potter said. He nodded at the "Deceptions" side of the bulletin board and LeBow jotted, *Handy told that HRT is in place.*

"You're asking me to hold off killing her?"

"I'm asking you not to kill anyone."

"I don't know. Should I, shouldn't I? You know how that happens sometimes, you just don't know what you want? Pizza or a Big Mac? Just can't fucking decide."

Potter's heart stuttered for a moment, for it seemed to him that Handy was being honest: that he really couldn't decide what to do, and that if he spared the girl it wouldn't be Potter's reasoned talk that saved her but whim, pure and simple, on Handy's part.

"I'll tell you what, Lou. I'm apologizing to you for the gunshot. I'll give you my word it won't happen again. In exchange for that, will you agree not to shoot that girl?"

He's smart, calculating, always thinking, the agent concluded. There wasn't a thing psychotic about Handy that Potter could identify. He wrote on a sheet of paper *IQ?* and pushed it toward LeBow.

Don't have it.

Handy's humming came through the phone. It was a song that Potter had heard a long time ago. He couldn't place it. Then through the speaker the man's amplified voice said, "Maybe I'll wait."

Potter sighed. LeBow gave him a thumbs-up and Budd smiled.

"I appreciate that, Lou. I really do. How's your food situation?"

Are you for real? Potter speculated.

"What're you, first you play cop, then you play nurse, now you're a fucking caterer?"

"I just want to keep everybody real calm and comfortable. Get you some sandwiches and sodas if you want. What do you say?"

"We're not hungry."

"Could be a long night."

Either: silence or *Won't be that long at all.*

"Don't think it's gonna be that long. Listen here, Art, you can chat me up 'bout food and medicine and any other crap you can think of. But the fact is we've got some things we're gonna want and we better have 'em without no hassles or I start killing. One by one."

"Okay, Lou. Tell me what they are."

"We'll do some talking here between us. And get back to you."

"Who's 'us,' Lou?"

"Aw, shit, you know, Art. There's me and Shep and my two brothers."

LeBow tapped Potter's arm. He was pointing to the screen. It read:

Handy is one of three brothers. Bench warrant out on Robert, 27. LKA, Seattle; failed to appear for grand larceny trial, fled jurisdiction. Eldest brother, Rudy, 40, was killed five years ago. Shot six times in the back of head by unknown assailant. Handy was suspected; never charged.

Potter thought of the delicate lines on his genealogy charts. What would Handy's look like; from whom did his blood descend? "Your brothers, Lou?" he said. "Is that right? They're inside with you?"

A pause.

"And Shep's four cousins."

"That's a lot of folk you got there. Anybody else?"

"Doc Holliday and Bonnie 'n' Clyde and Ted Bundy and a shitload of the gang from Mortal Kombat, and Luke Skywalker. And Jeffrey Dahmer's hungry ghost."

"Maybe we better surrender to *you,* Lou."

Handy laughed again. Potter was pleased at the sliver of rapport. Pleased too that he managed to say the magic word "surrender," plant it in Handy's thoughts.

"My nephew collects superhero comics," the agent said. "He'd love an autograph. Spider-Man wouldn't be in there too, would he?"

"Might just be."

The fax machine whirred and a number of sheets scrolled out. LeBow snatched them up and flipped through them rapidly, paused at one and then scribbled on the top, *HOSTAGES.* He pointed to a girl's name, followed by a block of handwritten text. It was preliminary data from Angie Scapello.

Hostage negotiation is the process of testing limits. Potter read the fax and noticed something. He said casually, "Say, Lou, like to ask you a question. One of those girls in there's got some serious health problems. Would you let her go?"

It was surprising how often direct requests of this sort worked. Ask a question and go silent.

"Really?" Handy sounded concerned. "Sick, huh? What's the trouble?"

"Asthma." Maybe the joking and the cartoon-character chat was having an effect on Handy.

"Which one is she?"

"Fourteen, short blond hair."

Potter listened to the background noise—just hollowness—as Handy, he assumed, looked over the hostages.

"If she doesn't get her medicine she could die," Potter said. "You release her, you do that for me, and when we get down to the serious negotiating I'll remember it. Tell you what, release her and we'll get you some electricity in there. Some lights."

"You'll turn the power on?" Handy asked so suddenly it startled Potter.

"We checked into that. The place is too old. It's not wired for modern current." Potter pointed to the "Deceptions" board and LeBow wrote. "But we'll run a line in and get you some lights."

"Do that and then we'll talk."

The balance of power was shifting subtly to Handy. Time to be tough. "All right. Fair enough. Now listen, Lou, I have to warn you. Don't try to get out of the building. There'll be snipers sighting on you. You're perfectly safe inside."

He'll be angry, Potter anticipated. A mini tantrum. Obscenities and expletives.

"Oh, I'm perfectly safe anywhere," Handy whispered into the phone. "Bullets pass right through me. I have strong medicine. When do I get some lights?"

"Ten minutes, fifteen. Give us Beverly, Lou. If you do—"

Click.

"Damn," Potter muttered.

"Little eager there, Arthur," LeBow said. Potter nodded. He'd made the classic mistake of negotiating against himself. Always wait for the other side to ask you for something. Understandably he'd pushed when he heard Handy's hesitation and upped the stakes himself. But he'd scared off the seller. Still, at some point he'd have to go through this exercise. Hostage takers can be pushed a certain distance, and bribed a certain amount further. Half the battle was finding out how far and when to do which.

Potter called Stillwell and told him he'd warned the takers about leaving the slaughterhouse. "You're greenlighted to contain them, as discussed."

"Yessir," Stillwell said.

Potter asked Budd, "What's the ETA on that power truck?"

"Should be just ten minutes." He was looking out the window morosely.

"What's the matter, Charlie?"

"Oh, nothing. I was just thinking that was good what you did there. Talking him out of shooting her."

Potter sensed there was something else on Budd's mind. But he said only, "Oh, Handy was the one who decided not to shoot. I had nothing to do with it. The problem is, I don't know why yet."

Potter waited five minutes, then pushed speed dial.

The phone rang a million times. "Could you please turn that down a little, Tobe?" Potter nodded at the speaker above his head.

"Sure. . . . Okay, uplink."

"Yeah?" Handy barked.

"Lou, you'll have a power line in about ten minutes."

Silence.

"What about the girl, Beverly?"

"Can't have her," he said abruptly, as if surprised that Potter hadn't figured this out yet.

Silence for a moment.

"Thought you said if you got power—"

"I'd think about it. I did, and you can't have her."

Never get drawn into petty bickering. "Well, have you done any thinking about what you fellows want?"

"I'll get back to you on that, Art."

"I was hoping—"

Click.

"Downlink terminated," Tobe announced.

Stillwell brought the trooper in, a short, swarthy young man. He leaned the offending weapon by the door, its black bolt locked back, and walked up to Potter.

"I'm sorry, sir, I was on this branch and there was this gust of wind. I—"

"You were told to unchamber your weapon," Potter snapped.

The trooper stirred and his eyes darted around the room.

"Here now," Stillwell said, looking faintly ridiculous with a bulky flak jacket on under his Penney's suit. "Tell the agent what you told me."

The trooper looked icily at Stillwell, resenting the new chain of command. He said to Potter, "I never received that order. I was locked and loaded from the git-go. That's SOP for us, sir."

Stillwell grimaced but he said, "I'll take responsibility, Mr. Potter."

"Oh, brother. . . ." Charlie Budd stepped forward. "Sir,"

he said formally to Potter, "I have to say—it's my fault. Mine alone."

Potter lifted an inquiring hand toward him.

"I didn't tell the snipers to unchamber. I should've, like you ordered me to. The fact is, I concluded that I wasn't going to have troopers in the field unprotected. It's my fault. Not this man's. Not Dean's."

Potter considered this and said to the sniper, "You'll stand down and assist at the rear staging area. Go report to Agent-in-Charge Henderson."

"But I slipped, sir. It wasn't my fault. It was an accident."

"There're no accidents in my barricades," Potter said coldly.

"But—"

"That's all, Trooper," Dean Stillwell said. "You heard your order. Dismissed." The man snagged his weapon then stormed out of the van.

Budd said, "I'll do the same, sir. I'm sorry. I really am. You should have Dean here assist you. I—"

Potter pulled the captain aside. He said in a whisper, "I need your help, Charlie. But what you did, it was a personal judgment call. That, I *don't* need from you. Understand?"

"Yessir."

"You still want to be on the team?"

Budd nodded slowly.

"Okay, now go on out there and give them the order to unchamber."

"Sir—"

"Arthur."

"I've got to go home and look my wife in the eye and tell her that I disobeyed an FBI agent's direct order."

"How long you been married?"

"Thirteen years."

"Get hitched in junior high?"

Budd smiled grimly.

"What's her name?"

"Meg. Margaret."

"You have children?"

"Two girls." Budd's face remained miserable.

"Go on now. Do what I asked." Potter held his eyes.

The captain sighed. "I will, yessir. It won't happen again."

"Keep your head down." Potter smiled. "And don't delegate this one, Charlie."

"No sir. I'll check everybody."

Stillwell looked on sympathetically as Budd, hangtail, walked out the door.

Tobe was stacking up audiocassettes. All conversations with the takers would be recorded. The tape recorder was a special unit with a two-second delay built in, so that an electronic voice added a minute-by-minute time stamp onto the recording yet didn't block out the conversation. He looked up at Potter. "Who was it who said, 'I've met the enemy and he is us'? Was that Napoleon? Or Eisenhower, or somebody?"

"I think it was Pogo," Potter said.

"Who?"

"Comic strip," Henry LeBow said. "Before your time."

12:33 P.M.

The room was growing dark.

It was only early afternoon but the sky had filled with purple clouds and the windows in the slaughterhouse were small. Need that juice and need it now, Lou Handy thought, peering through the dimness.

Water dripped and chains hung from the gloomy shadows of the ceiling. Hooks everywhere and overhead conveyors. There were rusted machines that looked like parts of cars a giant had been playing with and said fuck it and tossed down on the floor.

Giant, Handy laughed to himself. What the hell'm I talking about?

He wandered through the ground floor. Wild place. What's it like to make money knocking off animals? he wondered. Handy had worked dozens of jobs. Usually sweat labor. Nobody ever let him operate fancy equipment, which would have doubled or tripled his salary. The jobs always ended after a month or two. Arguments with the foreman, complaints, fights, drinking in the locker room. He had no patience to wait it out with people who couldn't understood that he wasn't your average person. He was *special*. Nofuckingbody in the world had ever caught on to this.

The floor was wood, solid as concrete. Beautifully joined oak. Handy was no craftsman, like Rudy'd been, but he could appreciate good work. His brother had laid flooring for a living. Handy was suddenly angry at that asshole Potter. For some reason the agent had brought Rudy to mind. It infuriated Handy, made him want to get even.

He walked to the room where they'd put the hostages. It was semicircular, sided in porcelain tile, windowless. The blood drain. He guessed that if somebody fired a gun in the middle of the room it'd be loud enough to shatter eardrums.

Didn't much matter with this buncha birds, he thought. He looked them over. What was weird was that these girls—most of 'em—were *pretty*. That oldest one especially, the one with the black hair. The one looking back at him with a go-to-fucking-hell expression on her face. She's what, seventeen, eighteen? He smiled at her. She stared back. Handy gazed at the rest of them. Yep, pretty. It blew him away. They're freaks and all and you'd think they'd look a little gross, like retards do—like no matter how pretty, there's still something wrong, the corners don't meet even. But no, they looked normal. But damn, they cry a lot. *That* was irritating . . . that sound their throats make. They're fucking deaf—they shouldn't be making those fucking sounds!

Suddenly, in his mind, Lou Handy saw his brother.

The red dot appearing where Rudy's skull joined his spine. Then more dots, the tiny gun bucking in his fingers. The shudder in his brother's shoulders as the man stiffened, did a spooky little dance, and fell dead.

Handy decided he hated Art Potter even more than he'd thought.

He ambled back to Wilcox and Bonner, pulled the remote control out of the canvas bag, and channel-surfed on
the tiny battery-powered TV that rested on an oil drum.
All the local stations and one network were reporting
about them. One newscaster said this would be Lou
Handy's fifteen minutes of fame, whatever the hell that
meant. The cops had ordered the reporters so far back
from the action that he couldn't see anything helpful on
the screen. He remembered the O. J. Simpson case,
watching the white Bronco cruise down the highway, park
at the man's house. The choppers were close enough to
see the faces of the guy who was driving and the cop in
his driveway. Everybody white in the prison rec room
thinking, Blow your fucking brains out, nigger. Everybody black thinking, Go, O.J.! We're with you, homes!

Handy turned down the sound on the TV. Fucking
place, he thought, looking around the slaughterhouse. He
smelled rotting carcasses.

A voice startled him, "Let them go. Keep me."

He wandered over to the tiled room. He crouched down
and looked at the woman. "Who're you?"

"I'm their teacher."

"You can do that sign language stuff, right?"

"Yes." She gazed at Handy with defiant eyes.

"Uck," Handy said. "Freaky."

"Please, let them go. Keep me."

"Shut up," Handy said, and walked away.

He looked out the window. A tall police van sat on the
crest of a hill. He bet that was where Art Potter was sitting. He took his pistol from his pocket and aimed at a
yellow square on its side. He compensated for the distance and the wind. He lowered the gun. "Coulda nailed
you, they wanted to," he called to Wilcox. "That's what
he told me."

Wilcox too was gazing out a window. "There's a lot of
'em," he mused. Then: "Who was he? Th'asshole you
were talking to."

"FBI."

Bonner said, "Oh, man. You mean we got a Feebie out
there?"

"Was a federal prison we broke outta. Who the fuck you think they'd have after us?"

"Tommy Lee Jones," Bonner said. The big man kept his eyes on the teacher for a moment. Then on the little girl in the flowered dress and white stockings.

Handy saw his eyes. That cocksucker. "Nup, Sonny. Keep it inside them stinky jeans of yours, you hear me? Or you'll lose it."

Bonner grunted. When accused of doing just what he was guilty of Bonner always got pissed. Fast as a hedge-hog rolls up. "Fuck you."

"Hope I gave one of 'em a new asshole," Wilcox said, but in his lazy-as-could-be voice, one of the reasons why Handy liked him.

"So what've we got?" Handy asked.

Wilcox answered, "The two shotguns. And close to forty shells. One Smitty only six rounds. No, make that five. But we've got the Glocks and beaucoup de ammo there. Three hundred rounds."

Handy paced around the slaughterhouse floor, dancing over the pools of standing water.

"Damn cryin's getting on my nerves," Handy snapped. "It's fucking with my mind. That fat one, shit. Lookit her. And I don't know what's going on out there. That agent sounded too slick. I don't trust his ass. Sonny, you stay with our girls. Shep 'n' me're gonna poke around."

"What about tear gas?" Bonner looked out the window uncertainly. "We shoulda got some masks."

"They shoot tear gas in," Handy explained, "just piss on the canisters."

"That works? To stop it?"

"Yep."

"How 'bout that."

Handy glanced into the tiled room. The older teacher gazed at him with her muddy eyes. Sort of defiant, sort of something else.

"What's your name?"

"Donna Harstrawn. I—"

"Tell me, Donna, what's her name?" he asked slowly, pointing to the oldest student, the pretty one with the long black hair.

Before the teacher could answer, the girl lifted her middle finger toward him. Handy roared with laughter.

Bonner stepped forward, lifting his arm. "You little shit."

Donna scrambled in front of the girl, who drew back her fists, grinning. The little girls made their fucking spooky bird noises and the scared blond teacher held up a pitiful, pleading hand.

Handy grabbed Bonner's hand and pushed him away. "Don't hit 'em 'less I tell you to." He pointed at the teenager and asked the teacher, "What's her fucking name?"

"Susan. Please, will you—"

"And what's hers?" Pointing at the blond, the younger teacher.

"Melanie."

Mel-a-nee. She was the one that really pissed him off. When he'd found her looking out the window just after the shooting he'd grabbed her arm and she'd gone apeshit, totally freaked. He'd let her wander around 'cause he knew she wouldn't cause any trouble. At first he'd thought it was funny, her being such a little mouse. Then it made him mad—that skittish light in her eyes that made him want to stamp his foot just to see her jump. It *always* pissed him off, seeing no spirit in a woman.

This little bitch was the opposite of Pris. Oh, he'd like to see the two of them tangle. Pris'd pull out that Buck knife she kept down her bra sometimes, hot against her left tit, open it up, and come after her. Little blondie here'd take a dump in her pants. She seemed a hell of a lot younger than that Susan.

Now, *she* interested him, Suze did. Good old Donna had her muddy eyes that told him nothing, and the younger teacher had her scared eyes that hid everything. But Miss Teenager here . . . well, her eyes said a lot and she didn't care if he read it. He figured that she was smarter than the other two put together.

And ballsier.

Like Pris, he thought, with approval. "Susan," Handy said slowly. "I like you. You've got spunk. You don't know what the fuck I'm saying. But I like you." To the older teacher he said, "Tell her that."

After a pause Donna gestured with her hands.

Susan gave him a drop-dead look and responded.

"What'd she say?" Handy barked.

"She said to please let the little girls go."

Handy grabbed the woman's hair and pulled hard. More little bird screeches. Melanie shook her head, tears streaming. "What the fuck did she say?"

"She said, 'Go to hell.' "

He pulled her hair harder; tufts of the dyed strands popped from her skull. She whined in pain. "She said," Donna gasped, "she said, 'You're an asshole.' "

Handy laughed hard and shoved the teacher to the ground.

"Please," she called. "Let them go, the girls. Keep me. What does it matter if you have one hostage or six?"

"Because, you stupid cunt, I can shoot a couple of 'em and still have some left over."

She gasped and turned away quickly, as if she'd just walked into a room and found a naked man leering at her.

Handy walked to Melanie. "You think I'm an asshole too?"

The other teacher started to move her hands but Melanie responded before she'd gotten the question out.

"What'd she say?"

"She said, 'Why do you want to hurt us, Brutus? We didn't hurt you.' "

"Brutus?"

"That's what she calls you."

Brutus. Sounded familiar but he couldn't remember where he'd heard it. He frowned slightly. "Tell her she knows the fucking answer to that question." As he walked out the doorway Handy called, "Hey, Sonny, I'm learning sign language. Lemme show you."

Bonner looked up.

Handy extended his middle finger. The three men laughed and Handy and Wilcox started down the corridor into the back of the slaughterhouse. When they were exploring the maze of hallways and butcher and processing rooms Handy asked Wilcox, "Think he'll behave?"

"Sonny? Fuck, I guess. Any other time he'd be on 'em like a rooster. But there ain't nothing like having a hundred armed cops outside your door to keep a pecker limp. What the fuck d'they do here?" Wilcox was gazing at the machinery, the long tables, gears and governors and belts.

"Whatta you think?"

"I don't know."

"It's a fucking slaughterhouse."

" 'Processing,' that's what it means?"

"Shoot 'em and gut 'em. Yeah. Processing."

Wilcox pointed to an old machine. "What's that?"

Handy walked over and looked at it. He grinned. "Shit. It's a old steam engine. Hell, lookit."

"What'd they use that for here?"

"See," Handy explained, "this is why the world's got itself into deep shit. Back then, see, that was a turbine." He pointed to an old rusted spine covered with rotting fan blades. "That was how things worked. It went around and did things. That was the steam age and it was like the gas age too. Then we got into the electric age and you couldn't see what things did too well. Like you can see steam and fire but you can't see electricity doing anything. That's what got us into World War Two. Now we're in the *electronic* age. It's computers and everything and it's fucking impossible to see how things work. You can look at a computer chip and not see a thing even though it's totally doing what it oughta do. We've lost control."

"It's all pretty fucked up."

"What? Life or what I'm saying?"

"I don't know. It just sounds all fucked up. Life, I guess."

They'd emerged into a large dim cavern. Must have been the warehouse. They tied or chocked shut the back doors.

"They can blow 'em open," Wilcox said. "A couple cutting charges'd do it."

"They could drop an A-bomb on us too. Either way them girls die. If that's what they want that's what they'll get."

"Elevator?"

"Nothing much we can do 'bout that," Handy said,

looking at the big service elevator. "They wanta come rappelling in, we can get the first half-dozen of 'em. You know, their necks. Always aim for their necks."

Wilcox glanced at him then drawled, "So, whatcha thinking?"

I do get that look in my eyes, Handy thought. Pris says so all the time. Damn, he missed her. He wanted to smell her hair, listen to the sound of her bracelet as she shifted gears in her car, wanted to feel her underneath him as they fucked on the shag carpet of her apartment.

"Let's send one back to 'em," Handy said.

"One of the girls?"

"Yeah."

"Which one?"

"I don't know. That Susan maybe. She's all right. I like her."

Wilcox said, "I'd vote her most likely to hump. Not a bad idea to get her out of Bonner's sight. He'd be sniffing her lickety-split 'fore sunset. Or that other one, Melanie."

Handy said, "Naw, let's keep her. We oughta hang on to the weak ones."

"Second that."

"Okay, it'll be Susan." He laughed. "Not many girls around can look me in the eye and tell me I'm an asshole, I'll tell you that."

Melanie kept her arm tight around Kielle's shoulders, which were oddly muscular for an eight-year-old, and reached out a little further to rub the arm of one of the twins.

The girls were sandwiched in between her and Susan, and Melanie admitted reluctantly to herself that her gesture was only partially to reassure the younger ones; she also wanted the comfort for herself, the comfort of being close to her favorite student.

Melanie's hands were still shaking. She'd been un-nerved when Brutus had grabbed her earlier as she was looking out the window, sending her message to the policeman in the field. And downright terrified when he'd pointed at her a few minutes ago and demanded to know her name.

She glanced at Susan and saw her looking angrily at Mrs. Harstrawn.

"What's the matter?" Melanie signed.

"My name. Giving it to him. Shouldn't have done that. Don't cooperate."

"We have to," the older teacher signed.

Melanie added, "Can't make them mad at us."

Susan laughed derisively. "What difference does it make if they're mad? Don't give in. They're assholes. They're worst type of Other."

"We can't—" Melanie began.

Bear stamped his foot. Melanie felt the vibrations and jumped. His fat lips were working fast and all she could make out was "Shut up." Melanie looked away. She couldn't stand the sight of his face, the way the black hairs at the edge of his beard curled outward, his fat pores.

His eyes kept returning to Mrs. Harstrawn. And Emily.

When he looked away Melanie slowly brought her hand up and switched from American Sign Language to Signed Exact English and fingerspelling. This was a clumsy way of communicating—she had to spell out words and put them into English word order. But it allowed the use of small hand motions and avoided the broad gestures necessary to communicate in ASL.

"Don't make them mad," she told Susan. "Take it easy."

"They're assholes." Susan refused to switch from ASL.

"Sure. But don't provoke!"

"They won't hurt us. We're no good to them dead."

Exasperated, Melanie said, "They can hurt us without killing us."

Susan just grimaced and looked away.

Well, what does she want us to do? Melanie thought angrily. Grab their guns away and shoot them? Yet at the same time she thought: Oh, why can't I be like her? Look at her eyes! How strong she is! She's eight years younger than me but I feel like the child when I'm around her.

Some of her envy could be attributed to the fact that Susan was the highest in the hierarchy of the world of the Deaf. She was prelingually deaf—born deaf. But more than that, she was Deaf of Deaf: both her parents had been deaf. Politically active in Deaf issues even at seventeen, accepted at Gallaudet in Washington, D.C., on a full scholarship, unyielding about the use of ASL versus SEE, militantly rejecting oralism—the practice of forcing the deaf to try to speak. Susan Phillips was the chic, up-to-the-minute Deaf young woman, beautiful and strong, and Melanie would rather have one Susan by her side at a time like this than a roomful of men.

She felt a small hand tug at her blouse.

"Don't worry," she signed to Anna. The twins hugged each other, their cheeks together, their remarkable eyes wide and tearful. Beverly sat by herself, her hands in her lap, and stared mournfully at the floor, struggling to breathe.

Kielle signed, "We need Jean Grey and Cyclops," referring to two of her favorite X-Men. "They'd tear them apart."

Shannon responded, "No, we need Beast. Remember? He had the blind girlfriend?" Shannon studied Jack Kirby's art religiously and intended to be a superhero-comic artist.

"Gambit too," Kielle signed. Pointing to Shannon's tattoo.

Shannon's own comics—surprisingly good, Melanie thought, for an eight-year-old—featured characters with disabilities, like blindness and deafness, that they could mutate to their advantage as they solved crimes and saved people. The two girls—Shannon, gangly and dark; Kielle, compact and fair—fell into a discussion of whether optic blasts, plasmoids, or psychic blades would be the weapons of choice to save them now.

Emily cried for a moment into the sleeve of her dress, printed with black and purple flowers. Then she bowed her head, praying. Melanie saw her two fists lift and open outward. It was the ASL word for "sacrifice."

"Don't worry," Melanie repeated to those girls who were looking at her. But no one paid attention. If they focused on anyone it was on Susan though the girl was signing nothing, merely gazing steadily at Bear, who stood near the entrance to the killing room. Susan was their rallying point.

Her presence alone gave them confidence. Melanie found herself struggling to keep from crying.

And it'll be so dark in here tonight!

Melanie leaned forward and looked out the window. She saw the grass bending in the wind. The Kansas wind, relentless. Melanie remembered her father telling her about the sea captain Edward Smith, who came to Wichita in the 1800s and got the idea of mounting sails on Conestoga wagons—literally prairie schooners. She'd laughed at the idea and at her father's humorous telling of the tale, never knowing whether to believe it or not. Now, she was stung at the memory of the storytelling and wished desperately for anything, mythical or real, to sweep her away from the killing room.

She thought suddenly: And what about that man outside? The policeman?

There had been something so reassuring in the way he'd stood up there on the hill after Brutus had fired his gun out the window and Bear was running around, his fat belly jiggling, ripping open boxes of bullets in a panic. The man stood on the hilltop waving his arms, trying to calm things down, stop the shooting. He was looking directly at her.

What would she call him? No animals came to mind. Nothing sleek and heroic anyway. He was old—twice her age probably. And he dressed frumpy. His glasses seemed thick and he was a few pounds heavy.

Then it occurred to her. De l'Epée.

That's what she'd call him. After Charles Michel de l'Epée, the eighteenth-century abbé who was one of the first people in the world to really care about the Deaf, to treat them as intelligent human beings. The man who created French Sign Language, the predecessor of ASL.

It was a perfect name for the man in the field, thought Melanie, who could read French and knew that the name itself meant a kind of sword. Her de l'Epée was brave. Just the way his namesake had stood up to the Church and the popular sentiment that the Deaf were retarded and freaks, he was standing up to Stoat and Brutus, up there on the hill, bullets flying around him.

Well, she *had* sent him a message—a prayer, in a way.

A prayer and a warning. Had he seen her? Could he understand what she'd said even if he had? She closed her eyes for a brief moment, concentrating all her thoughts on de l'Epée. But all she sensed was the temperature, which had grown cooler, her fear, and—to her dismay—the vibration of footsteps as a man, no, *two* men, approached slowly over the resonant oak floor.

As Brutus and Stoat appeared in the doorway Melanie glanced at Susan, whose face hardened once again, looking up at their captors.

I'll make my face hard too.

She tried but it trembled and soon she was crying again.

Susan! Why can't I be like you?

Bear walked up to the other men. He was gesturing to the main room. The light was dim and the phony science of lipreading gave her a distorted message. She believed he said something about the phone.

Brutus responded, "So let the fucker ring."

This was very strange, Melanie reflected, as the urge to cry diminished. Why, she thought again, can I understand *him* so well? Why him and not the others?

"We're going to send one back."

Bear asked a question.

Brutus answered, "Miss Deaf Teen." He nodded at Susan. Mrs. Harstrawn's face blossomed with relief.

My God, thought Melanie in despair, they're going to let her go! We'll be here all alone without her. Without Susan. No! She choked a sob.

"Stand up, honey," Brutus said. "Your . . . day. You're going home."

Susan was shaking her head. She turned to Mrs. Harstrawn and signed a defiant message, with her fast, crisp signing. "She says she isn't going. She wants you to release the twins."

Brutus laughed. "She wants me. . . ."

Stoat said, "Get . . . up." He pulled Susan to her feet.

And then Melanie's heart was pounding, her face burned red, for, to her horror, she realized that the first thought in her mind was: Why couldn't it have been me?

Forgive me, God. De l'Epée, please forgive me! But then she made her shameful wish once again. And again still. It looped through her mind endlessly. I want to go home. I want to sit down by myself with a big bowl of popcorn, I want to watch closed-captioned TV, I want to clap the Koss headsets around my ears and feel the vibrations of Beethoven and Smetana and Gordon Bok. . . .

Susan struggled away from Stoat's grip. She thrust the twins toward him. But he pushed the little girls aside and brutally tied Susan's hands behind her. Brutus stared out through the half-open window. "Hold up here," Brutus said, pushing Susan to the floor beside the door. He glanced back. "Sonny, go keep our lady friends company . . . that scattergun with you."

Susan looked back into the killing room.

In the girl's face Melanie saw the message: Don't worry. You'll be all right. I'll see to it.

Melanie held her gaze for only a moment then looked away, afraid that Susan would read her own thoughts and would see in them the shameful question: Why can't it be me, why can't it be me, why can't it be me?

1:01 P.M.

Arthur Potter gazed at the slaughterhouse and the fields surrounding it through the jaundice glass of the van's window. He was watching a trooper run the electrical line up to the front door. Five caged lights hung from the end of the cable. The officer backed away and Wilcox came out once more, pistol in hand, to retrieve the wire. He didn't, as Potter had hoped, run the line through the door, which would then have to remain open, but fed it through a window. He returned inside and the thick metal door swung tightly shut.

"Door is still secure," the negotiator said absently, and LeBow typed.

More faxes arrived. More background on Handy and on the hostages from the school the girls attended. LeBow greedily looked over the sheets and entered relevant data in the "Profiles" computer. The engineering and architect's diagrams had been transmitted. They were helpful only for the negatives they presented—how hard an assault would be. There were no tunnels leading into the slaughterhouse and if the P&Z variance documents from 1938 were accurate there had been significant construction on the roof of the building—with plans to create a fourth story—which would make a helicopter assault very difficult.

Tobe stiffened suddenly. "They've popped the cover on the phone." His eyes stared intently at a row of dials.

"Is it still working?"

"So far."

Looking for bugs.

The young agent relaxed. "It's back together again. Whoever did it knows his equipment."

"Henry, who?"

"No way of knowing yet. I'd have to guess Handy. The military training, you know."

"Downlink," Tobe called.

Potter lifted a curious eyebrow at LeBow and picked up the phone as it rang.

"Hello. That you, Lou?"

"Thanks for the lights. We checked 'em for microphones . . . the phone too. Didn't find a fucking thing. A man of your word."

Honor. It means something to him, Potter noted, trying once again to comprehend the unfathomable.

"Say, what are you, Art, a senior agent? Agent in Charge? That's what they call 'em, right?"

Never let the HT think you're in a position to make important decisions by yourself. You want the option to stall while you pretend to talk to your superiors.

"Nope. Just a run-of-the-mill special agent who happens to like talking."

"So you say."

"I'm a man of my word, remember?" Potter said, glancing at the "Deceptions" board.

Time to defuse things, build up some rapport. "So what about some food, Lou? We could start grilling up some burgers. How do you like 'em?"

Blood red, Potter speculated.

But he was wrong.

"Listen up, Art. I just want you to know what kind of nice fellow I am. I'm letting one of 'em go."

This news depressed Potter immeasurably. Curiously, with this act of spontaneous generosity, Handy had put them on the defensive. It was tactically brilliant. Potter was now indebted to him and he felt again a shift in the balance of power between predator and prey.

"I want you to understand that I ain't all bad."

"Well, Lou, I appreciate that. Is it Beverly? The sick girl?"

"Uh-uh."

Potter and the other cops craned forward to look outside. They could see a slight splinter of light as the door opened. Then a blur of white.

Keep his mind off the hostages, Potter thought. "You done any more thinking about what you folks're interested in? It's time to get down to some serious horse trading, Lou. What do you say—"

The phone clicked into dull static.

The door to the van suddenly swung open. Dean Stillwell's head poked in. The sheriff said, "They're releasing one of them."

"We know."

Stillwell disappeared outside again.

Potter spun about in the swivel chair. He couldn't see clearly. The clouds were very dense now and the fields dim, as if an eclipse had suddenly dipped the earth into shadow.

"Let's try the video, Tobe."

A video screen burst to life, showing in crisp black-and-white the front of the slaughterhouse. The door was open. They had all five lamps burning, it seemed.

Tobe adjusted the sensitivity and the picture settled.

"Who, Henry?"

"It's the older girl, Susan Phillips. Seventeen."

Budd laughed. "Hey, looks like it may be easier than we thought. If he's just gonna give 'em away."

On the screen Susan looked back into the doorway. A hand pushed her forward. Then the door closed.

"This is great," LeBow said enthusiastically, looking out the window, his head close to Potter's. "Seventeen. And she's a top student. She'll tell us a truckload of stuff about the inside."

The girl walked in a straight line away from the building. Through the glasses Potter could see how grim her face was. Her hands were tied behind her but she didn't seem to have suffered from the brief captivity.

"Dean," Potter said into the radio microphone, "send one of your men to meet her."

"Yessir." The sheriff was now speaking in a normal tone into his throat mike; he'd finally gotten the hang of the gear.

A state trooper in body armor and helmet slipped from behind a squad car and cautiously started in a crouch toward the girl, who'd made her way fifty feet from the slaughterhouse.

The gasp came from deep in Arthur Potter's throat.

As if his whole body'd been submerged in ice water he shuddered, understanding perfectly what was happening.

It was intuition probably, a feeling gleaned from the hundreds of barricades he'd negotiated. The fact that no taker had ever spontaneously released a hostage this early. The fact that Handy was a killer without remorse.

He couldn't say for sure what tipped him but the absolute horror of what was about to occur gripped his heart. "No!" The negotiator leapt to his feet, knocking the chair over with a huge crash.

LeBow glanced at him. "Oh, no! Oh, Christ, no."

Charlie Budd's head swiveled back and forth. He whispered, "What's wrong? What's going on?"

"He's going to kill her," LeBow whispered.

Potter tore the door open and ran outside, his heart slugging away in his chest. Snatching a flak jacket from the ground, he slipped between two cars and, gasping, ran straight toward the girl, passing the man Dean Stillwell had sent to meet her. His urgency made the troopers in the field uneasy but some of them smiled at the sight of the pudgy man running, holding the heavy flak jacket in one hand and waving a white Kleenex in the other.

Susan was forty feet from him, walking steadily over

the grass. She adjusted her course slightly so they would meet.

"Get down, drop down!" Potter cried. He released the tissue, which floated ahead of him on the fast breeze, and he gestured madly at the ground. "Down! Get down!"

But she couldn't hear, of course, and merely frowned.

Several of the troopers had heard Potter and stepped away from the cars they were using as cover. Reaching tentatively for their guns. Potter's shouts were joined by others. One woman trooper waved madly. "No, no, honey! Get down, for the love of God!"

Susan never heard a word of it. She'd stopped and was looking carefully at the ground, perhaps thinking that he was warning her about a hidden well or wire she might trip over.

Gasping, his middle-aged heart in agony, Potter narrowed the gap to fifteen feet.

The agent was so close that when the single bullet struck her squarely in the back, and a flower of dark red blossomed over her right breast, he heard the nauseating sound of the impact, followed by an unworldly groan from deep within a throat unaccustomed to speaking.

She stopped abruptly then spiraled to the ground.

No, no, no . . .

Potter ran to the girl and propped the flak jacket around her head. The trooper ran up, crouching, muttering, "My God, my God," over and over. He aimed his pistol toward the window.

"Don't shoot," Potter commanded.

"But—"

"No!" Potter lifted his gaze from Susan's dull eyes to the slaughterhouse. He saw in the window just to the left of the door the lean face of Lou Handy. And through the right, perhaps thirty feet inside the dim interior, the negotiator could make out the stunned face of the young teacher, the blond one, who'd sent him the cryptic message earlier and whose name he could not now recall.

You feel sounds.

Sound is merely a disturbance of air, a vibration, and it

laps upon our bodies like waves, it touches our brows like a lover's hand, it stings and it can make us cry.

Within her chest she still felt the sound of the gunshot.

No, Melanie thought. No. This isn't possible.

It *can't* be. . . .

But she knew what she'd seen. She didn't trust voices but her eyes were rarely wrong.

Susan, Deaf of Deaf.

Susan, braver than I could ever be.

Susan, who had the world of the Deaf and the world of the Others at her feet.

The girl had stepped into the horrible Outside and it had killed her. She was gone forever. A tiny hole opening in her back, kicking aside her dark hair. The abrupt halt as she walked the route that Melanie had shamefully prayed that she herself would be walking.

Melanie's breath grew shallow and the edges of her vision crumbled to blackness. The room tilted and sweat appeared in sheets on her face and neck. She turned slowly and looked at Brutus, who was slipping the still-smoking pistol into his waistband. What she saw filled her with hopelessness. For she could see no satisfaction, no lust, no malice. She saw only that he'd done what he planned to—and had already forgotten about the girl's death.

He clicked on the TV again and glanced toward the killing room, in whose doorway the seven girls stood or sat in a ragged line, some staring at Melanie, some staring at Mrs. Harstrawn, who had collapsed on the floor, sobbing, gripping her hair, her face contorted like a hideous red mask. The teacher had apparently seen the gunshot and understood what it meant. The other girls had not. Jocylyn wiped from her face a sheet of her dark hair, unfortunately self-cut. She lifted her hands, signing repeatedly, "What happened? What happened? What happened?"

I have to tell them, Melanie thought.

But I can't.

Beverly, the next oldest after Susan, understood something terrible had occurred but didn't quite know—or admit—what. She took Jocylyn's pudgy hand and gazed at Melanie.

She sucked air deep into her damaged lungs and put her other arm around the inseparable twins.

Melanie did not spell the name Susan. She couldn't, for some reason. She used the impersonal "she," accompanied by a gesture toward the field.

"She . . ."

How do I say it? Oh, God, I have absolutely no idea. It took her a moment to remember the word for "killed." The word was constructed by moving the extended index finger of the right hand up under the left hand, held cupped, palm down.

Exactly like a bullet entering the body, she thought.

She couldn't say it. Saw Susan's hair pop up under the impact. Saw her ease to the ground.

"She's dead," Melanie finally signed. "Dead" was a different gesture, turning over the flattened, palm-up right hand so that it was palm down; simultaneously doing the opposite with the left. It was at her right hand that Melanie stared, thinking how the gesture of this hand mimicked scooping earth onto a grave.

The girls' reactions were different but really all the same: the tears, the silent gasps, the eyes filling with horror.

Her hands trembling, Melanie turned back to the window. De l'Epée had picked up Susan's body and was walking back to the police line with it. Melanie watched her friend's dangling arms, the cascade of black hair, the feet—one shoe on, one shoe off.

Beautiful Susan.

Susan, the person I would be if I could be anybody.

As she watched de l'Epée disappear behind a police car, part of Melanie's silent world grew slightly more silent. And that was something she could scarcely afford.

"I'm resigning, sir," Charlie Budd said softly.

Potter stepped into the john of the van to put on the fresh shirt that had somehow appeared in the hands of one of Dean Stillwell's officers. He dropped his own blood-stained shirt into a wastebasket and pulled on the new one; the bullet that had killed Susan had spattered him copiously.

"What's that, Charlie?" Potter asked absently, stepping back to the desk. Tobe and Derek sat silently at their consoles. Even Henry LeBow had stopped typing and stared out the window, which from the angle at which he sat revealed nothing but distant wheat fields, distorted and tinted ocher by the thick grass.

Through the window on the other side of the van the ambulance lights flashed as they took the girl's body away.

"I'm quitting," Budd continued. "This assignment and the force too." His voice was steady. "That was my fault. It was because of that shot a half-hour ago. When I didn't tell the snipers to unchamber. I'll call Topeka and get a replacement in here."

Potter turned back, tucking the crisp shirt in. "Stick around, Charlie. I need you."

"Nosir. I made a mistake and I'll shoulder the consequences."

"You may have plenty of opportunity to take responsibility for your screwups before this night is through," Potter told him evenly. "But that sniper shot wasn't one of them. What Handy just did had nothing to do with you."

"Then why? Why in God's name would he do that?"

"Because he's putting his cards on the table. He's telling us he's serious. We can't buy him out of there cheap."

"By shooting a hostage in cold blood?"

LeBow said, "This's the hardest kind of negotiation there is, Charlie. After a killing up front, usually the only way to save any hostage is a flat-out assault."

"High stakes," Derek Elb muttered.

Extreme stakes, Arthur Potter thought. Then: Jesus, what a day this's going to be.

"Downlink," Tobe said, and a moment later the phone buzzed. The tape recorder began turning automatically.

Potter picked up the receiver. "Lou?" he said evenly.

"There's something you gotta understand 'bout me, Art. I don't *care* about these girls. They're just little birds to me that I used to shoot off my back porch at home. I aim to get outta here and if it means I gotta shoot nine more of 'em dead as posts then that's the way it's gonna be. You hear me?"

Potter said, "I do hear you, Lou. But we've got to get one other thing straight. I'm the only man in this universe can get you out of there alive. There's nobody else. So I'm the one to reckon with. Now do *you* hear *me*?"

"I'll call you back with our demands."

1:25 P.M.

This was tricky, this was dangerous, this was not about re-election.

This was about decency and life.

So Daniel Tremain told himself as he walked into the governor's mansion.

Standing upright as a birch rod, he headed through the surprisingly modest home into a large den.

Decency and life.

"Officer."

"Governor."

The Right Honorable Governor of the state of Kansas, A. R. Stepps, was looking at the faint horizon—fields of grain identical to those that had funded his father's insurance company, which had in turn allowed Stepps to be a public servant. Tremain believed Stepps was the perfect governor: connected, distrustful of Washington, infuriated about crime in Topeka and the felons that Missouri sloughed off into *his* Kansas City but able to live with it all, his eye no further than the low star of a retirement spent teaching in Lawrence and cruising Scandia Lines routes with the wife.

But now there was Crow Ridge.

The governor's eyes lifted from a fax he'd been reading and scanned Tremain.

Look me over if you want. Go right ahead. His blue-and-black operations gear certainly looked incongruous here among the framed prints of shot ducks, the Lemon-

Pledged mahogany antiques. Most frequently Stepps's eyes dipped to the large automatic pistol, which the trooper adjusted as he sat in the irritatingly scrolly chair.

"He's killed one?"

Tremain nodded his head, which was covered with a thinning crew cut. He noted that the governor had a tiny hole in the elbow of his baby-blue cardigan and that he was absolutely terrified.

"What happened?"

"Premeditated, looks like. I'm getting a full report but it looks like there was no reason for it. Sent her out like he was giving her up and shot her in the back."

"Oh, dear God. How young was she?"

"The oldest. A teenager. But still . . ."

The governor nodded toward a silver service. "Coffee? Tea? . . . No? You've never been here before, have you?"

"The governor's mansion? No." Though it wasn't a mansion; it was just a nice house, a house that rang with the sounds of family.

"I need some help here, Officer. Some of your expertise."

"I'll do whatever I can, sir."

"An odd situation. These prisoners escaped from a federal penitentiary. . . . What is it, Captain?"

"With all respect, sir, that prison at Callana's like it's got a revolving door in it." Tremain recalled four breakouts in the last five years. His own men had captured a number of the escapees, a record better than that of the U.S. marshals, who in Tremain's opinion were overpaid baby-sitters.

The governor began cautiously, like a man stepping onto November ice. "So they're technically federal escapees but they also're lined up for state sentences. Won't be till the year three thousand maybe but the fact is they're state felons too."

"But the FBI's in charge of the barricade." Tremain had been told specifically by the assistant attorney general that his services would not be required in this matter. The trooper was no expert on the hierarchy of state government but even schoolchildren knew that the AG and his underlings worked for the governor. Executive branch.

"We have to defer to them, of course. And maybe it's for the best."

The governor said, "This Potter's a fine man. . . ." His voice seemed not to stop but to deflate until it became a dwelling question mark.

Dan Tremain was a career law enforcer and had learned never to say anything that could be quoted back against him even before he'd learned how to cover two opposing doors when diving through a barricade window. "Pride of the FBI, I'm told," the trooper said, assuming that a tape recorder was running somewhere nearby, though it probably wasn't.

"But?" The governor raised an eyebrow.

"I understand he's taking a hard line."

"Which means what?"

Outside the window, threshers moved back and forth.

"It means that he's going to try to wear Handy down and get him to surrender."

"Will Potter attack eventually? If he has to?"

"He's just a negotiator. A federal hostage rescue team's being assembled. They should be here by early evening."

"And if Handy doesn't surrender they'll go in and . . ."

"Neutralize him."

The round face smiled. The governor looked nostalgically at an ashtray and then back to Tremain. "How soon after they get there will they attack?"

"The rule is that you don't assault except as a last resort. Rand Corporation did a study a few years ago and found that ninety percent of the hostages killed in a barricade are killed when the situation goes hot—when there's an assault. I was going to say something else, sir."

"Please. Speak frankly."

The corner of a sheet of paper peeked out from under the governor's repulsively blue sweater. Tremain recognized it as his own résumé. He was proud of his record with the state police though he wondered if he wasn't here now because the governor had read the brief paragraph referring to a "consulting" career, which had taken Tremain to Africa and Guatemala after his discharge from the Marines.

"The Rand Corporation study is pretty accurate as far

as it goes. But there's something else that bears on this situation, sir. That if there's a killing early in the barricade, negotiations rarely work. The HT—the hostage taker—has little to lose. Sometimes there's a psychological thing that happens and the taker feels so powerful that he'll just keep upping his demands so that they *can't* be met, just so he'll have an excuse to kill the hostages."

The governor nodded.

"What's your assessment of Handy?"

"I read the file on the way over here and I came up with a profile."

"Which is?"

"He's not psychotic. But he's certainly amoral."

The governor's thin lips twitched into a momentary smile. Because, Tremain thought, I'm a mercenary thug who used the word *amoral*?

"I think," Tremain continued slowly, "that he's going to kill more of the girls. Maybe all of them ultimately. If he goes mobile and gets away from us I think he'll kill them just for the symmetry of it."

Symmetry. How do you like *that,* sir? Check out the education portion of my résumé. I was cum laude from Lawrence. Top of my class at OCS.

"One other thing we have to consider," the captain continued. "He didn't try very hard to escape from that trooper who found them this afternoon."

"No?"

"There was just that one officer and the three takers, with guns and hostages. It was like Handy's goal wasn't so much to get away but to spend some time . . ."

"Some time what?"

"With the hostages. If you get what I'm saying. They *are* all female."

The governor lifted his bulky weight from the chair. He walked to the window. Outside the combines combed the flat landscape, two of the ungainly machines slowly converging. The man sighed deeply.

Fucking symmetrically amoral life, ain't it, sir?

"He simply isn't your typical hostage taker, Governor. There's a sadistic streak in him."

"And you really think he'd ... hurt the girls? You know what I mean?"

"I believe he would. If he could keep an eye out the window at the same time. And one of the fellows in there with him, Sonny Bonner, he's doing time for rape. Well, interstate transport. But rape was at the bottom of it."

On the governor's desk were pictures of his blond family, a black Labrador retriever, and Jesus Christ.

"How good is your team, Captain?" Whispering now.

"We're very, very good, sir."

The governor rubbed his sleepy eyes. "Can you get them out?"

"Yes. To know how many casualties, I'd have to do a preliminary plan of the tactical operation and then run a damage assessment."

"How soon could you do that?"

"I've asked Lieutenant Carfallo to obtain terrain maps and architectural drawings of the building."

"Where is he now?"

Tremain glanced at his watch. "He happens to be outside, sir."

The governor's eyes twitched again. "Why don't you ask him in?"

A moment later the lieutenant, a short, stocky young officer, was unfurling maps and old drawings.

"Lieutenant," Tremain barked, "give us your assessment."

A stubby finger touched several places on the architectural drawings. "Breachable here and here. Move in, use stun grenades, set up crossfire zones." The young man said this cheerfully and the governor seemed to grow uneasy again. As well he ought to. Carfallo was a scary little weasel. The lieutenant continued, "I'd estimate six to eight seconds, bang to bullets."

"He means," Tremain explained, "it's six seconds from the time the door blows until we acquire all three targets—um, have guns pointed at all the HTs."

"Is that good?"

"Excellent. It means that hostage casualties would be minimal or nonexistent. But of course I can't guarantee that there'd be none."

"God doesn't give us guarantees."

"No, He doesn't."

"Thank you, Lieutenant," the governor said.

"Dismissed," Tremain snapped, and the young man's face went still as he turned and vanished.

"What about Potter?" the governor asked. "He *is* in charge after all."

Tremain said, "And the related issue—there'd have to be some reason to green-light an assault."

"Some excuse," the governor mused, very carelessly. Then he stiffened and picked at a renegade powder-blue thread on his cuff.

"Say something happened to sever communications between Potter and Handy and the men in the field. And then say someone in my team observed a high-risk activity inside the slaughterhouse, some activity that jeopardized troopers or the hostages. Something Potter wasn't able to respond to. I'd think that—well, even legally—we'd be fully authorized to move in and secure the premises."

"Yes, yes. I'd think you would be." The governor lifted an inquiring eyebrow then thought better of saying whatever he'd been about to say. He slapped the desktop. "All right, Captain. My instructions: You're to move the state Hostage Rescue Unit to Crow Ridge and provide any backup assistance you can to Agent Potter. If for some reason Agent Potter is unable to remain in command of the situation and the convicts present an immediate threat to anyone—hostages or troopers or . . . just plain anyone—you're authorized to do whatever's necessary to neutralize the situation."

Entrust that to tape if you want. Who could argue with the wisdom and prudence of the words?

"Yessir." Tremain rolled up the maps and diagrams. "Is there anything else, sir?"

"I know that time is of the essence," the governor said slowly, applying his last test to the solemn trooper, "but do you think we could spend a moment in prayer?"

"I'd be honored, sir."

And the soldier took the sovereign's hand and they both dropped to their knees. Tremain closed his piercing blue eyes. A stream of words filled the room, rapid and articulate, as if they flowed straight from the heart of an Almighty worried sick about those poor girls about to die in the corridors of the Webber & Stoltz Processing Company, Inc.

So you'll be home then.

Melanie watched the lump of a woman and thought: it's impossible for someone to cry that much. She tapped Mrs. Harstrawn's arm but all the teacher did was cry even harder.

They were still in the little hellhole of the killing room. Scummy water on the floor, ringed like a rainbow from spilled oil. Filthy ceramic tile. No windows. It smelled of mold and shit. And decayed, dead animals in the walls. It reminded Melanie of the shower room in *Schindler's List.*

Her eyes kept falling on the center of the room: a large drain from which radiated spider legs of troughs. All stained brown. Old, old blood. She pictured a young calf braying then struggling as its throat was cut, the blood pulsing out, down the drain.

Melanie started to cry and once again heard her father's voice from last spring, *So you'll be home then. You'll be home then you'll be home then. . . .*

From there her thoughts leapt to her brother, lying in a hospital bed six hundred miles away. He'd have heard by now, heard about the murder of the couple in the Cadillac, the kidnaping. He'd be worried sick. I'm sorry, Danny. I wish I were with you!

Blood spraying through the air. . . .

Mrs. Harstrawn huddled and shook. Her face was a remarkable blue and Melanie's horror at Susan's death was momentarily replaced by the fear that the teacher was having a stroke.

"Please," she signed. "Girls are scared."

But the woman didn't notice or, if she did, couldn't respond.

So you'll . . .

Melanie wiped her face and lowered her head into her arms.

. . . be home then.

And if she'd been home, like her parents wanted (well,

her *father,* but her father's decision *was* her parents'), she
wouldn't be here now.

None of them would.

And Susan would still be alive.

Stop thinking about it!

Bear walked past the killing room and looked in. He
squeezed his crotch, half hidden beneath his belly, and
barked something at Shannon. He offered his knee, said
something about did she want to kick him again? She
tried to give him a defiant look but stared down at her
arm, rubbing the faded self-drawn tattoo of the superhero.

Brutus called something and Bear looked up. The big
man was afraid of him, Melanie understood suddenly,
seeing the look in Bear's eyes. He laughed humorlessly,
sneering. Glanced once at Mrs. Harstrawn. But his eyes
lingered longest on the little girls, especially the twins
and Emily, her dress, her white stockings and black
patent-leather shoes, the dress bought just for the occa-
sion of Melanie's performance at the Kansas State Theater of the Deaf Summer Recital. How long the gaze
coursed over the little girl. He reluctantly walked back
into the main room of the slaughterhouse.

Get them out, Melanie told herself. Whatever you have
to do, *get them out.*

Then: But I can't. Brutus will kill me. He'll rape me.
He's evil, he's the Outside. She thought of Susan and
wept again. He was right, her father.

So you'll be home then.

She'd be alive.

There'd have been no secret appointments after the
recital in Topeka. No lies, no hard decisions.

"Get back, against the wall," she signed to the girls.
She had to get them away from Bear, keep them out of
sight. They moved as instructed, tearful all of them except
lean, young Shannon, once more angry and defiant, the
tomboy. And Kielle too—though she was neither angry
nor defiant but eerily subdued. The girl troubled Melanie.
What was in her eyes? The shadow of exactly what had
been in Susan's? Here was a child with the visage of a
woman. My God, there's vindictiveness, chill, raw hatred.

Is she the one who's really Susan's heir? Melanie wondered.

"He's Magneto," Kielle signed matter-of-factly, glancing in Brutus's direction and addressing her comment to Shannon. It was her own nickname for Handy. The other girl disagreed. "No. He's Mr. Sinister. Not part of Brotherhood. Worst of the worst."

Kielle considered this. "But I think—"

"Oh, you two, stop!" Beverly burst into their conversation, her hands rising and falling like her struggling chest. "This isn't stupid game."

Melanie nodded. "Don't say anything more." Oh, Mrs. Harstrawn, Melanie raged silently, please . . . How you cry! Red face, blue face, quivering. Please don't do this! Her hands rose. "I can't do it alone."

But Mrs. Harstrawn was helpless. She lay on the tile floor of the killing room, her head against a trough where the hot blood of dying calves and lambs flowed and vanished and she said not a word.

Melanie looked up. The girls were staring at her.

I *have* to do something.

But all she remembered was her father's words—phantom words—as he sat on the front porch swing of their farmhouse last spring. A brilliant morning. He said to her, "This is your home and you'll be welcome here. See, it's a question of belonging and what God does to make sure those that oughta stay someplace do. Well, your place is here, working at what you can do, where your, you know, problem doesn't get you into trouble. God's will."

(How perfectly she'd made out the words then, even the impossible sibilants and elusive glottal stops. As clearly as she understood Handy—Brutus—now.)

Her father had finished. "So you'll be home then." And rose to hitch up the ammonia tank without letting her write a single word of response on the pad she carried around the house.

Suddenly Melanie was aware of Beverly's head bobbing up and down. A full-fledged asthma attack. The girl's face darkened and she closed her eyes miserably, struggling ferociously to breathe. Melanie stroked her damp hair.

"Do something," Jocylyn signed with her stubby, inept fingers.

The shadows reaching into the room, shadows of machinery and wires, grew very sharp, then began to sway. Melanie stood and walked into the slaughterhouse. She saw Brutus and Stoat rearranging the lights.

Maybe he'll give us one for our room. Please. . . .

"I hope he dies, I hate him," the blond fireball Kielle signed furiously, her round face contorted with hatred as she gazed at Brutus.

"Quiet."

"I want him to die!"

"Stop!"

Beverly lay down on the floor. She signed, "Please. Help."

In the outer room Brutus and Stoat sat close together under a swaying lamp, the light reflecting off Stoat's pale crew cut. They were watching the small TV, clicking through the channels. Bear stood at the window, counting. Police cars, she guessed.

Melanie walked toward the men. Stopped about ten feet from them. Brutus looked over the dark skirt, the ruddy blouse, the gold necklace—a present from her brother, Danny. He was studying her, that damn curious smile on his face. Not like Bear, not staring at her boobs and legs. Just her face and, especially, her ears. She realized it was the way he'd stared at devastated Mrs. Harstrawn—as if he was adding another specimen to a collection of tragedies.

She mimicked writing something.

"Tell me," he said slowly, and so loudly she felt the useless vibrations pelt her. "Say it."

She pointed to her throat.

"You can't talk neither?"

She wouldn't talk. No. Though there was nothing wrong with her vocal cords. And because she'd become deaf relatively late in life, Melanie knew the fundamentals of word formation. Still, following Susan's model, Melanie avoided oralism because it wasn't chic. The Deaf community resented people who straddled both worlds— the Deaf world and the world of the Others. Melanie hadn't tried to utter a single word in five or six years.

She pointed toward Beverly and breathed in hard.
Touched her chest.

"Yeah, the sick one. . . . What about her?"

Melanie mimicked taking medicine.

Brutus shook his head. "I don't give a shit. Go back and
sit down."

Melanie pushed her hands together, a prayer, a plea.
Brutus and Stoat laughed. Brutus called something to
Bear, and Melanie suddenly felt the firm vibrations of his
footsteps approach. Then an arm was around her chest
and Bear was dragging her across the floor. His fingers
squeezed her nipple hard. She yanked his hand away and
the tears came again.

In the killing room she pushed away from him and collapsed on the floor. Melanie grabbed one of the lights,
which rested on the ground, and clutched it, hot and oily,
to her chest. It burned her fingers but she clung to it like a
life preserver. Bear looked down, seemed to ask a question.

But just as she'd done that spring day with her father on
the farmhouse porch, Melanie gave no response; she simply went away.

That day last May, she'd climbed the creaking stairs
and sat in an old rocking chair in her bedroom. Now, she
lay on the killing room floor. A child again, younger than
the twins. Mercifully she closed her eyes and went away.
To anyone watching it seemed that she'd slipped into a
faint. But in fact she wasn't here at all; she'd gone someplace else, someplace safe, someplace not another living
soul knew about.

When he recruited hostage negotiators Arthur Potter
found himself in the peculiar position of interviewing
clones of himself. Middle-aged, frumpy, easygoing cops.

For a time it was thought that psychologists ought to be
used for negotiating; but even though a barricade resem-
bles a therapy session in many ways, shrinks just didn't
work out. They were too analytical, focused too much on
diagnostics. The point of talking to a taker isn't to figure
out where he fits in the *DSM IV* but to persuade him to
come out with his hands up. This requires common sense,

concentration, a sharp mind, patience (well, Arthur Potter worked hard at that), a healthy sense of self, the rare gift of speaking well, and the rarer talent of listening.

And most important, a negotiator is a man with controlled emotions.

The very quality that Arthur Potter was wrestling with at the moment. He struggled to forget the image of Susan Phillips's chest exploding before him, feeling the hot tap of blood droplets striking his face. There'd been many deaths in the barricades he'd worked over the years. But he'd never been so close to such a cold-blooded death as this one.

Henderson called. The reporters had heard a gunshot and were champing to get some information. "Tell them I'll make a statement within a half-hour. Don't leak it, Pete, but he just killed one."

"Oh, God, no." But the SAC didn't sound upset at all; he seemed almost pleased—perhaps because Potter had assumed point position on this megatragedy in progress.

"Executed her. Shot her in the back. Listen, this could all go bad in a big way. Get on the horn to Washington and push the HRT assembly, okay?"

"Why'd he do it?"

"No apparent reason," Potter said, and they hung up.

"Henry?" Potter said to LeBow. "I need some help here. What should we stay away from?"

Negotiators try to increase the rapport with their takers by dipping into personal matters. But a question about a sensitive subject can send an agitated taker into a frenzy, even prompting him to kill.

"There's so little data," the intelligence officer said. "I guess I'd avoid his military service. His brother Rudy."

"Parents?"

"Relation unknown. I'd steer clear on general principles until we learn more."

"His girlfriend? What's her name?"

"Priscilla Gunder. No problems there, it looks like. Fancied themselves a regular Bonnie and Clyde."

"Unless," Budd pointed out, "she dumped him when he went to prison."

"Good point," Potter said, deciding to let Handy bring up the girlfriend and just echo or reflect whatever he said.

"Definitely avoid the ex-wife. It seems there was some bad blood there."

"Personal relations in general, then," Potter summarized. It was typical in criminal takings. Usually mentally disturbed takers wanted to talk about the ex-spouse they were still in love with. Potter gazed at the slaughterhouse and announced, "I want to try to get one out. Who should we go for? What do we know about the hostages so far?"

"Just a few isolated facts. We won't have anything substantive till Angie gets here."

"I was thinking . . ." Budd began.

"Yes, go ahead."

"That girl with the asthma. You asked about her before but he's had a spell of her choking up a storm—if I know asthma. Handy's the sort who'd have a short fuse for something like that, seems to me. He's probably ready to boot her out."

"It's a good thought, Charlie," Potter said. "But the psychology of negotiating is that once you've had a refusal you have to go on to a different issue or person. For the time being Beverly's non-negotiable. It'd be weak of us to try to get her and too weak of him to give in when he's already refused. Henry, you have anything at all on the others?"

"Well, this girl Jocylyn Weiderman. I have a note from Angie that she's been in and out of counseling for depression. Cries a lot and has attacks of hysteria. She might try to panic and run. Get herself killed."

"I'll buy that," said Budd.

"Good," Potter announced. "Let's try for her."

As he was reaching for the phone Tobe held up a hand. "Downlink."

The phone buzzed; the recorder turned.

"Hello?" Potter asked.

Silence.

"How's everything doing in there, Lou?"

"Not bad."

The thick window of the command van was right next to him but Potter's head was up, gazing at what LeBow had mounted—the CAD diagram of the slaughterhouse. It was a hostage rescue team's nightmare. The spot where Handy seemed to be at the moment was a single large room—a holding pen for the livestock. But in the back of the slaughterhouse were three stories of warrens—small offices, cutting and packing rooms, sausage grinding and stuffing rooms and storage areas, interconnected with narrow corridors.

"You fellows must be pretty tired," Potter offered.

"Listen, Art. I'm gonna tell you what we want. You probably got a tape recorder going but're gonna pretend you don't."

"Sure, we're taking down every word. I'm not going to lie to you. You know the drill."

"You know, I hate the way I sound on tape. One of my trials they played a confession tape of me in court. I didn't like the way I sounded. I don't know why I confessed either. I guess I was just anxious to tell somebody what I done to that girl."

Potter, eager to learn everything about this man, asked, "What *did* you do exactly, Lou?" He speculated: *It was real nasty. I don't think you want to hear about it.*

"Oh, wasn't pleasant, Art. Not pretty at all. I was proud of my work, though."

"Asshole," Tobe muttered.

"Nobody likes how they sound on tape, Lou," Potter continued easily. "I've got to give this training seminar once a year. They tape it. I hate how I sound."

Shut the fuck up, Art. Listen.

"Don't much care, Art. Now, get your pencil ready and listen. We want a chopper. A big one. One that seats eight."

Nine hostages, three HTs, and the pilot. That leaves five left over. What's going to happen to them?

LeBow was writing all this down on his computer. He'd padded the keys with cotton so that they were nearly silent.

"Okay, you want a helicopter. The police and the Bureau only have two-seaters. It'll take some time until we can get—"

"Like I say, Art. Don't much care. Chopper and a pilot. That's number one. Got it?"

"Sure do, Lou. But like I told you before, I'm just a special agent. I don't have the authority to requisition a chopper. I'll have to get on the horn to Washington."

"Art, you ain't listening. That's *your* problem. It's gonna be my theme for the day. Don't. Much. Care. The clock's running, whether you gotta call the airport that's up the road a couple miles or the Pope in his holy city."

"Okay. Keep going."

"We want some food."

"You got it. Anything in particular?"

"McDonald's. Lots of it."

Potter motioned to Budd, who picked up his phone and began whispering orders.

"It's on its way."

Get into him. Get inside his head. He's going to ask for liquor next, Potter guessed.

"And a hundred rounds of twelve-gauge shells, double-ought, body armor, and gas masks."

"Oh, well, Lou, I guess you know I can't do that."

"I don't know that at all."

"I can't give you weapons, Lou."

"Even if I was to give you a girl?"

"Nope, Lou. Weapons and ammunition are deal breakers. Sorry."

"You use my name a lot, Art. Hey, if we *was* to do some horse trading, which one of the girls would you want? Anybody in particular? Say we weren't talking about guns and such."

LeBow raised his eyebrows and nodded. Budd gave Potter a thumbs-up.

Melanie, Potter thought automatically. But he believed their assessment was right and that they had to try for the girl most at risk—Jocylyn, the troubled student.

Potter told him there was one girl in particular they wanted.

"Describe her."

LeBow spun the computer around. Potter read the fine print on the screen then said, "Short dark hair, over-weight. Twelve. Her name's Jocylyn."

"Her? That weepy little shit. She whines like a pup with a busted leg. Good riddance. Thanks for picking her, Art. She's the one gets shot in five minutes, you don't agree to the guns 'n' ammo."

Click.

2:00 P.M.

Hell, Potter thought, slamming his fist on the table.

"Oh, brother," muttered Budd. Then: "Oh, Jesus."

Potter picked up the binoculars and saw a young girl appear in the window of the slaughterhouse. She was chubby and her round cheeks glistened with tears. When the muzzle of the gun touched her short-cut hair, she closed her eyes.

"Call it out, Tobe."

"Four minutes thirty."

"That's her?" Potter whispered to LeBow. "Jocylyn?"

"I'm sure."

"You've noted that the scatter guns are twelve-gauge?" Potter asked evenly.

LeBow said he had. "And that they're possibly low on ammo."

Derek glanced at them, shocked at this cold-blooded conversation.

"Jesus God," Budd rasped. "Do something."

"What?" Potter asked.

"Well, call him back and tell him you'll give him the ammo."

"No."

"Four minutes."

"But he's going to shoot her."

"I don't think he will." Will he, won't he? Potter debated. He honestly couldn't tell.

"Look at him," Budd said. "Look out there! That girl's got a gun to her head. I can see her crying from here."

"Which is just what he wants us to see. Calm down, Charlie. You never negotiate weapons or armor."

"But he's going to kill her!"

"Three minutes thirty."

"What if," Potter said, struggling to control his impatience, "he's completely out of ammo? He's sitting in there with two empty pistols and an empty scatter gun?"

"Well, maybe he's got one shell left and he's just about to use it on that girl."

A hostage situation is a homicide in progress.

Potter continued to gaze at the unhappy face of the child. "We have to assume there are nine fatalities right now—the girls inside. A hundred rounds of twelve-gauge shells? That could double the number of casualties."

"Three minutes," Tobe sang out.

Outside Stillwell shifted uncomfortably and ruffled his mop of hair. He looked at the van then back at the slaughterhouse. He hadn't heard the exchange but he, like all the other troopers, could see the poor girl's head in the window.

"Two minutes thirty."

"Send him some blanks. Or some shells that'll jam the guns."

"That's a good idea, Charlie. But we don't have any such thing. He won't waste another hostage this early." Is this true? Potter wondered.

"Waste a hostage?" The voice of another trooper—Derek the technician—cut through the van. Potter believed the man appended in a whisper, "Son of a bitch."

"Two minutes," Tobe said in his unflappable voice.

Potter hunched forward, gazing out the window. He saw the officers behind their Maginot line of cars, some looking back at the van uneasily.

"One minute thirty."

What's Handy doing? What's he thinking? I can't see into him. I need more time. I need to talk to him more. An hour from now I'd *know* whether he'd kill her or not. Right now, all I see is smoke and danger.

"One minute," Tobe called out.

Potter picked up the phone. Pressed the rapid-dial button.

Click.

"Uplink."

"Lou."

"Art, I've decided I want a hundred rounds of Glock ammo too."

"No."

"Make that a hundred and one rounds of Glock. I'm about to lose one in thirty seconds. I'll need something to replace it."

"No ammo, Lou."

Derek leapt forward and grabbed Potter's arm. "Do it. For God's sake!"

"Sergeant!" Budd cried, and pulled the man away, shoved him into the corner.

Handy continued, "Remember that Viet Cong dude got shot? It was on film? In the head? The blood squirting up into the air like a fucking fountain."

"I can't do it, Lou. Don't you follow? We have a bad connection, or something?"

"You're supposed to be negotiating!" Budd whispered. "Talk to him." Now he seemed to regret pulling Derek Elb off.

Potter ignored him.

"Ten seconds, Arthur," Tobe said, fingering his earring hole nervously. He'd turned away from his precious dials and was looking out the window.

The seconds passed, ten minutes or an hour. Absolute silence in the control van, except for the static on the open line, the sound bleeding through the van's speakers. Potter realized he was holding his breath. He resumed breathing.

"Lou, are you there?"

No answer.

"Lou?"

Suddenly the gun lowered and a hand grabbed the girl by the collar. She opened her mouth as she was dragged back into the slaughterhouse.

Potter speculated: *Yo, Art, what's happening, homes?*

"Hey, Art, how's it hanging?" Handy's cheerful voice crackled over the speakers.

"Fair to middlin'. How about you?"

"Doing peachy. Here's the deal. I shoot one an hour till

that chopper's here. On the hour, every hour, starting at four."

"Well, Lou, I'll tell you right now we're going to need more time than that to get a big chopper."

Potter guessed: *Fuck that. You'll do what I tell you.*

But with playful menace in his voice Handy said, "How much more time?"

"A couple of hours. Maybe—"

"Fuck no. I'll give you till five."

Potter paused for a judicious moment. "I think we can work with that."

A harsh laugh. Then: "And a whole 'nother thing, Art."

"What's that?"

A pause, tension building. At last, Handy growled, "With those burgers I want some Fritos. Lots of Fritos."

"You got it. But I want that girl."

"Oh, hey," Budd whispered, "maybe you shouldn't push him."

"Which girl?"

"Jocylyn. The one you just had in the window."

"Jocylyn," Handy said with sudden animation, again startling Potter. "Funny 'bout that name."

Potter snapped his fingers, pointed at LeBow's computer. The intelligence officer scrolled through the profile of Handy, and both men tried to find some reference to Jocylyn: mother, sister, probation officer. But there was nothing.

"Why's that funny, Lou?"

" 'Bout ten years ago I fucked a waitress named Jocylyn and enjoyed it very much."

Potter felt the chill run from his legs to his shoulders.

"She was tasty. Before I met Pris of course."

Potter listened to Handy's tone. He closed his eyes. He speculated: *She was a hostage too, that Jocylyn, and I killed her 'cause . . .* He couldn't guess the rest of what Handy might say.

"Haven't thought about her for years. My Jocylyn was a hostage too, just like this one. She didn't do what I told her. I mean, she just *didn't*. So I had to use my knife."

Some of this is part of his act, Potter thought. The cheerful reference to the knife. But there was something revealing in the words too. *Didn't do what I told her.* Potter wrote down the sentence and pushed it to LeBow to type in.

"I want her, Lou," Potter said.

"Oh, don't you worry. I'm faithful to my Pris now."

"When we get the food, let's exchange. How 'bout it, Lou?"

"She's not much good for anything, Art. I think she peed her pants. Or maybe she just don't shower much. Even Bonner wouldn't come close to her. And he's a horny son of a bitch as you probably know."

"We're working on your chopper and you'll have the food there soon. You owe me a girl, Lou. You killed one. You owe me."

Budd and Derek gazed at Potter in disbelief.

"Naw," Handy said. "Don't think so."

"You're only going to have room in the chopper for four or five hostages. Give me that one." Sometimes you have to lie down; sometimes you have to hit. Potter snapped, "Jesus Christ, Lou, I know you're willing to kill them. You made your damn point. So just let her go, all right? I'll send a trooper up with the food; let him come back with the girl."

A pause.

"You really want that one?"

Potter thought: *Actually, I'd like 'em all, Lou.*

Time for a joke? Or too early?

He gambled. "I'd really like them all, Lou."

A harrowing pause.

Then a raucous laugh from the speaker. "You're a pistol, Art. Okay, I'll send her out. Let's synchronize our Timexes, boys. The clock's running. You get the fat one for the food. Fifteen minutes. Or I might change my mind. And a big beautiful chopper at five in the p.m."

Click.

"All right!" Tobe shouted.

Budd was nodding. "Good, Arthur. That was good."

Derek sat sullenly at his control panel for a moment but finally cracked a smile and apologized. Potter, ever willing to forgive youthful enthusiasm, shook the trooper's hand.

Budd was smiling in relief. He said, "Wichita's the aviation capital of the Midwest. Hell, we can get a chopper here in a half-hour."

"We aren't getting him one," Potter said. He gestured to the "Promises/Deceptions" chart. LeBow wrote, *Helicopter seating eight, due on hourly deadlines. Commencing at 5 p.m.*

"You're not going to give it to him?" Budd whispered.

"Of course not."

"But you lied."

"That's why it's on the 'Deceptions' side of the board."

Typing again, LeBow said, "We can't let him go mobile. Especially in a chopper."

"But he's going to kill another one at five."

"So he says."

"But—"

"That's my *job,* Charlie," Potter said, finding patience somewhere. "It's what I'm doing here, to talk him out of it."

And poured himself a cup of extremely bad coffee from a stainless steel pot.

Potter slipped a cellular phone into his pocket and stepped outside, crouching until he was in the gully, which protected him from the slaughterhouse.

Budd accompanied him part of the way. The young captain had found out that the Hutchinson police were in charge of stopping the river traffic and had ordered them to do so, incurring the wrath of several charterers of container barges bound for Wichita, whose meters were running to the tune of two thousand dollars an hour.

"Can't please everybody," the negotiator observed, distracted.

It was growing even colder—an odd July indeed with temperatures in the mid-fifties—and there was a rich metallic taste to the air, perhaps from the diesel exhaust of the nearby threshers or harvesters or combines, whatever they were. Potter waved at Stillwell, who was walking back and forth among the troopers, grinning laconically, and ordering troops into position.

Leaving Budd, Potter climbed into a bureau car and

drove to the rear staging area. Already, all the networks and local stations from a three-state area were here, as were reporters or stringers from the big-city papers and the wire services.

He had a brief word with Peter Henderson, who—whatever his other failings and motives—had quickly put together an efficient transport pool, supply staging area, and press tent.

Potter was known to the press and they descended on him frantically as he walked from the car. They were as he expected them to be: aggressive, humorless, smart, blindered. They'd never changed in all the years Potter had been doing this. His first reaction, as always, was how he would hate to be married to one of them.

He climbed to the podium that Henderson had installed, and looked into the mass of white video lights. "At about eight-thirty this morning three escaped felons kidnaped and took hostage two teachers and eight students from the Laurent Clerc School for the Deaf in Hebron, Kansas. The felons had earlier in the day escaped from the Callana Federal Penitentiary.

"They're presently holed up in an abandoned factory along the Arkansas River about a mile and a half from here, on the border of the town of Crow Ridge. They are being contained by several hundred state, local, and federal law enforcers."

More like a hundred, but Potter would rather bend the truth to the fourth estate than risk nurturing overconfidence on the part of the takers—just in case they happened to catch a news report.

"There has been one fatality among the hostages. . . ."

The reporters gasped and bristled at this and their hands shot up. They barked questions but Potter said only, "The identity of the victim and those of the rest of the hostages will not be disclosed until all family members have been notified of the incident. We are in the midst of negotiations with the felons, who've been identified as Louis Handy, Shepard Wilcox, and Ray 'Sonny' Bonner. During the course of the negotiations there will be no press access to the barricade site. You'll be receiving updates as we get new information. That's all I have to say at this time."

"Agent Potter—"

"I'm not answering any questions now."

"Agent Potter—"

"Agent Potter, please—"

"Could you compare this situation to the Koresh situation in Waco?"

"We *need* the press copters released. Our lawyers have already contacted the director—"

"Is this like the Weaver situation a few years—"

Potter walked out of the press tent amid the silent flashes of still cameras and the blaring of videocam lights. He was almost to the car when he heard a voice. "Agent Potter, can I have a minute?"

Potter turned to see a man approaching. He had a limp. He didn't look like a typical newsman. He wasn't a pretty boy and while he seemed aggressive and sullen he was not indignant, which raised him—slightly—in Potter's estimation. Older than his colleagues, he was dark-complected, had a deeply lined face. At least he *looked* like a real journalist. Edward R. Murrow.

The negotiator said, "No individual statements."

"I'm not asking for one. I'm Joe Silbert with KFAL in Kansas City."

"Yessir, if you'll excuse me—"

"You're a prick, Potter," Silbert said with more exhaustion than anger. "Nobody's ever grounded press choppers before."

Extreme stakes, the agent thought. "You'll get the news as soon as anybody."

"Hold up. I know you guys could care less about us. We're a pain in the ass. But we've got our job to do too. This is big news. And you know it. We're going to need fucking more than just press releases and nonbriefings like the one we just had. The Admiral's going to be on your ass so fast you'll wish you were back in Waco."

Something about the way he uttered the rank suggested that Silbert knew the FBI director personally.

"There's nothing I can do. Security at the barricade site has to be perfect."

"I have to tell you that if you suppress too much, those youngsters're going to try some pretty desperate things to get inside your perimeter. They're going to be using descrambling scanners to intercept transmissions, they're going to be impersonating officers—"

"All of which is illegal."

"I'm just telling you what some of them have been talking about. There are rumblings out there. And I sure as hell don't want to lose an exclusive to some little asshole law-breaking journalism school graduate."

"I've given orders to arrest any non-law-enforcement personnel within sight of the plant. Reporters included."

Silbert rolled his eyes. "Arnett had it easier in Baghdad. Jesus Christ. You're a negotiator, I thought. Why won't you negotiate?"

"I should be getting back."

"Please! Just listen to my proposal. I want to start a press pool. You allow one or two journalists at a time up near the front. No cameras, radios, recorders. Just typewriters or laptops. Or pen and pencil."

"Joe, we can't risk the takers' getting any information about what we're doing. You know that. They might have a radio inside."

An ominous tone slipped into his voice. "Look, you start suppressing, we'll start speculating."

A barricade in Miami several years ago went hot when the takers heard on their portable radio a newscaster describing an HRT assault on the barricade site. It turned out the reporter was merely speculating as to what *might* happen but the takers thought it was real and began firing at the hostages.

"That's a threat, I assume," Potter said evenly.

"Tornadoes are threats," Silbert responded. "They're also facts of life. Look, Potter, what can I do to convince you?"

"Nothing. Sorry."

Potter turned toward the car. Silbert sighed. "Fuck. How's this? You can read the stories before we file them. You can censor them."

This was a first. Of the hundreds of barricades Potter had negotiated, he'd had good and bad relationships with the press as he tried to balance the First Amendment versus the safety of hostages and cops. But he'd never met a journalist who agreed to let him preview stories.

"That's a prior restraint," said Potter, fourth in his law school class.

"There've already been a half-dozen reporters talking about crossing the barriers. That'll stop if you agree to let a couple of us inside. They'll listen to me."

"And you want to be one of those two."

Silbert grinned. "Of course I fucking want to be one of them. In fact I want to be one of the first two. I've got a deadline in an hour. Come on, what do you think?"

What *did* he think? That half the problem at Waco had been press relations. That he was responsible not only for the lives of the hostages and troopers and fellow agents but for the integrity of the Bureau itself and its image, and that for all his negotiating skills he was an inept player of agency politics. He knew too that most of what Congress, senior Justice officials, and the White House learned about what happened here would be from CNN and the *Washington Post*.

"All right," Potter agreed. "You can set it up. You'll coordinate with Captain Charlie Budd."

He looked at his watch. The food was due. He should be getting back. He drove to the command van, told Budd to set up a small press tent behind it and to meet with Joe Silbert about the pooling arrangement.

"Will do. Where's the food?" Budd asked, gazing anxiously up the road. "Time's getting close."

"Oh," Potter said, "we've got a little flexibility. Once a taker's agreed to release a hostage you're past the biggest hurdle. He's already given Jocylyn up in his mind."

"You think?"

"Go set up that press tent."

He started back to the command van and found himself thinking not of food or helicopters or Louis Handy but rather of Melanie Charrol. And not of how valuable she as a hostage might be to him as a negotiator nor of how much of a benefit or liability she might be in a tactical resolution of the barricade. No, he was mulling over soft information, dicta. Recalling the motion of her mouth as she spoke to him from the dim window of the slaughter-house.

What could she have been saying?

Speculating mostly about what it would be like to have a conversation with her. Here was a man who'd made his way in the world by listening to other people's words, by talking. And here she was, a deaf-mute.

Lips, teeth, lips.

He mimicked her.

Lips, teeth . . .

Got it, he thought suddenly. And he heard in his mind: "Be forewarned."

He tried it out loud. "Be forewarned."

Yes, that was it. But why such an archaic expression? Of course: So *he* could lip-read it. The movement of the mouth was exaggerated with this phrase. It was obvious. Not "Be careful." Or "Look out." Or "He's dangerous."

Be forewarned.

Henry LeBow should know this.

Potter started toward the van and was only twenty feet from his destination when the limousine appeared silently beside him. It seemed to the agent that as it eased past it turned slightly, as if cutting him off. The door opened and a large, swarthy man climbed out. "Look at all this," he said boisterously. "It looks like D-Day, the troops have landed. You've got everything under control, Ike? Do you? Everything well in *hand*?"

Potter stopped and turned. The man walked up close and his smile, if a smile it had been, fell away. He said, "Agent Potter, we have to talk."

2:20 P.M.

But he didn't talk just at that moment.

He tugged his dark suit closed as a burst of chill wind shot through the gully and he strode to the rise, past Potter, and looked over the slaughterhouse.

The agent noted the state license plate, unhappily speculating as to who the visitor might be, and continued on to the van. "I'd step back," he said. "You're well within rifle range."

The man's large left hand reached out and gripped Potter's arm as they shook. He introduced himself as Roland Marks, the state's assistant attorney general.

Oh, him. Potter recalled the phone conversation earlier. The dusky man gazed at the factory again, still a clear target. "I'd be careful there," Potter repeated impatiently.

"Hell. They have rifles, do they? With laser scopes? Maybe phasers and photon torpedoes. Like *Star Trek,* you know."

I don't have time for this, Potter thought.

The man was tall and large, with a Roman nose, and his presence here was like the blue glow of plutonium in a reactor. Potter said, "One moment please." He stepped inside the command van, lifted an eyebrow.

Tobe nodded toward the slaughterhouse. "As a mouse," he said.

"And the food?"

Budd said it would arrive in a few minutes.

"Marks is outside, Henry. You find anything on him?"

"He's here?" LeBow grimaced. "I made a few calls. He's a hard-line prosecutor. Quick as a whip. Specializes in white-collar crimes. Excellent conviction ratio."

"Take-no-prisoners sort?"

"Exactly. But ambitious. Ran for Congress once. Lost, but still has his eye on Washington, the rumor is. My guess is he's trying to pry some media out of the situation."

Potter had learned long ago that hostage situations are also public relations situations and careers were as much on the line as were human lives. He decided to play Marks carefully.

"Oh, write down that I've translated the message from the hostage. 'Be forewarned.' Assume she's talking about Handy."

LeBow held his eye for a moment. He nodded and turned back to his keys.

Outside again, Potter turned to Marks, the second-most-powerful lawyer in the state. "What can I do for you?"

"So is it true then? What I heard? That he's killed one of them?" Potter nodded slowly. The man closed his eyes and sighed. His mouth tucked into a sorrowful wrinkle. "Why in the name of heaven do a crazy thing like that?"

"His way of telling us he's serious."

"Oh, my good Lord." Marks rubbed his face with large, blunt fingers. "The AG and I've been talking about this at some length, Agent Potter. We've been in a stew about the whole mess and I hightailed it down here to ask if there's anything we can do on the state level. I know about you, Potter. Your reputation. Everybody knows about you, sir."

The agent remained stone-faced. He thought he'd been rude enough on the phone to keep the lawyer out of his life. But it seemed that, to Marks, the earlier conversation had never taken place.

"Play it all close to your chest, do you? But I'd guess you have to. It *is* like playing poker, isn't it. High-stakes poker."

Extreme stakes, Potter thought again, and wished once more that this man would go away. "As I told you I don't really need anything else from the state at the moment. We've got state troopers for containment and I've enlisted Charlie Budd as my second-in-command."

"Budd?"

"You know him?"

"Sure I do. He's a good trooper. And I know all the good troopers." He looked around. "Where are the soldiers?"

"Hostage rescue?"

"I thought for sure they'd be in the thick of things by now."

Potter was still unsure of how the wind from Topeka was blowing. "I'm not using state HRT. The Bureau's team is assembling now and'll be here in the next few hours."

"That's troubling."

"Why's that?" Potter asked innocently, assuming that the man wanted the state rescue team to handle the tactical side.

"You're not thinking of an assault, I hope. Look at the Weaver barricade. Look at Waco. Innocent people killed. I don't want that to happen here."

"No one does. We'll attack only as a last resort."

Marks's boisterous facade fell away and he became deadly serious. "I know you're in charge of the situation, Agent Potter. But I want you to know that the attorney general's position is peaceful resolution at all costs."

Less than four months to the first Tuesday in November, Potter reflected.

"We're hoping things work out peacefully."

"What're his demands?" Marks asked.

Time to tug the leash? Not yet. Potter concluded that an offended Roland Marks could do much harm. "Typical. Chopper, food, ammo. All I'm giving him is food. I'm going to try to get him to surrender or at least get as many girls out as I can before HRT goes in."

He watched Marks's face turn darker than it already was. "I just don't want those little girls hurt."

"Of course not." Potter looked at his watch.

The assistant attorney general continued, "Here's a thought—have him give up the girls and take a chopper. You put one of those clever *Mission: Impossible* things inside and when they land you nail them."

"No."

"Why not?"

"We never let them go mobile if there's any way to avoid it."

"Don't you read Tom Clancy? There're all sorts of bugs and transponders you can use."

"It's still too risky. There's a known quantity of dead right now. The worst he can do is kill the nine remaining hostages, possibly one or two of the HRT." Marks's eyes widened in shock at this. Potter the cold fish continued, "If he gets out he could kill twice that. Three times, or more."

"He's just a bank robber. Hardly a mass murderer."

And how many bodies does it take to qualify somebody as a mass murderer? Potter gazed past the silent combines working their way over hills several miles away. Winter wheat was planted in November, he'd been told by the heli-

copter pilot, who added that the white man's way of bust-
ing sod for wheat planting had mortified the Potawatomi
Indians and helped bring on the Depression's dust bowl.

Where was the damn food? Potter thought, now nervous that minutes were slipping past.

"So that's what those girls are then?" Marks asked,
none too friendly now. "Acceptable casualties?"

"Let's hope it doesn't come to that."

The door opened and Budd looked out. "That food's almost here, Arthur. Oh, hello, Mr. Marks."

"Charlie Budd. Good luck to you. Tough situation.
You'll rise to meet it, though."

"We're doing our best," Budd said cautiously. "Mr.
Potter here's really an expert. Agent Potter, I should say."

"I'm going to call in," Marks said. "Brief the governor."

When the limo had vanished, Potter asked Budd, "You
know him?"

"Not too well, sir."

"He have an agenda?"

"Suppose he has his eye on Washington in a few years.
But he's pretty much a good man."

"Henry thought he might be running for office this
fall."

"Don't know 'bout that. But I don't think there's any
politics here. His concern'd be the girls. He's a real family man, I heard. A father himself a few times over, all
daughters. One of 'em's got some bad health problems so
I guess he's feeling this is pretty close to home, those
girls being deaf and all."

Potter had noticed Marks's well-worn wedding ring.

"Will he be a problem?"

"I can't imagine how. That way he is, joking and everything, it's kind of a front."

"It's not his sense of humor I'm worried about. How
connected is he?"

Budd shrugged. "Oh, well, you know."

"It won't go any further than me, Charlie. I have to
know if he can cause us any damage."

"Well, him saying he was going to call the governor?
Like they were best buddies?"

"Yes?"

"Doubt the man'll even take his call. See, there're Republicans and then there are *Republicans.*"

"Okay, thanks."

"Oh, hey, look, here we go now."

The state police car bounding over the rough road squealed to a stop. But it was not Handy's Big Macs and Fritos. Two women climbed out. Angie Scapello was in a mid-length navy suit, her weapon jutting from the thin blazer and her abundant black hair tumbling to her shoulders. She wore pale sunglasses in turquoise frames. Behind her emerged a young, short-haired brunette in a police uniform.

"Angie." Potter shook her hand. "Meet my right-hand man, Charlie Budd. Kansas State Police. Special Agent Angeline Scapello."

They shook hands and nodded to one another.

Angie introduced the other woman. "Officer Frances Whiting, Hebron PD. She'll be our sign language interpreter." The policewoman shook the men's hands and stole a fast glance at the slaughterhouse, grimaced.

"Please come inside," Potter said, nodding toward the van.

Henry LeBow was pleased by all the data Angie had brought. He rapidly began inputting the information. Potter had been right; the minute she'd heard about the barricade—before the DomTran Gulfstream was even fueled—she'd spoken with officials at the Laurent Clerc School and started compiling the profiles of the captives.

"Excellent, Angie," LeBow said, typing madly. "You're a born biographer."

She opened another folder, offering the contents to Potter. "Tobe," he asked, "could you please tape these up?" The young agent took the photographs of the girls and pinned them to the corkboard, just above the CAD diagram of the slaughterhouse. Angie had written the names and ages of the girls in the bottom margin in black marker.

Anna Morgan, 7
Suzie Morgan, 7

Shannon Boyle, 8
Kielle Stone, 8
Emily Stoddard, 10
Jocylyn Weiderman, 12
Beverly Klemper, 14

The picture of Susan Phillips remained face-up on the table.

"You always do this?" Frances waved at the wall.

Potter, eyes on the pictures, said absently, "You win by having better knowledge than the enemy." He found himself looking at the adorable twins, for they were the youngest. Whenever he thought of children he thought of them as being very young—perhaps because he and Marian never had any—and the image of the son or daughter that might have been was thus frozen in time, as if Potter were perpetually a young husband and Marian his bride of, say, twenty-five.

Look at them, he told himself. *Look at them.* And as if he'd spoken aloud, he realized that everyone except Derek and Tobe, who were hunched over their dials, had paused and was gazing up at the pictures.

Potter asked Angie for information about the girl who was about to be released, Jocylyn Weiderman.

Speaking from memory, Angie said, "Apparently she's a troubled girl. She was postlingually deaf—deaf after she learned to speak. You'd think that would make things easier and it *does* help with learning development. But psychologically what happens is people like that don't take to Deaf culture easily at all. You know what that means? 'Deaf' with a capital *D*?"

Potter, eye on the slaughterhouse, looking again for Melanie, said he didn't.

Angie lifted an eyebrow to Frances, who explained, "The word 'deaf,' small *d,* is the physical condition of not being able to hear. Deaf, upper-case *D,* is used by the Deaf to signify their community, their culture."

Angie continued, "In terms of Deaf status it's best to be born deaf of deaf parents and to shun all oral skills. If you're born hearing of hearing parents and know how to speak and read lips, you don't have the same status. But even that's a notch above someone deaf trying to pass for hearing—which is what Jocylyn's tried to do."

"So the girl has one strike against her to start with."

"She's been rejected by both the hearing and Deaf worlds. Add to that she's overweight. And has pretty undeveloped social skills. Prime candidate for a panic attack. If that happens Handy might think the girl was attacking him. She might even do it."

Potter nodded, thankful as always that Angie Scapello was assisting the threat management team. Her specialty was hostage psychology—helping them to recover and to remember observations that might be useful in future barricades and preparing former hostages to be witnesses at the trials of their takers.

Several years ago it had occurred to Potter to bring her along during ongoing barricades, analyzing the data that hostages reported and evaluating hostages and takers themselves. She often shared the podium with him when he lectured on negotiation strategy.

Potter observed, "Then we've got to try to keep her calm."

Panic during a hostage exchange was infectious. It often led to fatalities.

The negotiator asked Frances, "Could you teach our trooper something to tell her? Something that might help?"

Frances moved her hands and said, "That means 'Stay calm.' But signing's a very difficult skill to learn quickly and to remember. Slight mistakes change the meaning completely. I'd recommend if you have to communicate, use everyday gestures—for 'come here,' 'go there.' "

"And I'd suggest having him smile," Angie said. "Universal language, smiling. That's just what the girl needs. If he has to say something more complex, maybe write it down?"

Frances nodded. "That's a good idea."

"The reading age of prelingually deaf is sometimes below that of their chronological age. But with Jocylyn being postlingual and"—Angie stole back her notes from Henry LeBow, found what she sought—"and having a high IQ, she can read any commands fine."

"Hey, Derek, got any pens and writing pads?"

"Got 'em both right here," Elb replied, producing a stack of pads and a fistful of big black ink markers.

The agent then asked Angie if she happened to have a picture of the teachers. "No, I . . . Wait. I think I have one of Melanie Charrol. The younger of them."

She's twenty-five, Potter reminded himself.

"We're past the food deadline," Tobe announced.

"Ah, here it is," Angie said, handing him a picture.

Be forewarned. . . .

He was surprised. The woman it depicted was more beautiful than he'd thought. Unlike the other photos, this was in color. She had wavy blond hair, very curly bangs, smooth pale skin, radiant eyes. The picture seemed less like a staff photograph than like a model's head shot. There was something childlike about everything except the eyes. He himself pinned it up, next to the picture of the twins.

"Does she have family here?" Potter asked.

Angie looked at her notes. "The dean at Laurent Clerc told me her parents have a farm not far from the school but they're in St. Louis this weekend. Melanie's brother had an accident last year and he's having some kind of fancy surgery tomorrow. She was taking tomorrow off to go visit him."

"Farms," Budd muttered. "Most dangerous places on earth. You should hear some of the calls we get."

A console phone buzzed, a scrambled line, and Tobe pushed the button, spoke into his stalk mike for a moment. "It's the CIA," he announced to the room, then began speaking rapidly into the mike. He tapped several keys, conferred with Derek, and turned on a monitor. "Kwo got a SatSurv image, Arthur. Take a look."

A monitor slowly came to life. The background was dark green, like a glowing radar screen, and you could make out patches of lighter green, yellow, and amber. There was a faint outline of the slaughterhouse and a number of red dots surrounding it.

"The green's the ground," Tobe explained. "The yellow and orange, those are trees and natural thermal sources. The red are troopers." The slaughterhouse was a blue-green rectangle. Only toward the front was there any shift in the color, where the windows and doors were located. "There's probably a little heat rising from the lamps. Doesn't tell us much. Other than nobody's actually on the roof."

"Tell them to keep broadcasting."

"You know what it costs, don't you?" Tobe asked.

"Twelve thousand an hour," LeBow said, typing happily. "Now ask him if he cares."

Potter said, "Keep it on-line, Tobe."

"Will do. But I want a cost-of-living this year, we're so rich."

Then the door opened and a trooper entered, brown bags in his arms, and the van filled with the smell of hot greasy burgers and fries. Potter sat down at his chair, gripping the phone in his fingers.

The first exchange was about to begin.

2:45 P.M.

Stevie Oates again.

"Glutton for punishment?" Potter asked.

"Bored just sitting on my butt, sir."

"Nothing to pitch this time, Officer. You'll be going the distance."

Dean Stillwell stood beside the trooper as, Potter instructing, two FBI agents in flak jackets were suiting Oates up with two layers of thin body armor under his regular uniform. They were standing behind the van. Charlie Budd was nearby, directing the placement of the huge halogen spotlights, trained on the slaughterhouse. There was still plenty of summer light left in the day but the overcast had grown thicker and with every passing minute it seemed more like dusk.

"All set, Arthur," Budd announced.

"Hit 'em," Potter ordered, looking up from the trooper for a moment.

The halogens burst to life, shooting their streams of raw white light onto the front and sides of the slaughterhouse. Budd ordered a few adjustments and the lights focused on the door and the windows on either side of it. The wind was gusting sharply and the troopers had to anchor the legs of the lights with sandbags.

Suddenly a curious sound came from the field. "What's that?" Budd wondered aloud.

Stillwell said, "Somebody's laughing. Some of the troopers. Hank, what's going on out there?" the sheriff called over his radio. He listened, then looked at the slaughterhouse through field glasses. "Look in the window."

Potter ducked his head around the van. With the spotlights, nobody in the slaughterhouse would have a prayer of an effective sniper shot. He trained his Leicas on the window.

"Very funny," he muttered.

Lou Handy had put on sunglasses against the glaring lights. With exaggerated gestures he mopped his forehead and mugged for his laughing audience.

"Enough of that," Stillwell radioed sternly, speaking to his troops. "This isn't David Letterman."

Potter turned back to Oates, nodded at the thin armor. "You'll get a nasty bruise if you're shot. But it's important to look unthreatening."

HTs get very nervous, Angie explained, when they see troopers dressed up like alien spacemen plodding toward them. "You've got to dress for success."

"I'm about as unthreatening as can be. 'S'way I feel anyway. Should I leave my sidearm here?"

"No. But keep it out of sight," Potter said. "Your first responsibility is your own safety. Never compromise that. If it's between you and the hostage, save yourself first."

"Well—"

"That's an order, Trooper," Stillwell said solemnly. He'd grown into his role of containment officer like a natural.

Potter continued, "Walk up there slowly, carry the food at your side, in plain view. Don't move fast, whatever happens."

"Okay." Oates seemed to be memorizing these orders.

Tobe Geller stepped out of the doorway of the van, carrying a small box attached to a wire burgeoning into a stubby black rod. He hooked the box to the trooper's back, under the vest. The rod he clipped into Oates's hair with bobby pins.

"Couldn't use this with Arthur here," Tobe said. "Need a full head of hair."

"What is it?"

"Video camera. And earphone."

"That little thing? No foolin'."

Tobe ran the wire down Oates's back and plugged it into the transmitter.

"The resolution isn't very good," Potter said, "but it'll help when you get back."

"How's that?"

"You seem pretty cool, Stevie," LeBow said. "But at best you'll remember about forty percent of what you see up there."

"Oh, he's a fifty percenter," Potter said, "if I'm not mistaken."

"The tape won't tell us too much on its own," the intelligence officer continued, "but it should refresh your memory."

"Gotcha. Say, those burgers sure smell good," Oates joked, while his face said that food was the last thing on his mind.

"Angie?" Potter asked.

The agent walked up to the trooper and tossed the mass of dark, windblown hair from her face. "Here's a picture of the girl who's coming out. Her name's Jocylyn." Quickly, she repeated her assessment on how to best handle her.

"Don't talk to her," Angie concluded. "She won't understand your words and it might make her panic, thinking she's missing something important. And keep smiling."

"Smiling. Sure. Piece of cake." Oates swallowed.

Potter added, "Now, she's overweight and can't run very fast, I'd guess." He unfurled a small map of the grounds of the slaughterhouse. "If she could hustle I'd tell you to duck into that gully there, the one in front of the place, and then just run like hell. You'd be oblique targets. But as it is I think you'll just have to walk straight back."

"Like the girl who got shot?" Budd asked, and nobody was happy he had.

"Now, Stevie," Potter continued, "you should go up to the door. But under no circumstances are you to go inside."

"What if he says he won't release her 'less I do?"

"Then you leave her. Leave the food and walk away. But I think he'll let her go. Get as close as you can to the door. I want you to look inside. Look for what kinds of weapons they have, radios, any signs of blood, any hostages or hostage takers we might not know about."

Budd asked, "How could more've gotten in?"

"They might have been waiting inside for Handy and the others to arrive."

"Oh, sure." Budd looked discouraged. "Didn't think of that."

Potter continued to Oates, "Don't engage him in a dialogue, don't argue, don't say anything, except to answer his questions directly."

"You think he'll ask me stuff?"

Potter looked at Angie, who said, "It's possible. He might want to tease you a little. The sunglasses—he's got a playful streak in him. He might want to test you. Don't rise to the bait."

Oates nodded uncertainly.

Potter continued, "We'll be monitoring your conversations and I can feed you answers through your earphone."

Oates smiled a faint smile. "Those'll be the longest hundred yards of my life."

"There's nothing to worry about," Potter said. "He's a lot more interested in food right now than he is in shooting anybody."

This logic seemed to reassure Oates though the memory loomed in Potter's mind that some years ago he'd said similar words to an officer who a few moments later had been shot in the knee and wrist by a hostage taker who decided impulsively that he didn't want the painkillers and bandages the officer was bringing him.

Potter added an asthma inhaler to the bag of hamburgers. "Don't say anything about that. Just let him find it and decide to give it to Beverly or not."

Budd held up several pads of paper and the markers Derek had provided. "Should we include these?"

Potter considered. The pads and pens would give the hostages a chance to communicate with their captors and improve the Stockholming between them. But sometimes small deviations from what they expected set off HTs. The inhaler was one deviation. How would Handy feel about a second? He asked Angie's opinion.

"He may be a sociopath," she said after a moment. "But he hasn't had any temper tantrums or emotional outbursts, has he?"

"No. He's been pretty cool."

In fact he'd been frighteningly calm.

"Sure," Angie said, "add them."

"Dean, Charlie," Potter said, "come here a minute." The sheriff and the captain huddled. "Who're the best rifle shots you've got?"

"That'd be Sammy Bullock and—what do you think? Chris Felling? That's Christine. I'd say she's better'n Sammy. Dean?"

"If I was a squirrel sitting four hundred yards away from Chrissy and I saw her shoulder her piece, I wouldn't even bother to run. I'd just kiss my be-hind goodbye."

Potter wiped his glasses. "Have her load and lock and get a spotter with glasses to keep a watch on the door and windows. If it looks like Handy or one of the others is about to shoot, she's green-lighted to fire. But she's to aim for the doorjamb or windowsill."

"I thought you said there'd be no warning shots," Budd said.

"That's the rule," Potter said sagely. "And it's absolutely true—unless there's an exception to it."

"Oh."

"Go on and take care of that, Dean."

"Yessir." The sheriff hurried away, crouching.

Potter returned to Oates. "Okay, Trooper. Ready?"

Frances said to the young man, "Can I say 'Good luck'?"

"Please do," Oates said earnestly. Budd patted him on his Kevlared shoulder.

Melanie Charrol knew many Bible-school stories.

The lives of the Deaf used to be tied closely with religion, and many of them still were. The poor lambs of God . . . pat them on the head and force them to learn enough speech to struggle through catechism and Eucharist and confession (always among themselves of course so they didn't embarrass the hearing congregation). Abbé de l'Epée, goodhearted and brilliant though he was, created French Sign Language primarily to make sure his charges' souls could enter heaven.

And of course vows of silence by monks and nuns, adopting the "affliction" of the unfortunate as penance. (Maybe thinking that they could hear God's voice all the better though Melanie could have told them it didn't work worth squat.)

She leaned against the tile walls of the killing room, as horrible a part of the Outside as ever existed. Mrs. Harstrawn lay on her side, ten feet away, staring at the wall. No tears any longer—she was cried out, dry, empty. The woman blinked, she breathed but she might as well have been in a coma. Melanie rose and lifted her leg away from a pool of black water encrusted with green scum and the splintered bodies of a thousand insects.

Religion.

Melanie hugged the twins, feeling their delicate spines through identical powder-blue cowgirl blouses. She sat down beside them, thinking of some story she'd heard in Sunday school. It was about early Christians in ancient Rome, awaiting martyrdom in the Colosseum. They had, of course, refused to deny their faith. Men and women, children, happily praying on their knees while the centurions came for them. The story was ridiculous, the product of a simple-minded textbook writer, and it seemed inexcusable to adult Melanie Charrol that anyone would include it in a children's book. Yet like the cheapest melodrama the story had wrenched her heart then, at age eight or nine. And it wrenched her heart still.

Staring at the distant light, losing herself in the pulsing meditation of the yellow bulb, growing, shrinking, growing, shrinking, seeing the light turn into Susan's face, then into a beautiful young woman's body torn apart by lions' yellow claws.

Eight gray birds, sitting in dark . . .

But no, it's just seven birds now.

Was Jocylyn about to die too? Melanie peeked around the corner, seeing the girl standing at a window. She was sobbing, shaking her head. Stoat had her by the arm. They stood near the partially open door.

Motion nearby. She turned her head—the automatic reaction of a deaf person to the movement of gesturing hands. Kielle had closed her eyes. Melanie watched her hands move in a repetitive pattern, confused about the girl's message until she realized that she was summoning Wolverine, another of her comic-book heroes.

"Do something," Shannon signed. "Melanie!" Her tiny hands chopped the air.

Do something. Right.

Melanie thought of de l'Epée. She hoped the thought of him would restart her frozen heart. It didn't. She was as helpless as ever, staring at Jocylyn, who looked back toward the killing room and caught Melanie's eye.

"Going to kill me," Jocylyn signed, sobbing; her cheeks, round and pale as a honeydew, glistened from the tears. "Please, help."

The Outside . . .

"Melanie." Kielle's dark eyes flared. The girl had suddenly appeared beside her. "Do something!"

"What?" Melanie suddenly snapped. "Tell me. Shoot him? Grow wings and fly?"

"Then I will," Kielle said, and turned, bursting toward the men. Without thinking, Melanie leapt after her. The little girl was just past the doorway to the killing room when Bear loomed in front of them. Both Melanie and Kielle stopped abruptly. Melanie put her arm around the girl and looked down, eyes fixed on the black pistol in Bear's waistband.

Grab it. Shoot him. Don't worry what happens. You can do it. His filthy mind is elsewhere. De l'Epée would hear the shot and come running to save them. Grab it. Do it. She actually saw herself pulling the trigger. Her hands began to shake. She stared at the pistol butt, glistening black plastic.

Bear reached forward and touched her hair. The back of his hand, a gentle stroke. A lover's or father's touch.

And whatever strength was within Melanie vanished in that instant. Bear grabbed them by the collars and dragged them back into the killing room, cutting off her view of Jocylyn.

I'm deaf so I can't hear her screams.

I'm deaf so I can't hear her beg me to help her.

I'm deaf, I'm deaf, I'm deaf. . . .

Bear shoved them into the corner and sat down in the doorway. He gazed over the frightened captives.

I'm deaf so I'm dead already. What does it matter; what does anything matter?

Melanie closed her eyes, drew her beautiful hands into her lap, and, untethered, slipped away from the killing room once again.

"Run the HP, Tobe," Potter ordered.

Inside the van Tobe opened an attaché case, revealing the Hewlett-Packard Model 122 VSA, which resembled a cardiac-care monitor.

"These all one-ten, grounded?" He nodded at the outlets. Derek Elb told him yes.

Tobe plugged in and turned on the machine. A small strip of paper, like a cash-register receipt, fed out, and a grid appeared in green on the black screen. He glanced at the others in the room. LeBow pointed at Potter, himself, Angie, and Budd. "In that order."

Frances and Derek looked on curiously.

"Five says you're wrong," Potter offered. "Me, Angie, you, and Charlie."

Budd laughed uneasily. "What're you talking about?"

Tobe said, "Everybody, quiet." He pushed a microphone toward Angie.

"The rain in Spain falls—"

"That's enough," Tobe said, holding the microphone out to Potter.

He recited, "The quick brown fox . . ."

Henry LeBow was cut off during a lengthy quotation from *The Tempest*.

Budd nearly went cross-eyed gazing at the encroaching microphone and said, "That thing's making me pretty nervous."

The four FBI agents roared with laughter.

Tobe explained to Frances. "Voice stress analyzer. Gives us some clue about truth telling but mostly it gives us a risk assessment." He pushed a button and the screen divided into four squares. Wavy lines of differing peaks and valleys froze in place.

Tobe tapped the screen and said, "This is Arthur. He never gets rattled. Actually I think he pees his pants regularly but you'll never tell it by the sound of his voice. Then you're number two, Angie. Arthur was right. You get a Cool Cucumber Award. But Henry's not far behind." He laughed, tapping the final grid. "Captain Budd, you are one nervous fellow. Can I suggest yoga and breathing exercises?"

Budd frowned. "If you hadn't been poking that thing into my face I'da done better. Or told me what it was about in the first place. I get a second chance?"

The negotiator looked outside. "Let's make that phone call. Send him out, Charlie."

"Go ahead, Stevie," Budd said into the radio handset. They saw the trooper move into the gully and make his way toward the slaughterhouse.

Potter pressed the speed dial.

"Uplink."

"Hello, Lou."

"Art. We got the fat one all dressed up like a Thanksgiving turkey. We see your boy coming. He got my chocolate shake?"

"He's the same one who pitched the phone to you. Stevie's his name. Good man."

Potter thought: *Was he. one of them was shooting at us before?*

"Maybe," Handy said, "he was the one gave the signal to shoot at our Shep."

"I told you that was an accident, Lou. Say, how's everybody doing in there?"

Who gives a shit?

"Fine. I just checked on 'em."

Curious, the negotiator thought. He hadn't expected this response at all. Is he saying that to reassure me? Is he scared? Does he want to lull me into being careless?

Or did the bad-boy act fall away for a moment and was the real Lou Handy actually giving a legitimate response to a legitimate question?

"I put some of that asthma medicine in the bag."

Fuck her, who cares?

Handy laughed. "Oh, for the one sucking air. It's a pain, Art. How can anybody get any sleep with that little shit gasping for breath?"

"And some paper and pens. In case the girls want to say something to you."

Silence. Potter and LeBow glanced at each other. Was he angry about the paper?

No, he was just talking to someone inside.

Keep his mind busy, off the hostages, off Stevie. "How're those lights working?" Potter asked.

"Good. The ones you've got outside suck, though. Can I shoot 'em out?"

"You know what they cost? It'd come out of my paycheck."

Oates was fifty feet away, walking slowly and steadily. Potter glanced at Tobe, who nodded and pushed buttons on the HP.

"So you're a McDonald's fan, Lou? Big Macs, they're the best."

"How'd *you* know?" Handy asked sarcastically. "You never ate under the golden arches in your life, betcha."

Angie gave him a thumbs-up and Potter nodded, pleased. It's a good sign when the HT refers to the negotiator. The transference process was proceeding.

"Guess again, Lou. You're going to have exactly what I had for dinner twice last week. Well, minus the Fritos. But I did have a milk shake. Vanilla."

"Thought you fancy agents had gourmet meals every night. Steak and lobster. Champagne. Then you fuck the beautiful agent works for you."

"A bacon cheeseburger, not a glass of wine to be had. Oh, and instead of sex I had a second order of fries. I do love my potatoes."

In the faint reflection of the window Potter was aware that Budd was staring at him and he believed the expression was of faint disbelief.

"You fat too, like this little girl I got by her piggy arm?"

"I could lose a few pounds. Maybe more than a few."

Oates was fifty feet from the door.

Potter wanted to probe some more into Handy's likes and dislikes. But he was cautious. He sensed it would rile the man. There's a philosophy in barricade situations that tries to keep the HTs on edge—bombarding them with bad music or playing with the heating and cooling of the barricade site. Potter didn't believe in this approach. Be firm, but establish rapport.

Handy was too quiet. What was distracting him? What was he thinking? I need more control. That's the problem, it occurred to Potter. I can't get control of the situation away from him.

"I was going to ask you, Lou. . . . This is pretty odd weather for July. Must be cold in there. You want us to rig some heaters or something?"

Potter speculated: *Naw, we got plenty of bodies to keep us warm.*

But Handy responded slowly, "Maybe. How cold's it going to be tonight?"

Again, very logical and matter-of-fact. And behind the words: the implication that he might be planning on a long siege. That might give Potter the chance to push back some of Handy's deadlines. He jotted these impressions on a slip of paper and pushed it toward Henry LeBow to enter into his computer.

"Windy and chilly, I'm told."

"I'll think on it."

And listen to his voice, Potter thought. He sounds so reasonable. What do I make of that? Sometimes he's pure bravado; sometimes he sounds like an insurance salesman. Potter's eyes scanned the diagram of the slaughterhouse. Twelve yellow Post-Its, each representing a taker or a hostage, were stuck on the schematic. Ultimately, Potter hoped, they'd be placed in the exact position where each person was located. At the moment they were clustered off to the side.

"Lou, you there?"

"Sure I'm here. Where the fuck'd I be? Driving down I-70 to Denver?"

"Didn't hear you breathing."

In a low, chilling voice Handy said, "That's 'cause I'm a ghost."

"A ghost?" Potter echoed.

"I slip up quiet as a cat behind you and slit your throat and I'm gone before your blood hits the ground. You think I'm in that building there, that slaughterhouse you're looking at right now. But I'm not."

"Where'd you be?"

"Maybe I'm coming up behind you, that van of yours. See, I know you're in that there truck. Looking out your window. Maybe I'm right outsida that window. Maybe I'm in that stand of buffalo grass your man's walking by right now and I'm going to knife him in the balls when he passes."

"And maybe I'm in the slaughterhouse with you, Lou."

A pause. Potter thought, He'll laugh.

Handy did, a hearty belly laugh. "You get me lotsa Fritos?"

"Lots. Regular and barbecue."

Stevie Oates was at the building.

"Hey, shave and a haircut . . . Somebody's come acalling."

"Got a visual," Tobe whispered. He dimmed the van lights. They turned to the screen broadcasting the picture from the camera above Stevie Oates's right ear. The image wasn't good. The door of the slaughterhouse opened only several feet and the images inside—pipes, machinery, a table—were distorted by light flares. The only person in sight was Jocylyn, in silhouette, hands to her face.

"Here's your boy now. Stevie? I don't think I've ever

shot anyone named Stevie. He looks pretty *dayamm* un-comfortable."

What was probably a shotgun barrel protruded slowly and rested against Jocylyn's head. Her hands dropped to her sides, making fists. The sound of her whimpering floated from the speaker. Potter prayed that Stillwell's sniper would exercise restraint.

The video image quivered for a moment.

The shotgun turned toward Oates as a man's silhouette filled the doorway. Through the mike mounted above the trooper's ear came the words: "You got a gun on you?" A voice different from Handy's. Shepard Wilcox's, Potter guessed; Bonner would cast a far bigger shadow.

Potter looked down to make sure he was hitting the right buttons as he cut over to Oates's earphone. "Lie. Be insistent but respectful."

"No, I don't. Here's what you wanted. The food. Now, sir, if you'd let that girl go . . ." The trooper spoke without a quaver in his voice.

"Good, Stevie, you're doing fine. Nod if Jocylyn seems okay."

The picture dipped slightly.

"Keep smiling at her."

Another dip.

Handy asked Oates, "You got a microphone or camera?" Another silhouette had appeared. Handy's. "You recording me?"

"Your call," Potter whispered. "But there'll be no exchange if you say yes."

"No," the trooper said.

"I'll kill you if I find out you're lying to me."

"I don't," Oates said insistently, without hesitation.

Good, good.

"You alone? Anybody sneak up on either side of the door?"

"Can't you see? I'm alone. How's the girl?"

"Can't you see?" Handy mocked, stepping behind Wilcox, in plain view. "Here she is. Look for yourself."

There was no move to release her.

"Let her go," Oates said.

"Maybe you oughta come in and get her."

"No. Let her go."

"You wearing body armor?"

"Under my shirt, yeah."

"Maybe you oughta give me that. We could use it more'n you."

"How do you figure?" Oates said. His voice was no longer so steady.

" 'Cause it won't do you any good. See, we could shoot you in the face and take it offa you and you'd be just as dead as if we shot you in the back when you were walking away. So how 'bout you give it to us now?"

They'd find the video camera and radio transmitter if he gave up the armor. And probably kill him on the spot.

Potter whispers, "Tell him we had a bargain."

"We had a bargain," Oates said firmly. "Here's the food. I want that girl. And I want her now."

A pause that lasted eons.

"Put it on the ground," Handy finally said.

The image on the screen dipped as Oates set the bag down. Still, the trooper kept his head up and pointed directly into the crack of the open door. Unfortunately there was too much contrast in the image; the agents in the van could see virtually nothing inside.

"Here," Handy's voice crackled, "take Miss Piggy. Go wee, wee, wee all the way home." Laughter from several voices. Handy stepped away from the door. They lost sight of him and Wilcox. Was one of them raising the gun to shoot?

"Hiya, honey," Oates said. "Don't you worry, you're gonna be just fine."

"He shouldn't be talking to her," Angie muttered.

"Let's go for a walk, whatta you say? See your mommy and daddy?"

"Lou," Potter called into the throw phone, suddenly concerned that the takers were no longer in sight. No answer. To those in the van he muttered, "I don't trust him. Hell, I don't trust him."

"Lou?"

"Line's still open," Tobe called. "He hasn't hung up."

Potter said to Oates, "Don't say anything to her, Stevie. Might make her panic."

The screen dipped in response.

"Go on. Back on out of there. Go real slow. Then get behind the girl, turn around, and walk straight away. Keep your head up, so your helmet covers as much of your neck as possible. If you're shot, fall on top of the girl. I'll order covering fire and we'll get you out as fast as we can."

A faint disturbed whisper came through the speaker. But there was no other answer.

Suddenly the video screen went mad. There was a burst of light and motion and jiggling images.

"No!" came Oates's voice. Then a deep grunt, followed by a moan.

"He's down," Budd said, looking through the window with binoculars. "Oh, brother."

"Christ!" Derek Elb cried, gazing up at the video monitor.

They'd heard no gunfire but Potter was sure that Wilcox had shot the girl in the head with a silenced pistol and was firing repeatedly at Oates. The screen danced madly with grainy shapes and lens flares.

"Lou!" Potter cried into the phone. "Lou, are you there?"

"Look!" Budd shouted, pointing out the window.

It wasn't what Potter had feared. Jocylyn apparently had panicked and leapt forward. The big girl had knocked Oates flat on his back. She was bounding over the grass and bluestem toward the first row of police cars.

Oates rolled over and was on his feet, going after her.

Potter juggled more buttons. "Lou!" He slapped the console again, activating the radio to Dean Stillwell, who was watching through a night scope with a sniper beside him.

"Dean?" Potter called.

"Yessir."

"Can you see inside?"

"Not much. Door's open only about a foot. There's somebody behind it."

"Windows?"

"No one in 'em yet."

Jocylyn, overweight though she might be, was sprinting like an Olympian directly toward the command van, arms waving, mouth open wide. Oates was gaining on the girl but they were both clear targets.

"Tell the sniper," Potter said, desperately scanning the slaughterhouse windows, "safety off."

Should he order a shot?

"Yessir. Wait. There's Wilcox. Inside about five yards from the window. He's got a shotgun and's drawing a target."

Oh, Lord, Potter thought. If the sniper kills him Handy's sure to murder one of the hostages in retaliation.

Is he going to shoot or not?

Maybe Wilcox's just panicked too, doesn't know what's going on.

"Agent Potter?" Stillwell asked.

"Acquire."

"Yessir. . . . Wilcox's in Chrissy's sights. She's got a shot. Can't miss, she says. Crosshaired on his forehead."

Yes? No?

"Wait," Potter said. "Keep him acquired."

"Yessir."

Jocylyn was thirty yards from the slaughterhouse. Oates close behind her. Perfect targets. A load of twelve-gauge, double-ought buck would cut their legs off.

Sweating, Potter slammed his hand onto two buttons. Into the phone he said, "Lou, you there?"

There was the sound of static, or breathing, or an erratic heartbeat.

"Tell the sniper to stand down," Potter ordered Stillwell suddenly. "Don't shoot. Whatever happens, don't shoot."

"Yessir," Stillwell said.

Potter leaned forward, felt his head tap against the cool glass window.

In two leaps, Stevie Oates grabbed the girl and pulled her down. Her hands and legs flailed and together they tumbled behind the rise, out of sight of the slaughterhouse.

Budd sighed loudly.

"Thank God," muttered Frances.

Angie said nothing but Potter noticed that her hand had strayed to her weapon and now held the grip tightly.

"Lou, you there?" he called. Then again.

There was a crackle, as if the phone were being wrapped in crispy paper. "Can't talk, Art," Handy said through a mouthful of food. "It's suppertime."

"Lou—"

There was a click and then silence.

Potter leaned back in his chair and rubbed his eyes.

Frances applauded, joined by Derek Elb.

"Congratulations," LeBow said quietly. "The first exchange. A success."

Budd was pale. He slowly exhaled a cheekful of air. "Brother."

"All right, everybody, let's not pat ourselves on the back too much," Potter said. "We've only got an hour forty-five minutes till our first helicopter deadline."

Of all the people in the van only young Tobe Geller seemed disturbed.

Arthur Potter, childless father that he was, noticed it immediately. "What is it, Tobe?"

The agent pushed several buttons on the Hewlett-Packard and pointed to the screen. "This was your VSA grid during the exchange, Arthur. Lower anxiety than normal for a mildly stressful event."

"Mildly," Budd muttered, rolling his eyes. "Glad you didn't take mine."

"Here's Handy's average ten-second sequence for the entire exchange." He tapped the screen. It was nearly a flat line. "He was in the doorway with a dozen guns pointed at his heart and that son of a bitch was about as stressed out as most people get ordering a cup of coffee at 7-Eleven."

3:13 P.M.

She felt no thud of gunshots, no quiver of scream resonating in her chest.

Thank you thank you thank you.

The butterball Jocylyn was safe.

Melanie huddled with the twins in the back of the killing room, their long chestnut hair damp from tears, plastered to their faces. She looked up at the bare bulb, which—just barely—kept the crushing waves of the Outside from smashing her to death.

Her finger nervously entwining a strand of hair again. The hand shape for "shine." The word for "brilliance."

The word for "light."

A blur of motion startled her. The huge bearded form of Bear, chewing a hamburger, stormed up to Stoat and snapped a few words. Waited for an answer, got none, and shouted some more. Melanie couldn't read a single word of their conversation. The more emotional people became, the more ragged and fast their words, making them impossible to understand, as if just when it was the most important to say things clearly there could be no clarity.

Brushing his crew cut, Stoat stayed cool and looked back at Bear with a sneer of a smile. A real cowboy, Melanie thought, Stoat is. He's as cruel as the others but he's brave and he has honor and if those are good qualities even in bad people then there's some good in him. Brutus appeared and Bear suddenly stopped talking, grabbed a packet of fries in his fat hand, and wandered off to the front of the slaughterhouse, where he sat down and began shoveling food into his messy beard.

Brutus carried a paper-wrapped hamburger with him. He kept glancing at it in an amused way, as if he'd never had one before. He took a small bite and chewed carefully. He crouched in the doorway of the killing room, looking over the girls and the teachers. Melanie caught his eye once and felt her skin burn with panic. "Hey, miss," he said. She looked down quickly, feeling stomach sick.

She felt a thud and looked up, startled. He'd slapped the floor beside her. From his shirt pocket he took a small blue cardboard box and tossed it to her. It was an asthma inhaler. She opened it slowly and handed it to Beverly, who breathed in the medicine greedily.

Melanie turned to Brutus and was about to mouth "Thank you," but he was looking away, staring once

again at Mrs. Harstrawn, who'd fallen into another hysterical crying fit.

"Ain't that something—she ... keeps going and going."

How can I understand his words if I can't understand
him? Look at him—he crouches there and watches the
poor woman cry. Chewing, chewing, with that damn half-
smile on his lips. Nobody can be that cruel.

Or *do* I understand him?

Melanie hears a familiar voice. *So you'll be home
then. . . .*

Get up, she raged silently to the other teacher. Stop crying! Get up and do something! Help us. You're supposed
to be in charge.

So you'll be—

Suddenly her heart went icy cold and anger vaporized
her fear. Anger and ... what else? A dark fire swirling
within her. Her eyes met Brutus's. He'd stopped eating
and was looking at her. His lids never flickered but she
sensed he was winking at her—as if he knew exactly what
she was thinking about Mrs. Harstrawn and that the same
thing had occurred to him. For that instant the pathetic
woman was the butt of an inexcusable, mutual joke.

In despair she felt the anger vanishing, fear flooding in
to fill its place.

Stop looking at me! she begged him silently. Please!
She lowered her head and began to tremble, crying. And
so she did the only thing she could do—what she'd done
earlier: closing her eyes, lowering her head, she went
away. The place she'd escaped into from the slaughterhouse earlier today. Her secret place, her music room.

It is a room of dark wood, tapestries, pillows, smoky
air. Not a window in the place. The Outside cannot get in
here.

Here's a harpsichord carved of delicate rosewood, flo-
rets and filigree, inlaid with ivory and ebony. Here's a piano whose tone sounds like resonating crystal. A South
American berimbau, a set of golden vibes, a crisp, prewar
Martin guitar.

Here are walls to reflect Melanie's own voice, which is

an amalgam of all the instruments in the orchestra. Mezzo-sopranos and coloratura sopranos and altos.

It was a place that never existed and never would. But it was Melanie's salvation. When the taunts at school had grown too much, when she simply couldn't grasp what someone was saying to her, when she thought of the world she'd never experience, her music room was the only place she could go to be safe, to be comforted.

Forgetting the twins, forgetting gasping Beverly, forgetting the sobs of the paralyzed Mrs. Harstrawn, forgetting the terrible man watching her as he inhaled for sustenance the sorrow of another human being. Forgetting Susan's death, and her own, which was probably all too close.

Melanie, sitting on the comfortable couch in her secret place, decides she doesn't want to be alone. She needs someone with her. Someone to talk with. Someone with whom she can share human words. Whom should I invite?

Melanie thinks of her parents. But she's never invited them here before. Friends from Laurent Clerc, from Hebron, neighbors, students . . . But when she thinks of them she thinks of Susan. And of course she dares not.

Sometimes she invites musicians and composers—people she's read about, even if she's never heard their music: Emmylou Harris, Bonnie Raitt, Gordon Bok, Patrick Ball, Mozart, Sam Barber. Ludwig, of course. Ralph Vaughan Williams. Never Wagner. Mahler came once but didn't stay long.

Her brother used to be a regular visitor to the music room.

In fact, for a time, Danny was her only visitor, for he seemed to be the only person in the family not thrown by her affliction. Her parents struggled to coddle their daughter, keeping her home, never letting her go to town alone, scraping up money for tutors to come to the house, impressing on her the dangers of "her, you know, condition"—all the while avoiding any mention of her being deaf.

Danny wouldn't put up with her timidity. He'd roar into town on his Honda 350 with his sister perched on the back. She wore a black helmet emblazoned with fiery wings. Before her hearing went completely he'd take her

to movies and would drive audiences to rage by loudly re-
peating dialogue for her. To their parents' disgust the boy
would walk around the house wearing an airline me-
chanic's earmuffs, just so he'd know what she was going
through. Bless his heart, Danny even learned some basic
sign and taught her some phrases (naturally ones that she
couldn't repeat in the company of adult Deaf though they
would later earn her high esteem in the Laurent Clerc
schoolyard).

Ah, but Danny . . .

Ever since the accident last year, she hadn't had the
heart to ask him back.

She tries now but can't imagine him here.

And so today, when she opens the door, she finds a
middle-aged man with graying hair, wearing an ill-fitting
navy-blue jacket and black-framed glasses. The man from
the field outside the slaughterhouse.

De l'Epée.

Who else but him?

"Hello," she says in a voice like a glass bell.

"And to you." She pictures him taking her hand and
kissing it, rather bashfully, rather firmly.

"You're a policeman, aren't you?" she asks.

"Yes," he says.

She can't see him as clearly as she'd like. The power of
desire is unlimited but that of imagination is not.

"I know it's not your name but can I call you de
l'Epée?"

Of course he's agreeable to this, gentleman that he is.

"Can we talk for a little while? That's what I miss the
most, talking." Once you've spoken to someone, pelted
them with your words and felt theirs in your ears, signing
isn't the same at all.

"By all means, let's talk."

"I want to tell you a story. About how I learned I was
deaf."

"Please . . ." He seems genuinely curious.

Melanie had planned to be a musician, she tells him.
From the time she was four or five. She was no prodigy
but did have the gift of perfect pitch. Classical, Celtic, or
country-western—she loved it all. She could hear a tune

once and pick it out from memory on the family's Yamaha piano.

"And then . . ."

"Tell me about it."

"When I was eight, almost nine, I went to a Judy Collins concert."

She continues, "She was singing a cappella, a song I'd never heard before. It was haunting. . . ."

Conveniently, a Celtic harp begins playing the very tune through the imaginary speakers in the music room.

"My brother had the concert program and I leaned over and asked him what the name of the song was. He told me it was 'A Maiden's Grave.' "

De l'Epée says, "Never heard of it."

Melanie continues, "I wanted to play it on the piano. It was . . . It's hard to describe. Just a feeling, something I *had* to do. I had to learn the song. The day after the concert I asked my brother to stop by a music store and get some sheet music for me. He asked me which song. 'A Maiden's Grave,' I told him.

" 'What song's that?' he asked. He was frowning.

"I laughed. 'At the concert, dummy. The song she finished the concert with. *That* song. You told me the title.'

"Then *he* laughed. 'Who's a dummy? "A Maiden's Grave"? What're you talking about? It was "Amazing Grace." The old gospel. That's what I told you.'

" 'No!' I was sure I heard him say 'A Maiden's Grave.' I was positive! And just then I realized that I'd been leaning forward to hear him and that when either of us turned away I couldn't really hear what he was saying at all. *And* that when I was looking at him I was looking only at his lips, never his eyes or the rest of his face. The same way I'd been looking at everyone else I'd talked to for the last six or eight months.

"I ran straight to the record store downtown—two miles away. I was so desperate, I had to know. I was sure my brother was teasing me and I hated him for it. I swore I'd get even with him. I raced up to the folk section and flipped through the Judy Collins albums. It was true . . . 'Amazing Grace.' Two months later I was diagnosed with a fifty-decibel loss in one ear, seventy in the other. It's about ninety now in both."

"I'm so sorry," de l'Epée says. "What happened to your hearing?"

"An infection. It destroyed the hairs in my ear."

"And there's nothing you can do about it?"

She doesn't answer him. After a moment she says, "I think that you're Deaf."

"Deaf? Me?" He grins awkwardly. "But I can hear."

"Oh, you can be Deaf but hearing."

He looks confused.

"Deaf but hearing," she continues. "See, we call people who can hear the Others. But some of the Others are more like us."

"What sort of people are those?" he asks. Is he proud to be included? She thinks he is.

"People who live according to their own hearts," Melanie answers, "not someone else's."

For a moment she's ashamed, for she's not sure that she always listens to her own.

A Mozart piece begins to play. Or Bach. She isn't sure which. (Why couldn't the infection have come a year later? Think of all the music I could have listened to in twelve months. For God's sake, her father pumped easy-listening KSFT through the farm's loudspeakers. In my bio, they'll find I was reared on "Pearly Shells," Tom Jones, and Barry Manilow.)

"There's more I have to tell you. Something else I've never told anyone."

"I'd like to hear it," he says, agreeable. But then, in an instant, he disappears.

Melanie gasps.

The music room vanishes and she's back in the slaughter-house.

Her eyes are wide, she looks around, expecting to see Brutus approaching. Or Bear shouting, storming toward her.

But, no, Brutus is gone. And Bear sits by himself out-side the killing room, eating, an incongruous smile on his face.

What had dragged her from the music room?

A vibration from a sound? The light?

No, it was a smell. A scent had wakened her out of her daydream. But of what?

Something she detected amid the smell of greasy food, bodies, and oil and gasoline and rusting metal and old blood and rancid lard and a thousand other scents.

Ah, she recognized it clearly. A rich, pungent smell.

"Girls, girls," she signed emphatically to the students. "I want to say something."

Bear's head turned toward them. He noticed the signing. His smile vanished immediately and he climbed to his feet. He seemed to be shouting, "Stop that! Stop!"

"He doesn't like us to sign," Melanie signed quickly. "Pretend we're playing hand-shape game."

One thing Melanie liked about Deaf culture—the love of words. ASL was a language like any other. In fact it was the fifth most widely used language in America. ASL words and phrases could be broken down into smaller structural units (hand shape, motion, and relation of the hand to the body), just like spoken words could be broken down into syllables and phonemes. Those gestures lent themselves to word games, which nearly all Deaf people grew up playing.

Bear stormed up to her. "What the fuck . . . with . . ."

Melanie's hands began to shake violently. She managed to write in the dust on the floor, *Game. We're playing game. See? We make shapes with our hands. Shapes of things.*

"What things?"

This is animal game.

She signed the word "Stupid." With her index and middle fingers extended in a V, the shape vaguely resembled a rabbit.

"What's that . . . be?"

A rabbit, she wrote.

The twins ducked their heads, giggling.

"Rabbit . . . Doesn't . . . fucking rabbit to me," he said.

Please let us play. Can't hurt.

He glanced at Kielle, who signed, "You turd." Smiling, she wrote in the dust, *That was hippo.*

". . . out of your fucking minds." Bear turned back to his fries and soda.

The girls waited until he was out of sight then looked expectantly at Melanie. Kielle, no longer smiling, asked brusquely, "What do you have to say?"

"I'm going to get us out of here," Melanie signed. "That's what."

Arthur Potter and Angie Scapello were preparing to debrief Jocylyn Weiderman, who was being examined by medics at that moment, when they heard the first shot.

It was a faint crack and far less alarming than Dean Stillwell's urgent voice breaking over the speaker above their heads. "Arthur, we've got a situation here! Handy's shooting."

Hell.

"There's somebody in the field."

Before he even looked outside Potter pressed the button on the mike and ordered, "Tell everybody, no return fire."

"Yessir."

Potter joined Angie and Charlie Budd in the ocher window of the van.

"That son of a bitch," Budd whispered.

Another shot rang out from the slaughterhouse and the bullet kicked up a cloud of splinters from the rotting stockade post next to the dark-suited man about sixty yards from the command van. A voluminous handkerchief, undoubtedly expensive, billowed around the raised right hand of the intruder.

"Oh, no," Angie whispered in dismay.

Potter's heart sank. "Henry, your profile of the assistant attorney general neglected to mention he's out of his damn mind."

Handy fired again, hitting a rock just behind Roland Marks. The assistant AG stopped, cringing. He waved the handkerchief again. He continued slowly toward the slaughterhouse.

Potter pressed speed dial. As the phone rang and rang he muttered, "Come on, Lou."

No answer.

Dean Stillwell's voice came over the speaker. "Arthur,

I don't know what to make of it. Somebody here thinks it's—"

"It's Roland Marks, Dean. Is he saying anything to Handy?"

"Looks like he's shouting. We can't hear."

"Tobe, you have those Big Ears in place still?"

The young agent spoke into his stalk mike and punched buttons. In a few seconds, the mournful yet urgent sound of the wind filled the van. Then Marks's voice.

"Lou Handy! I'm Roland Marks, assistant attorney general of the state of Kansas."

A huge crack of a gunshot, overly amplified, burst into the van. Everyone cringed.

Tobe whispered, "The other Big Ear's trained on the slaughterhouse but we're not getting anything."

Sure. Because Handy's not saying anything. Why talk when you can make your point with bullets?

"This is bad," Angie muttered.

The AG's voice again: "Lou Handy, this isn't a trick. I want you to give up the girls and take me in their place."

"Jesus," Budd whispered. "He's doing that?" He sounded half impressed and Potter had to restrain himself from scowling at the state police captain.

Another shot, closer. Marks danced sideways.

"For the love of God, Handy," came the desperate voice. "Let those girls go!"

And all the while the phone inside the slaughterhouse rang and rang and rang.

Potter spoke into the radio mike. "Dean, I hate to say it but we've got to stop him. Hail him on the bullhorn and try to get him over to the sidelines. If he doesn't come, send out a couple of men."

"Handy's just playing with him," Budd said. "I don't think he's in any real danger. They could've shot him easy by now, they'd wanted to."

"*He's* not who I'm worried about," Potter snapped.

"What?"

Angie said, "We're trying to get hostages *out,* not in."

"He's making our job harder," Potter said simply, not explaining the terrible mistake Marks was now making.

With a whining ricochet, a bullet split a rock beside the

lawyer's leg. Marks remained on his feet. He turned and he was listening to Dean Stillwell, whose voice was being picked up by the Big Ear and relayed into the van. To Potter's relief the sheriff wasn't cowed by the man's authority. "You there, Marks, you're to get under cover immediately or you'll be arrested. Come back this way."

"We've got to save them." Marks's raw voice filled the van. It sounded resolute but terrified and for a moment Potter's heart went out to him.

Another shot.

"No, sir. Do you understand? You're about to be placed under arrest."

Potter called Stillwell and told him he was doing great. "Tell him he's *endangering* the girls doing this."

The sheriff's voice, mixing with the ragged wind, filled the van as he relayed this message.

"No! I'm saving them," the assistant AG shouted and started forward again.

Potter tried the throw phone again. No answer.

"Okay, Dean. Go get him. No covering fire under any circumstances."

Stillwell sighed. "Yessir. I've got some volunteers. I hope it's okay but I green-lighted pepper spray if he resists."

"Give him a blast for me," Potter muttered, and turned back to watch.

Two troopers in body armor and helmets slipped from the line of trees and, crouching, headed through the field.

Handy fired several more times. He hadn't noticed the troopers yet and was aiming only around Marks, the shots always near-misses. But one bullet hit a rock and ricocheted upwards, shattering the windshield of a squad car.

The two troopers kept low to the ground, running perpendicularly to the front of the slaughterhouse. Their hips and sides were easy targets if Handy decided to turn malicious and draw blood. Potter frowned. One of the men looked familiar.

"Who're those troopers?" Potter asked Stillwell. "Is one of them Stevie Oates?"

"Yessir."

Potter exhaled a deep sigh. "He just got *back* from a run, Dean. What's he thinking of?"

"Well, sir, he wanted to go out again. Was really insistent about it."

Potter shook his head.

Marks was now only forty yards from the slaughterhouse, the two troopers closing in slowly, scrambling through the buffalo grass. Marks saw them and shouted for them to get away.

"Sir," the voice through the speaker called—Potter recognized it as Oates's—"our orders're to bring you back."

"Fuck your orders. If you care about those girls just leave me alone."

They heard a whoop of distant laughter the Big Ear was picking up. "Turkey shoot," resounded Handy's voice, riding on the wind. Another deafening gunshot. A rock beside one of the troopers flew into the air. They both dropped to their bellies, began crawling like soldiers toward the assistant AG.

"Marks," Oates called, breathing hard. "We're bringing you back, sir. You're interfering with a federal operation."

Marks whirled around. "What're you going to do to stop me, Trooper? You work for *me*. Don't you forget it."

"Sheriff Stillwell has authorized me to use all necessary force to stop you, sir. And I aim to."

"You're downwind, son. Pepper-spray me and you're the only one who'll get a faceful of it."

Handy fired again. The bullet split an ancient post two feet from Oates's head. The convict, still in a playful mood, laughed hard.

"Jesus," somebody muttered.

"No, sir," Oates said calmly, "my orders're to shoot you in the leg and drag you back."

Potter and LeBow stared at each other. The negotiator's fervent thumb pressed the transmit button. "He *is* bluffing, isn't he, Dean?"

"Yep" was Stillwell's unsteady reply. "But . . . he sounds pretty determined. I mean, don't you think?"

Potter did think.

"Would he do it?" LeBow asked.

Potter shrugged.

Angie said, "He's drawn his weapon."

Oates was aiming steadily at Marks's lower extremities.

Well, this is escalating into a full-blown disaster, Potter thought.

"Sir," Oates called, "I will not miss. I'm an excellent shot and I'm just about to bring you down."

The assistant AG hesitated. The wind ripped the handkerchief from his fingers. It rose a few feet above his head.

A shot.

Handy's bullet struck the white cloth. It jerked and floated away on the breeze.

Again, through the Big Ear, the distant sound of Handy laughing. Marks looked back at the slaughterhouse. Called out, "You son of a bitch, Handy. I hope you rot in hell."

More laughter—or perhaps it was only the wind.

Standing tall, the assistant AG walked off the field. As if strolling through his own backyard. Potter was pleased to see that Stevie Oates and his partner kept low as terriers as they crawled after the man under cover of the sumptuous, windswept grass.

"You could've ruined everything," Arthur Potter snapped. "What the hell were you thinking?"

He had to look up into Marks's eyes—the man was well over six feet tall—but still felt he was talking to a snotty child caught misbehaving.

The assistant attorney general began firmly, "I was thinking—"

"You *never* exchange hostages. The whole point of negotiation is to devalue them. You were as good as saying to him, 'Here I am, I'm worth more than all of those girls combined.' If he'd gotten you it would've made my job impossible."

"I don't see why," Marks answered.

"Because," Angie said, "a hostage like you would have boosted his sense of power and control a hundred times.

He'd up his demands and stick to them. We'd never get him to agree to anything reasonable."

"Well, I kept thinking about those girls in there. What they were going through."

"He never would have let them go."

"I was going to talk him into it."

LeBow rolled his eyes and continued to type up the incident.

Potter said, "I'm not going to arrest you." He'd considered it and concluded that the fallout would be too thorny. "But if you interfere in any way with this barricade again I will and I'll have the U.S. Attorney make sure you do time."

To Potter's astonishment, Marks wasn't the least contrite. The witty facade was gone, yes; but he seemed, if anything, irritated that Potter had interfered with *his* plans. "You do things by the book, Potter." A large index finger pointed bluntly at the agent. "But the book doesn't say anything about a psycho who gets his kicks killing children."

The phone buzzed. LeBow took the call and said to Potter, "Jocylyn's gotten a clean bill of health from the medics. She's fine. You want to debrief her now?"

"Yes, thank you, Henry. Tell them to send her in. Stevie Oates too." To Marks he said, "I'll ask you to leave now."

Marks buttoned his suit jacket, brushed away the rock dust that had powdered his jacket from Handy's target practice. He strode to the door and muttered something. Potter believed he heard: "blood on your hands." But as to the other words, he didn't have a clue.

3:40 P.M.

For precious minutes she wept uncontrollably.

Angie Scapello and Arthur Potter sat with Jocylyn and struggled to look calm and reassuring while in their hearts they wanted to grab the girl by the shoulders and shake answers out of her.

Impatience, Arthur Potter's nemesis.

He kept a smile on his face and nodded with reassurance while the chubby twelve-year-old cried and cried, resting her round, red face in her hands.

The door opened and Stevie Oates stepped inside, pulled off his helmet. Despite the cold his hair was damp with sweat. Potter turned his attention from the girl to the trooper.

"You should stand down for a while, Stevie."

"Yessir, I think I will. Those last couple shots were kind of, well . . . close."

"Sobered you up pretty fast, did they?"

"Yessir. Sure did."

"Tell me everything you saw when you went up there with the food."

As Potter expected, even with the aid of the videotape from the camera perched over his ear, Oates couldn't provide much detail about the interior of the slaughterhouse.

"Any thoughts on Handy's state of mind?"

"Seemed calm. Wasn't edgy."

Like he was buying a cup of coffee at 7-Eleven.

"Anybody hurt?"

"Not that I could see."

LeBow dutifully typed in the paltry intelligence. Oates could recall nothing else. Potter pointed out to the discouraged officer that it was good news he *hadn't* seen blood or bodies. Though he knew his own face didn't mask the discouragement he felt; they wouldn't get anything helpful from the twelve-year-old girl, who continued to weep and twine her short dark hair around fingers that ended in chewed nails.

"Thanks, Stevie. That's all for now. Oh, one question. Were you really going to shoot Marks in the leg?"

The young man grew serious for a moment then broke into a cautious grin. "The best way I can put it, sir, is I wasn't going to know until I pulled the trigger. Or didn't pull the trigger. As the case might be."

"Go get some coffee, Trooper," Potter said.

"Yessir."

Potter and Angie turned their attention back to Jocylyn. Her eyes were astonishingly red; she huddled in the blanket one of Stillwell's officers had given her.

Finally the girl was calm enough that Potter could begin to question her through Officer Frances Whiting. The negotiator noted that while Frances's hands moved elegantly and with compact gestures Jocylyn's were broad and awkward, stilted: the difference, he guessed, between someone speaking smoothly and someone inserting "um"s and "you know"s into their speech. He wondered momentarily how Melanie signed. Staccato? Smooth?

"She isn't answering your questions," Frances said.

"What's she saying?" Angie asked, her quick, dark eyes picking up patterns in the signing.

"That she wants her parents."

"Are they at the motel?" he asked Budd.

The captain made a call and told him, "They should be, within the hour."

Frances relayed that information to her. Without acknowledging that she understood, the girl started another jag of crying.

"You're doing fine," Angie said encouragingly.

The negotiator glanced at his watch. A half-hour to the helicopter deadline. "Tell me about the men, Jocylyn. The bad men."

Frances's hands flew and the girl finally responded. "She says there are three of them. Those three there." The girl was gesturing at the wall. "They're sweaty and smell bad. The one there." Pointing at Handy. "Brutus. He's the leader."

"Brutus?" Potter asked, frowning.

Frances asked the question and watched a lengthy response, during which Jocylyn pointed to each of the takers.

"That's what Melanie calls him," she said. "Handy's 'Brutus.' Wilcox is 'Stoat.' And Bonner is 'Bear.' " The officer added, "Signing's very metaphoric. 'Lamb' is sometimes used for 'gentle,' for instance. The Deaf often think in poetic terms."

"Does she have any idea where they are in the slaughterhouse?" He asked this of Frances, and Angie said,

"Talk to her directly, Arthur. It'll be more reassuring, make her feel more like an adult. And don't forget to smile."

He repeated the question, smiling, to the girl, and Frances translated her response as she pointed to several locations near the front of the big room then touched Handy's and Wilcox's pictures. Tobe moved the Post-Its emblazoned with their names. LeBow typed.

Jocylyn shook her head. She rose and placed them more exactly. She signed some words to Frances, who said, "Bear—Bonner—is in the room with her friends."

Jocylyn put Bear's Post-It in a large semicircular room about twenty-five feet from the front of the slaughterhouse. Tobe placed all the hostage markers in there.

Jocylyn rearranged them too, being very precise.

"That's where everyone is, she says. Exactly."

Potter's eye strayed to Melanie's tab.

Jocylyn wiped tears, then signed.

"She says Bear watches them all the time. Especially the little girls."

Bonner. The rapist.

Potter asked, "Are there any other doorways or windows that aren't on the diagram?"

Jocylyn studied it carefully. Shook her head.

"Are you sure?"

"Yes."

"Did you see any guns?"

"They all have guns." The girl pointed to Tobe's hip.

He asked, "What kind were they?"

She frowned and pointed to the agent's hip again.

"I mean, were they like this, or did they have cylinders?" He found himself making a circular gesture with his finger. "Revolvers," he said slowly.

Jocylyn shook her head. Her awkward hands spoke again.

"No, she says they were black automatics. Just like that one." Frances smiled. "She asked why don't you believe her."

"You know what an automatic is?"

"She says she watches TV."

Potter laughed and told LeBow to write down that she'd

confirmed they were armed with three Glocks or similar weapons.

Jocylyn volunteered that they had two dozen boxes of bullets.

"Boxes?"

"This big," Frances said, as the girl motioned her hands about six inches apart. "Yellow and green."

"Remington," LeBow said.

"And shotguns. Like that. Three of them." Jocylyn pointed to a shotgun on the rack in the van.

"Any rifles?" Potter pointed to an M-16 resting against the wall.

"No."

"They're pretty damn prepared," Budd muttered.

Potter handed off to Angie, who asked, "Is anybody hurt?"

"No."

"Does Handy—Brutus—talk to anybody in particular? Any of the teachers or girls, I mean?"

"No. Mostly he just looks at us." This brought back some memory and, in turn, more tears.

"You're doing great, honey," Angie said, squeezing the girl's shoulder. "Have you been able to tell what the three men are talking about?"

"No. I'm sorry. I can't lip-read good."

"Is Beverly all right?"

"She can't breathe well. But she's had worse attacks. The worst problem is Mrs. Harstrawn."

"Ask her to explain."

Frances watched her hands and said, "It sounds like she's having a breakdown. She was fine until Susan was shot. All she does now is lie on her back and cry."

Potter thought: They're leaderless. The worst situation. They could panic and run. Unless Melanie has taken over.

"How's Melanie?"

"She just sits and stares. Sometimes closes her eyes." Frances added to Potter, "That's not good. The deaf never close their eyes in a tense situation. Their vision is the only warning system they have."

Angie asked, "Do the men fight among themselves?"

Jocylyn didn't know.

"Do they seem nervous? Happy? Scared? Sad?"

"They're not scared. Sometimes they laugh."

LeBow typed this into his computer.

"Okay," Potter said. "You're a very brave girl. You can go to the hotel now. Your parents will be there soon."

The twelve-year-old wiped her nose on her sleeve but didn't leave. She signed awkwardly.

"Is that all you want to ask me?" Frances translated.

"Yes. You can go."

But the girl signed some more. "She asked, 'Don't you want to know about the TV? And the other stuff?' "

Tobe, LeBow, and Budd turned their heads to Potter.

"They have a TV in there?" he whispered, dismayed. Frances translated and Jocylyn nodded.

"Where did they get it?"

"In the bags with the guns. They brought it in with them. It's a little one."

"Do they have a radio?"

"I didn't see one."

"Do they watch the TV a lot?"

She nodded.

"What other stuff do they have?"

"She says they have some tools. New ones. They're in plastic."

"What kind?"

"Silver ones. Wrenches. Pliers. Screwdrivers. A big shiny hammer."

"Offer her a job, Arthur," Henry LeBow said. "She's better than half our agents."

"Anything else you can think of, Jocylyn?"

Her red fingers moved.

"She misses her mommy."

"One more thing," Potter said. He hesitated. He wanted to ask something more about Melanie. He found he couldn't. Instead he asked, "Is it cold inside?"

"Not too bad."

Potter took the girl's round, damp hand and pressed it between his. "Tell her many thanks, Frances. She did a fine job."

After this message was translated Jocylyn wiped her face and smiled for the first time.

Angie asked Frances to tell the girl that she'd take her to the motel in a minute. Jocylyn went outside to wait with a woman state trooper.

LeBow printed out the list of what the men had inside the slaughterhouse with them. He handed it to Tobe, who pinned it up beside the diagram.

Tobe said, "It's like a computer adventure game. 'You're carrying a key, a magic sword, five stones, and a raven in a cage.'"

Potter sat back in his chair slowly, laughing. He looked at the list. "What do you make of it, Henry? Tools, a TV?"

"Knocked over a store on their way out of the prison?"

Potter asked Budd, "Any reports of a commercial burglary between here and Winfield, Charlie?"

"I'm outta that loop. I'll check." He stepped outside.

"I've never had such good intelligence from a hostage who'd been inside so short a time," Potter said. "Her powers of observation are remarkable."

"God compensates," Frances said.

Potter then asked Angie, "What do you think?"

"She's with us, I'd guess."

Because of the Stockholming process hostages have been known to give false information to negotiators and tactical teams. On one of Potter's negotiations—a week-long terrorist barricade—a released hostage left a handkerchief in front of the window where Potter was hiding so that the barricaded gunman would know where to shoot. A sniper killed the hostage taker before he could fire. Potter testified on the hostage's behalf at her subsequent trial; she got a suspended sentence.

Potter agreed with Angie's assessment. Jocylyn hadn't been inside long enough to skew her feelings about Handy and the others. She was just a scared little girl.

Angie said, "I'm going to take her to the motel. Make sure she's comfortable. Reassure the other parents."

Henry LeBow called, "Arthur, just got some info on Henderson."

Potter said to Angie as she stepped out the door, "While you're down there, check up on him. He makes me nervous."

"Pete Henderson we're talking, the Wichita SAC?"

"Yep."

"Why?"

"Gut feel." Potter told her about the threat. And added that he was more concerned that Henderson hadn't at first volunteered that he'd interviewed Handy after the S&L arson. "It's probably because his boys did a lousy job on the collar, letting the girlfriend get away and ending up with two wounded troopers." The postcollar interrogation too, which Potter now recalled had yielded only unimaginative obscenities on Handy's part. "But he should've told us up front he was involved."

"What do you want me to do?" Angie asked.

Potter shrugged. "Just make sure he's not getting into any trouble."

She offered a gimme-a-break look. Peter Henderson, as Special Agent in Charge of a resident agency, had the rank to get into as much trouble as he liked and it wasn't for underlings like Angie Scapello to do anything about it.

"Try. Please." Potter blew her a kiss.

LeBow handed Potter the printout, explaining with a sneer, "It's only résumé-quality data. But there *are* some details I'll bet he wants to keep under wraps."

Potter was intrigued. He read. Henderson had come up through the ranks, working as an investigator in the Chicago Police Department while he went to DePaul Law School at night. After he got his degree he joined the Bureau, excelled at Quantico, and returned to the Midwest, where he made a name for himself in southern Illinois and St. Louis, primarily investigating RICO crimes. He was a good administrator, fit the Feebie mold, and was clearly destined for a SAC job in Chicago or Miami or even the Southern District of New York. After which the career trajectory would have landed him in D.C.

If not for the lawsuit.

Potter read the press accounts and, supplemented by details from memos Henry LeBow had somehow managed to pry from the Bureau databases, he understood why Henderson had been shunted off to Kansas. Six years ago a dozen black agents had sued the Bureau for discrimination in doling out assignments, promotions, and raises. The St. Louis office was one of the targeted federal districts, and Henderson was quick to offer testimony supporting their claim. Too quick, some said. In the anticipated shakeup following the Title VII suit the then-current Bureau director was expected to resign and be replaced by a young deputy director, who would become the first black head of the FBI and who would—Henderson figured—remember those loyal to the cause.

But Henderson's scheming had blown up in his face. The steam went out of the suit as it bogged down in the federal courts. Some plaintiffs dropped out; others simply couldn't prove discrimination. For reasons stemming from ambition, not ideology, the young black deputy director chose to move to the National Security Council. The existing Bureau director simply retired, amid no scandal, and was replaced by the Admiral.

Turncoat Peter Henderson was administratively drawn and quartered. The man who'd once gotten a tap into syndicate boss Mario Lacosta's Clayton, Missouri, private den was sent packing to the state in which the geographic center of the country could be found and that was indeed known mostly for pilferings at McConnell Air Force Base and internecine battles with Indian Affairs and BATF. The career of the thirty-nine-year-old agent was at a complete standstill.

"Risks?" Potter asked LeBow. "He going to get in our way?"

"He's not in any position to do anything," the intelligence officer said. "Not officially."

"He's desperate."

"I'm sure he is. I said 'not officially.' We still have to keep our eyes on him."

Potter chuckled. "So, we've got an assistant attorney general ready to hand himself over to the takers and a SAC who wants to hand *me* over to them."

We have met the enemy . . .

He turned back to the window, thinking of Melanie, recalling what Jocylyn had said. *She just closes her eyes. Doesn't do anything.* What does that mean? he wondered.

Tobe broke into Potter's musings. "Handy's expecting a chopper in an hour, five minutes."

"Thank you, Tobe," Potter responded.

He looked out over the slaughterhouse and thought: A key, a magic sword, five stones, and a raven in a cage.

"Officer."

Charlie Budd was walking back to the van from his own unmarked car, where he'd just typed in a computer request for 211s in a four-county area. The only robberies today had been a convenience store, a gas station, and a Methodist church. The booty in none of them matched the weapons, TV, and tools that the HTs had brought with them.

"Come over here, Officer," the man's low voice said.

Oh, brother. What now?

Roland Marks leaned against the side of a supply van, smoking a cigarette. Budd thought he'd be ten miles away by now but there was purpose in his eyes and he looked like he was here to stay.

"You witnessed that little travesty," Marks announced.

Budd had been in the corner of the van as Potter read the riot act. Budd looked around then wandered through the grass to the dark-featured man and stood upwind of the smoke. He said nothing.

"I love summer afternoons, Captain. Remind me of growing up. I played baseball every day. Did you? You look like you could run like the wind."

"Track and field. Four-forty and eight-eighty mostly."

"All right." Marks's voice dropped again, softer than Budd thought it possibly could and still be audible. "We had the luxury, you and I'd dance around a bit like we were on a dinner cruise and you'd get my meaning and then go off and do what you ought to. But there's no time for that."

I was *never* cut out to be an officer, Budd thought, and replayed for the hundredth time the bullet cutting down seventeen-year-old Susan Phillips. He choked suddenly and turned it into an odd-sounding cough. "Say, I'm real busy right now, sir. I have to—"

"Answer me yes or no. Did I see something in your eyes in the van?"

"Don't know what you mean, sir."

"Sure, maybe what I did was out of line. I wasn't thinking too clearly. But you weren't completely sure *Potter* was right either. And—no, hold up there. I think if we took a vote more people in that van'd come down on my side than his."

Budd summoned his courage from somewhere and said, "It's not a popularity contest, sir."

"Oh, no, it's not. That's exactly right. It's a question about whether those girls live, and I think Potter doesn't care if they do or not."

"Noooo. That's not true. Not by a long shot. He cares a lot."

"What'm I seeing in your face, Officer? Just what I saw in the van, right? You're scared shitless for those little things in that slaughterhouse."

Our number-one priority isn't getting those girls out alive. . . .

Marks continued, "Come on now, Officer. Admit it."

"He's a good man," Budd said.

"I know he's a good man. What the fuck does that have to do with anything?"

"He's doing the best—"

"There is no way in hell," Marks said slowly, "I'm letting those girls in there die. Which is something he's willing to do . . . and that's been eating at you all day. Am I right?"

"Well—"

Marks's hand dug into his suit jacket and he pulled out a wallet, flipped it open. For a crazy moment Budd though he was going to display his AG's office ID. But what Budd found himself looking at had far more impact on him. Three photos in glossy sleeves of young girls. One had knitted eyebrows and slightly distorted features. The handicapped daughter.

"You're a father of girls, Budd. Am I right?"

The captain swallowed and tried to look away from the six dark eyes. He couldn't.

"Just imagine *your* little ones in there. And then imagine someone like Potter saying, 'Hell, they're expendable.' Imagine that, Captain."

Budd inhaled long. And finally managed to look away. The wallet snapped closed.

"We have to get him removed."

"What?"

"*He's* signing their death sentences. What did he say about meeting Handy's demands? Come on, Budd. Answer like an officer."

He looked into Marks's eye and ignored the slap, saying, "He said Handy wasn't leaving there except in cuffs or a body bag."

And that if those girls had to die, so be it.

"Is that acceptable to you, Officer?"

"It's not my job to say if it is or isn't."

" 'I was only following orders.' "

"That's about the size of it."

Marks spit the cigarette from his mouth. "For God's sake, Captain, you *can* take a moral position, can't you? Don't you have any higher values than running errands for a fat FBI agent?"

Budd said stiffly, "He's the senior officer. He's federal, and—"

"You just hold on to those words, Captain," Marks railed like a pumped-up evangelist. "Tuck 'em under your arm and bring 'em out at the funerals of those girls. I hope they make you feel better." He reached into Budd's soul and poked with a fingernail. "There's already one girl's blood on our hands."

He means your *hands.*

Budd saw Susan Phillips as she fell to her knees. The impact of that fall made her jaw drop open and distorted her beautiful face for a moment. It became beautiful once more as she died.

"What?" Budd whispered, his eyes on the buggish headlights of the harvesting threshers. "What do you want?" This sounded childish and shamed him but he couldn't stop himself.

"I want Potter out. You or I or somebody state'll take over the negotiations and give those cocksuckers their damn helicopter in exchange for the girls. We'll track 'em down when they land and blow 'em to hell. I've already checked. We can get a chopper here in a half-hour, fitted with a homing device that'll track 'em from a hundred miles away. They'll never know we're following."

"But he says Handy's too dangerous to let out."

"Of course he's dangerous," Marks said. "But once he's out he'll be up against professionals. Men and women who're paid to take risks. Those girls aren't."

Marks had tiny eyes and it seemed to Budd that they were on the verge of tears. He thought of the man's mentally retarded daughter, in and out of hospitals all her short life.

He observed that Marks had said nothing about the effect of Budd's decision on his career. If he had, Budd would have stonewalled. When it came to things like that, cheap shots, the young captain could be a mule. Then it discouraged him immensely to see that Marks had assessed that about him and had pointedly avoided any threats. Budd realized that he was already lying on the mat, shoulders pinned, staring at the ceiling. The count had begun.

Oh, brother.

"But how can we get Potter out?"

He said this to stymie Marks but of course the man was prepared. The small black box appeared in Marks's hand. For an absurd moment Budd actually thought it was a bomb. He stared at the tape recorder. "All I want is for you to get him to say that the hostages are expendable."

"You mean, record him?"

"Exactly."

"And . . . and then what?"

"I've got some friends at a St. Louis radio station. They'll run the tape on the news. Potter'll have to step down."

"That could be the end of his career."

"And it could be the end of *mine*, doing this. But I'm willing to risk it. For chrissake, I was willing to give myself up in exchange for them. You don't see Potter doing that."

"I just don't know."

"Let's save those nine poor girls in there, Captain. What do you say?"

Marks thrust the recorder into Budd's unhappy hands.

The officer stared at it then slipped it into his pocket and without a word turned away. His only act of defiance was to offer, "No, you're wrong. There are only eight people inside. He's gotten one out." But Marks was out of earshot when he said it.

4:10 P.M.

Captain Charles R. Budd stood in a gully not far from the command van.

He was delegating, yes, but mostly he was trying to ignore the weight of the tape recorder, a thousand pounds of hot metal, in his hip pocket.

I'll think about that later.

Delegate.

Phil Molto was setting up the press table: a folding fiberboard table, a small portable typewriter, paper and pencils. Budd was no news hog but he supposed this setup would be useless for today's high-tech reporters. Did they even know how to type, those pretty boys and girls? They seemed like spoiled high-school kids.

He guessed, though, that this arrangement had less to do with journalism than with politics. How did Potter know how to handle all these things? Maybe living in the nation's capital helped. Politics one way or another. The earnest young captain felt totally incompetent.

Shame too. The tape recorder melted into fiery plastic and ran down his leg.

Forget about it. Fifty minutes to five—fifty minutes to the deadline. He kept a meaningless smile on his face but he couldn't sweep from his mind the image of the teenage girl falling to ground, dying.

He somehow knew in his heart more blood would be spilled. Marks was right. In the van he *had* sided with the assistant attorney general.

Forty-nine minutes . . .

"Okay," he told his lieutenant. "Guess that'll do. You

ride herd on 'em, Phil. Make sure they sit tight. They can wander around a little behind the lines and take notes on whatever they want—"

Was that okay? he wondered. What would Potter say?

"—but suit 'em up in flak jackets and make sure they keep their heads down."

Quiet Phil Molto nodded.

The first car arrived a minute later, containing two men. They climbed out, flashed press credentials, and as they looked around hungrily the older of them said, "I'm Joe Silbert, KFAL. This is Ted Biggins."

Budd got a kick out of their dress—dark suits that didn't fit very well and black running shoes. He pictured them racing down the hall of a TV station, shouting, "Exclusive, exclusive!" while papers spun in their wakes.

Silbert looked at the press table and laughed. Budd introduced himself and Molto and said, "Best we could do."

"It's fine, Officer. Only I hope you don't mind if we use our own stone tablet to write on?"

Biggins hefted a large portable computer onto the table.

"Long as we see what you write before you send it." For so Potter had instructed him.

"File it," Silbert said. "We say 'file it,' not 'send it.' " Budd couldn't tell if he was making a joke.

Biggins poked at the typewriter. "What exactly is this?"

The men laughed. Budd told them the ground rules. Where they could go and where they couldn't. "We've got a couple troopers you can talk to if you want. Phil here'll send 'em over."

"They hostage rescue?"

"No. They're from Troop K, up the road."

"Can we talk to some hostage rescue boys?"

When Budd grinned Silbert smiled too, like a co-conspirator, and the reporter realized he wasn't going to catch the captain in any slip-ups about whether or not HRT was on the scene.

"We're going to want to talk to Potter sometime soon," Silbert groused. "He planning on avoiding us?"

"I'll let him know you're here," Budd said cheerfully, the Switzerland of law enforcers. "Meanwhile Phil here'll bring you up to date. He's got profiles of the escapees and pictures of them. And he'll get you suited up in body armor. Oh, and I was thinking you might want to get the human-interest angle from some troopers. What it's like to be on a barricade. That sort of thing."

The reporters' faces were solemn masks but Budd wondered again if they were laughing at him. Silbert said, "Fact is, we're mostly interested in the hostages. That's where the story is. Anybody here we can talk to about them?"

"I'm just here to set up the press table. Agent Potter'll be by to give you the information he thinks you oughta have." Is that the right way to put it? Budd wondered. "Now I got some things need looking after so I'll leave you be."

"But I won't," said Molto, cracking a rare smile.

"I'm sure you won't, Officer." Their computer whirred to life.

What Melanie had smelled in the air of the killing room, what had forced her from her music room: mud, fish, water, diesel fuel, methane, decaying leaves, wet tree bark.

The river.

The fishy breeze had been strong enough to start the lamp swaying. That told her that somewhere near the back of the slaughterhouse was an open doorway. It occurred to her that maybe de l'Epée had already sent his men around the slaughterhouse looking for places where the girls might get out. Maybe some were even cutting their way in right now to rescue them.

She thought back to their arrival at the slaughterhouse this morning. She remembered seeing groves of trees on either side of the building, a muddy slope down to the river, which glistened gray and cold in the overcast afternoon light, black wood pilings, dotted with tar and creosote, a dock leaning precariously over the water, dangling rotten tires for ship bumpers.

The tires . . . That's what had given her the idea. When she was a girl, every summer in the early evening she and Danny would race down to Seversen Corner on the farm, run over the tractor ruts and through a fog of wheat down to the pond. It was nearly an acre, surrounded by willows and grass and stiff reeds filled with cores like Styrofoam. She ran like the Kansas wind so that she'd be the first one to the hill overlooking the pond, where she'd leap into space, grab the tire swing hanging over the water and sail out above the mirrorlike surface.

Then let go and tumble into the sky and clouds reflected below her.

She and her brother had spent long hours at the pond— even now, that glassy water was often her first thought when she stepped outside into a warm summer evening. Danny had taught her to swim twice. The first time when she was six and he'd taken her hands and eased her into the water of the still but deep pond. The second time was far harder—after she'd lost her hearing and grown afraid of so many things. She was twelve then. But the lanky, blond boy, five years older, refused to let her dodge the swimming hole any longer and, using the sign language he alone in the Charrol family had learned, talked her into letting go her grip on the bald Goodyear. And he calmly trod water, supported her and kept her from panicking while she finally remembered the strokes she'd learned years before.

Swimming. The first thing she'd done that gave her back a splinter of self-confidence after her plunge into deafness.

Thank you, Danny, she thought. For then, and for now. Because it was this memory that she believed was going to save some, if not all, of her students.

The river was wide here. The surface was choppy and the current fast but she remembered a tangle of branches and garbage washed up against a fallen tree that hung into the choppy water maybe a hundred feet downstream. Melanie pictured the girls moving silently through the back corridors of the slaughterhouse, over the dockside, into the water, then drifting with the current to the tree, scrambling out through the branches. Running to safety. . . .

"Never underestimate a body of water," Danny had told her. "Even the calm ones can be dangerous."

Well, there was nothing calm about the Arkansas. Could they manage it? Donna Harstrawn can swim. Kielle and Shannon—superheroes that they are—can swim like otters. (Melanie pictures Kielle's compact body cannon-balling off the diving board, while Shannon's willowy frame leisurely completes her laps.) The twins love to play in the water. But they can't swim. Beverly knows how but with her asthma she can't. Melanie doesn't know about pretty Emily; the girl refuses to put her face underwater and always stands demurely in the shallow end of the pool when they go swimming.

She'll have to find something for the ones who can't swim, a paddleboard, a float. But what?

And how do I get them to the back of the slaughterhouse?

She thought of Danny. But Danny wasn't here to help. Panic edged in.

De l'Epée?

She sent her thoughts out to him but all he did was whisper his reassurance that there'll be police to find the girls that escape into the river. (They'll be there, won't they? Yes, she has to believe they will.)

Crap, Melanie thinks. I'm on my own here.

Then, suddenly, the smell changes.

Her eyes open and she finds herself staring into the face of Brutus, a few feet away from her. She no longer smells the river but rather meat and stale breath and sweat. He's so close that she sees, with horror, that the marks on his neck—what she thought were freckles—must be the blood from the woman with the purse, the woman he killed this afternoon. Melanie recoiled in disgust.

"Sit tight, missie," Handy said.

Melanie wondered again, Why can I understand him? *Sit tight.* A phrase almost impossible to lip-read, and yet she knows without a doubt that this is what he said. Brutus took her hands. She tried to resist him but she couldn't. "You were sitting there with your eyes closed . . . hands were twitching like a shot 'coon's paws. Talking to yourself? That what you doing?"

There was movement in the corner. Kielle had sat up and was staring at him. The little girl had an eerily adult look in her face. Her jaw was set. "I'm Jubilee!" Kielle signed. Her favorite X-Man character. "I'm going to kill him!" Melanie dared not sign but her eyes implored the girl to sit down.

Brutus glanced at the little girl, laughed then stepped into the main room of the slaughterhouse, motioning Bear after him. When he returned a moment later he was carrying a large can of gasoline.

Kielle's face went still as she stared at the red can.

"Don't nobody move." Brutus looked into Melanie's eyes as he said this. Then he set a heavy metal canister, a small rendering vat maybe, on top of a shelf above the girls and poured the gasoline into it. Melanie felt the thud as he pitched the gas can into the corner of the room. Then he tied a wire to the edge of the canister and ran it to the other room. Eerie shadows danced on the floor and wall as the light from the other room grew brighter and brighter and Brutus returned suddenly, swinging another of the lights. He unscrewed the cage and tied the unprotected fixture and bulb to a bolt in the floor, directly below the canister of gas.

Bear surveyed the workmanship with approval.

Kielle stepped toward Brutus.

"No," Melanie signed. "Get back!"

Brutus suddenly dropped to his knees and took Kielle by the shoulders. He put his face inches from hers and he spoke slowly.

"Here now, little bird . . . hassles from you . . . or somebody tries to save you, I'll pull that wire and burn you up."

He pushed hard and Kielle fell over one of the blood grooves in the floor.

"What one should I pick?" Brutus asked Bear. The fat man looked them over. His eyes lingered longest on Emily, her flat chest, her white stockings, her black-strapped shoes.

Bear gestured at Shannon. ". . . kicked me. Pick her, man."

Brutus looked down at the girl, tossing her long, dark hair. Like Kielle, she gazed back defiantly. But after a moment she looked down, tears filling her eyes. And Melanie could see the real difference between the girls. Shannon Boyle was one hell of an artist but she wasn't

Jubilee or any other kind of hero. She was an eight-year-old tomboy, scared to death.

"You're a kicker, are you?" Brutus asked. "Okay, let's go." They led her out.

What were they going to do with her? Release her, like Jocylyn? Melanie scooted toward the doorway of the killing room—as far as she dared. She looked out and saw Shannon in the greasy window in the front of the slaughterhouse. Brutus took his pistol from his back pocket. Rested the muzzle against the girl's head. No! Oh, no. . . .

Melanie started to rise. Bear's bulbous head swiveled toward her quickly and he raised the shotgun. She sank down to the cold floor and stared hopelessly at her student. Shannon closed her eyes and wrapped her fingers around the pink-and-blue-string friendship bracelet she'd tied on her wrist a month ago. The girl had promised to make a matching bracelet for her, Melanie now recalled, choking back tears, but had never gotten around to it.

Angie Scapello paused on her way back to the van from the rear staging area.

"Hey, Captain."

If he hadn't known it for a fact, Charlie Budd would never have guessed she was a federal agent. "Hi," he said.

She paused and fell into step beside him.

"You worked with Arthur much?" he asked suddenly, flustered. Just trying to make conversation.

"About thirty or forty barricades. Maybe a few more, I guess."

"Hey, you must've started out young."

"I'm older than I look."

He didn't think "older" was a word that applied to her at all.

"This isn't a line—I'm married." Budd awkwardly held up his glistening ring, which happened to match his wife's. "But you ever do any modeling? I only ask 'cause Meg, that's my wife, she gets these magazines. You know, *Vogue* and *Harper's Bazaar*. Like that. I was thinking maybe I saw you in an ad or two?"

"Could've been. I put myself through school doing print ads. Was a few years ago. Undergrad." She laughed.

"I was usually cast as a bride for some reason. Don't ask me why."

"Good hair for a veil," Budd suggested, and then went red because the comment sounded like a flirt.

"And I've been in one movie."

"No kiddin'?"

"I was a double for Isabella Rossellini. I stood outside in the snow for long angles."

"I was thinking you looked like her." Though Budd said this uneasily, having no idea who the actress was, and hoped that she wasn't some unknown who'd never appeared in a movie shown in America.

"You're kind of a celebrity in your own right, aren't you?" she asked.

"Me?" Budd laughed.

"They say you came up through the ranks real fast."

"They do?"

"Well, you're a captain and you're a young man."

"I'm older than *I* look," he joked. "And before today's over I'm going to be older still by a long shot." He looked at his watch. "I better be getting inside. Not long till the first deadline. How do you manage to stay calm?"

"I think it's all what you're used to. But what about you? That high-speed chase, the time you went after that sex offender in Hamilton?"

"How on earth d'you hear about that?" Budd laughed. Two years ago. He'd hit speeds of a hundred twenty. On a dirt road. "Didn't think my, you know, exploits made it into *National Law Enforcement Monthly*."

"You hear things. About certain people anyway."

Her brown eyes bored into Budd's, which were green, exceedingly embarrassed, and growing more and more flummoxed by the second. He rubbed his cheek with his left hand again, just to give her a view of his ring once more, then thought: Hey, get real. You actually think she's coming on to you? No way, he told himself. She's making polite talk to a local rube.

"Better see if there's anything Arthur needs," Budd said.

For some reason he stuck his hand out toward her. Wished he hadn't, but there it was and she reached out, took it in both of hers, and squeezed it hard, stepping close. He smelled perfume. It seemed entirely unnatural for FBI agents to be wearing perfume.

"I'm real glad we're working together, Charlie." She fired a smile at him, the likes of which he hadn't seen in years—since Meg, in fact, had crosshaired him at the junior prom with one of those flirtations that he never would've believed the president of Methodist Girls' Youth Group was capable of.

4:40 P.M.

"Twenty minutes to deadline," Tobe Geller called.

Potter nodded. He punched the speed-dial button. Handy answered by saying, "I've picked the next little bird, Art."

Get off the subject of the hostages; keep him thinking they're valueless. Potter said, "Lou, we're working on that helicopter. It isn't that easy to get one."

"This one's a little trouper, she is, Art. That fat one cried and cried. Man, did that bug me. This one's shedding a tear or two but she's a soldier. Got a fucking tattoo on her arm, you can believe it."

Share some observations. Show him you're concerned, find out a few things about him.

"You sound tired, Lou."

"Not me. I'm right as rain."

"Really? Would've guessed you were up all night planning your big getaway."

"Naw, got my full eight hours. 'Sides, there's nothing like a Mexican standoff to get the old juices flowing." In fact he didn't sound at all tired. He sounded relaxed and at ease. Potter nodded toward LeBow but the officer was already typing.

"So tell me. What's so hard about a chopper, Art?"

Potter trained the glasses out the window at the brown-haired, long-faced girl. He'd already memorized the names and faces. Punching the mute button, he said to Angie, "It's Shannon Boyle. Tell me about her." Then into the phone: "I'll tell you what's so hard, Lou," Potter snapped. "They don't grow on trees and they aren't free."

You're worried about fucking money at a time like this?

"Fuck, you got all the money you need. What with everything you assholes steal from us taxpayers."

"You a taxpayer, Lou?"

"We ain't buying nuclear bombs anymore so spend a little on a chopper and save some lives here."

Angie tapped his shoulder.

"Hold on a second, Lou. Word's coming in about that chopper right now."

"She's eight," Angie whispered, "prelingually deaf. No lip-reading skills to speak of. She's got a personality of her own. Very independent. She's marched in protests to get deaf deans at schools for the deaf in Kansas and Missouri. Signed the petition to increase the deaf faculty at Laurent Clerc and hers was the largest signature on the sheet. She's been in fistfights at school and she usually wins."

Potter nodded. So if they could distract him enough, and if she had an opportunity, the girl might make a run for freedom.

Or use the chance to attack Handy and get herself killed in the process.

He clicked the mute button off. Sounding exasperated: "Look, Lou. We're just talking about a little delay is all. You want a big aircraft. Well, we've got two-seaters galore. But the big ones're hard to find."

"That's your fucking problem, ain't it? I put a bullet into little Fannie Annie here in, lemme see, fifteen minutes by my clock."

Usually, you devalue the hostages.

Sometimes you just have to beg.

"Her name's Shannon, Lou. Come on. She's only eight years old."

"Shannon," Handy mused. "I guess you aren't catching on, Art. You're trying to get me to feel sorry for some poor kid's got a name. Shannon Shannon Shannon.

Those're your rules, right, Art? Written up in your Feebie handbook?"

Page 45, in fact.

"But see, those rules don't take into account somebody like me. The more I know them the more I *want* to kill 'em."

Walk that fine line. Chide, push, trade barbs. He'll back off if you hit the balance just right. Arthur Potter thought this but his hand cramped on the receiver as he said cheerfully, "I think that's bullshit, Lou. I think you're just playing with us."

"Have it your way."

A little edge in the agent's voice: "I'm tired of this crap. We're trying to *work* with you."

"Naw, you want to shoot me down. Why don't you have the balls to admit it? If I had you in my sights I'd drop you like a fucking deer."

"No, I don't want to shoot you, Lou. I don't want anybody to die. We've got a lot of logistic problems. Landing is a real hassle here. The field out front's filled with those old posts from the stockyard pens. And we've got trees everywhere. We can't set a chopper down on the roof because of the weight. We—"

"So you've got diagrams of the building, do you?"

Negotiate from strength—with a reminder to the HT that there's always a tactical solution in the back of your mind (we can kick in the door any time we want and nail you cold, and remember, there're a hell of a lot more of us than of you). Potter laughed and said, "Of course we do. We've got maps and charts and diagrams and graphs and eight-by-ten color glossy photos. You're a damn cover boy in here, Lou. This's no surprise, is it?"

Silence.

Push too far?

No, I don't think so. He'll laugh and sound cool.

It was a chuckle. "You guys're too fucking much."

"And the field to the south," Potter continued, as if Handy hadn't spoken, "look at it. Nothing but gullies and hummocks. To set an eight-person copter down'd be pretty dangerous. And this wind . . . it's a real problem. Our aviation advisor isn't sure what to do about it."

Budd frowned, mouthing, "Aviation advisor?" Potter shrugged, having just made up the job. He pointed to the "Deceptions" board and Budd wrote it down, sighing.

Silver tools, wrapped in plastic, new.

Potter desperately wanted to ask what they were for. But of course he couldn't. It was vitally important that Handy not realize what they knew about the inside of the barricade. Even more vital: if Handy suspected the released hostages were giving Potter quality information he'd think twice about releasing others.

"Art," Handy spat out, "I keep saying, them's your problems." But he was not as flippant now and part of him at least seemed to realize that this had become *his* problem.

"Come on, Lou. This's just a practical thing. I'm not arguing about the chopper. I'm telling you we're having trouble finding one and that I'm not sure where we can set it down. You got any ideas, I'll be happy to take 'em."

Hostage negotiation strategy calls for the negotiator to avoid offering solutions to problems. Shift that burden to the taker. Keep him in a problem-solving mode, uncertain.

A disgusted sigh. "Fuck."

Will he hang up?

Finally Handy said, "How 'bout a pontoon chopper? You can do that, can't you?"

Never agree too quickly.

"Pontoon?" Potter said after a moment. "I don't know. We'd have to look into it. You mean, set her down in the river."

"*Course* that's what I mean. Where'd you think, land in some fucking toilet somewhere?"

"I'll see about it. If there's a sheltered cove it might work out perfectly. But you'll have to give us more time."

You don't have more time.

"You haven't got any more time."

"No, Lou. Pontoons'd be perfect. It's a great idea. I'll get on it right away. But let me buy some time. Tell me something you want."

"A fucking helicopter."

"And you'll have it. It may just take a little longer than

we'd hoped. Name something else. Your heart's desire. Isn't there something you can think of you want?"

A pause. Potter thought: guns, X-rated tapes and a VCR, a friend busted out of prison, money, liquor . . .

"Yeah, I want something, Art."

"What?"

"Tell me 'bout yourself."

From out of left field.

Potter looked up into Angie's frown. She shook her head, cautious.

"What?"

"You asked me what I wanted. I want you to tell me about yourself."

You always want the HT to be curious about the negotiator but it usually takes hours, if not days, to establish any serious connection. This was the second time in just a few hours that Handy had expressed an interest in Potter, and the agent had never known an HT to ask the question so directly. Potter knew he was on thin ice here. He could improve the connection between the two or he could drive a wedge between them by not responding the way Handy wished.

Be forewarned. . . .

"What do you want to know?"

"Anything you wanta tell me."

"Well, there's nothing very exciting. I'm just a civil servant." His mind went blank.

"Keep going, Art. Talk to me."

And then, as if a switch had been flicked, Arthur Potter found himself desiring to blurt out every last detail of his life, his loneliness, his sorrow. . . . He wanted Lou Handy to know about him. "Well, I'm a widower. My wife died thirteen years ago, and today's our wedding anniversary."

He remembered that LeBow had told him there'd been bad blood between Handy and his ex; he turned to the intelligence officer, who had already called up a portion of Handy's profile. The convict had been married for two years when he was twenty. His wife had sued for divorce on the grounds of mental cruelty and had gotten a restraining order because he'd beaten her repeatedly. Just after that he'd gone off on a violent robbery spree. Potter was wishing he hadn't brought up the subject of marriage, but when Handy now asked what had happened to Potter's wife he sounded genuinely curious.

"She had cancer. Died about two months after we found out about it."

"Me, I was never married, Art. No woman'll ever tie me down. I'm a freewheelin' spirit, I go where my heart and my dick lead me. You ever get yourself remarried?"

"No, never did."

"What do you do when you want a little pussy?"

"My work keeps me pretty busy, Lou."

"You like your job, do you? How long you been doing it?"

"I've been with the Bureau all my adult life."

"All your adult life?"

My Lord, an amused Potter thought from a remote distance, he's echoing *me*. Coincidence? Or is he playing me the way I should be playing *him*?

"It's the only job I've ever had. Work eighteen hours a day a lot."

"How'd you get into this negotiating shit?"

"Just fell into it. Wanted to be an agent, liked the excitement of it. I was a pretty fair investigator but I think I was a little too easygoing. I could see both sides of everything."

"Oh, yessir," Handy said earnestly, "that'll keep you from moving to the top. Don't you know the sharks swim faster?"

"That's the God's truth, Lou."

"You must meet some real fucking wackos."

"Oh, present company excluded of course."

No laughter from the other end of the line. Only silence. Potter felt stung that the levity had fallen flat and he worried that Handy had heard sarcasm in Potter's voice and was hurt. He felt an urge to apologize.

But Handy just said, "Tell me a war story, Art."

Angie was frowning again. Potter ignored her. "Well, I did a barricade at the West German embassy in Washington about fifteen years ago. Talked for about eighteen hours straight." He laughed. "I had agents racing back and forth to the library bringing me books on political philosophy.

Hegel, Kant, Nietzsche . . . Finally I had to send out for Cliff Notes. I was camped out in the backseat of an unmarked car, talking on a hard-wired throw phone to this maniac who thought he was Hitler. Wanted to dictate a new version of *Mein Kampf* to me. I still have no idea what the hell we talked about all that time."

Actually, the man hadn't claimed to be Hitler but Potter felt the urge to exaggerate, to make sure Handy was amused.

"Sounds like a fucking comedy."

"He was funny. His AK-47 was pretty sobering, I have to say."

"You a shrink?"

"Nope. Just a guy who likes to talk."

"You must have a pretty good ego."

"Ego?"

"Sure. You gotta listen to somebody like me say, 'You scurvy piece of dogshit, I'm going to kill you the first chance I get,' and then still ask him if he'd like Diet Coke or iced tea with his burgers."

"You want lemon with that tea, Lou?"

"Haw. This's all you do?"

"Well, I teach too. At the military police school at Fort McClellan. In Alabama. Then I'm head of hostage and barricade training at Quantico in the Bureau's Special Operations and Research Unit."

Now Henry LeBow offered an exasperated expression to Potter. The intelligence officer had never heard his fellow agent give away so much personal information.

Slowly Handy said in a low voice, "Tell me something, Art. You ever done anything bad?"

"Bad?"

"Really bad."

"I suppose I have."

"Did you mean to do it?"

"Mean to do it?"

"Ain't you listening to me?" Testy now. Echoing too frequently can antagonize the hostage taker.

"Well, the things I've done aren't so much intentional, I suppose. One bad thing is that I didn't spend enough time with my wife. Then she died, pretty fast, like I told you, and I realized there was a lot I hadn't said to her."

"Fuck," Handy spat out with a derisive laugh. "That's not bad. You don't know what I'm talking about."

Potter felt deeply hurt by the criticism. He wanted to cry out, "I do! And I *did* feel that I'd done something bad, terribly bad."

Handy continued, "I'm talking about killing somebody, ruining somebody's life, leaving a widow or widower, leaving children to grow up alone. Something *bad*."

"I've never killed anyone, Lou. Not directly."

Tobe was looking at him. Angie scribbled a note: *You're giving away a lot, Arthur.*

He ignored them, wiped the sweat from his forehead, kept his eyes focused outside on the slaughterhouse. "But people have died because of me. Carelessness. Mistakes. Sometimes intent. You and I, Lou, we both work flip sides of the same business." Feeling the overwhelming urge to make himself understood. "But you know—"

"Don't skip over this shit, Art. Tell me if they bother you, some of the things you've done?"

"I . . . I don't know."

"What about them people dying you was talking about?"

Take his pulse, Potter told himself. What's he thinking? I can't see a thing. Who the hell knows?

"Yo, Art, keep talkin'. Who were they? Hostages you couldn't save? Troopers you sent in when you shouldn't've?"

"Yes, that's who they were."

And takers too. Though he doesn't say this. Ostrella, he thinks spontaneously, sees her long, beautiful face, serpentine. Dark eyebrows, full lips. *His* Ostrella.

"And that bothers you, huh?"

"Bothers me? Sure it does."

"Fuck," Handy seemed to sneer. Potter again felt the sting. "See, Art, you're proving my point. You've never done anything bad and you and me, we both know it. Take those folks in the Cadillac this afternoon, that couple I killed. *Their* names were Ruth and Hank, by the way. Ruthie and Hank. You know why I killed them?"

"Why, Lou?"

"Same reason I'm putting that little girl—*Shannon*—in the window in a minute or two and shooting her in the back of the head."

Even cool Henry LeBow stirred. Frances Whiting's elegant hands moved to her face.

"Why's that?" Potter asked calmly.

"Because I didn't get what I was owed! Pure and simple. This afternoon, in that field, they fucked up my car, ran right into it. And when I went to take theirs they tried to get away."

Potter had read the report from the Kansas State Police. It looked as if Handy's car had run a stop sign and been hit by the Cadillac, which had the right of way. Potter did not mention this fact.

"That's fair, isn't it? I mean, what could be clearer? They had to die, and it woulda been more painful than it was if I'd had more time. They didn't give me what I shoulda had."

How cold and logical he sounds.

Potter reminded himself: No value judgment. But don't approve of him either. Negotiators are neutral. (And it broke his heart that he didn't in fact feel the disgust that he ought to have been feeling. That a small portion of him believed Handy's words made sense.)

"Man, Art, I don't get it. When I kill somebody for a reason they call me bad. When a cop does it for a reason they give him a paycheck and call him good. Why're some reasons okay and others ain't? You kill when people don't do what they're supposed to. You kill the weak because they'll drag you down. What's wrong with that?"

Henry LeBow typed his notes calmly. Tobe Geller perused his monitors and dials. Charlie Budd sat in the corner, eyes on the floor, Angie beside him, listening carefully. And Officer Frances Whiting stood in the corner, uneasily holding a cup of coffee she'd lost all taste for; police work in Hebron, Kansas, didn't involve the likes of Lou Handy.

A laugh over the speaker. He asked, "Admit it, Art. . . . Haven't you ever wanted to do that? Kill someone for a bad reason?"

"No, I haven't."

"That a fact?" He was skeptical. "I wonder. . . ."

Silence filled the van. A trickle of sweat flowed down Potter's face and he wiped his forehead.

Handy asked, "So, you look like that guy in the old FBI show, Efrem Zimbalist?"

"Not a bit. I'm pretty ordinary. I'm just a humble constable. I eat too many potatoes—"

"Fries," Handy remembered.

"Mashed are my favorite, actually. With pan gravy."

Tobe whispered something to Budd, who wrote down on a slip of paper: *Deadline*.

Potter glanced at the clock. Into the phone he said, "I fancy sports coats. Tweed are my favorite. Or camel's hair. But we have to wear suits in the Bureau."

"Suits, huh? They cover up a lot of fat, don't they? Hold on a second there, Art."

Potter dipped out of his reverie and trained his Leicas on the factory window. A pistol barrel appeared next to Shannon's head, which was covered with her long, brown hair, now mussed.

"That son of a bitch," Budd whispered. "The poor thing's terrified."

Frances leaned forward. "Oh, no. Please . . ."

Potter's fingers tapped buttons. "Dean?"

"Yessir," Stillwell answered.

"Can one of your snipers acquire a target?"

A pause.

"Negative. All they can see is a pistol barrel and slide. He's behind her. There's no shot he can make except into the window frame."

Handy asked, "Hey, Art, you really never shot anyone?"

LeBow looked up, frowning. But Potter answered anyway, "Nope, never have."

His hands stuffed deep into his pockets, Budd began pacing. It was very irritating.

"Ever fired a gun?"

"Of course. On the range at Quantico. I enjoyed it."

"Didja? You know, if you enjoyed shooting you might enjoy shooting some*body*. Killing somebody."

"Sick son of a bitch," Budd muttered.

Potter waved the captain quiet.

"You know something, Art?"

"What's that?"

"You're all right. I mean it."

Potter felt a pleasing burst—from the man's approval.

I *am* good, he thought. He knew that it was the empathy that makes the difference at this job. Not the strategy, not the words, not the calculation or intelligence. It's what I can't teach in the training courses. I was always good, he reflected. But when you died, Marian, I became great. I had nowhere for my heart to go and so I gave it to men like Louis Handy.

And to Ostrella . . .

A terrorist takeover in Washington, D.C. The Estonian woman, blond and brilliant, walking out of the Soviet embassy after twenty hours of negotiating with Potter. Twelve hostages released, four more inside. Finally she'd surrendered, come out with her hands not outstretched but on her head—a violation of the hostage surrender protocol. But Potter knew she was harmless. Knew her as well as he knew Marian. He'd stepped unprotected from the barricade and walked toward her, to greet her, to embrace her, to make sure that when she was arrested the cuffs weren't too tight, that her rights were read to her in her native language. And he'd had to endure the copious spatter of her blood from the sniper who shot her in the head when she pulled the hidden pistol from her collar and shoved it directly toward Potter's face. (And his reaction? To scream to her, "Get down!" And fling his arms around her to protect his new love, as bits of her skull snapped against his skin.)

Have you ever wanted to do something bad?

Be . . .

Yes, Lou, I have. If you must know.

. . . forewarned.

Potter was unable to say anything for a moment, afraid to offend Handy, afraid that he'd hang up. Almost as afraid of that as of Handy's killing the girl. "Listen to me, Lou. I tell you in good faith we're working on this chopper and I asked you to tell me something that you'll accept to buy another hour." Potter added, "We're trying to work out a deal. Help me out here."

There was a pause and the confident voice said, "It's thirsty work, here."

Ah, let's play a game. "Diet Pepsi?" the agent asked coyly.

"You know what I'm talking about."

"Lemonade, made out of fresh Sunkist?"

LeBow hit several keys and showed the screen to Potter, who nodded.

"Glass of mother's milk?" Handy sneered.

Reading Wilcox's profile, Potter said, "I don't think liquor's a real good idea, Lou. Shep has a bit of a problem, doesn't he?"

A pause.

"You boys sure seem to know a lot about us."

"That's what they pay me my meager salary for. To know everything in the world."

"Well, that's the deal. One hour for some booze."

"Nothing hard. No way."

"Beer's fine. 'S'more to my liking anyway."

"I'll send in three cans."

"Hold up there. A case."

"No. You get three cans of light beer."

A snicker. "Fuck light beer."

"That's the best I can do."

Frances and Budd were plastered against the window, watching Shannon.

Handy's voice sang, "This little piggy went to market, this little piggy stayed home. . . ." Moving the gun from one of the girl's ears to the other.

Stillwell came on the air to ask what he should tell the snipers.

Potter hesitated. "No fire," he said. "Whatever happens."

"Copy," Stillwell said.

They heard the whimper of the girl as Handy pressed the gun against her forehead.

"I'll give you a six-pack," Potter said, "if you let me have that girl."

Budd whispered, "Don't push it."

A pause. "Give me a reason why I'd want to do that."

LeBow dropped the cursor to a paragraph in the evolving *Biography of Louis Handy*. Potter read, then said, " 'Cause you *love* beer."

Handy had been reprimanded by one of his wardens for whipping up some home brew in prison. Later, his privileges were suspended after he'd smuggled in two cases of Budweiser.

"Come on," Potter chided, "what can it hurt? You'll have plenty of hostages left over." Potter took the chance. "Besides, she's a little pain in the ass, isn't she? That's her reputation at school."

Angie's eyes sprang open. It's a risk to refer to the hostages in any way because it gives them more value to the taker than they already have. You *never* suggest that they have some liability that might irritate or endanger him.

A pause.

Now, set the hook.

The agent said, "What's your favorite brand? Miller? Bud?"

"Mexican."

"You got it, Lou. A six-pack of Corona, you let that girl go and we get another hour for the chopper. Everybody's happy."

"I'd rather shoot her."

Potter and LeBow glanced at each other. Budd was suddenly standing close to Potter, his hands in his pocket, fidgeting.

The negotiator ignored the young captain and said to Handy, "Okay, Lou, then shoot her. I'm tired of this bullshit."

From the corner of his eye he saw Budd shift and for a moment Potter tensed, thinking the captain was going to leap forward, grab the phone, and agree to whatever Handy wanted. But he just kept his hands in his back pockets and turned away. Frances gazed at the negotiator in utter shock.

Potter hit buttons on the phone. "Dean, he may shoot the girl. If he does, make sure nobody returns fire."

A hesitation. "Yessir."

Potter was back on the line with Handy. The man hadn't hung up but he wasn't talking either. Shannon's head swiveled back and forth. The black rectangular pistol was still visible.

Potter jumped inches when Handy's staccato laugh shot into the van. "This's sorta like Monopoly, ain't it? Buying and selling and all?"

Potter struggled to remain silent.

Handy growled, "Two six-packs or I do it right now." Shannon's head bent forward as Handy pressed the gun into it.

"And we get an extra hour for the chopper?" Potter asked. "Makes it about six-fifteen."

"Safety's off," Dean Stillwell sang out.

Potter closed his eyes.

Not a single sound in the van. Complete silence. This is what Melanie lives with day after day after day, Potter thinks.

"Deal, Art," Handy said. "By the way, you *are* one bad motherfucker."

Click.

Potter slumped into the chair, closed his eyes for a moment. "You get all that, Henry?"

LeBow nodded and typed away. He rose and started to lift Shannon's marker out of the slaughterhouse schematic.

"Wait," said Potter. LeBow paused. "Let's just wait."

"I'll get that beer," Budd said, exhaling a sigh.

Potter smiled. "Getting a little hot for you, Captain?"

"Yeah. Some."

"You'll get used to it," Potter said, just as Budd said, "I'll get used to it." The captain's voice was far less optimistic than Potter's. The agent and the trooper laughed.

Budd started like a rabbit when Angie squeezed his arm. "I'll come with you to see about that beer, Captain. If that's all right with you."

"Uh, well, sure, I guess," he said uncertainly, and they left the van.

"One more hour," LeBow said, nodding.

Potter swiveled around in his chair, staring out the window at the slaughterhouse. "Henry, write down: 'It's the negotiator's conclusion that the stress and anxiety of the initial phase of the barricade have dissipated and subject Handy is calm and thinking rationally.' "

"That makes one of us," said Frances Whiting, whose shaking hands spilled coffee on the floor of the van. Derek Elb, the red-haired trooper, gallantly dropped to hands and knees to clean up the mess.

5:11 P.M.

"What's he doing with Shannon?" Beverly signed, her chest rising and falling as she tried to breathe.

Melanie leaned forward. Shannon's face was emotionless. She was signing and Melanie caught the name Professor X, the founder of the X-Men. Like Emily, the girl was summoning her guardian angels.

Bear and Brutus were talking and she could see their lips. Bear gestured to Shannon and asked Brutus, "Why . . . giving them away?"

"Because," Brutus answered patiently, "if we don't they'll break in the fucking door and . . . shoot us dead."

Melanie scooted back, said, "She's just sitting there. She's all right. They're going to let her go."

Everyone's face lit up.

Everyone except Mrs. Harstrawn's.

And Kielle's. Little Kielle, a blond, freckled bobcat. An eight-year-old with twenty-year-old eyes. The girl glanced impatiently at Melanie and turned away, bent down to the wall beside her, working away at something. What was she doing? Trying to tunnel her way out? Well, let her. It'll keep her out of harm's way.

"I think I'm going to be sick," signed one of the twins, Suzie. Anna signed the same but then she usually echoed everything her very slightly older sister said.

Melanie signed to them that they wouldn't be sick. Everything would be fine. She scooted over beside Emily, who was tearfully examining a rip in her dress. "You and

I'll go shopping next week," Melanie signed. "Buy you new one."

And that was when de l'Epée whispered in her useless ear. "The gas can," he said, and vanished immediately.

Melanie felt the chill run down her back. The gas can, yes. She turned her head. It sat beside her, red and yellow, a big two-gallon one. She eased toward it, snapped closed the cover and the pressure hole cap. Then looked around the killing room for the other thing she'd need.

There, yes.

Melanie slid around to the front of the room, examined the back of the slaughterhouse. There were two doors— she could just make them out in the dimness. Which one led to the river? she wondered. She happened to glance down at the floor, where she'd written the messages in the dust about the hand-shape game. Squinting, she looked at the floor in front of each door—there was much less dust in front of the left. That's it—the river breeze blows through that one and has swept away the dust. Enough wind for there to be, just possibly, a window or door open far enough for a little girl to scoot through.

Beverly choked and started a crying fit. She lay on her side, struggling for breath. The inhaler hadn't done her much good. Bear frowned and looked at her, called something.

Shit. Melanie signed to Beverly, "It's hard, honey, but please be quiet."

"Scared, scared."

"I know. But it'll be all—"

Oh, my God. Melanie's eyes went wide and her signing hands stopped in midword as she looked across the room.

Kielle was holding the knife in front of her, an old hook-bladed knife. That's what she'd seen underneath a pile of trash; that's what she'd been digging out.

Melanie shuddered. "No!" she signed. "Put it back."

Kielle had murder in her gray eyes. She slipped the weapon into her pocket. "I'm going to kill Mr. Sinister. You can't stop me!" Her hands slashed the air in front of her as if she were already stabbing him.

"No! Can't do it that way!"

"I'm Jubilee! He can't stop me!"

"That's character in comic book," Melanie's staccato hands shot out. "Not real!"

Kielle ignored her. "Jubilation Lee! I'm going to blow him apart with plasmoids! He's going to die. No one can stop me!" She crawled through the door and disappeared through the shower of water tumbling from the ceiling.

The huge main room of the Webber & Stoltz slaughter-house, in the front portion of which were clustered the three convicts, had been a series of holding pens and walkways for the beasts that had died here. The space was now used for storing slaughterhouse equipment—butcher blocks, one- and three-bay decapitation guillotines, gutting machines, grinders, huge rendering vats.

It was into this gruesome warehouse that Kielle disappeared, intending, it seemed, to circle around to the front wall, where the men lounged in front of the TV.

No. . . .

Melanie half-rose, looked at Bear—the only one of the three with a clear view of the killing room—and froze. He wasn't looking their way but he had only to turn his greasy head inches to see them. In a panic she looked over the main room. Caught a glimpse of Kielle's blond hair vanishing behind a column.

Melanie eased closer to the doorway, still crouching. Brutus was at the window, beside Shannon, looking out. Bear started to glance toward the room but turned back to Stoat, who was laughing at something. Bear, stroking the shotgun he held, reared back and laughed, closing his eyes.

Now. Do it.

I can't.

Do it, while he can't see you.

A deep breath. Now. Melanie slipped out of the room and crawled under a rotting walkway, indented and bowed from a million hoofprints. She paused, looking through the cascade of tumbling water. Kielle . . . Where are you? You think you can stab him and just vanish? You and your damn comic books!

She slipped through the water—it was freezing cold

and slimy. Shivering in disgust, she made her way into the cavernous room.

What would the girl do? Circle around, she supposed, come up behind him, stab him in the back. Past the machinery, rusting scraps of metal and rotting wood. Piles of chains and meat hooks, stained with blood and barbed with sharp bits of dried flesh. The vats were disgusting. From them emanated a sickening smell and Melanie couldn't rid her mind of the image of animals sinking down into simmering fat and fluid. She felt her gorge rising, started to retch.

No! Be quiet! The least sound'll tell them you're here.

She struggled to control herself, dropping to her knees to breathe the cool moist air from the floor.

Glancing under the legs of a large guillotine, its angular blade rusty and pitted, Melanie saw the little girl's shadow across the room as she scrambled from one column to another.

Melanie started forward quickly. And got only two feet before she felt the numbing thud of her shoulder running into a piece of steel pipe, six feet long, resting against a column. It began a slow fall to the floor.

No!

Melanie flung her arms around the pipe. It must have weighed a hundred pounds.

I can't hold it, can't stop it!

The pipe fell faster, pulling her after it. Just as her grip was about to go she dropped to the floor, rolled under the rusty metal, and took the impact of it on her tensed stomach muscles. She gasped at the pain that surged through her body, praying that the wind and the cascade of water made enough noise to cover the grunting from her throat. She lay stunned for a long moment.

Finally she managed to ease out from underneath the pipe and roll it to the floor—silently, she hoped.

Oh, Kielle, where are you? Don't you understand? You can't kill them all. They'll find us, they'll kill us. Or Bear'll take us into the back of the factory. Haven't you seen his eyes? Don't you know what he wants? No, you probably don't. You don't have a clue—

She risked a look toward the front of the room. The

attention of the men was mostly turned toward the TV. Occasionally Bear glanced at the killing room but didn't seem to notice that two of the captives were missing.

Glancing again beneath the legs of the machinery, Melanie caught a glimpse of blond hair. There she was, Kielle, making her way inexorably toward the three men near the window. Crawling, a smile on her face. She probably *did* think she could kill all three.

Struggling to catch her breath from the blow of the pipe, Melanie scrabbled down a corridor, hid behind a rusted column. She turned the corner and saw the blond girl, only twenty or thirty feet from Brutus, whose back was to her as he continued to gaze out the window. His hand casually gripping Shannon's collar. If any one of the three men had stood and walked toward the girl, they'd only have to look down over one of the large vats, which lay on its side, to see her.

Kielle was tensing. About to leap over the vat and charge Brutus.

Melanie thought, Should I just let her do it? What is the worst that would happen? She'd get a few feet toward them, Bear would see her, take the knife away. They'd slap her once or twice, shove her back into the killing room.

Why should I risk my life? Risk Bear's hands on me? Risk Brutus's eyes?

But then Melanie saw Susan. Saw the dot appearing on her back and the puff of black hair, like smoke, rise up.

She saw Bear looking over Emily's boyish body, grinning.

Shit.

Melanie pulled her black shoes off, pushed them under a metal table. She started to sprint. Flat out, down the narrow corridor, dodging overhanging hunks of metal and rods and pipes, leaping over a piece of butcher block.

Just as Kielle stood and reached for the top of the vat Melanie tackled her. One hand around her stomach, the other around her mouth. They went down hard and knocked into the hinged lid of a vat, which slammed closed.

"No!" the little girl signed. "Let me—"

Melanie did something she'd never in her life done: drew back her open palm and aimed directly at the girl's cheek. Kielle's eyes went wide. The teacher lowered her hand and glanced through the crack between two over-turned vats. Brutus had turned, looking in their direction. Stoat was shrugging. "Wind," she saw him say. Unsmil-ing Bear was on his feet, carrying the shotgun, walking toward them.

"Inside," Melanie signed fiercely, gesturing toward a large steel vat nearby, resting on its side. The girl hesi-tated for a moment and they climbed inside, pulling the lid closed, like a door. The sides were coated with a waxy substance that disgusted Melanie and made her skin crawl. The smell was overpowering and she struggled once again to keep from vomiting.

A shadow fell over the vat and she felt a vibration as Bear stepped into the corridor. He was only two feet from them.

Halfheartedly, he glanced around and then stepped back toward Shannon and the other men.

Kielle turned to her. In the dim light Melanie could just make out the girl's words. "I'm going to kill him! Don't stop me, or I'll kill you too!"

Melanie gasped as the little girl lifted the razor-sharp blade and pointed it at her. "Stop it!" Melanie signed bru-tally. What should I do? she wondered. Images of Susan were flashing through her mind. Mrs. Harstrawn, her fa-ther, her brother.

And de l'Epée.

Susan, help me.

De l'Epée . . .

Then Melanie thought suddenly: There *is* no Susan. She's dead. Dead and already cold.

And Mrs. Harstrawn may as well be.

De l'Epée? He's just a lie. A phony visitor to your phony little room. Another of your sick, imaginary friends, one of the dozens you grew up talking to, going out with, making very solitary love to while you hid from everything real. I get everything wrong! I hear music when there is no music, I hear nothing when people speak to me inches away, I'm afraid when I have to be brave. . . .

A Maiden's Grave.

The little girl reached for the lid of the vat.

"Kielle!" Melanie signed angrily. "Jubilee . . . All right. Listen."

The girl looked at her cautiously, nodded.

"You really want to kill him?"

"Yes!" Kielle's eyes glowed.

"Okay. Then we'll do it together. We'll do it the right way."

A ragged smile blossomed in Kielle's face.

"I'll distract him. You go behind pipe there. See it? Go over there and hide."

"What should I do?"

"Wait until I give you signal to come out. He'll be talking to me, won't look for you."

"And then?"

"Stab him as hard as you can in back. Okay?"

"Yes!" The little girl smiled, her eyes no longer fiery but cold as stone. "I'm Jubilee! No one can stop me!"

Brutus had his back to the interior of the slaughterhouse but he must have seen her reflection in a pane of cracked glass. He turned. "Whatta we got here?"

Melanie had slipped from the vat and circled back toward the killing room. Now she walked toward them, smiled at Shannon.

She looked at Handy and mimicked writing. He handed her a yellow pad and pen. She wrote, *I don't want you to hurt her.* She nodded toward Shannon.

"Hurt her? I'm giving . . . away. Understand?"

Why not both her and the sick girl? she wrote. Mention her name, Melanie thought. Maybe he'll be more sympathetic. *Beverly,* she added.

Brutus grinned and nodded at Bear. "My friend . . . wants to keep the pretty ones . . . for a while."

He's saying this just to be cruel, she thought. Then reflected: He *is* cruel, yes. But what else is he, what else do I feel about him? Something strange; there's some connection. Is it because I can understand his words? Or do I understand him *because* of the connection?

Stoat stepped away from the window and said, ". . . coming . . . two . . . packs." He winked and continued to chew on a toothpick. But Brutus wasn't looking out the window; he was scanning the slaughterhouse, looking around, squinting.

What can I do to keep him from seeing Kielle?

Try to seduce him? she thought suddenly.

What she knew of love she knew from books, movies, and girl talk. Melanie had had boyfriends but had never slept with any of them. Always, the fear . . . Of what, she didn't know. The dark maybe. Trusting somebody that much. Of course there was the problem that she'd never met anyone interested in making love with her. Oh, there'd been plenty of boys who wanted to fuck her. But that was so different. Look at the two terms: Saying "fuck" pinched the nose and made your features tight and lonely. "Making love" . . . it was soft and opened up your face.

Suddenly Brutus laughed and stepped forward, grabbed her and pulled her close. Maybe he was far smarter than he seemed. Or maybe her eyes could keep nothing secret; in any event he knew exactly what she was thinking. He stroked her hair.

She waited for the hands on her breasts, between her legs. She remembered how she'd recoiled when a boyfriend had slipped his hand up there quickly. She'd leapt off his knee like lightning, smacking her head on the car's hot dome light.

Then Brutus turned his head and said something she didn't catch.

Bear and Stoat were laughing.

Abruptly he shoved her away, leaned his face close, and said, "Why'd I want you? A busted little thing like you? You're like a boy. I want women only." His black eyes bored into hers and she broke into sobs. With satisfaction he looked over the horror and shame in her face. "I got me a real woman. Pris's all I need. She's got herself a woman's body and a woman's eyes. We fuck for hours. You have a boyfriend?"

Melanie couldn't answer. Her arms were weak and hung at her side. In the corner of her eye she saw Kielle slip through the shadows of machinery. She struggled to stop the tears, refused to wipe them away.

"Pris's a real character. A ballbuster . . . Think I'm bad? She's badder. You hate me? You wouldn't like her one bit. Now, *she* might fuck you. She's a bit that way and I'd like to watch. If we get out of this we'll do that, her and me and you."

Melanie stepped away but he took her by the arm. The grip cut off the blood to her hands and she felt them tingle painfully.

Stoat, hand on his crew cut, was calling something. Brutus turned to the window, looked out. Melanie felt a vibration in the air. Brutus looked toward the phone. Smiling, he let go of Melanie's arm and picked up the receiver.

"Hello . . ."

Was he talking to de l'Epée? What were they saying?

Behind the pipes near the door was Kielle's shadow. The girl held the knife in her hand.

". . . almost here," Stoat called, pointing his gun out the window.

Brutus lowered his head and kept talking into the phone, fiddling with the pistol stuffed in his belt. He looked bored; he grimaced and hung up. Picked up a shotgun, pulled back a lever on it, and stepped to the doorway. His back was to Kielle, perhaps ten feet away. The girl leaned her head out. Light from outside, a shaft of brilliant white light, glinted off the blade in her hand. Melanie signed, "Wait."

Stoat grabbed Shannon by the arm and pulled her to the door. Brutus stepped back, pointing the gun outward, and Stoat eased the door open.

A figure appeared in the doorway—a trooper dressed in black. He handed in two six-packs of beer. Stoat shoved the girl out the door.

Now!

Melanie stepped slowly behind Brutus. She smiled at Kielle, who frowned, confused. Then Melanie reached down and simply scooped the little girl off the ground, grabbing the knife from her hand.

Kielle shook her head violently.

But Melanie spun around, moving so fast that Brutus froze in confusion, staring at them, no idea what was going on. Melanie continued to smile as she stepped around him, firmly gripping the astonished girl.

Then flung Kielle out the door into the chest of the trooper.

For an instant no one moved. Melanie, still smiling at Stoat, slowly eased the door closed, shooing her hand lethargically at the astonished cop as if he were a bluetail fly.

"Fuck," Brutus spat out. Stoat started forward, but Melanie slammed the door completely closed and wedged it tight with Kielle's knife. Stoat tugged at the large knob but it wouldn't budge.

Then Melanie dropped to her knees and covered her face, trying to cushion herself from the blow as Stoat's bony fist slammed into her neck and jaw. He pulled her arms away and struck her hard on the forehead and chin.

"You fucking bitch!" Brutus's tendons and jaw quivered.

He hit her once hard and she fell against the floor. Trying to scrabble away, she pulled herself up by the windowsill, glanced outside and saw the trooper carrying both the young X-Men with him, tucked under his arms. Jogging awkwardly through the gully away from the slaughterhouse.

On her neck she heard the vibrations of a man's voice shouting in anger. Brutus was running to the window on the other side of the door. He stepped back from it then aimed the shotgun outside.

Melanie ran at him.

It seemed that her feet didn't even touch the ground. Stoat grabbed for her but caught only a shred of silk collar that tore away. As she collided with Brutus's shoulder she had the satisfaction of seeing his pain and surprise and fear as he fell sideways into a square of butcher block. The gun hit the floor but didn't go off.

Melanie looked out the window once more and saw the

two girls and the trooper disappear over a small hill. And then Stoat's gun caught her above the ear that had first gone deaf, years ago, and she dropped to her knees. She fainted not so much from the pain as from the terror that the darkness taking her vision was from a broken nerve and that she would now be blind as well as deaf forever and ever.

5:34 P.M.

"You gave us a bonus, Lou. Thanks much."

"Wasn't me," Handy grumbled.

"No? What happened?"

"Listen here, I'm pissed."

"Why's that?"

"Just shut up and listen, Art. I don't wanta hear your bullshit." His voice was colder than it'd been all day.

"Forty-five minutes for that helicopter. That's all you got and I'll tell you, mister, I'm itching to kill somebody. I almost hope it don't show up. I'm not doing any more bargaining with you."

"How's your beer?"

"I picked the little bitch already. She's ten or eleven. Wearing a pretty dress."

"Emily," Angie said.

"And I'm gonna let Bonner have her first. You know 'bout Bonner, don't you? You got your fucking files on us. You must know all 'bout his little problem."

A negotiator never imposes his own values on the situation—either approval or criticism. Doing so suggests that there are standards of what is and isn't acceptable and is apt to irritate the taker or make his bad behavior seem justified. Even offering reassuring clichés can be dangerous, suggesting that you're not taking the situation seriously.

Reluctantly Potter now said in as blasé a voice as he could muster, "You don't want to do that, Lou. You know you don't."

The cackle of vicious laughter filled the van. "Everybody's telling me what I don't want to do. I *hate* that!"

"We're working on the chopper, Lou. Look outside. We've got twenty-mile-an-hour winds, low overcast, and fog. You wanted pontoons. Well, pontoons don't grow on trees."

"You got twelve-mile-an-hour winds, ceilings of two thousand feet, and no fucking fog that I can see."

The television, Potter remembered, angry with himself for forgetting. Maybe Handy was watching the *Live at Five* weather report at that moment. A long minute of silence. Potter, staring at the speaker above his head, decided they were too focused on the mechanics of the negotiating. It was time for something personal.

"Lou?"

"Yeah."

"You asked me what *I* looked like. Let me ask you about yourself."

"Fuck, you've got pictures in there, I'll bet."

"What do mug shots show?" Potter asked, and laughed.

When Handy spoke, his voice had calmed considerably. "What do I look like?" he mused. "Let me tell you a story, Art. I was in a prison riot one time. All kindsa shit was going down like usual in things like that. What the fuck happens but I find myself in the laundry room with a fellow I'd had it in for for a long time. Now, you know where you hide things when you're inside, don't you? So I crapped this glass knife, unwrapped it, and started to work on him. You know why?"

Echo his questions and comments, Arthur Potter the negotiator thought. But Arthur Potter remained silent.

" 'Cause when I first was in he come up to me, all macho and that shit, and said he didn't like the way I looked."

"So you killed him." A matter-of-fact statement.

"Fuck yes, but that's not my point. While he was dying there, his gut all split open, I leaned down. See, I was curious. I leaned down real close and I asked him what exactly it was he didn't like about the way I looked. And you know what he said? He said, 'You looked like cold death.' Know something, Art? I was sorry I killed him after he told me that. Yessir, cold death."

Don't play his game, Potter thought suddenly. You're
falling under his spell. With an edge to his voice he asked,
"Lou, give us until seven. You do me that, I think we'll
have some good news for you."

"I—"

"That's all. What difference does it make?" Potter kept
all supplication from his voice. He made it sound that
Handy was being unreasonable. It was a risk but Potter
assessed that the man would have no respect at all for
whiners.

Still, he was very surprised when Handy said, "All
right. Jesus! But have the chopper here, Art. Or the little
one in the dress goes."

Click.

Potter calmly instructed Tobe to adjust the deadline
clock accordingly.

The door to the van opened and a trooper looked in. "The
two girls are here, sir. They're in the medical tent."

"Are they okay?"

"One fell and scraped her elbow. Otherwise they're
fine."

"I'll go over there. I could use some fresh air. Frances,
could you translate? Henry, get yourself unplugged and
come with us. Angie too?"

In a grove of trees not far from the van Potter ushered
the girls into folding chairs. Henry LeBow joined them,
portable computer in hand. He sat down and smiled at the
girls, who stared at the Toshiba.

Potter tried to recall what Frances had taught him and
spelled their names in sign language. S-H-A-N-N-O-N
and K-I-E-L-L-E, bringing a smile to Shannon's face.
They were the same age, Potter knew—eight—but Shannon was taller. Kielle, however, with her grim face and
cynical eyes, gave the impression of being far older.

"What's the matter?" Potter asked Kielle.

Frances's face went cold when she received a response.
"She said she tried to kill him."

"Who?"

"Handy, I think she means. She calls him Mr. Sinister."

Potter produced the flyer of the fugitives. Kielle's face screwed into a tight mask and she poked a finger at Handy's picture.

"She says he killed Susan and she was going to kill him. Melanie betrayed her. Melanie is a Judas."

"Why?" Angie asked.

More brutal signing.

"She threw her out the door."

"Melanie did that?"

Potter felt the chill down his spine. He knew there'd be a payback of some kind.

Shannon confirmed that the men didn't seem to have any rifles, only shotguns—her father hunted and she knew something about guns. Beverly's asthma was bad, though Handy had given her the medicine. She reiterated that the "big man," Bonner, hovered over the girls and kept looking at Emily because she was "prettier and looked more like a girl."

Angie asked delicately, "Has anyone touched any of you?"

Shannon said that they had. But Kielle waved her hand and signed, "Not the way you mean. But Bear looks a lot."

So, Potter reflected, Bonner's a discrete threat, separate from Handy. And probably more dangerous. Lust-driven criminals always are.

"Who picked you to be released?" Angie asked Shannon.

"Him." She pointed at Handy.

"The one Melanie calls Brutus, right?"

Shannon nodded. "We call him Mr. Sinister. Or Magneto."

"Why did he pick you, do you think? Was there any reason?"

"Because Bear"—Shannon pointed at Bonner's picture—"told him to." Frances looked at Angie and said, "Shannon kicked him and he was mad."

"I didn't mean to kick him. I just didn't think. . . . And then I got really scared. I thought it was my fault he was going to burn us up."

"Burn you up? Why'd you think that?"

Shannon told them about the gas can rigged right above their heads.

Frances's face went pale. "He wouldn't."

"Oh, yes he would," Angie said. "Fire. His new toy."

"Damn," Potter muttered. This virtually eliminated the possibility of an HRT rescue. Henry LeBow's concession to the horror was to pause before he typed a description of the device.

Potter walked to the doorway of the van, called Budd out, and then motioned Dean Stillwell over. The negotiator said to them both, "We've got a hot trap inside—"

"Hot?" Budd asked.

"Armed," Potter continued. "We can't give him the least excuse to trip it. There's to be absolutely no action that could be construed as offensive. Double-check—all weapons unchambered."

"Yessir," Stillwell said.

Potter then asked Shannon if there was anything else she could remember about the men and what they did inside.

"They watch TV," Frances translated. "They walk around. Eat. Talk. They're pretty relaxed."

Relaxed. Jocylyn had said the same. Well, this was a first for a barricade.

"You saw the tools they have?"

Shannon nodded.

"Have they used them?"

"No."

"Do you remember what tools they had?"

She shook her head no.

"Can you tell what they talk about?" Potter asked.

"No," Frances explained. "Neither of them can lip-read."

"They watch you all the time?" Angie asked.

"Pretty much. He's scary. Him." Shannon was pointing at Handy. Kielle reached forward viciously and grabbed the picture. She tore it up and signed violently.

"She says she hates Melanie. She could have killed him. And now he's alive to kill more people. She says she wouldn't have minded dying. But Melanie's a coward and she hates her."

As he had done with Jocylyn, Potter warmly shook the girls' hands and thanked them. Shannon smiled; Kielle did not but it was with a strong, self-assured grip that the little girl grasped the agent's hand. Then he sent the two girls off with a trooper, to meet their parents at the motel in Crow Ridge. He conferred with Angie for a few minutes then climbed into the van. She followed him.

The negotiator rubbed his eyes and leaned back and took the cup of the dreadful coffee Derek set beside him. "I don't get it," he said to no one in particular.

"What?" Budd asked.

"A hostage escaped and he's angry. That part I understand. But he doesn't seem angry because he lost a bargaining chip. He's angry for some other reason." He looked across the van. "Angie? Our resident psychologist? Have any ideas?"

She organized her thoughts, then said, "I think Handy's big issue is control. He says he's killed people because they didn't do what he wanted. I've heard that before. A convenience store clerk didn't put the money in the robber's bag as fast as he wanted so *she's* the one guilty of an offense, not him. That gave him, in effect, permission to kill her."

"Is that why he killed Susan?" Budd asked.

Potter rose and paced. "Ah, a very good question, Charlie."

"I agree," Angie said. "A key question."

"Why her?" Potter continued.

"Well, what I actually meant," Budd said, "was why did he *kill* her? Why go to that extreme?"

"Oh, when somebody breaks his rules, however slightly," Angie said, "any punishment's fair. Death, torture, rape. In Handy's world, even misdemeanors are capital offenses. But let's ask *Arthur's* question. Why *her?* Why Susan Phillips? That's the important issue. Henry, tell us about the girl."

LeBow's finger clattered. He read from the screen. "Seventeen. Born of deaf parents. IQ of one hundred and forty-six."

"This is hard to listen to," Budd muttered. Potter nodded for LeBow to go on.

"First in her class at the Laurent Clerc School. And listen to this. She's got a record."

"What?"

"She was a protestor last year at Topeka School for the
Deaf, a part of Hammersmith College. They wanted a
deaf dean. Fifty students got arrested and Susan slugged
a cop. They dropped the charges for assault but gave her a
suspended for trespass."

LeBow continued, "Volunteered at the Midwest Bicul-
tural/Bilingual Center. There's an article here—in the material Angie brought." He skimmed it. "Apparently it's an
organization that opposes something called 'mainstream-
ing.' "

Angie said, "The dean of the Clerc School told me
about that. It's a movement to force the Deaf into regular
schools. It's very controversial. Deaf activists oppose it."

"All right," Potter said. "Let's file that away for a moment. Now, who's Handy given up so far?"

"Jocylyn and Shannon," Angie said.

"Anything in common about them?"

"Doesn't seem to be," Budd said. "In fact, looks like
they're opposites. Jocylyn's a timid little thing. Shannon's feisty. She's a little Susan Phillips."

"Angie?" Potter said. "What do you think."

"Control again. Susan was a direct threat to him. She
had an in-your-face attitude. She probably challenged his
control directly. Now, Shannon, with her kicking Bonner . . . Handy'd sense the same threat but on a smaller
scale. He wouldn't feel the need to kill her—to reassert
control in the most extreme way possible—but he'd want
her out. Jocylyn? She was crying all the time. Sniveling.
She got on his nerves. That's a way to eat at his control
too."

"What about the adults?" LeBow asked. "I'd think
they'd be more of a threat than the children."

"Oh, not necessarily," Angie said. "The older teacher,
Donna Harstrawn, is half-comatose, it sounds like. No
threat there."

"And Melanie Charrol?"

Angie said, "The dean at the school told me that she's got a reputation for being very timid."

"But look at what she just did," Potter said. "Getting Kielle out."

"A fluke, I'd guess. Probably impulse." She gazed out the window. "He's an odd one, Handy is."

"Unique in my experience," Potter said. "Say, Henry, read to us from your opus. Tell us what we know about him so far."

LeBow sat up slightly and read in a stiff voice. "Louis Jeremiah Handy is thirty-five years old. Mother raised him after his alcoholic father went to jail when the baby was six months. The mother drank too. Child protective services considered placing him and his brothers in foster homes several times but nothing ever came of it. No evidence he was abused or beaten, though when his father returned from prison—Lou was eight—the man was arrested several times for beating up his neighbors. The father finally took off when Handy was thirteen and was killed a year later in a barroom fight. His mother died a year after that."

Officer Frances Whiting shook her head with undirected sympathy.

"Handy killed his first victim at age fifteen. He used a knife though he apparently had a gun on him and could have used the more merciful weapon. It took the victim, a boy his age, a long time to die. Six years in juvenile for that then out long enough to earn a string of GTA arrests, carjackings, assault, D&D. Suspected in ATM stickups and bank robberies. Was almost convicted twice for major jobs but the witnesses were killed before trial. No link to him could be proved.

"His two brothers were in and out of trouble with the law over the years. The eldest was killed five years ago, as I mentioned before. It was thought Handy might have done it. No known whereabouts for the younger brother.

"As Handy's career's progressed," LeBow said to his audience, "he's gotten more violent." It was the severity and randomness of his crimes that seemed to escalate, the intelligence officer explained. Recently he'd taken to killing for no apparent reason and—in the robbery in which he'd most recently been convicted—started committing arson.

Potter interrupted to say, "Tell us specifically what happened at the Wichita robbery. The Farmers & Merchants S&L."

Henry LeBow scrolled through the screen, then continued, "Handy, Wilcox, a two-time felon named Fred Laskey, and Priscilla Gunder—Handy's girlfriend—robbed the Farmers & Merchants S&L in Wichita. Handy ordered a teller to take him into the vault but she moved too slow for him. Handy lost his temper, beat her, and locked her and another woman teller inside the vault, then went outside and got a can of gas. Doused the inside of the bank and lit it. The fire was the reason he was caught. If they'd just run with the twenty thousand they'd have made it but it took him another five minutes or so to torch the place. That gave the cops and Pete Henderson's men time to roll up, silent."

He summarized the rest of the drama: There was a shootout in front of the bank. The girlfriend got away and Handy, Wilcox, and Laskey stole another car but got stopped by a roadblock a mile away. They'd climbed out and walked toward the cops. Handy fired a hidden gun through Laskey's back, killing him and wounding two of the arresting officers before being wounded himself.

"Pointless." Budd shook his head. "That fire. Burning up those women."

"Oh, no, the fire was one way to regain control of the situation," Angie said.

Potter quoted, " 'They didn't do what I wanted. When I wanted it.' "

"Maybe people like Handy'll become your specialty, Arthur," Tobe said.

Two years until retirement; as if I need a specialty, thought Potter. *And one that includes the Lou Handys of the world.*

Budd sighed.

"You all right, Captain?" Potter asked.

"I don't know if I'm exactly made for this kind of work."

"Ah, you're doing fine."

But of course the young trooper was right. He wasn't made for this line of work; nobody was.

"Listen, Charlie, the troopers're probably getting antsy by now. I want you to make the rounds, you and Dean. Calm 'em down. See about coffee. And for God's sake make sure their heads're down. Keep yours that way too."

"I'll come with you, Charlie," Angie said. "If it's okay with Arthur."

"Catch up with him, Angie. I want to talk to you for a moment."

"I'll meet you outside," she called, and pulled her chair closer to Potter.

"Angie, I need an ally," Potter said. "Someone inside."

She glanced at him. "Melanie?"

"Was that really just a fluke, what she did? Or can I count on some help?"

Angie thought for a minute. "When Melanie was a high-school student there, Laurent Clerc was an oralist school. Signing was forbidden."

"It was?"

"It was a mainstream school. But Melanie realized that was stifling her—which is what all educators are now coming to realize. What she did was to develop her own sign language, one that was very subtle—basically just using the fingers—so the teachers didn't notice it the way you'd see people signing in ASL. Her language spread through the school like wildfire."

"She created a language?"

"Yep. She found that the ten fingers alone weren't enough for a working vocabulary and syntax. So the variable element she introduced was brilliant. It had never been done in sign language before. She used rhythm. She overlaid a temporal structure on the finger shapes. Her inspiration was apparently orchestral conductors."

Arthur Potter, who, after all, made his living with language, was fascinated.

Angie continued, "Right around that time there were protests to shift to a curriculum where ASL was taught and one of the reasons cited by the deaf teachers in favor of doing so was that so many students were using Melanie's language. But Melanie wouldn't have anything to do with the protests. She denied that she'd invented the language—as if she was afraid the administration would punish her for it. All she wanted to do was study and go home. Very talented, very smart. Very scared. She had a chance to go to Gallaudet College in Washington this summer on a fellowship. She turned it down."

"Why?"

"Nobody knew. Her brother's accident maybe."

Potter recalled that the young man was having surgery tomorrow. He wondered if Henderson had gotten in touch with the family. "Maybe," he mused, "there's just a certain timidity that goes along with being deaf."

"Excuse me, Agent Potter." Frances Whiting leaned forward. "Is that like a certain amount of fascism goes along with being a federal agent?"

Potter blinked. "I'm sorry?"

Frances shrugged. "Stereotyping. The Deaf have had to deal with it forever. That they're kings of the beggars. That they're stupid. Deaf and *dumb*. That they're timid. . . . Helen Keller said that blindness cuts you off from *things,* deafness cuts you off from *people*. So the Deaf compensate. There's no other defining physical condition that's given rise to a culture and community the way deafness has. There's a huge diversity among—pick a group: gays, paraplegics, athletes, tall people, short people, the elderly, alcoholics. But the Deaf community is militantly cohesive. And it's anything but timid."

Potter nodded. "I stand chastised." The officer smiled in response.

He looked out over the scruffy field beside them. He said to Angie, "My feeling is that I can get only so far with Handy through negotiations. It could save three or four lives if somebody inside was helping us."

"I'm not sure she's the one who can do it," Angie said.

"Noted," he said. "You better go find Charlie now. He's probably wondering what's become of you."

Angie left the van, Frances too, on her way to the hotel to check on the hostages' families. Potter sat back in the desk chair, picturing the photo of Melanie's face, her wavy blond hair.

How beautiful she is, he mused to himself.

Then he sat up, laughing to himself.

A beautiful face? What was he thinking of?

A negotiator must never Stockholm with hostages. That's the first rule of barricades. He has to be ready to sacrifice them if need be. Still, he couldn't stop thinking about her. This was ironic, for nowadays he rarely thought cf women in terms of physical appearance. Since Marian died he'd had only one romantic involvement. A pleasant woman in her late thirties. It was a liaison doomed from the start. Potter now believed you could return successfully to romantic love at age sixty and above. But in your forties and fifties, he suspected, the process was doomed. It's the inflexibility. And the pride. Oh, and always the doubts.

Gazing at the slaughterhouse, he thought: In the past fifteen years, since Marian, the most meaningful conversations I've had have been not with my surrogate cousin Linden or her clansmen or the women who've hung chastely on my arm at functions in the District. No, they've been with men holding oiled guns at the heads of hostages. Women with short black hair and Middle Eastern faces, though very Western code names. Criminals and psychopaths and potential suicides. I've spilled my guts to them and they to me. Oh, they'd lie about tactics and motives (as I did) but everyone told the exquisite truth about themselves: their hopes, their dreams dead and dreams living still, their families, their children, their scorching failures.

They told their stories for the same reasons Arthur Potter told his. To wear the other side down, to establish bonds, to "transfer the emotive response" (as his own highly circulated hostage negotiation guidebook, eighth printing, explained).

And simply because someone seemed to want to listen.

Melanie . . . will we ever have a conversation, the two of us?

He saw Dean Stillwell wave to him and stepped into the fragrant gully to meet the sheriff. He glanced at the shreds of fog wafting around the van. So Handy's weather report wasn't up to date after all. It gave him a fragment of hope—unreasonable perhaps, but hope nonetheless. He looked up at the late-afternoon sky, in which strips of yellow and bruise-colored clouds sped past. In a break between two of the vaporous shapes he saw the moon, a pale crescent sitting over the slaughterhouse, directly above the blood-red brick.

6:03 P.M.

They appeared suddenly, the dozen men.

The slippery wind covered the noise of their approach and by the time the agent was aware of them they'd surrounded him and Dean Stillwell, who was telling Potter about the dock behind the slaughterhouse. Stillwell had looked over the river and the dock and concluded that, even though the current was fast, as Budd had reported, it was too tempting an escape route. He'd put some armored troops in a skiff and anchored them twenty yards offshore.

Potter noticed Dean Stillwell look up and stare at something behind the agent. He turned.

The team was dressed in black and navy-blue combat gear. Potter recognized the outfits—the American Body Armor plated vests, the rubberized ducking uniforms and hoods, the H&K submachine guns with laser sights and flashlights. It was a Hostage Rescue Team, though not his, and Arthur Potter didn't want these men within a hundred miles of the Webber & Stoltz Processing Company.

"Agent Potter?"

A nod. Be gracious. Don't jerk leashes until leashes need to be jerked.

He shook the hand of the crew-cut man in his forties.

"I'm Dan Tremain. Commander of the state police Hostage Rescue Unit." His still eyes were confident. And challenging. "I understand you're expecting a Delta team."

"The Bureau's HRT actually. Jurisdiction, you know."

"Course."

Potter introduced him to Stillwell, whom Tremain ignored.

"What's the status?" Tremain asked.

"They're contained. One fatality."

"I heard," Tremain said, rubbing a gold pinky ring on which was a deep etching of a cross.

"We've gotten three girls out unhurt," Potter continued. "There are four other girls inside and two teachers. The HTs've asked for a chopper, which we aren't going to give them. They've threatened to execute another hostage at seven unless we have it here by then."

"You're not going to give him one?"

"No."

"But what'll happen?"

"I'm going to try to talk him through it."

"Well, why don't we deploy just the same? I mean, if it comes down to him killing her, I know you'll want to move in."

"No," Potter said, looking over at the press table, where Joe Silbert and his assistant were diligently typing away on a computer. The reporter looked up glumly. Potter nodded and glanced back at Tremain.

The state police commander said, "You're not saying that you'd let him kill the girl, are you?"

"Let's hope it doesn't come to that."

Acceptable casualties . . .

Tremain held his eye for a moment. "I'm thinking we really ought to move into position. Just in case."

Potter glanced at the men and gestured Tremain aside. They walked into the shadow of the command van. "If it comes down to an assault, and I certainly hope it doesn't, then my team'll be the one doing it—and only my team. Sorry, Captain, that's just the way it is."

Was this going to explode? Shoot straight to the governor and the Admiral in Washington?

Tremain bristled but he shrugged. "You're in charge, sir. But those men are state felons too and our regulations require us to be on the scene. And *that's* just the way it is too."

"I have no objection at all to your presence, Captain. And if they come out, guns ablazing, I'd sure welcome your firepower. But as long as it's understood that you're taking orders from me."

Tremain relented. "Fair enough. Fact is, I told my men that we'll probably be spending three hours drinking coffee and then pack up and go home."

"Let's hope so for all our sakes. If you want to go into position as part of the containment crew, Sheriff Stillwell here's in charge of that."

The two men nodded at each other coolly and every soul within earshot knew there was no way an HRT commander would put his men under the orders of a small-town sheriff. Potter hoped this would guarantee that Tremain would hightail it out of here.

"I think we'll just hang back. Stay out of sight. If you need us we'll be around."

"Whatever you want, Captain," Potter said.

Budd and Angie appeared, striding up the hill, and stopped suddenly. "Hey, Dan," Budd said, recognizing Tremain.

"Charlie." They shook hands. Tremain's eyes took in Angie's hair and face but it was a chaste examination, one of curiosity, and when his eyes dipped downward to her chest it was simply to confirm from her necklace ID that she was in fact an FBI agent.

"You boys heard about our little situation, did you?" Budd said.

Tremain laughed. "How 'bout, anybody watches TV knows about it. Who's working the CP?"

"Derek Elb."

"Derek the Red?" Tremain laughed. "I gotta say hi to him." Now jovial, Tremain said to Potter, "That boy wanted to join HRU but we took one look at that hair on him and thought he'd be just a little too prominent in a sniper's scope."

Potter smiled agreeably, pleased that there'd been no confrontation. Usually state and federal negotiators get along well enough but there's invariably tension between negotiators and tactical units from other branches. As Potter explained in class, "There're talkers and there're shooters. That's night and day and it won't ever change."

Tremain stepped into the van. Potter eyed the dozen

men. Somber, artful, and oh-so-pleased to be here. He thought of Robert Duvall in *Apocalypse Now* and supposed these men too loved the smell of napalm in the morning. Potter finished his conversation with Stillwell. When he turned back he was surprised to find that the HRU, to a man, was gone. When he climbed into the van he saw that Tremain too had left.

LeBow entered the information about Stillwell's skiff into his electronic memory.

"Time, Tobe?" Potter was staring at the "Promises/Deceptions" board.

The young man glanced at the digital clock.

"Forty-five minutes," Tobe muttered, then said to LeBow, "You tell him."

"Tell me what?"

The intelligence officer said, "We've been playing with the infrared monitor. We caught a glimpse of Handy a minute ago."

"What was he doing?"

"Loading the shotguns."

The Kansas State Police Hostage Rescue Unit, led by Captain Daniel Tremain, slipped silently into a stand of trees a hundred yards from the slaughterhouse.

The trees, Tremain noted at once, were not unoccupied. There were a state police sniper and two or three local deputies in position. Using hand signals Tremain directed his men through the trees and down into a gully that would take them around the side of the slaughterhouse. They passed undetected through the small forest. Tremain looked about and saw—fifty yards toward the river—an abandoned windmill, forty feet high, sitting in the middle of a grassy field. Beside it were two state troopers, standing with their backs to the HRU as they gazed warily at the slaughterhouse. Tremain ordered the two men into a line of trees out of sight of both the north side of the slaughterhouse and the command post.

From the windmill, the HRU team walked into a gully and made their way closer to the slaughterhouse. Tremain held up his hand and they stopped. He tapped his helmet twice and the men responded to the signal by switching on their radios. Lieutenant Carfallo opened the terrain map and the architectural drawings. From his pocket Tremain took the diagram of the inside of the slaughterhouse that Derek the Red, Derek the trooper, Derek the spy, had just slipped him inside the van. It was marked with the location of the hostages and the HTs.

Tremain was encouraged. The girls weren't being held in shield positions by the windows or in front of the HTs. There were no booby traps. Derek reported that the men inside were armed with pistols and shotguns only, no automatic weapons, and they had no flak jackets, helmets, or flashlights. Of course the hostages weren't as far away from the takers as he would have liked, and the room in which they were being kept had no door. But still Handy and the others were twenty or so feet from the girls. It would take a full five seconds for Handy to get to the hostages, and that was assuming he'd already decided that he would kill them the instant he heard the cutting charges. As a rule, in an assault, there were four to ten seconds of confusion and indecision while the takers tried to scope out what was happening before they could take up effective defensive positions.

"Listen up." Hands tapped ears and heads nodded. Tremain pointed at the chart. "There are six hostages inside. Three HTs—located here, here, and here, though they're pretty mobile. One checks on the girls with some frequency." Tremain nodded to one trooper. "Wilson."

"Sir."

"You're to proceed through this gully along the side of the building here and surveil from one of these two windows."

"Sir, can you get them to shift that light?" Trooper Joey Wilson nodded toward the halogens.

"Negative. This is a clandestine operation and you're not to expose yourself to the friendlies."

"Yessir," the young man barked. No questions asked.

"The middle window is hidden by that tree and the school bus. I'd suggest that one."

"Yessir."

"Pfenninger."

"Sir."

"You're to return to the command van and your orders are consistent with what you and I discussed earlier. Is that understood?"

"Yessir."

"The rest of us are moving to this point here. Using those bushes and trees for cover. Harding, you take point. All officers move out now."

And they dispersed into the dusky afternoon, as fluid as the dark river flowing past, more silent than the wind that bent the grass around them.

"Let's have a smoke," Potter said.

"Not me," Budd answered.

"An imaginary one."

"How's that?"

"Let's step outside, Captain."

They wandered away from the van twenty feet into a stand of trees, the agent adjusting his posture automatically to stand more upright; being in the presence of Charlie Budd made you want to do this. Potter paused and spoke with Joe Silbert and the other reporter.

"We've got two more out."

"Two more? Who?" Silbert seemed to be restraining himself.

"No identities," Potter said. "All I'll say is that they're students. Young girls. They've been released unharmed. That leaves a total of four students and two teachers left inside."

"What did you trade for them?"

"We can't release that information."

He'd expected the reporter would be grateful for the scoop but Silbert grumbled, "You're not making this very fucking easy."

Potter glanced at the computer screen. The story was a human-interest piece about an unnamed trooper, waiting for action—the boredom and the edginess of a barricade. Potter thought it was good and told the reporter so.

Silbert snorted. "Oh, it'd sing like poetry if I had some hard news to put in. When can we interview you?"

"Soon."

The agent and the trooper wandered down into a grove

of trees out of the line of fire. Potter called in and told Tobe where he was, asked for any calls from Handy to be patched through immediately.

"Say, Charlie, where'd that attorney general get himself to?"

Budd looked around. "I think he went back to the hotel."

Potter shook his head. "Marks wants Handy to get his helicopter. The governor told me he wants Handy dead. The Bureau director'll probably be on the horn in the next half-hour—and there've been times when I've gotten a call from the president himself. Oh, and mark my words, Charlie, somebody's writing the script right at this moment and making *me* out to be the villain."

"You?" Budd asked, with inexplicable glumness. "You'll be the hero."

"Oh, not by a long shot. No, sir. Guns sell advertising, words don't."

"What's this about imaginary cigarettes?"

"When my wife got cancer I quit."

"Lung cancer? My uncle had that."

"No. Pancreas."

Unfortunately the party with whom Potter had been negotiating for his wife's recovery had reneged on the deal. Even so, Potter never took up smoking again.

"So you, what, imagine yourself smoking?"

Potter nodded. "And when I can't sleep I imagine myself taking a sleeping pill."

"When you're, you know, depressed you imagine yourself happy?"

That, Arthur Potter had found, didn't work.

Budd, who'd perhaps asked the question because of the funk he'd been in for the last hour, forgot his dolor momentarily and asked, "What brand aren't you smoking?"

"Camels. Without the filter."

"Hey, why not?" His face slipped and he seemed sad again. "I never smoked. Maybe I'll have me an imaginary Jack Daniel's."

"Have a double while you're at it." Arthur Potter drew hard on his fake cigarette. They stood among flowering catalpa and Osage orange and Potter was looking down at what appeared to be the deep tracks of wagon wheels. He asked Budd about them.

"Those? The real thing. The Santa Fe Trail itself."

"Those're the *original* tracks?" Potter was astonished.

"They call 'em swales. Headed west right through here."

Potter, genealogist that he was, kicked at the deep, rocklike tread mark cut into the dirt, and wondered if Marian's great-great-grandfather Ebb Schneider, who had traveled with his widowed mother from Ohio to Nevada in 1868, had been an infant asleep in the wagon that had made this very track.

Budd nodded toward the slaughterhouse. "The reason that was built was because of the Chisholm Trail. It went south to north right through here too, from San Antonio to Abilene—that's *our* Abilene, in Kansas. They'd drive the longhorns along here, sell off and slaughter some for the Wichita market."

"Got another question," Potter said after a moment.

"I'm not much of a state historian. That's 'bout all I know."

"Mostly, Charlie, I'm wondering why you're looking so damn uneasy."

Budd lost interest in the swales at his feet. "Well, I guess I wonder what exactly you wanted to talk to me about."

"In about forty minutes I've got to go talk Handy out of killing another of the girls. I don't have a lot of ideas. I'd like to get your opinion. What do you think of him?"

"Me?"

"Sure."

"Oh, I don't know."

"We never *know* in this business. Give me an educated guess. You've heard his profile. You've talked to Angie. . . . She's quite a lady, isn't she?"

"Say, 'bout that, Arthur . . . the thing is, I'm a married man. She's been chatting me up an awful lot. I mentioned Meg must've been a dozen times and she doesn't seem to pay any attention to it."

"Consider it flattery, Charlie. You're in control of the situation."

"Sorta in control." He looked back at the van but didn't see the dark-haired agent anywhere.

Potter laughed. "So now, give me some thoughts."

Budd fidgeted with his fingers, maybe thinking he should actually be pretending to hold his glass of whisky. Potter smoked as he had come to do so much else in recent years—not actually doing it, not pantomiming, only imagining. It was for him a type of meditation.

"I guess what I'm thinking," Budd said slowly, "is that Handy's got a plan of some kind."

"Why?"

"Partly it's what Angie was saying. Everything he does has a purpose. He's not a crazed kick killer."

"What sort of plan were you thinking of?"

"Don't know exactly. Something he thinks is gonna outsmart us."

Budd's hands slipped into his rear pockets again. The man's nervous as a fifteen-year-old at his first school dance, Potter reflected.

"Why do you say that?"

"I'm not sure exactly. Just an impression. Maybe because he's got this holier-than-thou attitude. He doesn't respect us. Every time he talks to us what I hear is, you know, contempt. Like he knows it all and we don't know anything."

This was true. Potter had noticed it himself. Not a shred of desperation, no supplication, no nervous banter, no tin defiance; all the things you usually heard from hostage takers were noticeably absent here.

Along with the flattest VSA line Potter had ever seen.

"A breakout," Budd continued. "That's what I'd guess. Maybe setting fire to the place." The captain laughed. "Maybe he's got fireman outfits in there—in those bags he brought in with him. And he'll sneak out in all the confusion."

Potter nodded. "That's happened before."

"Has it?" Budd asked, incredulous that he'd thought of this strategy and, accordingly, very pleased with himself.

"Medical-worker outfits one time. And police uniforms another. But I'd given all the containment officers handouts, like what I distributed earlier, so the HTs were spotted right away. Here, though, I don't know. It doesn't seem to be his style. But you're right on about his attitude. That's the key. It's saying something to us. I just wish I knew what."

Again Budd was fiddling nervously with his pockets.

"Those tools," Potter mused, "might have something to do with it. Maybe they'll set a fire, hide in a piece of machinery or even under the floor. Then climb out when the rescue workers are there. We should make sure that everybody, not just the troopers, has a copy of the profile flyers."

"I'll take care of it." Budd laughed nervously again. "I'll delegate it."

Potter had calmed considerably. He thought of Marian. The infrequent evenings he was home they used to sit together by the radio listening to NPR and share one cigarette and a glass of sherry. Occasionally, once a week, perhaps twice, the cigarette would be stubbed out and they would climb the stairs to their ornate bed and forgo the musical programming for that evening.

"This negotiation stuff," Budd said. "It's pretty confusing to me."

"How so?"

"Well, you don't seem to talk to him about what I'd talk to him about—you know, the stuff he wants and the hostages and everything. Business. Mostly, it seems that you just chat."

"You ever been in therapy, Charlie?"

The young officer seemed to snicker. He shook his head. Maybe analysis was something Kansans didn't go in for.

Potter said, "I was. After my wife died."

"I was going to say, I'm sorry to hear that happened."

"You know what I talked to the therapist about? Genealogy."

"What?"

"It's my hobby. Family trees, you know."

"You were paying good money to a doctor to talk about hobbies?"

"And it was the best money I ever spent. I started to feel what the therapist was feeling and vice versa. We moved closer to each other. What I'm doing here—with Handy—is the same. You don't click a switch and make Handy give up the girls. Just like the doctor doesn't click a switch and make everything better. The point is to create a relationship between him and me. He's got to know me, and I've got to know him."

"Hey, like you're dating?"

"You could say that," Potter said without smiling. "I want to get him into my mind—so he'll realize it's a hopeless situation. So he'll give me the girls and surrender, to make him feel that it's pointless to go on. Not to understand it intellectually, but to *feel* it. You can see it's working a bit. He's given us two and hasn't killed anyone else, even when that other girl snuck out." Potter drew a final breath of his imaginary Camel. Stubbed it out.

He started to imagine climbing stairs, Marian's hand in his. But this image faded quickly.

"And I do it to get into his mind. To understand him."

"So you become his friend?"

"Friend? Not a friend. I'd say that we become linked."

"But, I mean, isn't that a problem? If you have to order HRT to green-light him, you'd be ordering the death of somebody you're close to. Betraying them."

"Oh, yes," the negotiator said softly. "Yes, it's a problem."

Budd blew air out of his cheeks and again studied the harvesting. "You said . . ."

"What?"

"You said before that you're willing to sacrifice those girls to get him. Is that really true?"

Potter looked at him for a moment while Budd's distraught eyes gazed at the steadfast threshers miles away. "Yes, it is. My job is to stop Handy. Those're my orders. And yes, there may have to be sacrifices."

"But they're little girls."

Potter smiled grimly. "How can you make a value judgment? These aren't the days of women and children first. A life is a life. Are those girls more deserving than the family Handy might kidnap and kill next year if he escapes today? Or the two traffic cops he shoots when they stop him for speeding? I have to keep thinking that those hostages are dead already. If I can save some, so much the better. But I can't look at it any other way and still function."

"You're good at what you do, seems."

Potter didn't answer.

"You think there'll be more deaths?"

"Oh, yes, I'm afraid so. Just an educated guess but I do think so."

"The girls?"

Potter didn't answer.

"Our immediate problem, Charlie—what can we use to buy another hour with?"

Budd shrugged. "No guns or ammo, right?"

"That's not negotiable."

"Well, he thinks he's getting his imaginary helicopter, right?"

"Yes."

"As long as we're lying to him 'bout that, why don't we lie to him 'bout something else? Promise him something to go along with it."

"Can't give a kid a toy without giving him batteries, is that what you're saying?"

"I guess I am."

"That's brilliant, Charlie. Let's go kick it around with Henry."

As they climbed into the van Potter clapped the trooper on the shoulder and Budd responded with as hangtail a smile as the agent had ever in his life encountered.

They would divide into three teams, Alpha, Bravo, Charlie.

The HRU officers, under Dan Tremain, were gathered in a cluster on the left side, the northwest side, of the slaughterhouse, hidden in a grove of trees. The men were now wearing black assault coveralls over their body armor. Nomex hoods and gloves. Their goggles rested on the crest of their foreheads.

Alpha and Bravo teams had four men each, two armed with Heckler & Koch MP-5 submachine guns, fitted with B.E.A.M. mounts and halogen flashlights, two armed with H&K Super 90 semiautomatic shotguns. The two

HRU troopers in Charlie team had MP-5s as well but were also carrying Accuracy Systems M429 Thunderflash stun grenades and M451 Multistarflash grenades.

Two other troopers had been deployed. Chuck Pfenninger—Outrider One—was in standard uniform beside the command van. Joey Wilson—Outrider Two—in ops armor and camouflage was beneath the middle window to the left of the main door of the slaughterhouse. He was hidden from view of the command post and the troopers in the field by the Laurent Clerc School bus and a ginkgo tree.

Tremain went over the plan one more time in his mind. As soon as Wilson reported that the HTs were as far away from the hostages as they could hope for, Pfenninger would blow the generator in the command van, using an L210 charge, known informally as a mini-Molotov. It was a small gasoline bomb sealed in a special fiberboard container, like single-serving boxes of grape juice or fruit punch. The container would disintegrate under the heat from the blast and would be virtually undetectable by crime-scene technicians. Properly placed, it would cut off all communications and seal the troopers inside the van. The vehicle had been designed to be driven through flames, was well insulated, and had an internal oxygen system. As long as the door remained closed, no one inside would be injured.

Tremain would officially take charge and "declare" that the situation had gone hot.

As soon as this happened HRU's three teams would move into the slaughterhouse. Charlie team would use Model 521 cutting charges to blast a hole in the roof and drop two stun grenades onto the takers. Alpha and Bravo would blow the side and loading-dock doors simultaneously and enter the building while Charlie dropped the second—the flash—grenades, which would explode in a huge burst of blinding light, and then rappel through the opening in the roof. Bravo team would head straight to the hostages, and Alpha and Charlie would advance on the HTs, neutralizing them if there was any resistance.

They were now waiting for three troopers who'd gone to check out the side door, the loading dock, and the roof.

Dan Tremain lay prone beside the steely Lieutenant Carfallo and gazed at the slaughterhouse, which rose above them like a medieval castle, toothy and dark. The captain said to his troops, "You'll be using four-man entry. The first two men will be the key shooters. Machine guns first, followed by shotgun backup. This will be a dynamic shooting entry. You will proceed until all hostile targets have been successfully engaged and neutralized and the premises have been secured. There are six hostages inside, located where I indicated on the map. They're all female, and four are young girls, who may panic and run. You will exercise absolute muzzle control of your weapons at all times you are inside. Do you copy?"

Affirmative answers.

Then came the bad news.

One by one the surveillance troopers called in. The reconnaissance revealed that the side door was far thicker than the diagram indicated: three-inch oak with a sheet steel face. They would have to use four cutting charges. For safety, Alpha team would have to be farther away when it blew than originally planned. That would add as much as six seconds to the time it would take to get to the girls.

It turned out too that there'd been some construction on the roof not reflected in the original architectural drawings—a series of steel plates, covering virtually the entire roof, had been bolted into place years ago. The men on the roof would have to use a large amount of C4 to cut through them. In an old building like this, that much plastic explosive could bring down girders—possibly even major portions of the roof.

Tremain then learned from the third scout that the loading-dock door was jammed open only about eight inches. It was a huge steel sheet, too large to blow.

The captain conferred with Carfallo and they revised their plans. They decided they'd have to forgo the roof and loading-dock assaults and go with a two-team, single-door entry through the north door. Wilson, standing by the front window, would toss in a stun grenade, followed by the flash. This was risky because it would expose him to both the police line and the HTs; he might get shot by either. But Tremain concluded there was no choice.

He needed another hour, he decided, for an effective attack—time to find another unbarred door or window and time to weaken the hinges on the fire door so they could use smaller charges.

But he didn't have an hour. He had twenty minutes until the next deadline.

Until the next girl would die.

Well, then, a single-entrance assault it would be. Tremain said, "Code word 'filly' means green light. Code word 'stallion' means stand down. Acknowledge."

The men responded. Tremain led them into the gully beside the slaughterhouse. There they plastered themselves against the damp earth and fell into absolute stillness and silence, for so they had been instructed, and these were men who lived by their orders before anything else.

6:40 P.M.

Joe Silbert had taught himself to type with two fingers on an Underwood upright that smelled of oil and ink and the bittersweet scent of eraser shavings clogging the carriage.

Technology hadn't changed things for him much and he now pounded away with only his index digits thudding loudly on the large portable Compaq. The orange light of the screen illuminated both him and Ted Biggins, made them look jaundiced and depleted. Silbert supposed that, being almost double Biggins's age, he looked twice as bad.

Philip Molto stood his diligent guard, as instructed by nervous Captain Budd.

"What do you think?" Silbert asked Biggins.

Biggins looked over his colleague's shoulder at the dense single-spaced type on the screen and grunted. "Mind if I take over?" He nodded at the screen.

"Be my guest."

Biggins could touch-type like a demon and his fingers moved quietly and invisibly over the keys. "Hey, I'm a fucking natural at this," he said, his hair perfectly coiffed although he was only an engineer and Silbert was in fact the on-camera reporter.

"Hey, Officer," Silbert called to Molto, "our shift's almost up. We're just going to leave the computer here for the next team. They'll pick up the story where we left it off."

"You guys do that?"

"It's a cooperative thing, you know. You'll keep an eye on the computer?"

"Sure thing, yessir. What's the matter?"

Silbert was frowning, looking out into the stand of trees and juniper bushes behind the police line. "You hear something?"

Biggins was standing up, looking around uneasily. "Yeah."

Molto cocked his head. There were footsteps. A snap of branch, a shuffle.

"There's nobody behind there," the lieutenant said, half to himself. "I mean, nobody's *supposed* to be."

Silbert's face had the cautious look of a man who'd covered combat zones before. Then he broke into a wry grin. "That son of a bitch. Lieutenant, I think we've got a trespasser here."

The trooper, hand on his pistol, stepped into the bushes. When he returned he was escorting two men in black jogging suits. Press credentials bounced on their chests.

"Well, look who it is," Silbert said. "Walter Cronkite and Chet Huntley."

Biggins said to Molto, "If you're going to arrest them, forget trespassing. Charge 'em with being first-degree assholes."

"You boys know each other?"

One of the captives grimaced. "Silbert, you're a son of a bitch. You blow the whistle on us? And don't even let that little shit with you say a word to me."

Silbert said to Molto, "They're with KLTV. Sam Kellog

and Tony Bianco. They seem to've forgotten that we're press-pooling."

"Fuck you," Bianco snapped.

Silbert spat out, "I gave up an exclusive just like you did, Kellog. You would've had your turn."

"I'm supposed to arrest you," Molto said to Kellog and Bianco.

"Bullshit, you can't do that."

"I'll think about it on the way back to the press tent. Come on."

"Look, Officer," Kellog said, "as long as we're here . . ."

"How'd you get here anyway, Kellog?" Biggins said. "Crawl on your belly?"

"Fuck you too."

Molto led them away. As soon as the squad car vanished Silbert barked to Biggins, "Now. Do it."

Biggins unhooked the casing of the computer monitor and pulled it open. From it he took a Nippona LL3R video camera—the subminiature model, which cost one hundred and thirty thousand dollars, weighed fourteen ounces, and was equipped with a folding twelve-inch parabolic antenna and transmitter. It produced a broadcast-quality picture in virtual darkness and had a telescopic lens as smooth as a sniper's riflescope. It had an effective range of three miles, which would be more than enough to reach the KFAL mobile transmitting center, where Silbert's colleagues (Tony Bianco and Sam Kellog, as it turned out, not too coincidentally) would soon—if they weren't actually under arrest—be waiting for the transmission. In case they were in fact sacrifices to the First Amendment other technicians were ready to wade into the breach.

Silbert opened his attaché case and took out two black nylon running suits—identical to those that Kellog and Bianco had been wearing, except for one difference: on the back were stenciled the words *U.S. Marshal*. They pulled these on.

"Wait," Silbert said. He bent down to the screen and erased the entire file that Biggins had written—which consisted of the sentence *The quick brown fox jumped over the lazy dog*, written about three hundred times. Shift-F3. He switched screens to the generic cop-on-a-

stakeout story, which Silbert had filed about three years
ago and had called up tonight as soon as they got the computer booted up. The story that prick Arthur Potter had
admired.

The two men slipped into the gully behind the command van and hurried through the night in the direction
that Dan Tremain and his silent Hostage Rescue Unit had
gone.

The gas can.

This was the first thing in her thoughts as she opened
her eyes and looked around the killing room.

Emily, on her knees, playing good Christian nurse,
brushed the blood away from Melanie's eye. It was
swollen, though not closed. The girl ripped the hem of her
precious Laura Ashley dress and wiped more of the blood
away.

Melanie lay still, as the terrible pain in her head less-
ened and her vision improved. One of the twins, Suzie
(she *thought* it was Suzie), brushed her hair with her tiny,
perfect fingers.

The gas can. There it was.

Finally Melanie sat up and crawled over to Beverly.

"How are you?" she asked the girl.

Sweat had plastered Beverly's blond Dutch-boy hair to
her face. She nodded, though her chest continued to rise
and fall alarmingly. She used the inhaler again. Melanie
had never seen her this sick. The device seemed to be
having no effect.

Mrs. Harstrawn still lay on the floor, on her back. She'd
been crying again but was now calm. Melanie gently
worked the woman's colorful sweater over her shoulders.
She muttered some words. Melanie thought she said,
"Don't. I'm cold."

"I have to," Melanie signed. Her fingers danced in front
of the woman's face but she didn't see the message.

A minute later Mrs. Harstrawn's sweater was off.
Melanie looked around and pitched it casually against the
wall of the killing room, near the place where the arched
opening met the floor toward the rear of the slaughterhouse. Then she scooted forward until she could look into

the main room. Bear glanced toward them occasionally but the men were concentrating on the television. Melanie looked at the twins and in faint gestures signed to them, "Go over to gas can."

They looked uneasily at each other, their heads moving identically.

"Do it. Now!" Her signs were urgent—sharp, compact stabs of her fingers.

They rose and crawled slowly toward the red-and-yellow can.

When Suzie looked at her she told the girl to pick up the sweater. Mrs. Harstrawn's mother in Topeka had knitted it. The colors were red and white and blue, very visible—bad news for now; good news once the girls got outside. But Suzie wasn't moving. Melanie repeated the command. There was no time for caution, she explained. "Move! Now!"

Why is she hesitating? She's just staring at me.

No, not at me. . . .

Then the shadow fell over her.

She gasped as Brutus took her by the shoulders and spun her around.

"You think . . . a fucking hero, do you? Why, I've shot people for a lot less'n what you did."

She thought for a terrible moment that Brutus could actually read her mind, had an animal's sixth sense, and knew what she was planning with the gas can. But then she understood he was talking about her pitching Kielle out the door. Maybe being pistol-whipped wasn't enough punishment. He pulled his gun and rested it against her head.

Filled with a burst of rage that shocked her, she pushed the gun aside, stood, and walked into the main room of the plant, feeling the vibrations of his shouts on her back. She ignored him and continued to the oil drum that served as a table. Bear rose and stepped toward her but she ignored him too. She picked up the pen and paper and returned to the killing room.

She wrote: *You work real hard to prove you're a bad guy, don't you?* Thrust it in his face.

Brutus laughed. He ripped the pad from her hands,

tossed it on the floor. He studied her for a long, long moment, then, eerily calm, he said, ". . . you and me chew
the fat. I don't talk much . . . not many people I can talk
to. But you I can. Why's that? . . . you can't talk back, I
guess. It's good when a woman don't talk back. Pris,
she's got a mind of her own. . . . I approve of that. But
sometimes she's off someplace else, you know? . . . I just
don't get what she's saying. You, I look into your face
and I can understand you. You seem like a little mouse,
but maybe there's more to you. There is, ain't there?"

Melanie was horrified to find, somewhere in her heart,
a splinter of pleasure. This terrible, terrible man was ap-
proving of her. He killed Susan, he killed Susan, he killed
Susan, she told herself. He'd kill me in an instant if he
wanted to. These things she knew but all she sensed at
this moment was his approval.

He put the gun away and fiddled with his shoelaces.
"You think I'm bad for . . . to your friend. Well, by your
thinkin' I am bad. I ain't . . . smart and I don't have no
particular talents. But the one thing I am is bad. I'm not
saying I don't have a heart or that I haven't cried in my
day. I cried for a week when somebody shot my brother.
Yes, I did." Brutus paused, his pointy teeth rising from his
thin lips, "Now, that sonofabitch out there . . ." He nodded toward the phone.

De l'Epée? Does he mean de l'Epée?

"Him and me, we're in a battle right now. And he's going to lose. . . . Why? Because bad is simple and good is
complicated. And the simple always wins. That's what
everything comes down to in the end. Simple always
wins. That's just nature and you know what kind of trouble people get into ignoring nature. Look at you, all you
deaf people. You'll die out before people like me. I need
something, I can say, 'Give it to me.' I open my mouth
and somebody does what I want. But you, you have to do
funny things with your hands. You have to write it down.
That's complicated. You're a freak . . . you'll die and I'll
live. It's nature.

"Me, I'm taking that girl over there, that flower-dress
one, and shooting her in about ten minutes if . . . helicopter don't get here. Which I don't think it will. To me,

that's no worse'n scratching an itch or buying a soda pop when you're thirsty."

He looked at Emily, his mouth curling into that faint smile of his.

And in his glance, Melanie suddenly saw much more than a look of a captor toward his victim. She saw all the taunts of her classmates, the grinding frustrations of trying to understand what can be understood only by the miracle of hearing. She saw an empty life without a lover. She saw the cover of a piece of sheet music entitled "Amazing Grace" and inside, merely blank pages.

God's will . . .

Brutus's glance . . .

And so it made sense that she went for his eyes.

Melanie leapt forward, her perfect fingernails clawing at his face.

He gave a gasp of surprise and stumbled backwards, groping for his gun. He pulled it from his belt and she lunged for it. The pistol flew from his grip and slid across the floor. She was out of control, crazed, driven by a consuming anger unlike any she'd ever experienced. An anger that poured from her too quickly, ripping her open, hurting the way the fever had burned her skin when she was eight and took away the simple and made her life so terribly complicated.

Her long fingers, muscular from years of signing, tipped with pearl nails, ripped into his cheek; she slapped his nose, she dug for his eyes. As he fell onto his back she leapt upon his chest, her knee crunching into his solar plexus. He gasped as the breath was forced from his lungs. He struck her once in the chest and she recoiled from him but he had no leverage and his blow was painless.

"Jesus Christ . . . !" His wiry hands reached for her throat but she punched them aside and got a grip on his windpipe, her strong arms fending off his; he couldn't quite reach her. Where was this strength coming from? she wondered, as she banged his head into the concrete and watched his face turn blue.

Perhaps Stoat and Bear were running toward her, perhaps they were aiming their guns at her. Or maybe because Brutus had no air in his lungs he was silent, maybe he was too proud to call for help. She didn't know—or care. Nothing existed for her but this man and his evilness—not the other girls, not Mrs. Harstrawn, not the soul of Susan Phillips, who agnostic Melanie believed floated above them at this moment, a beautiful seraph.

She was going to kill him.

Then suddenly he went limp as a towel. His tongue protruded from his pale lips. And she thought, My God, I've done it! Exultant and terrified, she sat back, looking at the twins, sobbing Emily, gasping Bev.

When his knee rose fast she had no time to deflect it and it caught her between the legs, crashing into her with a raging pain. She inhaled fiercely and cradled her groin as Brutus's fist drove into her chest just below the breastbone. Melanie doubled over, breathless.

He rose easily and she saw that, aside from the scratches on his cheek, he wasn't hurt at all. He'd been playing with her. Roughhousing.

Then he had her by the hair and was dragging her into the front room.

She dug her nails into his hand and he slapped her face hard. Her vision exploded with light and her arms went limp. The next thing she knew she was in the window of the slaughterhouse, staring out at the windy field and the brilliant lights trained on the building.

Her face was against the glass and she thought it might break and slice through her eyes. No, no, not *that* kind of darkness. Permanent darkness. No, please. . . .

Stoat stepped forward but Brutus waved him off. He pulled his pistol out. He spun her around so she could see him speak. "If you could talk like a normal person, maybe you could say something to save yourself. But you can't. No, no. You're a freak of nature and if they don't come through with that chopper you're going to be even more of a freak. Shep, how much time . . . ?"

Stoat seemed to hesitate and said something she didn't understand.

"How much fucking *time*?" Brutus's bloody face was distorted with rage.

He received the answer and lifted the gun to her cheek.

Then slowly his hand entwined in her hair and turned her around so that she was facing into the blinding white lights once again.

Melanie. Potter saw her face through his thick field glasses. Melanie was the next victim.

Budd, LeBow, and Frances stared out the window. Stillwell came on the radio and said, "One of my snipers reports that Handy's bleeding. Doesn't seem serious but his face is cut."

"Twelve minutes to deadline," Tobe said. "Downlink coming in."

The phone rang and Potter answered at once. "Lou, what—?"

"I've got a new one, Art," Handy's voice raged. "She's got some spirit. I was gonna forgive her after she gave you that little troublemaker. But the slut got it into her mind she wanted to have a little fun. Go for a roll in the hay with me."

Stay calm, Potter told himself. He's playing you again. He tamped down his own rage, which mimicked Handy's.

"She's into some sick stuff, Art. One of them S&M pups, looks like. She'll learn, she'll learn. You've got 'bout ten minutes, Art. I don't hear that chopper overhead we're gonna do some nine-millimeter plastic surgery on this here girl. Now I want that fucking helicopter. You got it?"

"We have to bring one in from Topeka. There—"

"There's a goddamn airport three miles west of here. Why the fuck don't you *bring one in* from there?"

"You said you—"

"Ten minutes."

Click.

Potter closed his eyes and sighed.

"Angie?"

"I think we have a problem," the psychologist answered. "He wants to hurt her."

This was a real setback. Potter could probably have gotten an extension of the deadline from a Lou Handy who was in a good frame of mind and in control. Vindictive Lou Handy, embarrassed and angry Lou Handy, wasn't

inclined to give them anything and was now in the mood
for bloodshed.

Oh, Melanie, why couldn't you have just left well
enough alone? (Yet what else did he feel? Pride that she
had the guts to resist Hardy when he tried to beat her for
saving Kielle? Admiration? And what else?)

Angie's beautiful, exotic face was frowning.

"What is it?" Budd asked her.

"What Handy was saying about plastic surgery. What
does he mean?"

"He doesn't want to kill anyone else just yet, I think,"
Potter said slowly. "He's worried that he's losing too
many hostages and we haven't given him anything substantive. So he's going to wound her. Maybe blind her in
one eye."

"Lord," Budd whispered.

Tobe called, "Arthur, I'm picking up scrambled signals
from nearby."

"What frequency?"

"What megahertz, you mean?"

"I don't care about the numbers. Whose would they
be?"

"It's an unassigned frequency."

"Two-way?"

"Yep. And they're retrosignals."

Some operations are so secret that the law enforcers'
radios use special coordinated scramblers that change the
code every few seconds. Derek confirmed that the state
police radios didn't have this feature.

"How nearby?"

"Within a mile radius."

"Press?"

"They don't usually use scramblers but it could be."

Potter couldn't waste time on this now. He made a fist
and stared out the window through the Leicas. He saw
Melanie's blond hair, the black speck of the pistol. Struggling to keep his voice calm, he said, "Well, Charlie . . .
you thought any more about what kind of imaginary batteries he wants for his toy?"

Budd lifted his hands helplessly. "I can't think. I . . . I

just don't know." Panic edged into his voice. "Look at the time!"

"Henry?"

LeBow scrolled slowly through the now-lengthy profile of Louis Handy. To nervous Charlie Budd he said, "The more urgent the task, Captain, the more slowly you should perform it. Let's see, there was a lot of grand theft auto when he was a kid. Maybe he's into cars. Should we push that button?"

"No. Charlie's got a point. Let's think about something having to do with his escape."

"What else does he spend his money on?" Angie asked.

"Not much. Never owned property. Never knocked over a jewelry store. . . ."

"Any interests?" Potter wondered.

Angie said suddenly, "His probation reports. You have those in there?"

"I've scanned them in."

"Read them. See if he's ever asked permission to leave a jurisdiction and why."

"Good, Angie," Potter said.

Keys tapped. "Okay. Yes, he has. Twice he left Milwaukee, where he was living following his release, to go fishing in Minnesota. Up near International Falls. And three times up to Canada. Returned all times without incident." LeBow squinted. "Fishing. That reminds me of something. . . ." He typed in a search request. "Here, a prison counselor's report. He likes to fish. Loves it. Worked up merit points for a leave to a trout stream on the grounds at Pennaupsut State Pen."

Potter thought, Minnesota. His home state. Land of a Thousand Lakes. Canada.

Budd—standing tall with his perfect posture—continued to fidget. "Oh, brother." He looked at his watch twice, five seconds apart.

"Please, Charlie."

"We've got seven minutes!"

"I know. You had the brainstorm. What was in your mind?"

"I don't *know* what I meant!"

Potter was staring at Melanie once again. Stop it, he ordered. Forget about her. He sat up suddenly. "Got it. He likes to fish and has a fondness for the north?"

"Right," Budd said. Asking, in effect, So what?

But LeBow understood. He nodded. "You're a poet, Arthur."

"Thank Charlie here. He got me thinking of it."

Budd looked merely perplexed.

"Five minutes," Tobe called.

"We're going to cut a phony escape deal," Potter said quickly, pointing to the "Deceptions" half of the board. LeBow rose to his feet, grabbed the marker. Potter thought for a moment. "Handy's going to want to check what I tell him. He's going to call the FAA regional headquarters. Where is that, Charlie?"

"Topeka."

To Tobe, Potter said, "I want an immediate routing of all calls into the main FAA number sent to that phone right there." He pointed to a console phone. It would be an arduous task, Potter knew, but without a word Tobe set to work pushing buttons and speaking urgently into his headset mike.

"No," Budd protested. "There's no time. Just give him that number. How will *he* know it's not the FAA?"

"Too risky if he checks." Potter picked up the phone and hit redial.

An enthusiastic voice answered, "Yo."

"Lou?"

"Hello, Art. My ears're peeled but I don't hear no chopper. You see my girlfriend here in the window?"

"Say, Lou," Potter said calmly, looking into the window. "I've got a proposition for you."

"Ten, nine, eight . . ."

"Listen—"

"Hey, Art, I just had a thought. Maybe this is your way of doing something bad. Maybe you *are* a son of a bitch."

"The chopper's just about ready."

"And this here girl is just about bleedin'. She's crying a stream, Art. I've had it. I've just fucking had it with you people. You don't take me seriously." He raged, "You don't do what I fucking *want!*"

Angie leaned forward. Charlie Budd's lips moved in a silent prayer.

"All right, Lou," Potter growled. "I know you'll shoot her. But you know I'll let you do it."

Static filled the van.

"Hear me out at least."

"By my clock I'll hear you out for another minute or two."

"Lou, I've been working on this for an hour. I didn't want to say anything until it was in place but I'll tell you anyway. It's almost done."

Let the anticipation build up.

"Well, what? Tell me."

"Give me another hour, don't hurt the girl, and I'll get you a priority FAA-cleared flight plan into Canada."

Silence for a second.

"What the fuck does that mean?"

"You can deal with the FAA directly. We'll never know where you go."

"But the pilot will."

"The pilot'll have handcuffs for himself and the hostages. You set down wherever you want in Canada, disable the chopper and the radio, and you'll be gone hours before we find them."

Silence.

Potter looked at Tobe desperately, eyebrows raised. The young man, sweating heavily, exhaled long and mouthed, "Working on it."

"We'll stock the chopper with food and water. You want backpacks, hiking boots? Hell, Lou, we'll even give you fishing rods. This is a good deal. Don't hurt her. Give us another hour and you'll get the clearance."

"Lemme think."

"I'll get the name of the FAA supervisor and call you right back."

Click.

Unflappable Tobe gazed at his inert dials then hit the console with his fist and said, "Where the fuck is our transfer?"

Potter folded his hands together and stared out the window at the configuration that was Melanie Charrol—tiny glowing shapes of color and light, like pixels on a TV screen.

Captain Dan Tremain leaned forward, pushing aside a branch, silent as snow.

From this angle he could just see the corner of the window in which the young woman was being held. Tremain was one of the best sniper shots in the HRU and often regretted that his command position didn't give him the chance to strap up a Remington and, with the aid of his spotter, acquire and neutralize a target eight hundred, a thousand yards away.

But tonight was a door-entry operation. Snipers would be useless and so he turned his thoughts from the vague target in the window to the job at hand.

Tremain's watch showed seven. "Deadline," he said. "Outrider One. Report."

"Charge loaded in generator."

"Await green-light command."

"Roger."

"Outrider Two, report."

"The subjects are all in the main room, hostages are unattended, except for the woman in the window."

"Roger," Tremain said. "Teams A and B, status?"

"Team A to home base. Loaded and locked."

"Team B, loaded and locked."

Tremain chocked his foot against a rock and eased to one knee. Eyes on Handy. He looked like a sprinter waiting for the gun—which was exactly what he would become in a matter of minutes.

"Done," Tobe called.

He added, "Theoretically, at least."

Potter wiped his palm. He transferred the phone to his other hand, then called Handy back and said the helicopter clearance was arranged. He gave him the number of the FAA office.

"What'sa name?" Handy growled. "Who should I talk to?"

Potter said, "Don Creswell." It was the name of his

cousin-in-law Linden's husband. LeBow scrawled it on the nearly filled "Deceptions" board.

"We'll see, Art. I'll call you back. The girl stays right beside me and my big G till I'm satisfied."

Click.

Potter spun around and looked at Tobe's screen. He said, "It'll have to be you, Henry. He knows my voice."

LeBow grimaced. "I could have used time to prepare, Arthur."

"So could we all."

A moment later Tobe said, "Uplink from slaughter-house. . . . Not coming here . . . digits . . . . one, nine-one-three, five-five-five, one-two-one-two. Topeka directory assistance."

They heard Handy's voice ask for the number of the FAA regional office. The operator gave it to him. Potter exhaled in relief. Budd said, "You were right. He didn't trust you."

"Uplink terminated," Tobe whispered unnecessarily. "Uplink from slaughterhouse to Topeka, downlink transfer from trunk line to . . ." He pointed to the phone on the desk, and it began to ring. "Curtain up."

LeBow took a deep breath and nodded.

"Wait," Budd said urgently. "He'll be expecting a secretary or receptionist."

"Damn," Potter spat out. "Of course. Angie?"

She was the closest to the phone.

Third ring. Fourth.

She nodded brusquely, snatched up the receiver. "Federal Aviation Administration," she said breezily. "May I help you?"

"I wanta talk to Don Creswell."

"One moment please. Who's calling?"

A laugh. "Lou Handy."

She clapped her hand to the mouthpiece and whispered, "What's hold?"

Tobe took the phone from her and tapped it with a fingernail, then handed it to LeBow. Potter winked at her.

Again LeBow inhaled and said, "Creswell here."

"Hey, Don. You don't know me."

A brief pause. "This is that fellow the FBI called me about? Louis Handy?"

"Yeah, this's that *fellow*. Tell me, is this bullshit he's feeding me? It is, isn't it?"

Pudgy, benign Henry LeBow snapped, "Well, sir, I'll tell you, it's more bullshit for me. 'Cause frankly it's making my life pure hell. I got sixty planes an hour coming into our airspace and this's going to mean rerouting close to three-quarters of them. And that's just the commercial flights. I told the agent no way at first but he's a grade-A pain in the ass, and a FBI pain in the ass to boot. He told me he'd fuck up my life royal if I don't do exactly what you want. So, yeah, it's bullshit but, yeah, I'm going to give him what he asked for."

"What the fuck is that, exactly?"

"Didn't he tell you? An M-4 priority airspace clearance straight into western Ontario."

Good job, Henry, Potter thought, his eyes on Melanie's silhouette.

"A what?"

"It's the highest priority there is. It's reserved for Air Force One and visiting heads of state. We call it 'papal clearance' because it's what the Pope gets. Now listen, you might want to write this down. What you have to do is make sure the helicopter pilot shuts off the transponder. He'll point it out to you and you can shut it off or smash it or whatever, and we won't be able to track you on radar."

"No radar?"

"That's part of the M-4. We do that so radar-seeking missiles can't lock onto a dignitary's jet."

"The transponder. I think I heard about them. How long do we have?"

LeBow looked at Potter, who held up eight fingers.

"We can keep the airspace open for eight hours. After that there's too much commercial traffic and we'd have to rewrite the airspace requirements."

"Okay. Do it."

"It's being done. It'll be effective in, let me see . . ."

Potter held up two fingers.

"About two hours."

"Fuck that. One hour tops, or I kill this pretty little thing next to me."

"Oh, my God. Are you seri—? Well, sure. One hour. But I need a full hour. Only please, mister, don't hurt anybody."

Handy's cold chuckle came through the speaker. "Hey, Don, lemme ask you a question."

"Sure."

"You in Topeka right now?"

Silence in the room.

Potter's head turned away from the window, stared at LeBow.

"Sure am."

Potter snapped his fingers and pointed to LeBow's computer. The intelligence officer's eyes went wide and he nodded. He punched silent buttons. The message came on: "Loading Encyclopedia." The words blinked repeatedly.

"Topeka, huh?" Handy said. "Nice place?"

Loading . . . loading . . .

Come on, Potter thought desperately. Come *on!*

"I like it."

The screen went blank; at last a colorful logo appeared. LeBow typed madly.

"How long you been there?"

How calm Handy sounds, Potter reflected. Holding a gun to a girl's eye and he's still working all the angles, cool as can be.

"About a year," LeBow ad-libbed. "You work for Uncle Sam, they move you around a lot." He typed rapidly. His fingers stopped. An error message appeared. "Invalid Search Request."

The more urgent the task . . .

He started again. Finally a map and text appeared and in the corner of the screen a color photo of a skyline.

"Imagine they do. Like that FBI agent who called you. Andy Palmer. He must move a bunch too."

LeBow took a breath to answer but Potter scrawled on a sheet of paper, "Don't respond to name."

"Hell, I'd guess so."

"That *is* his name, right? Andy?"

"I think so. I don't remember. He just told me the code that let me know it was a real call."

"You got codes? That you use like spies?"

"You know, sir, I really oughta get on this project for you."

"What's that river there?"

"In Topeka, you mean?"

"Yeah."

LeBow leaned forward and read the blurb about the city. "The Kaw, you mean. The Kansas River. The one cuts the town in half?"

"Yeah. That's it. Used to go fishing there. Had a uncle lived in that old neighborhood. It was all la-di-da, fancy old houses. Cobblestoned roads, you know."

Henry LeBow was sitting so far forward he was in danger of tumbling off his chair. He read frantically. "Oh, Potwin Place. He's a lucky man, your uncle. Nice houses. But the streets aren't cobblestoned, they're brick." The agent's bald head glistened with silver beads of sweat.

"What's your favorite restaurant there?"

A pause.

"Denny's. I have six children."

"You son of a bitch," Handy growled.

Click.

"Downlink terminated," Tobe called.

LeBow, hands shaking, stared at the phone.

Four heads jammed into the window.

"Did it work?" Frances muttered.

No one ventured a guess. Only Charlie Budd said anything and the most he dared utter was "Oh, brother."

"Home base to Outrider Two."

"Outrider Two," whispered Lieutenant Joey Wilson, standing just beneath the window of the slaughterhouse, in the shadow of the school bus.

"Positions of subjects?"

The trooper lifted his blackened face quickly, glanced inside, then dropped down again.

"Two takers in the main room by the window, Handy's got a gun on one hostage. A Glock. Right against her head. Can't tell if it's cocked. Wilcox doesn't have a weapon in his hands but's got a Glock in his belt. Bonner's got a Mossberg semiauto twelve-gauge. But he's thirty feet from the hostage room. It's a good scenario. Except for the girl in the window."

"Can you take out Handy?"

"Negative. He's behind pipes. Have no clear shot. Bonner keeps going back and forth. Maybe I can acquire him. I don't know."

"Stand by."

They were well past deadline now. Handy could shoot the poor woman at any moment.

"Outrider One? Report."

"Outrider One. I'm at the generator. Charge is armed."

Lord, let us not fail, Tremain thought, and took a deep breath.

"Outrider One?" Tremain called to Pfenninger, whom he pictured beside the command van's generator, the detonating cord to the L-210 in his hand.

"Outrider One here."

"Code word—"

"Outrider Two to home base!" Wilson's energetic voice cut through the airwaves. "Hostage is safe. Repeat. Outrider Two to home base. Subject Handy is standing down. He's put his weapon away. Subject Bonner's taking the girl back to the room with the rest of the hostages."

Tremain looked. The girl was being pulled out of the window.

"Subject Bonner has left her in the hostage room and has returned to the front of the factory."

"Code word Stallion," Tremain said. "All outriders, all teams, Stallion, Stallion, Stallion. Confirm transmission."

They all did.

Dan Tremain—senior HRU commander and a man who had a reputation for thinking fast—composed and then offered a silent prayer to his just and merciful Lord in Christ, thanking Him for sparing the girl's life. But mostly he gave thanks for providing the extra time in which to prepare for the assault that He had assured Tremain would free the poor lambs from the hands of the barbaric Romans.

"Downlink," Tobe announced. "From him."

Potter let the phone ring twice then answered it. "Art?"

"Lou. Creswell just called."

"He thinks you're a prick. He doesn't even know your fucking name."

"I have my enemies. More of them within the government than without, I'm sorry to say. What about it?"

"Okay, it's a deal," Handy said cheerfully. "You got one more hour."

Potter paused, let the silence build up.

"Art," Handy asked uncertainly, "you still there?"

A subtle sigh issued from the negotiator's mouth.

"What'sa matter? You sound like your fucking dog just died."

"Well . . ."

"Come on, talk to me."

"I don't know how to ask this. You were real good about agreeing to give us the extra time. And . . ."

Test the bonds, Potter was thinking. What exactly *is* Handy thinking about me? How close are we?

"Well, ask me what you gotta, Art. Just fucking do it."

"Creswell said he'll need at least until nine-thirty to do the clearance right. He's got to coordinate with the Canadian authorities. I told him to do it within an hour. But he said they can't do it that fast. I feel like I'm letting you down. . . ."

And part of him did, yes—at the lie he was telling, so blatantly, so coldly.

"Nine-thirty?"

A long hesitation.

"Fuck, I can live with that."

"Really, Lou?" Arthur Potter asked, surprised. "Appreciate it."

"Hey, anything for my good buddy Art."

Take advantage of the good mood. He said, "Lou, let me ask you another question."

"Shoot."

Should I push or not?

Angie was watching him. Their eyes met and she mouthed, "Go for it."

"Lou, how about if you let her go? Melanie."

Okay. Art, I'm in a good mood. I'm going to Canada, so you just bought yourself one.

Handy's voice was like a cold razor blade. "Sometimes you ask for too fucking much, you asshole. I'm the one person in the fucking universe you *don't* want to do that to."

The phone went dead.

Potter raised his eyebrows at the outburst. But the room erupted into applause and laughter. Potter hung up the phone and joined in.

Potter clapped LeBow on the back. "Excellent job." He looked at Angie. "Both of you."

Budd said, "You deserve an Oscar for that. Yessir, I'd vote for you."

"M-4?" Potter said. "What's an M-4 priority?"

"Doris and I went to England last year," LeBow explained. "That was a highway, I seem to recall. Did sound good, didn't it?" He was very pleased with himself.

"That radar missile tracking," Budd said. "That sounded pretty cool."

"All made up."

"Oh, brother. He bought it all."

Then they went somber again as Potter gazed out the window at the place where six hostages still remained, safe for at least a couple of hours—if Handy kept his word. Then simultaneously the entire crowd in the van all laughed once more as Tobe Geller, maven of electronics and coldly rational science, whispered reverently, "Papal clearance," and crossed himself expertly like the good Catholic that he apparently was.

7:15 P.M.

"Well, Charlie, what's the news from the front?"

Budd stood outside the van in a gully. He held his cellular phone pressed hard into his ear—as if that would keep anyone from overhearing. Roland Marks's voice tended to boom.

The assistant attorney general was down at the rear

staging area. Budd said, "I'll tell you, it's been a real roller coaster here. Up and down, you know. He's doing some real remarkable things—Agent Potter, I mean."

"Remarkable?" Marks asked sarcastically. "He's brought that girl back to life, has he? A regular Lazarus situation, is it?"

"He's gotten a couple more out safe and he just bought us another couple of hours. He's—"

"Do you have that present for me?" Marks asked evenly.

The door of the van opened and Angie Scapello stepped out.

"Not yet," Budd said, and decided the lie was credible. "Soon. I should go."

"I want that tape within the hour. My friend from the press'll be here then."

"Yessir, that's right," he said. "I'll talk to you later."

He pushed disconnect. And said to Angie, "Bosses. We could do without 'em."

She was carrying two cups of coffee and offered one to him.

"Milk, no sugar. That's how you like it?" she said.

"Agent LeBow has my file too, huh?"

"You live near here, Charlie?"

"My wife and I bought a house about fifteen miles away."

That was good. Work in Meg again.

"I have an apartment in Georgetown. I travel so much it doesn't make sense for me to buy. And just being by myself."

"Never been married?"

"Nope. I'm an old maid."

"Old, there you go again. You must be all of twenty-eight."

She laughed.

"You like life out here in the country?" Angie asked him.

"Sure do. The girls have good schools—I showed you the pictures of my family?"

"You did, yes, Charlie. Twice."

"They have good schools and good teams to be on.

They live for soccer. And it's not expensive, really. I'm thirty-two and own my own house on four acres. You couldn't do that on the East Coast, I don't imagine. I went to New York once and what people pay for apartments there—"

"You faithful to your wife, Charlie?" She turned her warm, brown eyes on him.

He gulped down coffee he had absolutely no taste for. "Yes, I am. And as a matter of fact I've been meaning to talk to you. I think you're an interesting person and what you're doing to help us is real valuable. And I'd have to be a blind man not to see how pretty you are—"

"Thank you, Charlie."

"But I'm not even unfaithful in my mind—like that president was, Jimmy Carter? Or somebody, I don't remember." This was all rehearsed and he wished he didn't have to swallow so often. "Meg and I've had our problems, that's for sure. But who hasn't? Problems're part of a relationship and you get through them just like you get through the good times, and you keep going." He stopped abruptly, forgetting completely the end of his speech, which he improvised as "So there. I just wanted to say that."

Angie stepped closer and touched his arm. She leaned up and kissed his cheek. "I'm very glad you told me that, Charlie. I think fidelity is the most important trait in a relationship. Loyalty. And you don't see much of it nowadays."

He hesitated. "No, I guess you don't."

"I'm going down to the motel and visit the girls and their parents. Would you like to come with me?" She smiled. "As a friend and fellow threat management team member?"

"I'd be delighted." And to Budd's unbounded relief she didn't slip her arm through his as they walked to the van to tell Potter where they would be and then proceeded to the squad car for the short drive to the Days Inn.

They sat in the killing room, the entrance to hell, tears on all their faces.

What was happening now—only a few feet in front of

them—was worse than they'd ever imagined. Let it be over soon, Melanie thought, her fingers twitching this mute plea. For the love of God.

"Don't look," she finally signed to the girls. But they all did look—no one could turn away from this terrible spectacle.

Bear lay atop poor Mrs. Harstrawn, her blouse open, her skirt up to her waist. Numb, Melanie watched the man's naked ass bob up and down. She watched his hands grip one of Mrs. Harstrawn's breasts, as white as his own bloated skin. She watched him kiss her and stick his wet tongue into her unresponsive mouth.

He paused for a moment and looked back into the main room. There, Brutus and Stoat sat before the TV, drinking beer. Laughing. Like Melanie's father and brother would sit around the TV on Sunday, as if the small black box were something magic that allowed them to talk to one another. Then Bear reared up, hooked his arms beneath Mrs. Harstrawn's knees and lifted her legs into the air. He began his ungainly motion once again.

Melanie grew calm as death.

It's time, she decided. They couldn't wait any longer. Never looking away from Bear's closed eyes, she wrote a note on the pad of paper that Brutus had torn from her hands earlier. She folded it tightly and slipped it into Anna's pocket. The girl looked up. Her twin did too.

"Go into corner," Melanie signed. "By gas can."

They didn't want to. They were terrified of Bear, terrified of the horrible thing he was doing. But so emphatic was Melanie's signing, so cold were her eyes that they moved steadily into the corner of the room. Once again Melanie told them to take Mrs. Harstrawn's sweater.

"Tie it around gas can. Go—"

Suddenly Bear leapt up off the teacher and faced Melanie. His bloody organ was upright and glistened red and purple. The overwhelming scent of musk and sweat and woman's fluid made her gag. He paused, his groin only a foot from her face. He reached down and touched her hair. "Stop that fucking spooky shit. Stop . . . with your hands . . . that bullshit." He mimicked signing.

Melanie understood his reaction. It was common. People

have always been frightened by signing. It was why there was such a strong desire to force the deaf to speak and not use sign language—which was a code, a secret language, the hallmark of a mysterious society.

She nodded slowly and lowered her eyes once more to the glistening, erect penis.

Bear strode back to Mrs. Harstrawn, squeezed her breasts, knocked her legs apart, and plunged into her once again. She lifted a hand in a pathetic protest. He slapped it away.

Don't sign. . . .

How could she talk to the girls? Tell the twins what they had to do?

Then she happened to recall her own argot. The language that she had created at age sixteen, when she'd risked getting her knuckles slapped by the teachers—most of them Others—for using ASL or SEE at the Laurent Clerc School. It was a simple language, one that had occurred to her while watching Georg Solti conduct a silent orchestra. In music the meter and rhythm were as much a part of the piece as the melody; she'd kept her hands close to her chin and spoke to her classmates through the shape *and* rhythm of her fingers, combined with facial expressions. She'd shown all her students the basics of the language—when she compared different types of signing—but she didn't know if the twins recalled enough to understand her.

Yet she had no choice. She lifted her hands and moved her fingers in rhythmic patterns.

Anna didn't understand at first and began to respond in ASL.

"No," Melanie instructed, frowning for emphasis. "No signing."

It was vital that she convey her message, for she believed she could save the twins at least, and maybe one more—poor gasping Beverly, or Emily, whose thin white legs Bear had been staring at for long moments before he pulled Donna Harstrawn toward him and spread her legs like a hungry man opening up a package of food.

"Take gas can," Melanie communicated. Somehow. "Tie sweater around it."

After a moment the girls understood. They eased for-

ward. Their tiny hands went to work enwrapping the can
with the colorful sweater.

The can was now enwrapped by the sweater.

"Go out back door. One on left."

The doorway swept clean of dust by the breeze from the
river.

"Afraid."

Melanie nodded but persisted. "Have to."

A faint, heartbreaking nod. Then another. Emily stirred
beside Melanie. The girl was terrified. Melanie took her
hand, behind their backs, out of Bear's view. She finger-
spelled in English. "Y-o-u w-i-l-l b-e n-e-x-t. D-o n-o-t
w-o-r-r-y."

Emily nodded. To the twins Melanie said, "Follow
smell of river." She flared her nostrils. "River. Smell."

A nod from both girls.

"Hold on to sweater and jump into water."

Two no shakes. Emphatic.

Melanie's eyes flared. "Yes!"

Then Melanie looked at the teacher and back to the
girls, explaining silently what could happen to them. And
the twins understood. Anna started to whimper.

Melanie would not allow this. "Stop!" she insisted.
"Now. Go."

The twins were behind Bear. He'd have to stand up and
turn to see them.

Afraid to use her hands, Anna timidly lowered her face
and wiped it on her sleeve. They shook their heads no. In
heartbreaking unison.

Melanie's hand rose and she risked fast fingerspellings
and hand signs. Bear's eyes were closed; he missed the
gestures. "Abbé de l'Epée is out there. Waiting for you."

Their eyes went wide.

De l'Epée?

The savior of the Deaf. A legend. He was Lancelot, he
was King Arthur. For heaven's sake, he was *Tom Cruise!*
He *couldn't* be outside. Yet Melanie's face was so serious, she was so insistent that they offered faint nods of
acquiescence.

"You must find him. Give him note in your pocket."

"Where is he?" Anna signed.

"He's older man, heavy. Gray hair. Glasses and blue sports coat." They nodded enthusiastically (though this was hardly how they pictured the legendary abbé). "Find him and give him note."

Bear looked up and Melanie continued to lift her hand innocently to wipe her red, but dry, eyes as if she'd been crying. He looked down again and continued. Melanie was grateful she couldn't hear the piggish grunts she knew issued from his fat mouth.

"Ready?" she asked the girls.

Indeed they were; they would leap into flames if it meant they could meet their idol. Melanie looked again at Bear, the sweat dripping off his face and falling like rain on poor Mrs. Harstrawn's cheeks and jiggling breasts. His eyes closed. The moment of finishing was near—something Melanie had read about but couldn't quite comprehend.

"Take shoes off. And tell de l'Epée to be careful."

Anna nodded. "I love you," she signed. Suzie did too.

Melanie looked out the doorway and saw Brutus and Stoat, far across the slaughterhouse, staring at the TV. She nodded twice. The girls picked up their gas-can life preserver and vanished around the corner. Melanie watched Bear to see if their passage was silent. Apparently it was.

To distract him she leaned forward, enduring the ugly man's ominous stare, and slowly, cautiously, with her burgundy sleeve wiped the sheen of his sweat from the teacher's face. He was perplexed by the gesture then angered. He shoved her back against the wall. Her head hit the tile with a thud. There she sat until he finished and lay gasping. Finally he rolled off her. Melanie saw a slick pool on the woman's thigh. Blood too. Bear glanced furtively into the other room. He had escaped undetected; Brutus and Stoat hadn't seen. He sat up. He zipped his filthy jeans and pulled down Mrs. Harstrawn's skirt, roughly buttoned her blouse.

Bear leaned forward and put his face inches from Melanie's. She managed to hold his eye—it was terrifying but she would do anything to keep him from looking around the room. He spat out, "You . . . word about . . . you're . . ."

Delay, stall. Buy time for the twins.

She frowned and shook her head.

He tried again, words spitting from his mouth.

Again she shook her head, pointed to her ear. He boiled in frustration.

Finally, she leaned away and pointed to the dusty floor. He wrote, *Say anything and your dead.*

She nodded slowly.

He obliterated the message and buttoned his shirt.

Sometimes all of us, even Others, are mute and deaf and blind as the dead; we perceive only what our desires allow us to see. This is a terrible burden and a danger but can also be, as now, a small miracle. For Bear rose unsteadily, tucked in his shirt, and looked around the killing room with a glazed look of contentment on his flushed face. Then he strode out, never noticing that only four shoes remained in place of the twins and that the girls were gone, floating free of this terrible place.

For a few years I was nothing but Deaf.

I lived Deaf, I ate Deaf, I breathed it.

Melanie is speaking to de l'Epée.

She has gone into her music room because she cannot bear to think about Anna and Suzie, leaping into the waters of the Arkansas River, dark as a coffin. They're better off, she tells herself. She remembers the way Bear looked at the girls. Whatever happens, they're better off.

De l'Epée shifts in his chair and asks what she meant by being nothing but Deaf.

"When I was a junior the Deaf movement came to Laurent Clerc. Deaf with a capital *D*. Oralism was out and at last the school began teaching Signed Exact English. Which is sort of a half-assed compromise. Eventually, after I graduated, they agreed to switch to ASL. That's American Sign."

"I'm interested in languages. Tell me about it." (Would he say this? It's *my* fantasy; yes, he would.)

"ASL comes from the world's first school for the deaf, founded in France in the 1760s by your namesake. Abbé

Charles Michel de l'Epée. He was like Rousseau—he felt that there was a primordial human language. A language that was pure and absolute and unfalteringly clear. It could express every emotion directly and it would be so transparent that you couldn't use it to lie or deceive anyone."

De l'Epée smiles at this.

"With French Sign Language, oh, the Deaf came into their own. A teacher from de l'Epée's school, Laurent Clerc, came to America in the early 1800s with Thomas Gallaudet—he was a minister from Connecticut—and set up a school for the deaf in Hartford. French Sign Language was used there but it got mixed with local signing—especially the dialect used on Martha's Vineyard, where there was a lot of hereditary deafness. That's how American Sign Language came about. That, more than anything, allowed the Deaf to live normal lives. See, you have to develop language—some language, either sign or spoken—by age three. Otherwise you basically end up retarded."

De l'Epée looks at her somewhat cynically. "It seems to me that you've rehearsed this."

She can only laugh.

"Once ASL hit the school, as I was saying, I lived for the Deaf movement. I learned the party line. Mostly because of Susan Phillips. It was amazing. I was a student teacher at the time. She saw my eyes flickering up and down as I read somebody's lips. She came up to me and said, 'The word "hearing" means only one thing to me. It's the opposite of who I am.' I felt ashamed. She later said that the term 'hard of hearing' should infuriate us because it defines us in terms of the Other community. 'Oral' is even worse because the Oral deaf want to pass. They haven't come out yet. If somebody's Oral, Susan said, we have to 'rescue' them.

"I knew what she was talking about because for years I'd tried to pass. The rule is 'Plan ahead.' You're always thinking about what's coming, second-guessing what questions you'll be asked, steering people toward streets with noisy traffic or construction, so you'll have an excuse to ask them to shout or repeat what they say.

"But after I met Susan I rejected all that. I was anti-Oral, I was anti-mainstreaming. I taught ASL. I became a poet and gave performances at theaters of the deaf."

"Poet?"

"I did that as a substitute for my music. It seemed the closest I could hope for."

"What are signed poems like?" he asks.

She explains that they "rhymed" not sonically but because the hand shape of the last word of the line was similar to that of the last words in preceding lines. Melanie recited:

"Eight gray birds, sitting in dark.
Cold wind blows, it isn't kind.
Sitting on wire, they lift their wings
And sail off into billowy clouds."

"Dark" and "kind" share a flat, closed hand, the palm facing the body of the signer. "Wings" and "clouds" involve similar movements from the shoulders up into the air above the signer.

De l'Epée listens, fascinated. He watches her sign several other poems. Melanie puts almond-scented cream on them every night and her nails are smooth and translucent as lapidaried stones.

She stopped in mid line. "Oh," she muses, "I did it all. The National Association of the Deaf, the Bicultural Center, the National Athletic Association of the Deaf."

He nods. (She wishes he'd tell her about his life. Is he married? [Please no!] Does he have children? Is he older than I imagine, or younger?)

"I had my career all laid out before me. I was going to be the first deaf woman farm foreman."

"Farm?"

"Ask me about dressing corn. About anhydrous ammonia. You want to know about wheat? Red wheat comes from the Russian steppes. But it's name isn't political—oh, not in Kansas, nosir. It's the color. 'Amber waves of grain . . .' Ask me about the advantages of no-till planting and how to fill out UCC financing statements to collateralize crops that haven't grown yet. 'All the accretions and appurtenances upon said land . . .' "

Her father, she explains, owned six hundred and sixty

acres in south-central Kansas. He was a lean man who wore an exhaustion that many people confused with ruggedness. His problem wasn't a lack of willingness but a lack of talent, which he called luck. And he acknowledged—to himself alone—that he needed help from many quarters. He of course put most of his stock in his son but farms are big business now. Harold Charrol planned to invest both son, Danny, and daughter, Melanie, with third-share interests and watch them all prosper as a corporate family.

She had been reluctant about these plans but the prospect of working with her brother had an appeal to it. The unfazable boy had become an easygoing young man, nothing at all like their embittered father. While Harold would mutter darkly about fate when a thresher blade snapped and he stood paralyzed with anger, staring at the splintered wood, Danny might jump down out of the cockpit, vanish for a time, and return with a six-pack and some sandwiches for an impromptu picnic. "We'll fix the son of a bitch tonight. Let's eat."

For a time she believed this could be a pleasant life. She took some ag extension courses and even sent an article to *Silent News* about farm life and Deafness.

But then, last summer, Danny'd had the accident, and lost both the ability, and the will, to work the place. Charrol, with the desperate legitimacy of a man needing heirs, turned to Melanie. She was a woman, yes (this a handicap somewhat worse than her audiologic one), but an educated, hardworking one at least.

Melanie, he planned, would become his full partner. And why not? Since age seven she'd ridden in the air-conditioned cab of the big John Deere, helping him shift up through the infinite number of gears. She'd donned goggles and mask and gloves like a rustic surgeon and filled the ammonia tank, she'd sat in on his meetings with United Produce, and she'd driven with him to the roadside stops, known only to insiders, where the illegal migrant workers hid, waiting for day jobs at harvest.

It's a question of belonging and what God does to make sure those that oughta stay someplace do. Well, your place is here, working at what you can do, where your,

*you know, problem doesn't get you into trouble. God's
will. . . . So you'll be home then.*

Tell him, Melanie thinks.

Yes! If you never tell another soul, tell de l'Epée.

"There's something," she begins, "I want to say."

His placid face gazes at her.

"It's a confession."

"You're too young to have anything to confess."

"After the poetry recital in Topeka I wasn't going back
to the school right away. I was going to see my brother in
St. Louis. He's in the hospital. He's having some surgery
tomorrow."

De l'Epée nods.

"But before I went to see him there was something I
planned to do in Topeka. I had an appointment to see
somebody."

"Tell me."

Should she? Yes, no?

Yes, she decides. She has to. But just as she is about to
speak, something intrudes.

The smell of the river?

The thud of approaching feet.

Brutus?

Alarmed, she opened her eyes. No, there was nothing.
The slaughterhouse was peaceful. None of their three captors was nearby. She closed her eyes and struggled back
into the music room. But de l'Epée was gone.

"Where are you?" she cried. But realized that though
her lips were moving she could no longer hear any words.

No! I don't want to leave. Come back, please. . . .

Then Melanie realized that it wasn't the breeze from
the river that booted them out of the room; it was her own
self. She had grown timid once again, ashamed, and could
not confess.

Even to the man who seemed more than willing to listen to anything she wanted to say, however foolish, however dark.

They caught the glint of light about fifty yards away.

Joe Silbert and Ted Biggins walked silently through the
field on the left flank of the slaughterhouse. Silbert

pointed to the light, a flash off the field glasses or a piece of equipment dangling from the belt of one of the hostage rescue troopers, a reflection from the brilliant halogen lights.

Biggins grumbled that the lights were too bright. There'd be lens flare, he was worried.

"You want me to go fucking shut them off?" Silbert whispered. He wanted a cigarette badly. They continued through the woods until they broke into an open field. Silbert looked through the camera, pushing the zoom button. The troopers, he could see, were clustered on a brush-filled ridge overlooking the slaughterhouse. One of them—hidden behind the school bus—was actually at the slaughterhouse, hovering just below a window.

"Damn, they're good," Silbert whispered. "One of the best teams I've ever seen."

"Fucking lights," muttered Biggins.

"Let's get going."

As they walked through the field Silbert looked for patrolling troops. "I thought we had baby-sitters all over the place."

"Those lights're really a pain."

"This is almost too easy," Silbert muttered.

"Oh, my God." Biggins was looking up in the air.

"Perfecto," Silbert whispered, laughing softly.

The men gazed up at the top of the windmill.

"It'll get us above the lights," Biggins the sticking record said.

Forty feet in the air. They'd have a spectacular view of the field. Silbert grinned and began to climb. At the top they stood on the rickety platform. The mill was long abandoned and the blades were missing. It rocked back and forth in the wind.

"That going to be a problem?"

Biggins pulled a retractable monopod from his pocket and extended it, screwing the joints tight. "So what can I do about it? Like, I've got a Steadicam in my fucking pocket?"

The view was excellent. Silbert could see troopers were clustered on the left side of the slaughterhouse. With grim respect he thought of Agent Arthur Potter, who'd looked

him in the eye and said there'd be no assault. It was obvious the troopers were getting ready for an imminent kick-
in.

Stillwell took a small sponge-covered microphone from
his pocket and held it in his hand. He spoke into his
scrambled cellular phone and called the remote transmission van, which was back near the main press tent. "You
cocksucker," he said to Kellog when the man answered.
"I was hoping they'd bust your ass."

"Naw, I told that trooper they could fuck your wife and
they let me go."

"The other guys, they're at the press table?"

"Yep."

Silbert had in fact never told any of the other reporters
about the press pool arrangement. He and Biggins, Kellog
and Bianco and the two reporters now sitting at the pool
site, pretending to type stories on the gutted Compaq,
were all employees of KFAL in Kansas City.

Biggins plugged the mike into the camera and unfolded
the parabolic antenna. He clipped it to the handrail of the
windmill and began speaking into the mike, "Testing,
testing, testing . . ."

"Cut the crap, Silbert, you gonna give us some pictures?"

"Ted's sending the level now." Silbert gestured toward
the antenna and Biggins adjusted it while he spoke. "I'm
switching to radio," the anchorman said, then took the
microphone and shoved an earphone in his left ear.

After a moment Kellog said, "There. Five by five. Jesus H.
Christ, we got the visual. Where the fuck are you? In a helicopter?"

"The pros know," Silbert said. "Cut into the feed. I'm
ready to roll. Let's do it before we get shot down."

There was a staticky click and he heard a Toyota commercial suddenly cut off in mid-disclaimer. "And now
from Crow Ridge, Kansas," the baritone announcer said,
"we have a live report from Channel 9 anchorman Joe Silbert with exclusive footage from the kidnaping scene,
where a number of students from the Laurent Clerc
School for the Deaf and two teachers are being held by escaped convicts. Let's go live to you, Joe."

"Ron, we're overlooking the slaughterhouse in which the girls and their teachers are being held. As you can see, there are literally hundreds of troopers surrounding the building. The police have set up a series of those brilliant halogen lights to shine into the slaughterhouse windows, presumably to prevent any sniping from inside.

"The lights and the presence of the troopers, however, didn't prevent the murder of one of the hostages on that spot right about there, in the center of your screen, about six hours ago. A trooper told me that the girl was released by the fugitives and was walking down to join her family and friends when a single shot rang out and she was hit squarely in the back. She was, as you said, Ron, deaf, and the trooper told me he believed she'd used sign language to plead for help and to tell her family that she loved them."

"Joe, do you know the identity of that girl?"

"No, we don't, Ron. The authorities are being very slow in releasing any information."

"How many hostages are involved?"

"At this point it seems there are four students remaining inside and two teachers."

"So some have gotten out?"

"That's right. Three have been released so far, in exchange for demands by the kidnapers. We don't know what concessions the authorities have made."

"Joe, what can you tell us about those policemen off to the side there?"

"Ron, those are members of the elite Kansas State Police Hostage Rescue Unit. We've had no official word about an attempted rescue but I've covered a number of situations like this before and my impression is that they're preparing for an assault."

"What will happen, do you think, Joe? In terms of the assault? How will it proceed?"

"It's hard to say without knowing where the hostages are being kept, what the firepower of the men inside is, and so on."

"Could you speculate for us?"

"Sure, Ron," Silbert said. "I'd be happy to."

And he signaled to Biggins, using the hand gestures

they'd developed between them. The sign meant "Zoom in."

They got down to the business at hand, for they didn't know how much time remained until the next deadline.

Captain Dan Tremain spoke on the scrambled radio to Bravo team and learned that they had found a breachable door near the dock in the back of the slaughterhouse but it was in full view of a skiff containing two armed troopers. The boat was anchored about twenty yards offshore.

"They'll see us if we get any closer."

"Any other access to the door?"

"Nosir."

Outrider Two, however, had some good news. Glancing into the plant, Trooper Joey Wilson had scanned the far wall—the southeast side—of the slaughterhouse and saw that, just opposite the fire door that Alpha team was going to breach, was a large piece of sloppily mounted plasterboard. He wondered if it covered a second fire door. The initial exterior surveillance hadn't revealed it. Tremain sent another trooper under the dock to the far side of the building. He made his way to the place Wilson mentioned and reported that it was in fact a door, invisible because it was overgrown with ivy.

Tremain ordered the trooper to drill through the door with a silenced Dremel tool fitted with a long, thin titanium sampling bit. Examining the core samples he found that the door was only an inch thick and had been weakened with wet rot and termite and carpenter ant tunneling. There was a two-inch gap and then he struck plasterboard, which proved to be only three-eighths inch thick. The whole assembly was far weaker than the door on the opposite side. Small cutting charges would rip it open easily.

Tremain was ecstatic. This was even better than going through the loading-dock door, because opposing door entry allowed for immediate dynamic crossfire. The takers wouldn't have a chance to respond. Tremain conferred with Carfallo and divided the men into two new teams. Bravo would make its way under the dock to the southeast side of the slaughterhouse. Alpha would position itself at the north door, further to the back but closer to the hostages.

Upon entry, Alpha would split in two groups, three men going for the hostages, three advancing on the takers, while the four-man Bravo team would enter through the south door and engage the HTs from behind.

Tremain considered the plan: Deep gullies to cover their approach, absolute surprise, stun then flash grenades, crossfire. It was a good scenario.

"Home base to all teams and outriders. On my mark it will be forty-five minutes to green-light order. Are you ready? Counting from my five. . . . Five, four, three, two, one, mark."

The troopers acknowledged the synchronization.

He would—

An urgent, staticky message: "Bravo leader to home base. We have movement here. From the loading dock. Somebody's rabbiting."

"Identify."

"Can't tell. They're slipping out from under the loading-dock door. I can't see clearly. It's just motion."

"An HT?"

"Unknown. The dock's shot to hell and there's crap all over it."

"Mount your suppressors."

"Yessir."

The men had suppressors on their H&Ks—big tubes of silencers. For at least a clip or two of ammunition the sound of the guns would be merely a whispering rattle and with this wind the troopers in the skiff would probably not hear a sound.

"Acquire target. Semiauto fire."

"Acquired."

"What's it look like, Bravo leader?"

"Real hard to make him out but he's wearing a red, white, and blue shirt. I can probably neutralize but can't make a positive ID. Whoever it is, he's staying real low to the ground. Advise."

"If you can make a positive ID on a taker you've got a green light to take him out."

"Yessir."

"Keep him acquired. And wait."

Tremain called Outrider Two, who risked a look through the window. The Trooper responded, "If anybody's bolting, it's Bonner. I can't see him. Only Handy and Wilcox."

Bonner. The rapist. Tremain would love the chance to bring God's revenge down upon him.

"Bravo leader. Status? He's going into the water?"

"Wait, yeah, there he goes. Just slipped in. Lost him. No, got him again. Should I tell the officers in the boat? He'll float right past them."

Tremain debated.

"Home base, do you copy?"

If it was Bonner he might get away. But at least he wouldn't be inside for the assault. One less person to worry about. If—though it seemed impossible—it was a hostage there was a chance she might drown. The current was swift here and the channel deep. But to rescue her he'd have to give away his presence, which would mean calling off the operation and jeopardizing the other hostages. But no, he thought. It couldn't be a hostage. There was no way a little girl could escape from three armed men.

"Negative, Bravo team leader, do not advise the troopers in the boat. Repeat, do not advise of subject's presence."

"I copy, home base. By the way, I don't think we have to worry about him. He's going straight out to mid-river. Doubt we'll ever see him again."

III

ACCEPTABLE
CASUALTIES

7:46 P.M.

"What's that?"

Crow Ridge sheriff's deputy Arnold Shaw didn't know and he didn't care.

The lean thirty-year-old, a law enforcer all his young working life, had been in his share of boats. Dropping stinkers for catfish, trolling for bass and muskie. He'd even been water-skiing a couple of times down at Lake of the Ozarks. And he'd never once been as seasick as he was right now.

Oh, man. This is torture.

He and Buzzy Marboro were anchored twenty yards or so into the river, keeping their eyes "glued like epoxy" on the dock of the slaughterhouse, as their boss, Dean Stillwell, had commanded. The wind was bad, even for Kansas, and the shallow skiff bobbed and twisted like a Tilt-A-Whirl carnival ride.

"I'm not doing too well," Shaw muttered.

"There," Marboro said. "Look."

"I don't want to look."

But look he did, where Marboro was pointing. Ten yards downstream, something was floating away from them. The men were armed with battered Remington riot guns and Marboro drew a lazy target at the bobbing mass.

They'd heard a splash coming from the dock not long ago and had looked carefully but found no takers escaping through the water.

"If somebody did jump in—"

"We woulda seen him," Shaw muttered through the wind.

"—he'd be right about there by now. Just where that thing is. *Whatever* it is."

Shaw struggled to rid himself of memories of last night's dinner—his wife's tuna casserole. "I'm not feeling too well here, Buzz. What's your point, exactly?"

"I see a hand!" Marboro was standing up.

"Oh, no, don't do that. We're moving round enough as it is. Sit your heinie down."

Tuna and cream of mushroom soup and peas and those canned fried onions on top.

Oh, man, can't keep it down much longer.

"Looks like a hand and look at that thing—it's red and white—hell, I think it's one of the hostages got away!"

Shaw turned and looked at the debris, just above the surface of the choppy water, rising and falling. Each glimpse lasted no more than a few seconds. He couldn't tell what it was exactly. It looked sort of like a net float, except, as Buzz Marboro had pointed out, it was red and white. Blue too, he now saw.

And moving away from them, straight into midstream, pretty damn fast.

"Don't you see a hand?" Marboro said.

"No. . . . Wait. You know, it *does* look like a hand. Sorta." Reluctantly, and to the great distress of his churning gut, Arnie Shaw rose to his feet. That made him feel, he estimated, about a thousand times worse.

"I can't tell. A branch maybe."

"I don't know. Look how fast it's moving. It'll be in Wichita 'fore too long." Shaw decided he'd rather have a tooth pulled than be seasick. No—two teeth.

"Maybe it's just something the takers threw out to, you know, distract us. We go after it and they get away out the back door."

"Or maybe it's just trash," Shaw said, sitting down. "Hey, what're we thinking of? If they were friendlies they wouldn't've just floated past without calling for help. Hell, we've got our uniforms on. They'd know we're deputies."

"Sure. What'm I thinking of?" Marboro said, sitting down too.

One pair of vigilant eyes returned to the ass end of the slaughterhouse. The other pair closed slowly, as their owner swallowed in a desperate effort to calm his stomach. "I'm dying," Shaw whispered.

Exactly ten seconds later the eyes opened. "Oh, son of a bitch," Shaw spat out slowly. He sat up straight.

"You just remembered too?" Marboro was nodding.

Shaw *had* in fact just remembered—that the hostages were deaf and mute and wouldn't be able to call out for help to save their souls, no matter how close they'd passed by the skiff.

That was one of the reasons for his dismay. The other was that Shaw knew that while he himself had been an intercollegiate state finals swim champion three years running, Buzz Marboro couldn't dog-paddle more than ten yards.

Breathing deeply—not for the impending swim but merely to keep his turbulent stomach at bay—Shaw shed his weapons, body armor, helmet, boots. A final breath. He dove headfirst into the raging, murky water and streaked toward the disappearing flotsam as it headed rapidly southeast in the ornery current.

Arthur Potter gazed at the window where he'd first seen Melanie.

Then at the window where he'd almost seen her shot.

"I think we're moving up against the wall here," he said slowly. "If we're lucky we're going to get maybe one or two more out but that's it. Then we'll either have to get him to surrender or have HRT go in. Somebody tell me the weather." Potter was hoping for a hellsapoppin' storm to justify a longer delay in finding a helicopter.

Derek Elb turned a switch and the Weather Channel snapped on. Potter learned that the rest of the night would be much the same—windy, with clearing skies. No rain. Winds would be out of the northwest at fifteen to twenty miles an hour.

"We'll have to rely on the wind for an excuse," LeBow said. "And even that's going to be dicey. Fifteen miles an hour? In the service Handy's probably flown in Hueys that've landed in gusts twice that."

Dean Stillwell called in for Henry LeBow, his laconic voice tripping out of the speaker above their heads.

"Yes?" the intelligence officer answered, leaning into his microphone.

"Agent Potter said to relay any information about the takers to you?"

"That's right," LeBow said.

Potter picked up the mike and asked what Stillwell had learned.

"Well, one of the troopers here has a good view inside, sort of an angle. And he said that Handy and Wilcox are walking around inside, looking the place over real carefully."

"Looking it over?"

"Pushing on pipes and machinery. It's like they're looking for something."

"Any idea what?" LeBow asked.

"Nope. I thought maybe they're checking out places to hide."

Potter nodded at Budd, recalling it had been the captain's idea that the takers might don rescue-worker uniforms during the surrender or HRT assault. It also wasn't unheard of for takers to, say, leave a back window open, then hide inside closets or crawl spaces for a day or two until law enforcers concluded they were long gone.

LeBow wrote down the information and thanked Stillwell. Potter said, "I want to make sure everybody's got pictures of the takers. And we'll have to tell Frank and the HRT to go through the place with a fine-tooth comb if it looks like an escape."

He sat in his chair once more, staring out at the factory.

"By the way," Stillwell returned over the radio. "I'm having chow brought in for the troopers and the Heartland's delivering you all's supper any time now."

"Thank you, Dean."

"Heartland? All right," Derek Elb said, looking particularly pleased.

Potter's mind, though, wasn't on food. He was thinking something far graver—whether or not he should meet with Handy. He felt the deadlines compressing, sensed somehow that Handy was growing testy and would start making nonnegotiable ultimatums. Face to face, Potter might be able to wear the convict down more efficiently than through their phone conversations.

Thinking too: It might give me a chance to see Melanie.

It might give me a chance to save her.

Yet a meeting between the taker and the incident commander was the most dangerous form of negotiating. There was the physical risk, of course; hostage takers' feelings, both positive and negative, are their most extreme about the negotiator. They often believe, sometimes subconsciously, that killing the negotiator will give them power they don't otherwise have, that the troopers will fall into chaos or that someone less daunting will take the negotiator's place. Even without violence, however, there's a danger that the negotiator will, in the taker's eyes, shrink in authority and stature and lose his opponent's respect.

Potter leaned against the window. What's inside you, Handy? What's making the wheels go round?

Something's happening in that cold brain of yours.

When you talk I hear silence.

When you don't say a word I hear your voice.

When you smile I see . . . what? What *do* I see? Ah, that's the problem. I just don't know.

The door swung open and the smell of food filled the room. A young deputy from the Crow Ridge Sheriff's Department brought in several boxes, filled with plastic containers of food and cartons of coffee.

Potter's appetite returned suddenly as the trooper set out the containers. He expected tasteless diner fare—hot beef sandwiches and Jell-O. But the trooper pointed to each of the dishes as he laid them out and said, "That's cherry mos, that's zwieback, bratwurst, goat and lamb pie, sauerbraten, dill potatoes."

Derek Elb explained, "Heartland's a famous Mennonite restaurant. People drive there from all over the state."

For ten minutes, they ate, largely in silence. Potter tried to remember the names of the dishes to tell Cousin Linden when he returned to the Windy City. She collected exotic recipes. He was just finishing his second cup of coffee when, from the corner of his eye, he saw Tobe stiffen as a radio transmission came in. "What?" the young agent said in shock into his microphone. "Repeat that, Sheriff."

Potter turned to him.

"One of Dean's men just fished the twins out of the river!"

A collective gasp. Then, spontaneous applause erupted in the van. The intelligence officer plucked the two Post-It tabs representing the girls off the chart and moved them to the margin. He took down their pictures, which joined Jocylyn's, Shannon's, and Kielle's in the "Released" folder of hostage bios.

"They're being checked for hypothermia but they look fine otherwise. Like drowned rats, he said, but we're not supposed to tell the girls that."

"Call the hotel," Potter instructed. "Tell their parents."

Tobe, listening into his headset, laughed. He looked up. "They're on their way over, Arthur. They're insisting on seeing you."

"Me?"

"If you're an older man with glasses and a dark sports coat. Only they think your name is de l'Epée. . . ."

Potter shook his head. "Who?"

Frances laughed briefly. "Abbé de l'Epée. He created the first widely used sign language."

"Why would they call me that?"

Frances shrugged. "I have no idea. He's sort of a patron saint for the Deaf."

The girls arrived five minutes later. Adorable twins, wrapped up in colorful Barney blankets, no less (another of Stillwell's miracles). They no longer resembled wet rodents at all but girls more awestruck than scared as they stared at Potter. In halting sign language they explained through Frances about how Melanie had gotten them out of the slaughterhouse.

"Melanie?" Angie asked, nodding toward Potter. "I was wrong. Seems you do have an ally inside."

Did Handy know what she'd done? Potter wondered. How much more resistance would he tolerate before the payback? And how lethal would it be this time?

His heart froze as he saw Frances Whiting's eyes go wide with horror. She turned to him. "The girls didn't understand exactly what was going on but I think one of them was raping the teacher."

"Melanie?" Potter asked quickly.

"No. Donna Harstrawn."

"Oh, my good Lord, no," Budd muttered. "And they saw it, those girls?"

"Bonner?" Angie asked.

Potter's face showed none of the anguish he felt. He nodded. Of course it would be Bonner. His eyes strayed to the pictures of Beverly and Emily. Both young, both feminine.

And then to the photo of Melanie.

Angie asked the girls if Handy had, in effect, set Bonner on the woman, or if the big man had been acting by himself.

Frances watched the signing, then said, "Bear—that's what they're calling Bonner—looked around a lot while he was doing it. Like he didn't want to get caught. They think Brutus—Handy—would have been mad if he'd seen him."

"Is Brutus friendly with any of you?" Angie asked the twins.

"No. He's terrible. He just looks at us with cold eyes, like somebody in one of Shannon's cartoons. He beat up Melanie."

"Is she all right?"

One girl nodded.

Angie shook her head. "This isn't good." She looked at the diagram of the factory. "They're not that far apart, the hostages and the takers, but there doesn't seem to be *any* Stockholming going on with Handy."

The more I know about them the more I want to kill them.

Potter asked about guns and the tools and the TV. But the little girls could offer nothing new. Then one of them handed him a slip of paper. It was soggy but the lettering, written in the waterproof markers Derek had provided, was clear enough. "It's from Melanie," he said, then read out loud: *"Dear de l'Epée: There is so much to write to*

*you. But no time. Be very careful of Handy. He's evil—
more evil than anything. You should know: Handy and
Wilcox are friends. Handy hates Bear (the fat one). Bear
is greedy."*

LeBow asked for the paper so he could type it into the
computer. "It's disintegrating," Potter told him. He read
aloud again as the intelligence officer typed.

One of the twins stepped forward and signed timidly.
Potter smiled and glanced queryingly at Frances.

"They want your autograph," she said.

"Mine?"

In perfect unison they nodded. Potter took a pen from
his shirt pocket, the silver fountain pen that he always
carried with him.

"They're expecting," Frances continued, " 'Abbé de
l'Epée.' "

"Ah, yes. Of course. And that's what they'll have. One
for each."

The girls looked at the two slips of paper and carried
them reverently when they left. One girl paused and
signed to Frances.

She said, "Melanie said something else. She said to tell
you to be careful."

Be forewarned. . . .

"Show me how to say 'Thank you. You're very
brave.' "

Frances did, and Potter mimicked the words with halting gestures. The girls broke into identical smiles then
took Frances's hands as she escorted them to a trooper
outside for the drive to the Days Inn.

Budd sat down next to Potter. "Why," he asked, "would
Melanie tell us that?" He pointed to the note. "About
Bonner being greedy, about the other two being friends?"

"Because she thinks there's something we can do with
it," Angie said.

"What?"

Potter looked down at the soggy slip of paper. It was
signed, *"Love, Melanie C."*—which was the reason he
hadn't shown the note itself to Henry LeBow. He now
folded it up, put the damp paper in his pocket.

"Look up Bonner," Potter instructed.

He read from the screen. Ray "Sonny" Bonner had led a useless life. He'd done time for sex offenses and minor robberies, domestic violence, public disorderliness. Lust-driven, not bright. He was a snitch too; he'd testified against his partner at a robbery trial ten years ago.

Potter and Angie looked up at each other. They smiled.

"Perfect."

The decision had been made. Potter would not meet with Handy face to face. A new strategy had presented itself. Riskier, yes. But perhaps better.

Charlie Budd was suddenly aware that both Angie and Potter were looking at him, studying him.

"What do *you* think, Henry?" Potter asked.

"Say—" Budd began uneasily.

"I think he's perfect," LeBow offered. "Earnest, straightforward. And he's got a great baritone."

Potter said, "You've got quite a performance ahead of you, Charlie."

"Me?" The young captain looked stricken. "How d'you mean that, exactly?"

"You're taking over the negotiation."

"What?"

"And I want you to talk to Handy about surrendering."

"Yessir," Budd answered Potter. Then: "You're kidding."

"You're perfect, Charlie," Angie said.

Potter said, "I've brought up the subject with him. Now it's time to raise surrender as a realistic possibility. Of course he'll say no. But it'll be in his mind as an option. He'll start to weigh the possibilities."

"There'll be a little more to it than that, though," LeBow said, eyes as ever on his screen.

"We're upping the ante," Potter said, and began to jot notes on a yellow pad.

"You know, I'm thinking I wouldn't be very good at this."

"You ever do any acting?" Angie asked.

"I dress up like Santa on Christmas for my kids and my brother's. That's it. Never been on stage, never wanted to be."

"I'll give you a script." Potter thought for a moment,

then tore off the top sheets of the yellow pad and began again, writing meticulous notes: two pages' worth of dense writing.

"This is the gist of it. Just ad-lib. Can you read it okay?"

Budd scanned the sheets. "Sure, only I don't think I'm ready. I should practice or something."

"No time for practice," Potter told him. "Just let me give you a few pointers in negotiations."

"You're serious about this, aren't you?"

"Listen, Charlie. Concentrate. You've got to break through his barriers quickly and get him to believe this." He tapped the yellow paper.

Budd's face grew still and he sat forward in front of the desk on which rested the cellular phone.

"Now I want you to echo things he says. He'll say he wants ice cream. You say, 'Ice cream, sure.' He'll say he's angry. You say, 'Angry, are you?' It shows you're interested in what he says without expressing judgment. It wears him down and makes him think. Do it selectively, though. Not every comment or you'll antagonize him."

Budd nodded. He was sweating fiercely.

Angie offered, "Acknowledge his feelings but don't sympathize with him."

"Right," Potter continued. "He's the enemy. We don't sanction violence and therefore he's doing something wrong. But you should explain that you understand why he feels the way he does. Got it? Don't ramble. You have to be aware of how you sound and how fast you're talking. I'll tell you right now you'll be going way too fast. Make a conscious effort to talk slowly and deliberately. To you it'll feel like you're underwater."

Angie said, "If you ask him a question and he doesn't respond just let the silence run up. Don't let pauses rattle you."

"Don't let him manipulate you. He'll do it intentionally and subconsciously—using threats, fast speech, craziness, and silence. Just keep your mind on your goal." Again Potter, rather solemnly this time, tapped the yellow paper. "Most important, don't let him get to you. Let him rant and say terrible things but don't get shook up. Let him laugh at you. Let him insult you. It rolls off you. You're above it all." Potter leaned forward and whispered, "He might tell you he's going to kill all those girls. He may even fire the gun off and let you think he's shot someone. He might tell you he's going to torture them or rape them. Don't let it affect you."

"What do I say?" Budd said desperately. "If he says that, what do I say?"

"It's best not to say anything at all. If you feel compelled to respond you say simply that it wouldn't be in the best interests of a solution to do that."

"Oh, brother."

Potter looked at his watch. "Let's get this show on the road. Ready?" Potter asked.

The young captain nodded.

"Push button one."

"What?"

"It's on speed dial," Tobe explained. "Push number one."

"And then I just talk to him?"

"You understand the script?" Potter asked.

Budd nodded again. Potter pointed to the phone. "Oh, brother." He reached for the phone, dialed.

"Uplink," Tobe whispered.

"Hey. How you doing, Art?" The voice came through the speakers above their heads. Handy seemed to be smirking.

"This is Charlie Budd. Is this Lou Handy?"

"The fuck're you?"

Budd's eyes were on the sheet in front of him. "I'm with the U.S. attorney's office."

"The hell you say."

"I'd like to talk to you for a few minutes."

"Where's Art?"

"He's not here."

"What the fuck's going on?"

Budd swallowed. Come on, Charlie, Potter thought. No time for stage fright. He tapped the pad before Budd. "Going on?" the captain echoed. "What do you mean?"

"I only want to talk to *him*."

"To who?"

"Art Potter. Who the fuck do you think?"

Budd took a deep breath. "Well, why don'tcha talk to me? I'm not such a bad guy."

"U.S. attorney?"

"That's right. I want to talk to you about surrendering."

Slow down, Potter wrote.

"Oh, a shyster with a sense of humor. Well, fuck you."

Budd's face was relaxing. "Hey, don'tcha like lawyers?"

"I love 'em."

Budd said, "You wanta hear a joke, Lou?"

Potter and LeBow looked at each other, eyebrows raised.

"Sure, Charlie."

"A woman goes to her gynecologist and asks can somebody get pregnant by having anal sex. And the doctor says sure you can, where do you think lawyers come from?"

Handy roared with laughter. Budd's face burned crimson.

Potter had never in twenty years of negotiating shared a joke with a taker. Maybe he'd rewrite his instruction book.

Budd continued. "Arthur's seeing about getting you some helicopter or 'nother. Something about pontoons. It should be here soon."

"It fucking well better be here in one hour and twenty fucking minutes."

"Well, all I know is, Lou, he's doing what he can. But look here, even if you get the chopper they're gonna find you sooner or later." Budd stared at the sheet in front of him. "Soon as somebody finds out who you are, the fact you shot a girl in the back, you know what'll happen. They'll collar you and somehow you'll be riding in the back of a meat wagon and some accident'll happen."

"You threatening me?"

"Hell, no. I'm trying to save you. I'm just saying the way it is. The way you *know* it is."

"Ain't nobody gonna find me. So fuck that surrender shit. It ain't gonna happen. You assholes'll have to come in and get me 'fore I'd do that. And you'd find me atop six dead hostages."

Potter pointed to the pictures of the twins. LeBow frowned. Why didn't Handy know they were gone?

Budd continued, "Listen, Lou, we can offer you a deal."

"A deal? What kind of deal?"

"Some immunity. Not complete, but—"

"You know what I done here?"

"What you've done?" Echoing like a pro, Potter thought.

"I killed me a few people today. We're not talking immunity, we're talking . . . what the fuck's that thing priests give you?"

Budd looked up at Potter, who whispered, "Dispensation."

"Dispensation."

"So I don't think so, Charlie the butt-fucked lawyer. I think I need a helicopter or I'm going to turn my good friend Bonner here loose on a girl or two. You know Bonner? He stays hard twenty-four hours a day. Re-fucking-markable. Never seen anybody like him. You should've seen him in prison. Kid comes in for GTA and, bang, there's Bonner next to him 'fore the fingerprints're dry, saying, 'Bend over, pretty boy. Spread 'em.' "

Potter clamped his hand down on Budd's arm, seeing the anguish in his face. He tapped the yellow sheet once more.

"Where's Art?" Handy said suddenly. "I like him better'n you."

"He's out rustling up your helicopter, like I said."

"Fuck if he isn't listening to this right now on the squawk box. How close is he? He could probably stick his dick in your mouth without either of you moving. Hey, you a faggot, Charlie? Sound like one to me."

Budd adjusted his grip on the phone. "Agent Potter's trying to get you what you've been asking for."

They died because they didn't give me what I wanted. Potter nodded approval.

"I want that chopper or Bonner gets a girl."

"You don't need to do that, Lou. Come on. We're all working together here, aren't we?"

"Oh, I wasn't on your team last time I looked, Charlie."

Budd wiped sweat from his forehead. Potter, feeling

very much like an orchestra conductor, gestured at Budd and pointed to a portion of the yellow sheet.

"My team?" Budd responded. "Hey now, that's wrong, Lou. I *am* on your team. And I want to offer you a deal. You and Wilcox."

Potter held his finger to his lips, indicating for Budd to pause. The captain swallowed. Angie handed him a cup of water. He drank it down, gave her a rueful smile.

Handy was silent.

Budd started to speak; Potter shook his head.

Finally Handy said, "Me and Shep?"

"That's right."

Cautiously: "What kinda deal?"

Budd looked down at the sheet. "We'll go for life only. No death penalty."

"For us two?"

Potter heard the uncertainty in Handy's voice. Beautiful, he thought. For the first time all night he's not sure what's going on. He gave Budd a thumbs-up.

"Just you and Wilcox," he said firmly.

"What about Bonner?"

Potter held up his wavering hands, indicating uncertainty.

"Well, I'm just talking about you two."

"Why aren't you talking about Bonner?"

Potter frowned angrily. Budd nodded and in a testy voice said, "Because I don't want to talk about Bonner. I'm offering you and Wilcox a deal."

"You're an asshole, Charlie."

"An asshole?"

"You're not telling me everything."

Potter touched his lips.

Silence.

Perfect, thought Potter. He's doing great. Finally he nodded to Budd.

"I *am* telling you everything." Budd gave up on the yellow sheet and stared out the window at the slaughterhouse. "And I'm telling it to you for your benefit as much as anybody's. You oughta surrender, sir. Even if you get out of here in that helicopter you'll be the most wanted man in North America. Your life's gonna be pure hell and

if you get caught you'll get death. You know that. No
statute of limitations for murder."

"What'm I supposed to say to Bonner?"

Potter made an angry fist.

"I don't much care what you say to him," Budd said
gruffly. "He's not included in—"

"Why not?"

Hesitate, Potter wrote.

Handy broke the interminable silence. "What aren't
you fucking telling me?"

"Do you want a deal or not? You and Wilcox. It'll save
you from lethal injection."

"I want a fucking helicopter and that's what I'm going
to get. Tell Art that. Fuck you all."

"No, wait—"

Click.

Budd closed his eyes and rested the phone on the table.
His hands shook fiercely.

"Excellent, Charlie." Potter clapped him on the back.

"Good job," Angie said, winking at him.

Budd looked up, perplexed. "Excellent? He's all pissed
off. He hung up on me."

"No, he's just where we want him." LeBow typed up
the incident in the log and noted the time. On the "Deceptions" side of the board he wrote, *Federal plea bargain by
"U.S. Attorney Budd"—Handy and Wilcox. Life sentences
in lieu of death.*

Budd stood up. "You think?"

"You planted the seeds. We'll have to see if they take."
Potter caught Angie's eye and they exchanged a solemn
glance. The negotiator made a point of looking away before Budd noticed.

8:16 P.M.

"Five minutes and counting."

Dan Tremain had called the governor and together they

had decided that the HRU rescue would go ahead as planned. Over the scrambled frequency he radioed this to his men.

Outrider One, Chuck Pfenninger, was in position near the command van, and Outrider Two, Joey Wilson, hidden behind the school bus, was prepared to lob the stun grenades through the front window. Alpha and Bravo teams were ready to make the dynamic entry through the northwest and southeast doors as planned.

Tremain was very confident. Although the HTs might be anticipating an attack through the one well-marked fire exit, they'd never expect the assault through the hidden southeast door.

In five minutes it would all be over.

Lou Handy stared down at the phone and felt it for the first time that day: doubt.

Son of a bitch.

"Where is he?" he snarled, looking through the slaughterhouse.

"Bonner? In with the girls," Wilcox answered. "Or eating. I don't know. What's up?"

"Something's funny going on." Handy paced back and forth. "I think maybe he cut a deal." He told Wilcox what the U.S. attorney had said.

"They're offering *us* a deal?"

"Some deal. Life in Leavenworth."

"Beats that little needle. The worst part is you piss. You know that? There's nothing you can do to stop it. I tell you, I'm going out, I don't want to piss my pants in front of everybody."

"Hey, homes." Handy dropped his head, gazed coolly at his partner. "We're getting out. Don't you forget it."

"Right, sure."

"I think that prick's been with 'em all along."

"Why?" Wilcox asked.

"Why the fuck you think? Money. Cut down his hard time."

Wilcox cast his eyes into the dim back of the slaughterhouse. "Sonny's an asshole but he wouldn't do that."

"He did a while back."

"What?"

"Give up somebody. A guy he did a job with."

"You *knew* that?" Wilcox asked, surprised.

"Sure, I knew that," Handy said angrily. "We needed him."

But how had Bonner gotten to the feds? Almost every minute of the big man's time was accounted for from the moment of the breakout.

Though not all of it, Handy now recalled. Bonner was the one who'd gone to pick up the car. After they'd gotten out of the prison Bonner had been gone for a half-hour while he picked up the wheels. Handy remembered thinking that it was taking him a long time and thinking, If he skips on us he's going to die real fucking slow.

Gone a half-hour to get a car eight blocks away. Plenty of time to call the feds.

"But he's a short-timer," Wilcox pointed out. Bonner's interstate transport sentence was four years.

"The kind," Handy countered, "they'd be most likely to cut a deal with. Feds never chop off sentences more'n a couple years."

Besides, Bonner had an incentive: sex offenders were the prisoners who most often woke up with glass shards shoved down their throat, or a tin-can-lid knife in their gut—or who didn't wake up at all.

Uncertainly Wilcox looked into the dim slaughter-house. "Whatta you think?"

"I think we oughta talk to him."

They walked through the main room, over the rotting ramps the livestock had once ambled along, past the long tables where the animals had been cut apart, the rusting guillotines. The two men stood in the doorway of the killing room. Bonner wasn't there. They heard him standing not far away, pissing a solid stream into a well or sump pump.

Handy stared at the room—the older woman, lying curled into a ball. The gasping girl and the pretty girl. And then there was Melanie, who stared back with eyes that tried to be defiant but were just plain scared. Then he realized something.

"Where," Handy said softly, "are the little ones?"

He gazed at two empty pairs of black patent-leather shoes.

Wilcox spat out, "Son of a bitch." He ran into the hallway, following the tiny footprints in the dust.

Melanie put her arms around the girl with the asthma and cowered against the wall. Just then Bonner came around the corner and stopped. "Hey, buddy." He blinked uneasily, looking at Handy's face.

"Where are they, you fuck?"

"Who?"

"The little girls. The twins?"

"I—" Bonner recoiled. "I was watching 'em. All this time. I swear."

"All this time?"

"I took a piss is all. Look, Lou. They gotta be here someplace. We'll find 'em." The big man swallowed uneasily.

Handy glared at Bonner, who started toward Melanie, shouting, "Where the fuck are they?" He pulled his pistol from his pocket and walked up to her.

"Lou!" Wilcox was calling from the main room. "Jesus Christ."

"What?" Handy screamed, spinning around. "What the fuck is it?"

"We got a worse problem than that. Look here."

Handy hurried back to Wilcox, who was pointing at the TV.

"Holy Christ. Potter, that lying son of a bitch!"

On the screen: A newscast, showing the perfect telephoto image of the front and side of the slaughterhouse. The reporters had snuck through the police line and had set up the camera on something close and tall—maybe that old windmill just to the north. The camera was a little shaky but there was no doubt that they were looking at a fucking SWAT trooper at a front window—only twenty feet away from where Handy and Wilcox now stood.

"Is that more there?" Wilcox cried. He pointed to some bumps in a gully to the north of the slaughterhouse.

"Could be. Shit yes. Must be a dozen of them."

The newscaster said, "It looks like an assault could be imminent. . . ."

Handy looked up at the fire door on the north side of

the factory. They'd wedged it shut but he knew that explosive charges could take it down in seconds. He shouted
to Bonner, "Get that scatter gun, we got a firefight."

"Shit." Bonner pulled the slide back on the Mossberg,
let it snap back.

"The roof?" Wilcox asked.

Those were the only two ways a hostage rescue team
could get in quickly—the side door and the roof. The
loading dock was too far back. But as he stared at the ceiling he saw a thick network of ducts and vents and conveyors. Even if they blew through the roof itself they'd have
to cut through those utility systems.

Handy glanced out over the field in front of the slaughterhouse. Aside from the trooper by the window—hidden
from the police lines by the school bus—no other cops
seemed to be approaching from that direction.

"They're coming through that side door there."

Handy moved slowly toward the window where the
trooper was hiding. He gestured to Wilcox's gun. The
lean man grinned and pulled his pistol from his belt,
pulled the slide, chambering a round.

"Go behind him," Handy whispered. "Other window.
Get his attention."

Wilcox nodded, dropped suddenly to his belly, and
crawled off to the far window. Handy too crawled—to the
open window outside of which the trooper was hiding.
Wilcox put his mouth next to a hole in a shattered pane
and gave the warble of a wild turkey. Handy couldn't suppress his smile.

When Wilcox warbled again Handy looked outside
quickly. He saw the trooper, only two feet away, turning
toward the sound in confusion. Handy reached out the
window, grabbed the trooper's helmet, and, jerking hard,
lifted him off the ground. The man let go of his machine
gun, which dangled from his shoulder by a leather thong,
and grasped Handy's wrists, struggling fiercely as the helmet strap choked him. Wilcox leapt to Handy's side and
together they muscled the trooper through the window.

As Handy held him in a full nelson Wilcox kicked him
in the groin and pulled his machine gun, pistol, and
grenades away. He crumpled and fell to the floor.

"You son of a bitch," Handy raged, kicking the man violently. "Lemme look at you!" He ripped off the trooper's
helmet, hood, and goggles. He bent his face low. Handy
pulled his knife from his pocket and flicked it open, held
the blade against the young man's cheek. "Shoot me in
the back? That's the kind of balls you have? Come up behind a man like a fucking nigger!"

The trooper struggled. Handy slashed the knife downward, drawing a streak of blood along his jawline. He
slammed his fist into the man's face once, then again, a
dozen times, stepped away and turned back, kicking him
in the belly and groin.

"Hey, Lou, take it—"

"Fuck him! He was going to shoot me in the back! He
was going to shoot me in the fucking back! Is that what
kind of man you are? That's what you think of honor?"

"Fuck *you*," the trooper gasped, rolling on the floor,
helpless. Handy turned him over, slugged him in the
lower back, handcuffed him with the boy's own cuffs.

"Where are the rest of 'em?" Handy poked the knife
into the trooper's thigh, a shallow cut. "Tell me!" he
raged. He pushed further. The man screamed.

Handy leaned his face close, inches away from the
trooper's face.

"Straight to hell, Handy. That's where *you* can go."

The knife slipped further in. Another scream. Handy
reached out and touched a tiny sphere of the tear. It clung
to his finger, which he lifted to his tongue. Pushed the
knife into the thigh a little bit more. More screaming.

Let's see when this boy breaks.

"Oh, Jesus," the man moaned.

Have to happen sooner or later. Just work our way
north with this little bit o' Buck steel and see when he
starts squealing. He began to saw slowly with the blade,
working his way toward the trooper's groin.

"I don't *know* where the rest of 'em are! I'm just fucking reconnaissance."

Handy suddenly got tired of the knife and beat him
again with his fist, angrier than ever. "How many?
Where're they coming in through?"

The trooper spat on his leg.

And suddenly Handy was back years ago, seeing Rudy sneer at him—well, it was probably a sneer. Seeing him turn away, Handy's two hundred dollars in his brother's wallet—he *thought* it was there, probably was. Seeing Rudy walk away like Handy was a piece of dried shit. The anger cutting through him like a carbon-steel blade in somebody's hot belly.

"Tell me!" he screamed. His fist rose again and again and smashed into the trooper's face. Finally, he stood back. "Fuck him. Fuck 'em all." Handy ran into the killing room and tipped the pot containing the gasoline over. The room filled with the chill liquid, splashing on the women and girls. Melanie the scared mouse-cunt pulled them into a corner but still they were doused.

Handy held the trooper's submachine gun toward the side door. "Shep, they're gonna come through there fast. As soon as they do I'm going to shoot a couple of 'em in the legs. You pitch that"—nodding at the grenade—"into the room, set off the gas. I want to keep some of them cops alive to tell everybody what happened to those girls. What it looked like when they burnt up."

"Yo, homes. You got it." Wilcox pulled the pin out of the smooth black grenade and, holding the delay handle, stepped into the doorway of the killing room. Handy pulled back the bolt of the H&K, aimed it at the door.

"Arthur, we have some movement by the window," Dean Stillwell said over the radio. "The one second to the left from the front door."

Potter acknowledged his transmission and looked out the window with field glasses. His vision of that window was blocked by the school bus and a tree.

"What was it, Dean?"

"One of my men said it looked like somebody going through the window."

"One of the HTs?"

"No, I meant going *in* the window."

"In? Any confirmation?"

"Yessir, another trooper said she saw it too."

"Well—"

"Oh, Jesus," Tobe whispered. "Arthur, look."

"Who are they?" Angie snapped. "Who the hell *are* they?"

Potter turned and glanced at the TV monitor she was gazing at. It took a moment to realize he was looking at a newscast—the monitor that had been tuned to the Weather Channel. To his horror he realized he was watching an assault on the slaughterhouse.

"Wait a minute," Budd said. "What's going on?"

". . . exclusive footage. It appears that one of the troopers outside the slaughterhouse has just been kidnaped himself."

"Where's the camera?" an astounded LeBow said.

"Can't worry about that now," Potter said. The involuntary thought popped into his mind: Is this Henderson's revenge?

"Tremain," LeBow called out. "It's Tremain."

"Fuck," said good Catholic Tobe. "*Those* were the scrambled messages we were picking up. He's put an operation together."

"The trap inside! Tremain doesn't know about it."

"Trap?" Derek asked nervously.

Potter looked up, shocked. He understood instantly the depth of the betrayal. Derek Elb had been feeding the Hostage Rescue Unit information about the barricade. Had to be. "What's Tremain's frequency?" he shouted, leaping over the table and grabbing the young trooper by the collar.

Derek was shaking his head.

"Tell him, goddamnit!" Budd shouted.

"I don't have access. It's field-set. There's no way to break in."

"I can crack it," Tobe said.

"No, it's retrosignaling, it'll take you an hour. I'm sorry, I didn't know. . . . I didn't know anything about a trap." Potter recalled that they had been outside when they'd learned about the bomb—at the field hospital.

Budd raged, "He's got a firebomb rigged up in there, Sergeant."

"Oh, God, no," Derek muttered.

Potter grabbed the phone. He dialed. There was no answer. "Come on, Lou. Come on! . . . Tobe, is SatSurv still on line?"

"Yep." He slammed his finger into a button. A monitor burst to life. It was essentially the same green-and-blue image of the grounds they'd seen before, but now there were ten little red dots clustered on either side of the slaughterhouse.

"They're in those gullies there. Probably going in through the northwest and southeast windows or doors. Give me a high-speed printout."

"You got it. Black-and-white'll be faster."

"Do it!" As the machine buzzed, Potter pressed the phone to his ear, hearing the calm, unanswered ringing on the other end. "Lou, Lou, Lou, come on. . . . Answer!"

He slammed it down. "Henry, what'll they do?"

LeBow leapt up and stared at the printout as it spewed from the machine. "Blow in the door here, on the left. But I don't know what they're doing on the right side. There's no door. You can't use cutting charges to breach a structural wall." He pointed at the mounted diagram of the processing plant. "Look there. That dotted line. That might've been a door at one time. Tremain must have found it. They're going in from both sides."

"Single-file?"

"Two-man entry but tandem, yeah. They'll have to."

"It's—"

The bang was very soft. Suddenly the van went dark. Frances gave a short scream. Only an eerie yellow glow from the thick windows and the twin blue screens of Henry LeBow's computers illuminated the pungent interior.

"Lost power," Tobe said. "We—"

"Arthur!" LeBow was pointing out the window at the flames that were rolling up the side of the van.

"What happened? Jesus, did Handy hit us?"

Potter ran to the door. He pulled it open and cried out, leaping back from the tongue of flames and the searing heat that flowed into the van. Slammed the door.

"We can't power up," Tobe said. "Backup's gone too."

"How long do I have?" he raged at Derek.

"I—"

"Answer me or you'll be in jail in an hour. How long from the time the power goes out till they attack?"

"Four minutes," Derek whispered. "Sir, I was just do-ing what—"

"No, Arthur," Angie called, "don't open it!"

Potter flung the door open. He flew backwards as his sleeves ignited. Outside all they could see was an ocean of flame. Then the black smoke of burning rubber and oil poured inside, sending them to the floor in search of air.

Disengaging his scrambler, Dan Tremain broadcast, "Agent Potter, Agent Potter! This is Captain Tremain. Come in, please. Are you all right?"

Tremain watched the fire on the hill. It was alarming, the orange flames and the black smoke, swirling in a tor-nado. He knew all about the van, had used it himself of-ten, and knew that those inside were safe as long as they kept the door closed. Still, it was a terrible conflagration.

No time to think about that now. He called again, "Agent Potter . . . Derek? Is anyone in the command van? Please report."

"This is Sheriff Stillwell, who's calling?"

"Captain Dan Tremain, state police. What's going on?"

"The van's on fire, sir. We don't know. Handy may've made a lucky shot."

Thank you, Sheriff, Tremain thought. The conversa-tions were being recorded at state police headquarters. Stillwell's comment would more than justify Tremain's action.

"Is everyone all right?" the HRU commander asked.

"We can't get close to the van. We don't—"

Tremain cut off the transmission and ordered, on the scrambled frequency, "Alpha team, Bravo team. Code word Filly. Code word Filly. Arm the cutting charges. Sixty seconds to detonation."

"Alpha. Armed."

"Bravo. Armed."

"Fire in the hole," Tremain called, and lowered his head.

Arthur Potter, fifteen pounds overweight and never ath-letic, rolled to the ground just past the flames that two troopers were trying unsuccessfully to douse with fire ex-tinguishers.

He hit the ground and stared in alarm at his flaming sleeves. One trooper cried out and blasted him with carbon dioxide. The icy spray stung his hands more than the burn had though he saw the wounds on his skin and knew what kind of agony he could anticipate later.

If he lived to later.

No time, no time at all . . .

He rolled to his feet and ignored the embers smoldering on his jacket, the pain searing his skin. He began to jog, clicking on the bullhorn.

Potter struggled across the field, through the line of police cars and directly toward the slaughterhouse. He gasped as he shouted, "Lou Handy, listen to me! Listen. This is Art Potter. Can you hear me?"

Sixty yards, fifty.

No response. Tremain's men would be moving in at any minute.

"Lou, you're about to be attacked. It's an unauthorized operation. I had nothing to do with it. Repeat: It's a mistake. The officers are in two gullies to the north and the south of the slaughterhouse. You can set up a crossfire from the two windows on those sides. Do you hear me, Lou?"

He was gasping for breath and struggling to call out. A pain shot through his chest and he had to slow down.

A perfect target, he stood on the crest of a hill—the very place where Susan Phillips had been shot in the back—and shouted, "They're about to blow the side doors but you can stop them before they get inside. Set up crossfire positions in the southeast and the northwest windows. There's a door on the south side you don't know about. It's covered up but it's there. They're going to blow their way in from there too, Lou. Listen to me. I want you to shoot for their legs. They have body armor. Shoot for their legs! Use shotguns. Shoot for their legs."

No movement inside the slaughterhouse.

Oh, please. . . .

"Lou!"

Silence. Except for the urgent wind.

Then he noticed movement from the gully to the north of the slaughterhouse. A helmet rising from a stand of buffalo grass. A flash as a pair of binoculars turned his way.

Or was it the telescopic sight of an H&K MP-5?

"Lou, do you hear me?" Potter called again. "This is an unauthorized operation. Set up crossfire positions on the north door and the south door. There'll be plasterboard or something covering the doorway on the south."

Nothing . . . silence.

Somebody please . . .

For God's sake, talk to me. Somebody!

Then: movement. Potter looked toward it—just to the north of the slaughterhouse.

On the crest of a hill seventy-five, eighty yards away a man in black stood, his hip cocked, an H&K on a strap at his side, staring at Potter. Then one by one the troopers in the gullies on either side of the slaughterhouse rose and slithered away from the doors. The helmeted heads bobbed up and retreated into the bushes. HRU was standing down.

From the slaughterhouse there was nothing but silence. But Arthur Potter still was heartsick. For he knew that there would have to be a reparation. As amoral and cruel as Handy was, the one thing he'd done consistently was keep his word. Handy's world may have run on a justice of his own making, an evil justice, but justice it was nonetheless. And it was the good guys who'd just broken faith.

Potter, LeBow, and Budd stood back, arms crossed, while Tobe desperately ran wires, cutting and splicing.

Potter watched Derek Elb being escorted away by two of Pete Henderson's agents and asked Tobe, "Sabotage?"

Tobe—nearly as good at ballistics as he was at electronics—couldn't say for certain. "Looks like a simple gasoline fire. We were running a lot of juice out of the generator. But somebody could've slipped in an L210 and we'd be none the wiser. Anyway I can't look for anything now." And he stripped, joined, and taped a dozen wires at once, it seemed.

LeBow said, "You know it is, Arthur."

Potter agreed, of course. Tremain had probably left a remote-controlled incendiary device in the generator of the van.

Incredulous, Budd asked, "He'd do something like that? What are you going to do?"

The negotiator said, "Nothing right now." In his heart he lived too far in the past; in his career, he lived there hardly at all. Potter had no time or taste for revenge. Now he had the hostages to think about. Hurry, Tobe, get the lines running again.

Officer Frances Whiting returned to the van. She'd been inhaling oxygen at the medical tent. Her face was smudged and she breathed with some difficulty, but otherwise she was okay.

"Little more excitement than you're used to in Hebron?" Potter asked her.

"Not counting traffic citations, my last collar was when Bush was in office."

The smell of scorch and burnt rubber and plastic was overwhelming. Potter's arms were streaked with burn. The hair on the backs of his hands was gone and one searing patch on his wrist raged with pain. But he couldn't take the time to see the medics just yet. He had to make contact with Handy first, try to minimize whatever payback was undoubtedly fermenting in Handy's mind.

"Okay," Tobe called. "Got it." The miracle worker had run a line from the remote generator truck and the van was up and running again.

Potter was about to tell Budd to prop the door open to air the place out when he realized there was no door. It had been burned away. He sat down at the desk, grabbed the phone, and dialed.

The electronic sound of a ringing phone filled the van.

No answer.

Behind them Henry LeBow had begun to type again. The sound of the muted keys more than anything else restored Potter's confidence. Back in business, he thought. And turned his attention to the phone.

Answer, Lou. Come on. We've got too much behind us to let it fall apart now. There's too much history, we've gotten too close. . . .

Answer the damn phone!

A loud squeal outside, so close that Potter thought at first it was feedback. Roland Marks's limo bounded to a stop and he leapt from the car, glancing briefly at the scorched van. "I saw the news!" he shouted to no one in particular. "What the fuck happened?"

"Tremain went rogue," Potter said, pressing redial once more and eyeing the lawyer coldly.

"He *what?*"

LeBow explained.

Budd said, "We didn't have a clue, sir."

"I want to talk to that fellow, oh, yes I do," Marks grumbled. "Where—?"

Then there was a rush of motion from the doorway and Potter was knocked sideways. He fell heavily on his back, grunted.

"You son of a bitch!" Tremain cried. "You fucking son of a bitch!"

"Captain!" Marks roared.

Budd and Tobe grabbed the HRU commander's arms, pulled him off. Potter rose slowly. He touched his head where he'd banged it in the fall. No blood. He gestured for the two men to release Tremain. Reluctantly they did.

"He's got one of my men, Potter. Thanks to you, you fucking Judas."   •

Budd stiffened and stepped forward. Potter waved him down and straightened his tie, glancing at the burns on the backs of his hands. Large blisters had formed and the pain was really quite remarkable.

"Tobe," he said calmly, "run the tape, would you please? The KFAL tape."

There was a hum of a VCR and a monitor burst to life. A red-white-and-blue TV station logo appeared on the bottom of the screen, along with the words *Reporting Live . . . Joe Silbert.*

"Oh, that's brilliant," Marks said sourly, staring at the screen.

"He's got one of your men," Potter said, "because you dismissed the troopers who were preventing reporters from getting near the site."

"What?" Tremain stared at the newscast.

LeBow continued to type. Without looking up he said, "Handy saw you moving in. He's got a TV inside."

Tremain didn't answer. Potter wondered if he was thinking, Name, rank, serial number.

"Expected better of you, Dan," the assistant attorney general said.

"The governor—" he blurted before he thought better of it. "Well, even if he did, we could've saved those girls. They'd be out by now. We still could have gotten them out safe!"

Why aren't I angry? Potter wondered. Why aren't I raging at him, this man who nearly ruined everything? Who nearly killed the girls inside, who nearly killed Melanie? *Why?*

Because it's crueler this way, Potter understood suddenly. To tell him the truth starkly and without emotion.

Ever done anything bad, Art?

"Handy rigged a booby trap, Captain," Potter said, calm as a deferential butler. "A gasoline bomb on a hair trigger. Those girls would've burned to death the instant you blew those doors."

Tremain stared at him. "No," he whispered. "Oh, no. God forgive me. I didn't know." The sinewy man looked like he was going to faint.

"Downlink," Tobe called.

An instant later the phone rang. Potter snatched it up. "Lou?"

That sucked, Art. I thought you were my friend.

"Well, Art. That was pretty fucking low. Some goddamn friend you are."

"I had nothing to do with it." Potter's eyes were on Tremain. "We had an officer here go rogue."

"These boys have some nice equipment. We've got some grenades and a machine gun now."

Potter pointed to LeBow, who pulled Tremain aside and asked the numb captain what kind of armament the captured trooper had with him.

A figure appeared in the doorway. Angie. Potter waved her in.

"Lou," the negotiator said into the phone, "I'm apologizing for what happened. It won't happen again. You have my word on that. You heard me out there. I gave you good tactical information. You know it wasn't anything I'd planned."

"I suppose you've got those girls by now. The little ones."

"Yes, we do, Lou."

"That U.S. attorney, Budd . . . he set us up, didn't he, Art?"

Again a hesitation. "I have no knowledge to that effect."

He's going to be very reasonable, Potter surmised.

Or go totally nuts.

"Ha. You're a kicker, Art. Well, okay, I believe you about this D-Day shit. You tell me there was some crazy cop doing things he shouldn't oughta've. But you should've been more in charge, Art. It's the way the law works, isn't that right? You're responsible for things people work for you do."

Angie was frowning.

"What?" Budd asked, seeing the hopeless expression on her face. It matched that on Potter's.

"What's the matter?" Frances Whiting whispered.

Potter grabbed the field glasses, wiped the greasy smoke residue off them, and looked out.

Oh, Christ, no . . . Desperately Potter said, "Lou, it was a *mistake*."

"You shoot at Shep it was a mistake. You don't get me my chopper on time it's not your fault. . . . Don't you know me by now, Art?"

Only too well.

Potter set down the glasses. He turned away from the window, glanced up at the pictures above the diagram of the slaughterhouse. Who will it be? he wondered.

Emily?

Donna Harstrawn?

Beverly?

Potter thinks suddenly: Melanie. He's going to pick Melanie.

Frances understood and cried out, "No, please no. Do something!"

"There's nothing *to* do," Angie whispered.

Tremain leaned his miserable face down to the window and looked out.

Handy's voice filled the van. He sounded reasonable,

wise. "You're a lot like me, Art. Loyal. That's what I think. You're loyal to them that do what they're supposed to and you don't have time for those that don't." A pause. "You know just what I'm saying, don't you, Art? I'll leave the body outside. You can come get it. Flag of truce."

"Lou, isn't there anything I can do?" Potter heard the desperation in his own voice. Hated it. But it was there just the same.

Who will it be?

Angie had turned away.

Budd shook his head sorrowfully. Even boisterous Roland Marks could find nothing to say.

"Tobe," Potter said softly, "please turn down the volume."

He did. But still everyone jumped at the stark sound of the gunshot, which filled the van as a huge metallic ring.

As he stumbled toward the slaughterhouse, where the body lay pale in the halogen lights, he pulled off his flak jacket and dropped it on the ground. His helmet too he left behind.

Dan Tremain walked on, tears in his eyes, gazing at the still body, the bloody body, lying in the posture of a rag doll.

He crested the rise and saw from the corner of his eye troopers standing from their places of cover. They were staring at him; they knew he was responsible for what had happened, for this unconscionable death. He was walking up Calvary Hill.

And in the window of the processing plant: Lou Handy, a gun pointed directly at Tremain's chest. It made no difference, he was no threat; the captain had dropped the utility belt holding his Glock service pistol some yards back. On he stumbled, nearly falling, then just catching his balance like a drunk with some irrepressible sense of survival. His despair was deepened by Lou Handy's face—the red eyes, set back under bony brows, the narrow jaw, the five o'clock shadow. He was smiling, an innocuous smile of curiosity, as he gazed at the sorrow on the cop's face. Sampling, tasting.

Tremain gazed at the body lying there in front of him. Fifty feet away, forty. Thirty.

I'm mad, Tremain thought. And continued to walk, staring into the black eye of the muzzle of Handy's gun.

Twenty feet. Blood so red, skin so pale.

Handy's mouth was moving but Tremain could hear nothing. Maybe God's judgment is to make me deaf as those poor girls.

Ten feet. Five.

He slowed. The troopers were standing now, all of them, staring at him. Handy could pick any of them off, as they could him, but there would be no shooting. This was the Christmas Eve during World War I when the enemy troops shared carols and food. And helped each other collect and bury the shattered bodies strewn throughout no-man's-land.

"What have I done?" he muttered. He dropped to his knees and touched the cold hand.

He cried for a moment then hefted the body of the trooper in his arms—Joey Wilson, Outrider Two—and lifted it effortlessly, looking into the window. At Handy's face, which was no longer smiling but, oddly, curious. Tremain memorized the foxlike cast of his face, the cold eyes, the way the tip of his tongue lay against his upper lip. They were only feet apart.

Tremain turned and started back to the police line. In his mind he heard a tune, floating aimlessly. He couldn't think of what it might be for a minute then the generic instrument turned into the bagpipe he remembered from years ago and the tune became "Amazing Grace," the traditional song played at the funerals of fallen policemen.

8:45 P.M.

Arthur Potter thought about the nature of silence.

Sitting in the medical tent. Staring at the floor as medics attended to his burnt arms and hands.

Days and weeks of silence. Silence thicker than wood, perpetual silence. Is that what Melanie's day-to-day life was like?

He himself had known quiet. An empty house. Sunday mornings, filled only with the faint tapping of household motors and pumps. Still summer afternoons by himself on a back porch. But Potter was a man who lived in a state of anticipation and for him the silence was, on good days at least, the waiting state before his life might begin again— when he would meet someone like Marian, when he would find someone other than takers and terrorists and psychos with whom he might share his thoughts.

Someone like Melanie? he wondered.

No, of course not.

He felt a chill on the back of his hand and watched the medic apply some kind of ointment, which had the effect of dulling most of the stinging immediately.

Arthur Potter thought of Melanie's photograph, saw it hanging over the diagram of the slaughterhouse. He thought of his reaction when he understood, a few minutes ago, that Handy was going to kill another hostage. She was the first person in his mind.

He stretched. A joint somewhere in his back popped softly and he admonished himself: Don't be a damn fool. . . .

But in another part of his lavish mind Arthur Potter English-lit major thought, If we have to be foolish it ought to be in love. Not in our careers, where lives hang in the balance; not with our gods or in our lust for beauty and learning. Not with our children, so desirous and so unsure. But in love. For love is nothing but the purest folly and we go there for the purpose of *being* impassioned and half-crazy. In matters of the heart the world will always be generous with us, and forgiving.

Then he laughed to himself and shook his head as reality descended once more—like the dull ache that returned along his seared arms. She's twenty-five—less than half your age. She's deaf, both lower- and upper-case. And, for heaven's sake, it's your wedding anniversary today. Twenty-three years. Not a single one missed. Enough nonsense. Get back to the command van. Get to work.

The medic tapped him on the shoulder. Potter looked up, startled.

"You're all set, sir."

"Yes, thank you."

He rose and walked unsteadily back to the van.

A figure appeared in the doorway.

Potter looked up at Peter Henderson. "You all right?" the SAC asked.

He nodded cautiously. Tremain might have been the main perp but Potter would have bet a week's salary that Henderson had played some role in the assault. Ambition? A desire to get back at the Bureau, which betrayed him? Yet this would be even harder to prove than the existence of the suspected gas bomb in the generator. Forensics of the heart are always elusive.

Henderson looked at the burns. "You'll get yourself a medal for this."

"My first wound in the line of duty." Potter smiled.

"Arthur, I just wanted to apologize for losing my temper before. It gets dull down here. I was hoping for some action. You know how it is."

"Sure, Pete."

"I miss the old days."

Potter shook the man's hand. They talked about Joe Silbert and his fellow reporters. They'd refer the matter to the U.S. attorney but concluded there was probably nothing to hold them for. Obstruction of justice is a tricky charge and absent interfering with an ongoing criminal prosecution judges usually come down on the side of the First Amendment. Potter had contented himself by walking ominously up to Silbert, who stood in a circle of troopers, cool as a captured revolutionary leader. The agent had told him that he was going to cooperate in every way with the widow of the dead trooper, who would undoubtedly be bringing a multimillion-dollar wrongful-death action against the TV station and Silbert and Biggins personally.

"I intend to be a plaintiff's witness," Potter explained to the reporter, whose facade cracked momentarily, revealing beneath it a very scared, middle-aged man of questionable talents and paltry liquidity.

The negotiator now sat back in his chair and gazed at the slaughterhouse through the yellow window.

"How many minutes to the next deadline?"

"Forty-five."

Potter sighed. "That's going to be a big one. I'll have to do some thinking about it. Handy's mad now. He lost control in a big way."

Angie said, "And what's worse is that you helped him get it back. Which is a form of losing control in itself."

"So he's resentful in general and resentful at me in particular."

"Though he probably doesn't know it," Angie said.

"It's lose-lose." Potter's eyes were on Budd, gazing mournfully at the slaughterhouse.

The phone buzzed. Tobe picked it up, blew soot off the receiver, and answered. "Yeah," the young man said. "I'll tell him." He hung up. "Charlie, that was Roland Marks. He asked if you could come see him right away. He's got his friend with him. Somebody he wants you to meet. He said it's critical."

The captain kept his eye on the battlefield. "He's . . . Where is he?"

"Down by the rear staging area."

"Uh-huh. Okay. Say, Arthur, can I talk to you for a minute?"

"Sure you can."

"Outside?"

"Taken up imaginary smoking, have you?" Potter asked.

"Arthur started a trend in Special Ops," Tobe said. "Henry's taken up imaginary sex."

"Tobe," barked LeBow, typing away madly.

The young agent added, "I'm not being critical, Henry. *I'm* going to imaginary AA."

Budd smiled wanly and he and Potter stepped outside. The temperature had dropped ten degrees and it seemed to the negotiator that the wind was worse.

"So, what's up, Charlie?"

They stopped walking. The men gazed at the van and the burnt field around it—the devastation that the fire had caused.

"Arthur, there's something I have to tell you." He reached into his pocket and pulled out a tape recorder. He looked down and turned it over and over in his hands.

"Oh," the agent said. "About this?" Potter held up a small cassette.

Budd frowned and flipped open the recorder. There was a cassette inside.

"That one's blank," Potter said. "It's a special cassette. Can't be recorded on."

Budd pushed the play button. The hiss of static brayed from the tiny speaker.

"I knew all about it, Charlie."

"But—"

"Tobe has his magic wands. They pick up magnetic recording equipment. We're always sweeping locations for bugs. He told me somebody had a recorder. He narrowed it down to you."

"You knew?" He stared at the agent, then shook his head in disgust with himself—for having been outsmarted at something he didn't think was very smart to begin with.

"Who was it?" Potter asked. "Marks? Or the governor?"

"Marks. Those girls . . . he's really in a state about them. He wanted to give Handy whatever he wanted in order to get them released. Then he was going to track him down. He had this special homing device he was going to put in the chopper. You could track 'em from a hundred miles away and they'd never know."

Potter nodded at the crestfallen captain. "I figured it was something like that. Any man willing to sacrifice himself is willing to sacrifice somebody else."

"But how'd you swap the cassettes?" Budd asked.

Angie Scapello stepped down through the open doorway of the van and nodded a greeting to the men. She walked past Budd, touching his arm very lightly as she passed.

"Hi, Charlie."

"Hey, Angie," he said, not smiling.

"Say, what time do you have?" she asked him.

He lifted his left wrist. "Hell, it's gone. My watch. Damn. And Meg just gave it to me for my—"

Angie held up the Pulsar.

Budd was nodding, understanding it all. "Got it," he said, and hung his head even lower, if that was possible. "Oh, brother."

"I used to teach the pickpocket recognition course at Baltimore PD," she explained. "I borrowed the recorder when we were strolling around in the gully—having our loyalty talk—and switched cassettes."

Budd smiled miserably. "You're good. I'll give you that. Oh, man. I've been messin' up all night long. I don't know what to say. I've let you down."

"You confessed. No harm done."

"It was Marks?" Angie asked.

"Yep." Budd sighed. "At first I was thinking like him— that we should do anything to save those girls. I gave Arthur an earful about that this morning. But you were right, a life's a life. Doesn't matter if it's a girl or a trooper. We gotta stop him here."

"I appreciate that Marks had noble motives," Potter said. "But we have to do things a certain way. Acceptable losses. Remember?"

Budd closed his eyes. "Man, I almost ruined your career."

The negotiator laughed. "You didn't come close, Captain. Believe me, you were the only one at risk. If you'd given that tape to anyone *your* career in law enforcement would've been over."

Budd looked very flustered then stuck out his hand.

Potter shook it warmly though Budd didn't grip it very hard, either out of shame or out of concern about the fluffy pads of bandages on the agent's skin.

They all fell silent as Potter gazed up at the sky. "When's the deadline?"

Budd looked again at his wrist blankly for a moment then he realized that he was holding his watch in his right hand. "Forty minutes. What's the matter?" The captain's eyes lifted to the same jaundiced cloud that Potter was targeting.

"I'm getting a bad feeling about this one. This deadline."

"Why?"

"I just am."

"Intuition," Angie said. "Listen to him, Charlie. He's usually right."

Budd looked down from the sky and found Potter looking at him. "I'm sorry, Arthur. I'm plumb outta ideas."

Potter's eyes zipped back and forth over the grass, blackened by the fire and by the shadow of the van. "A helicopter," he blurted suddenly.

"What?"

Potter felt a keen sense of urgency seize him. "Get me a helicopter."

"But I thought we weren't going to give him one."

"I just need to show him one. A big one. At least a six-seater—eight- or ten- if you can find one."

"If *I* can find one?" Budd exclaimed. "Where? How?"

A thought slipped into Potter's mind from somewhere. *Airport.*

There was an airport nearby. Potter tried to remember. How did he know that? Had somebody told him? He hadn't driven past it. Budd hadn't told him; SAC Henderson hadn't said anything. Where—

It was Lou Handy. The taker had mentioned it as a possible source of a helicopter. He must've driven by it on the way here.

He told this to Budd.

"I know it," the captain said. "They got a couple choppers there but I don't know if there's anybody there who can even fly one. I mean, if we found one in Wichita they might make it here in time. But hell, it'll take more'n forty minutes to track down a pilot."

"Well, forty minutes is all we have, Charlie. Get a move on."

"The truth . . ." Melanie is crying.

And de l'Epée is the one person she doesn't want to cry in front of. But cry she does. He rises from his chair and sits on the couch next to her.

"The truth is," she continues, "that I just don't like who I am, what I've become, what I'm a part of."

It's time to confess and nothing can stop her now.

"I told you about how I lived for being Deaf. It became my whole life?"

"Miss Deaf Farmhand of the Year."

"I didn't want any of it. Not. One. Bit." She grows ve-
hement. "I got so damn tired of the self-consciousness of
it all. The politics of being part of the Deaf world, the
prejudice the Deaf have—oh, it's there. You'd be surprised. Against minorities and other handicapped. I'm
tired of it! I'm tired of not having my music. I'm tired of
my father . . ."

"Yes, what?" he asks.

"I'm tired of him using it against me. My deafness."

"How does he do that?"

"Because it makes me more scared than I already am! It
keeps me at home. That piano I told you about? The one I
wanted to play 'A Maiden's Grave' on? They sold it when
I was nine. Even though I could still hear enough to play
and could for a couple years more. They said—well, *he*
said, my father said—they didn't want me to learn to love
something that would be taken away from me." She adds,
"But the real reason was that he wanted to keep me on the
farm."

So you'll be home then.

Melanie looks into de l'Epée's eyes and says what she's
never said to anyone. "I can't hate him for wanting me to
stay at home. But selling the piano—that hurt so much.
Even if I'd had only one day of playing music it would
have been better than nothing. I'll never forgive him for
that."

"They had no right to do that," he agrees. "But you
managed to break away. You've got a job away from
home, you're independent. . . ." His voice fades.

And now for the hard part.

"What is it?" de l'Epée asks softly.

"A year ago," she begins, "I bought some new hearing
aids. Generally they don't work at all but these seemed to
have some effect with certain pitches of music. There was
a recital in Topeka I wanted to go to. Kathleen Battle. I'd
read in the paper that she was going to sing some spiritu-
als as part of the program and I thought . . ."

"That she'd sing 'Amazing Grace'?"

"I wanted to see if I could hear it. I was desperate to go.
But I had no way of getting there. I can't drive and the

buses would have taken forever. I begged my brother to take me. He'd been working all day on the farm but he said he'd take me anyway.

"We got there just in time for the concert. Kathleen Battle walked out on stage wearing this beautiful blue dress. She smiled to the audience. . . . And then she began to sing."

"And?"

"It was useless." Melanie breathes deeply, kneads her fingers. "It . . ."

"Why are you so sad?"

"The hearing aids didn't work at all. Everything was muddled. I could hardly hear anything and the notes I could hear were all off key to me. We left at intermission. Danny was doing his best to cheer me up. He . . ."

She falls silent.

"There's more, isn't there? There's something else you want to tell me."

It hurts so much! She only thinks these words but according to the fishy rules of her music room de l'Epée can hear them perfectly. He leans forward. "What hurts? Tell me?"

And there's so much to tell him. She could use a million words to describe that night and never convey the horror of living through it.

"Go ahead," de l'Epée says encouragingly. As her brother used to do, as her father never did. "Go ahead."

"We left the concert hall and got into Danny's car. He asked if I wanted some dinner but I couldn't eat a thing. I asked him just to drive home."

De l'Epée scoots forward. Their knees meet. He touches her arm. "What else?"

"We left town, got onto the highway. We were in Danny's little Toyota. He rebuilt it himself. Everything. He's so good with mechanical things. He's amazing, really. We were going pretty fast."

She pauses for a moment to let the tide of sadness subside. It never does but she takes a deep breath—remembering when she had to take a breath before saying something—and finds herself able to continue. "We were talking in the car."

De l'Epée nods.

"But that means we were signing. And that means we had to look at each other. He kept asking me what I was sad about, that the hearing aids didn't work, was I discouraged, had Dad been hassling me about the farm again? . . . He . . ."

She must breathe deeply again.

"Danny was looking at me, not at the road. Oh, God . . . it was just there, in front of us. I never saw where it came from."

"What?"

"A truck. A big one, carrying a load of metal pipes. I think it changed lanes when Danny wasn't looking and . . . oh, Jesus, there was nothing he could do. All these pipes coming at us at a thousand miles an hour . . ."

The blood. All the blood.

"I know he braked, I know he tried to turn. But it was too late. No . . . Oh, Danny."

Spraying, spraying. Like the blood from the throat of a calf.

"He managed to steer mostly out of the way but one pipe smashed through the windshield. It . . ."

De l'Epée kneads her hand. "Tell me," he whispers.

"It . . ." The words are almost impossible to say. "It took his arm off."

Like the blood running down the gutters into the horrible well in the center of the killing room.

"Right at the shoulder." She sobs at the memory. Of the blood. Of the stunned look on her brother's face as he turned to her and spoke for a long moment, saying words she couldn't figure out then and never had the heart to ask him to repeat.

The blood sprayed to the roof of the car and pooled in his lap, while Melanie struggled to get a tourniquet around the stump and screamed and screamed. She, the vocal one. While Danny, still conscious, nodding madly, sat completely mute.

Melanie says to de l'Epée, "The medics got there just a few minutes later and stopped most of the bleeding. They saved his life. They got him to a hospital and the doctors got his arm reattached within a couple of hours. For the past year he's had all sorts of operations. He's having one tomorrow—that's where my parents are. In St. Louis, visiting him. They think he'll get back maybe fifty percent use of his arm eventually. If he's lucky. But he lost all interest in the farm after that. He's pretty much stayed in bed. He reads, watches TV. That's about all. It's like his life is over with. . . ."

"It wasn't your fault," he says. "You're taking the blame, aren't you?"

"A few days after it happened my father called me out on the porch. There's something about him that's funny— I can lip-read him perfectly."

(Like Brutus, she thinks, and wishes she hadn't.)

"He sat on the porch swing and looked up at me and he said, 'I guess you understand what you've done now. You had no business talking Danny into doing something as foolish as that. And for a selfish reason all your own. What happened was your fault, there's no two ways about it. You might just as well've turned the engine over on a corn picker when Danny was working on a jam inside.

" 'God made you damaged and nobody wants it. It's a shame but it's not a sin—as long as you understand what you have to do. Come home now and make up for what you done. Get that teaching of yours over with, get that last year done. You owe your brother that. And you owe me especially.

" 'This is your home and you'll be welcome here. See, it's a question of belonging and what God does to make sure those that oughta stay someplace do. Well, your place is here, working at what you can do, where your, you know, problem doesn't get you into trouble. God's will.' And then he went to spray ammonia, saying, 'So you'll be home then.' It wasn't a question. It was an order. All decided. No debate. He wanted me to come home this last May. But I held off a few months. I knew I'd give in eventually. I *always* give in. But I just wanted a few more months on my own." She shrugs. "Stalling."

"You don't want the farm?"

"No! I want my music. I want to *hear* it, not just feel vibrations. . . . I want to hear my lover whisper things to me when I'm in bed with him." She can't believe she's saying these things to him, intimate things—far more intimate than she's ever told anyone. "I don't want to be a virgin anymore."

Now that she's started it's all pouring out. "I hate the poetry, I don't care about it! I never have. It's stupid. Do you know what I was going to do in Topeka? After my recital at the Theater of the Deaf? I had that appointment afterwards." Then his arms are around her and she is pressing against his body, her head on his shoulder. It's an odd experience, doubly so: being close to a man, and communicating without looking at him. "There's something called a cochlear implant." She must pause for a moment before she can continue. "They put a chip in your inner ear. It's connected by wire to this *thing,* this speech processor that converts the sounds to impulses in the brain . . . I could never tell Susan. A dozen times I was going to. But she would've hated me. The idea of trying to cure deafness— she hated that."

"Do they work, these implants?"

"They can. I have a ninety percent hearing loss in both ears but that's an average. In some registers I can make out sounds and the implants can boost those. But even if they don't work there are other things to try. There's a lot of new technology that in the next five or six years'll help people like me—grass-roots deaf and peddlers and just ordinary people who want to hear."

She thinks: And I *do.* I want to hear . . . I want to hear you whisper things in my ear while we make love.

"I . . ." He's speaking, his mouth is moving, but the sound dwindles to nothing.

Fading, fading.

No! Talk to me, keep talking to me. What's wrong?

But now it's Brutus who is standing in the doorway of her music room. What are you doing here? Leave! Get out! It's *my* room. I don't want you here!

He smiles, looks at her ears. "Freak of nature," he says.

Then they were back in the killing room and Brutus wasn't talking to her at all but to Bear, who stood with his arms crossed defensively. The tension between them was like thick smoke.

"You give us up?" Brutus asked Bear.

Bear shook his head and said something she didn't catch.

"They picked them up outside, those little girls."

The twins! They were safe! Melanie relayed this to Beverly and Emily. The younger girl burst into a smile and her fingers stuttered out a spontaneous prayer of thanks.

"You let them go, didn't you?" Brutus asked Bear. "Your plan all along."

Bear shook his head. Said something she didn't catch.

"I talked to . . ." Brutus snarled.

"Who?" Bear seemed to ask.

"The U.S. attorney you cut a deal with."

Bear's face grew dark. "No way, man. No fucking way."

Wilcox came up behind him and said something. Bear stabbed a finger at Melanie. "She's the one. . . ."

Brutus turned toward her. She gazed back coldly at him then rose and walked slowly over the wet tiles, almost choking on the smell of gasoline. She stopped and stood directly over Donna Harstrawn. With her finger she gestured Brutus forward. Her eyes locked into Bear's, Melanie lifted the woman's skirt a foot or two, revealing bloody thighs. She nodded at Bear.

"You little bitch!" Bear took a step toward her but Brutus caught his arm, pulled Bear's gun from his belt, tossed it to Stoat.

"You stupid asshole!"

"So? I fucked her, so what?"

Brutus lifted an eyebrow and then pulled a gun from his pocket. He pulled the slide and let it snap forward then pushed a button and took out the little metal tube that held the rest of the bullets. He put the pistol in Melanie's hand. It was cold as a rock, it gave her power like raw electrical current and it terrified her.

Bear was muttering something; in the corner of Melanie's eye she saw his lips moving. But she couldn't take her eyes from the gun. Brutus stood behind her and directed the barrel toward Bear's chest. He wrapped her hands in his. She smelled him, a sour scent of unwashed skin.

"Come on!" Bear's face was grim. "Quit fooling . . ."

Brutus was speaking to her; she felt the vibrations on the flesh of her face but she couldn't understand him. She sensed he was excited, almost aroused, and she felt it too—like a fever. Bear raised his hands. He was muttering something. Shaking his head.

The gun burned, radioactive. Bear eased away and Brutus adjusted the pistol to keep the muzzle pointed directly at his chest. Melanie pictured him lying atop Mrs. Harstrawn. She pictured him gazing at the twins' thin legs, their flat chests. Pull the trigger, she thought. Pull it! Her hand started to shake.

She again felt the vibrations of Brutus's words. In her mind, she heard his voice, an oddly soothing voice, the phantom voice. "Go ahead," he said.

Why isn't it firing? I'm ordering my finger to pull.

Nothing.

Bear was crying. Tears down his fat cheeks, running into his beard.

Melanie's hand was shaking badly. Brutus's firm hand curled around hers.

Then the gun silently bucked in her hand. Melanie gasped as the hot wind from the muzzle hit her face. A tiny dot appeared in Bear's chest and he gripped the wound with both hands, looked into the air, and fell backwards.

No, it fired by itself! I didn't do it, I didn't!

I *swear!*

She screamed those words to herself, over and over. And yet . . . yet she wasn't sure. She wasn't sure at all. For an instant—before the horror of what had happened hit home—she was enraged that she might *not* have been the one responsible for his death. That Brutus, not she, had applied the final ounce of pressure.

Brutus stepped away and reloaded the gun, pulled a lever, and the slide snapped forward.

Bear's mouth moved, his eyes darkened. She watched his miserable face, which looked as if all the injustice of the earth were conspiring to cheat a good man out of his life. Melanie didn't even try to figure out what he was saying.

She thought: Every once in a while deafness is a bless-ing.

Handy stepped past Melanie. He looked down at Bear. Muttered something to him. He fired one shot into the man's leg, which kicked violently in reaction. Bear's face contorted with pain. Then Handy fired again—into his other leg. Finally he aimed leisurely at the huge gut; the gun exploded once more. Bear shuddered once, stiffened, and went still.

Melanie sank to the floor, put her arms around Emily and Beverly.

Brutus bent down and pulled her close. His face was only inches away. "I didn't do that 'cause he fucked that woman. I did it 'cause he didn't do what I'd told him. He let those girls get away and was gonna snitch on us. Now you just sit on back there."

How can I understand his words if I can't understand him?

How? Melanie wonders. I hear him so perfectly, just like I hear my father.

So you'll be home—

How? she wonders.

Handy's eyes looked Melanie up and down as if he clearly knew the answer to her question and was simply waiting for her to catch on. Then he looked at his watch, bent down, grabbed Emily by the arm. He dragged the little girl, hands pressed together in desperate prayer, into the main room.

Handy was singing.

Potter had called and said, "Lou, how're things going in there? Thought we heard a few gunshots."

To the tune of "Streets of Laredo" Handy sang in a half-decent voice, "I see by my Timex you got fifteen minutes. . . ."

"You sound like you're in a bright mood, Lou. You do-ing okay foodwise?"

His voice didn't reveal his concern. *Were* they gun-shots?

"I'm feeling pretty chipper, sure am. But I don't want to talk about my moods. That's fucking boring, isn't it?

Tell me about my golden helicopter that's flying through the air right now. You get me one with diamond rotors, Art? Some babe with huge tits in the cockpit?"

What were those shots?

Looking at the monitor, the telescopic camera fixed on the window, he could see ten-year-old Emily Stoddard's waved blond hair, her big eyes, heart-shaped face. The silver glint of Handy's blade rested on her cheek.

"He's going to cut her," Angie whispered. For the first time that day her voice cracked with emotion. Because she, like Potter, knew he'd do it.

"Lou, we *have* your chopper. It's on its way."

Why won't he wear down? Potter wondered. After this much time most criminal takers're climbing the walls. They'll do anything to cut a deal.

"Hold on, Lou. I think that's the pilot now. I'm going to put you on hold. I'll be right back."

"No need. Just get me that chopper in fourteen minutes."

"Just hold on."

Potter hit the mute button and asked, "What do you think, Angie?"

She gazed out the window. Suddenly she announced, "He's serious. He's going to do it. He's tired of the bargaining. And he's still mad about the assault."

"Tobe?"

"It's ringing, there's no answer."

"Damn it. Doesn't he keep the phone in his pocket?"

"You still there, Lou?"

"Time's awasting, Art."

Potter tried to sound distracted as he asked, "Oh, hey, tell me, Lou. What *about* those shots?"

A low chuckle. "You sure are curious about that."

"*Were* they shots?"

"I dunno. Maybe it was all in your head. Maybe you were feeling guilty 'bout that trooper of yours getting accidentally shot after you accidentally tried to attack me. And you heard it, you know, like a delusion."

"Sounded real to us."

"Maybe Sonny accidentally shot himself cleaning his gun."

"That what happened?"

"Be a shame if anybody was counting on him to be a witness and all and what happens but he goes and cleans a Glock without looking to see if there was a round inside."

"There is no deal between him and us, Lou."

"Not now there ain't. I'll guaran-fucking-tee that."

LeBow and Angie looked up at Potter.

"Bonner's dead?" the negotiator asked Handy.

Have you ever done anything bad, Art?

"You got twelve minutes," Handy's cheerful voice said. *Click.*

Tobe said, "Got him. Budd."

Potter grabbed the offered phone. "Charlie, you there?"

"I'm at the airport and they've got a helicopter here. But I can't find anybody to fly it."

"There's got to be somebody."

"There's a school here—an aviation school—and some guy lives in the back but he won't answer the door."

"I need a chopper here in ten minutes, Charlie. Just buzz the river and set it down in that big field to the west. The one about a half-mile from here. That's all you've got to do."

"That's *all*? Oh, brother."

Potter said, "Good luck, Charlie." But Charlie was no longer on the line.

Charlie Budd ran underneath the tall Sikorsky helicopter. It was an old model, a big one, the sort that had plucked dripping astronauts from the ocean during the Gemini and Apollo days at NASA. It was orange and red and white, Coast Guard colors, though the insignias had long ago been painted over.

The airport was small. There was no tower, just an air sock beside a grass strip. A half-dozen single-engine Pipers and Cessnas sat idle, tied down securely against Land of Oz twisters.

Budd slammed his fist onto the door of a small shack behind the airport's one hangar. The sign beside the door said, *D. D. Pembroke Helicopter School. Lessons, Rides. Hourly, Daily.*

Despite that claim, however, the place was mostly a residence. A pile of mail sat on the doorstep and through the window in the door Budd could see a yellow light burning, a pile of clothes in a blue plastic hamper, and what appeared to be a man's foot hanging off the end of a cot. A single toe protruded from a hole in his sock.

"Come on!" Budd pounded hard. He shouted, "Police! Open up!"

The toe moved—it twitched, swung in a slow circle—then fell still.

More pounding. "Open up!"

The toe was fast asleep once more.

The window shattered easily under Budd's elbow. He unlocked the door and pushed inside. "Hey, mister!"

A man of about sixty lay on the cot, wearing overalls and a T-shirt. His hair was like straw and spread out from his head in all directions. His snore was as loud as the Sikorsky's engine.

Budd grabbed his arm and shook violently.

D. D. Pembroke, if D. D. Pembroke this was, opened his wet, red eyes momentarily, gazed through Budd, and rolled over. The snoring, at least, stopped.

"Mister, I'm a state trooper. This's an emergency. Wake up! We need that chopper of yours right now."

"Go away," Pembroke mumbled.

Budd sniffed his breath. He found the empty bottle of Dewar's cradled beneath the man's arm like a sleeping kitten.

"Shit. Wake up, mister. We need you to fly."

"I can't fly. How can I fly? Go away." Pembroke didn't move or open his eyes. "How'd you get in here?" he asked without a trace of curiosity.

The captain rolled him over and shook him by the shoulders. The bottle fell to the concrete floor and broke.

"You Pembroke?"

"Yeah. Shit, was that my bottle?"

"Listen, this is a federal emergency." Budd spotted a jar of instant coffee on a filthy, littered tabletop. He ran water in the rusted sink and filled a mug, not waiting for it to turn hot. He dumped four heaping tablespoons into the cold water and thrust the dirty cup into Pembroke's hands. "Drink this, mister. We gotta get going. I need you to fly me to that slaughterhouse up the road."

Pembroke, eyes still closed, sat up and sniffed at the cup. "What slaughterhouse? What's this shit in here?"

"The one by the river."

"Where's my bottle?"

"Drink this down, it'll wake you up." The instant grounds hadn't dissolved; they floated on the top like brown ice. Pembroke sipped it, spit a mouthful onto the bed, and flung the cup away. "Jeeeez!" Only then did he realize that there was a man in a blue suit and body armor standing over him.

"Who the fuck're you? Where's my—"

"I need your helicopter. And I need it now. It's a federal emergency. You gotta fly me to that slaughterhouse by the river."

"There? The old one? It's three fucking miles away. You can drive faster. Fuck, you can walk! God in Hoboken . . . my head. Oooooh."

"I need a chopper. And I need it now. I'm authorized to pay you whatever you want."

Pembroke sagged back onto the bed. His eyes kept closing. Budd figured even if they managed to take off, he'd crash and kill them both.

"Let's go." The trooper pulled him up by his Oshkosh straps.

"When?"

"Now. This instant."

"I can't fly when I'm sleepy like this."

"Sleepy. Right. What do you charge?"

"A hundred twenty an hour."

"I'll pay you five hundred."

"Tomorrow." He started to lie down again, eyes closed, patting the dingy sheets for his bottle. "Get the hell outta here."

"Mister. Open your eyes."

He did.

"Shit," Pembroke muttered as he looked down the barrel of the black automatic pistol.

"Sir," Budd said in a low, respectful voice, "you're going to stand up and walk out to that helicopter and fly it exactly where I tell you. Do you understand me?"

A nod.

"Are you sober?"

"Stone cold," Pembroke said. He kept his eyes open for a whole two seconds before he passed out once more.

Melanie lay against the wall, caressing Beverly's sweaty blond hair, the poor girl gasping with every breath.

The young woman leaned forward and looked out. Emily, crying, stood in the window. Now Brutus turned suddenly and looked at Melanie, gestured her forward.

Don't go, she told herself. Resist.

She hesitated for a moment then walked out of the killing room toward him.

I go because I can't stop myself.

I go because he wants me.

She felt the chill sweeping into her from the floor, from the metal chains and meat hooks, from the cascade of slick water, from the damp walls spattered with mold and old, old blood.

I go because I'm afraid.

I go because he and I just killed a man together.

I go because I can understand him. . . .

Brutus pulled her close. "You think you're better'n me, right? You think you're a good person." She could tell he was whispering. People's faces change when they whisper. They look like they're telling you absolute truths but really they're just making the lie more convincing.

"Why're we selling it? Honey, you know what the doctor said. It's your ears. You can still hear now some, sure, but that'll go, remember what they said. You don't really want to start something you'll have to give up in a few years. We're doing it for you."

"See, I'm going to cut her in about three minutes, that chopper don't show up. I'd kill her I had more hostages. But I can't afford to lose another one. Least not yet."

Emily stood, hands still clasped together, staring out at the window, shaking as she sobbed.

"See"—Brutus closed his fiercely strong fingers around Melanie's arm—"if you were a good person, you were really good, you'd say, 'Take me, not her.' "

Stop it!

He slapped her. "No, keep your eyes open. So if you're

not like totally good you must have some bad inside you.
Somewhere. To let this little one get cut instead of you.
It's not like you'd die. I ain't gonna kill her. Just a little
pain. Make sure those assholes out . . . know I mean business. You won't put up with a little pain for your friend,
huh? You . . . bad. Just like me?"

She shook her head.

His head swiveled. Stoat's too. She guessed the phone
was ringing.

"Don't answer it," he said to Stoat. "Too much talking.
I'm sick and tired. . . ." He thumbed the blade. Melanie
was frozen. "You? You for her?" He moved the blade of
the knife one way then the other. Figure eights.

What would Susan have done?

Melanie hesitated though she knew the answer clearly.
Finally she nodded.

"Yeah," he said, eyebrows raised. "You mean it?"

"Two minutes," Stoat called.

Melanie nodded then embraced sobbing Emily, lowered
her head to the girl's cheek, directed her gently away
from the window.

Handy leaned close, his head inches from Melanie's,
his nose beside her ear. She couldn't hear his breath, of
course, but she had the impression he was inhaling something—the scent of her fear. Her eyes were fixed on the
knife. Which hovered over her skin: her cheek, her nose,
then her lips, her throat. She felt it caress a breast and
slide down her belly.

She felt the vibration of his voice, turned to look at his
lips. ". . . should I cut you? Your tit? No loss there—you
don't have no boyfriend to feel you up, do you? Your ear?
Hey, that wouldn't matter either. . . . You see that flick,
Reservoir Dogs?"

The blade lifted, slipped over her cheek. "How 'bout
your eye? Deaf and blind. You'd be a real freak then."

Finally she could take it no longer and she closed her
eyes. She tried to think of the tune of "Amazing Grace"
but it was nowhere in her memory.

A Maiden's Grave . . .

Nothing, nothing, all silence. Music can be vibrations
or sound, but not both.

And for me, neither.

Well, she thought, do whatever the fuck you're going to do and get it over with.

But then the hands pushed her brutally away and she opened her eyes, staggering across the floor. Brutus was laughing. She understood that this little sacrifice scene had been just a game. He'd been playing with her once again. He said, "Naw, naw, I've got other plans for you, little mouse. You're a present for my Pris."

He handed her off to Stoat, who held her firmly. She struggled but he gripped her like a vise. Brutus pulled Emily back into the window. The girl's eyes met Melanie's momentarily, and Emily pushed her hands together, praying, crying.

Brutus caught Emily's head in the crook of his left arm and lifted the tip of the knife to her eyes.

Melanie struggled futilely against Stoat's iron grip.

Brutus looked at his watch. "Time."

Emily sobbed; her joined fingers twitched as they uttered fervent prayers.

Brutus tightened his grip on Emily's head. He drew back a few inches with the knife, aimed right for the center of her closed right eye.

Stoat looked away.

Then suddenly his arms jerked in surprise. He looked straight up at the murky ceiling.

Brutus did too.

And finally Melanie felt it.

A huge thudding overhead, like the roll of a timpani. Then it grew closer and became the continuous sound of a bowed upright bass. An indiscernible pitch that Melanie felt on her face and arms and throat and chest.

Music is sound or vibration. But not both.

Their helicopter was overhead.

Brutus leaned out the window and looked up at the sky. With his bony fingers he dramatically unlocked the blade of his knife and closed it with what Melanie supposed was a loud snap. He laughed and said something to Stoat, words that Melanie was, for some reason, furious to realize she could not understand at all.

9:31 P.M.

"You're looking a little green around the gills there, Charlie."

"That pilot," Budd said to Potter, climbing into the van unsteadily. "Brother, I thought I'd bought the farm. He missed the field altogether, set her down in the middle of Route 346, almost on top of a fire truck. Now, there's an experience for you. Then he puked out the window and fell asleep. I kept shutting stuff off till the engine stopped. This smell in here isn't helping my stomach any." The captain's exemplary posture was shot to hell; he slumped into a chair.

"Well, you did good, Charlie," Potter told him. "Handy's agreed to give us a little more time. HRT'll be here any minute."

"Then what?"

"We shall see what we shall see," Potter mused.

"When I was driving up," Budd said, his eyes firmly on Potter's, "I heard a transmission. There was a shot inside?"

LeBow stopped typing. "Handy shot Bonner," the intelligence officer said. "We think."

"I think Handy and Wilcox," Potter continued, "took our strategy a little more seriously than I'd expected—about Bonner cutting a separate deal. They figured him for a snitch."

"Wasn't anything we could do about it," LeBow said offhandedly. "You can't second-guess stuff like that."

"Couldn't have been foreseen," Tobe recited like a cyborg in one of the science fiction novels he was always reading.

Charlie Budd—the faux U.S. attorney, a naif in the state police—was the only honest one in the group, for he was silent. He continued to look at Potter and their eyes met. The young man's gaze said he understood that Potter had known what would happen when he gave Budd the script; it'd been Potter's intent all along for Budd to plant the seed of distrust that would set Handy against Bonner.

But in Budd's glance was another message. His eyes

said, Oh, I get it, Potter. You used me to kill a man. Well, fair's fair; after all, I spied on you. But now our sins have canceled each other out. Mutual betrayals, and what's happened? Well, we're one hostage taker down, all to the good. But listen here: I don't owe you anything anymore.

A phone buzzed—Budd's own cellular phone. He took the call. He listened, punctuating the conversation with several significant "ums," and then clamped a hand over the mouthpiece.

"Well, how 'bout this? It's my division commander, Ted Franklin. He says there's a trooper in McPherson, not too far from here. A woman. She negotiated Handy's surrender five years ago in a convenience store holdup that went bad. He wants to know if he should ask her to come down here and help."

"Handy surrendered to her?"

Budd posed the question and listened for a moment. Then he said, "He did, yes. Seems there were no hostages. They'd all escaped and HRU was about to go in. A lot different from this, sounds like."

Potter and LeBow exchanged glances. "Have her come anyway," the negotiator said. "Whether she can help us directly or not, I can see Henry's licking his chops at the thought of more info on the bad guys."

"Yes indeed."

Budd relayed this to his commander and Potter was momentarily heartened at the thought of having an ally. He sat back in the chair and mused out loud, "Any way we can get another one or two out before HRT gets here?"

Angie asked, "What can we give him that he hasn't asked for? Anything?"

LeBow scrolled through the screen. "He's asked for transportation, food, liquor, guns, vests, electricity. . . ."

Angie said, "All the classic things. What every taker wants."

"But not money," Budd said suddenly.

Frowning, Potter glanced at the "Promises" side of the board, where the things they'd actually given Handy were recorded. "You're right, Charlie."

Angie asked, "He hasn't?" Surprised.

LeBow scrolled through his files and confirmed that

Handy had not once mentioned money. He asked the captain, "How'd you think of that?"

"I saw it in a movie," Budd explained.

"It's an opportunistic taking," LeBow offered. "Handy's not out to make a profit. He's an escaping criminal."

"So was this fellow," Budd said. Potter and LeBow glanced at the captain, who, blushing, added, "In the movie, I mean. I think it was Gene Hackman. Or maybe he was the one playing your role, Arthur. He's a good actor, Hackman is."

Angie said, "I agree with Charlie, Henry. It's true that a lot of criminal takers don't want money. But Handy's got a mercenary streak in him. Most of his underlying raps're larceny."

"Let's try to buy a couple of them," Potter said. "What've we got to lose?" He asked Budd, "Can you get your hands on any cash?"

"This time of night?"

"Immediately."

"Geez, I guess so. HQ's got petty cash. Maybe two hundred. How's that?"

"I'm talking about a hundred thousand dollars in small bills, unmarked. Within, say, twenty minutes."

"Oh," Budd said. "In that case, no."

LeBow said, "I'll call the DEA. They've got to have some buy money in Topeka or Wichita. We'll do an interagency transfer." He nodded at Tobe, who flipped through a laminated phone book and pushed in a phone number. LeBow began speaking through his headset in a voice as soft and urgent as his key strokes.

Potter picked up his phone and rang Handy.

"Hey, Art."

"How you doing, Lou? Ready to leave?"

"You bet I am. Go to a nice warm cabin. . . . Or a hotel. Or a desert island."

"Whereabouts, Lou? Maybe I'll come visit."

You got yourself quite a sense of humor, Art.

"I like cops with a sense of humor, you old son of a bitch."

"Where's my chopper?"

"Close as we could get it, Lou. In that field just over the

trees. Turned out the river was too choppy after all. Now
listen, Lou. You saw that chopper. It's a six-seater. I
know you wanted an eight- but that's all we could rustle
up." He hoped the man hadn't gotten a very good look at
it; you could fit half the Washington Redskins in an old
Sikorsky. "So, I've got a proposition. Let me buy a couple
of the hostages."

"Buy?"

"Sure. I'm authorized to pay up to fifty thousand each.
There just isn't room for the six of you and the pilot. No
overhead racks for carry-ons, you know. Let me buy a
couple of them."

*Shit, Art, I could shoot one of 'em. Then we'd have
plenty of space.*

But he'll laugh when he says it.

"Hey, I got an idea. 'Stead of giving one of 'em to you,
I could shoot her. Then we'd have plenty of room. For us
and our matched sets of American Tourister."

The laugh was almost a cackle.

"Ah, but Lou, if you kill her you don't get any money.
That'd be a bummer, as my nephew says." Potter said
this good-naturedly, for he felt the rapport had been re-
established. It was solid, fibrous. The negotiator knew
that the man was seriously considering the offer.

"Fifty thousand?"

"Cash. Small, unmarked bills."

A hesitation. "Okay. But only one. I keep the rest."

"Make it two. You'll still have two left. Don't want to
be greedy."

*Fuck it, Art. Gimme a hundred for one. That's the best
I'll do.*

"Nope," Handy said. "You get one. Fifty thousand.
That's the deal."

Potter glanced at Angie. She shook her head, perplexed.
Handy wasn't bargaining. After some feigned horse trading, Potter had been prepared to turn over the full one
hundred for a single girl.

"Well, all right, Lou. I accept."

"Only, Art?"

There was a tone in Handy's voice Potter hadn't yet

heard and it troubled him. He had no idea what was coming next. Where had he left himself exposed?

"Yes?"

"You have to tell me which one."

"How do you mean, Lou?"

The chuckle again. "Pretty easy question, Art. Which one do you want to buy? You know how it works, good buddy. You go to a car lot and say, I'll take that Chevy or that Ford. You pays your money, you takes your choice. Which one you want?"

His heart. That's where Potter had left himself unprotected. In his heart.

Budd and Angie stared at the agent.

Tobe kept his head down, focusing on his animate dials.

"Well, Lou, now . . ." Potter could think of nothing else to say. For the first time today, indecision crept into Potter's soul. And, worse, he heard it in his voice. This *couldn't* happen. Hesitation was deadly in a negotiation. Takers picked up on it immediately and it gave them power, deadly power. With someone like Handy, a control freak, hearing even a one-second pause in Potter's voice might make him feel invincible.

In the delay Potter sensed he was signing the death warrants for all four hostages. "Well, that's a tough question," Potter tried to joke.

"Must be. Fact, sounds like you're pretty damn flummoxed."

"I just—"

"Lemme help you, Art. Let's take a stroll through the used-hostage lot, why don't we? Well, here's the old one—that teach. Now, she's gotta lot of mileage on her. She's pretty run-down. A clunker, a lemon. That was Bonner's doing. He rode her hard, I tell you. Radiator's still leaking."

"Jesus," Budd muttered.

"That son of a bitch," placid Angie said.

Potter's eyes were firmly fixed on the yellow, homey windows of the slaughterhouse. Thinking: No! Don't do this to me! No!

"Then there's the pretty one. The blond one. Melanie."

Why does he know her name? Potter thought. Unreasonably angry. Did she tell him? Does she talk to him?

Has she fallen for him?

"I myself've taken a shine to her. But she's yours if you want her. Then we have this little shit that can't breathe. Oh, and finally we got the pretty one in the dress just about became Miss One-Eye. Take your pick."

Potter found himself looking at Melanie's picture. No, stop it, Potter commanded himself. Look away. He did. Now think! Who's the most at risk?

Who threatens his control the most?

The older teacher? No, not at all. The little girl, Emily? No, too frail and feminine and young. Beverly? Her illness would, as Budd had suggested, irritate Handy.

And what of Melanie? Handy's comment about taking a shine to her suggested that some Stockholming was going on. Was it enough to make him hesitate to kill her? Probably not. But she's older. How could he ask for an adult before a child?

Melanie, Potter's heart cried helplessly, I want to save you! And the same heart burned with rage for Handy's laying the decision in his lap.

He opened his mouth; he couldn't speak.

Budd frowned. "There isn't much time. He may back down if we don't pick right now."

LeBow touched his arm. He whispered, "It's okay, Arthur. Pick who you want. It doesn't really matter."

But it did. Every decision in a barricade incident mattered. He found himself staring at Melanie's picture again. Blond hair, large eyes.

Be forewarned, de l'Epée.

Potter sat up straight. "Beverly," he said suddenly into the phone. "The girl with the asthma." He closed his eyes.

"Hmmm. Good choice, Art. Her wheezing's gettin' on my nerves. I was getting close to doing her on general principles 'cause of that fucking wheeze-wheeze shit. Okey-dokey, when you get the cash, I'll send her out."

Handy hung up.

No one spoke for a long moment. "I hate that sound," Frances finally muttered. "I never want to hear a phone hang up again."

Potter sat back. LeBow and Tobe were looking at him. Slowly he swung to the window and looked out.

Melanie, forgive me.

"Hello, Arthur. This's a bad one, to hear tell."

Frank D'Angelo was a lanky, mustachioed man, calm as a summer pond. The head of the Bureau's Hostage Rescue Team had been in charge of the hot work in fifty or sixty negotiations Potter had run. The tactical agents—pulled off the Florida and Seattle barricades—had just arrived and were assembled in the gully behind the command van.

"It's been a long day, Frank."

"He's got a booby trap rigged?"

"So it seems. I'm inclined to get him out on a short leash and then apprehend or neutralize. But that's your speciality."

D'Angelo asked, "How many hostages left?"

"Four," Potter answered. "We're getting another one out in about ten minutes."

"You going to make a surrender pitch?"

The ultimate goal of all negotiations is to get the takers to surrender. But if you make your case to them just before they get their helicopter or other means of escape, they might conclude, reasonably, that an offer to surrender is actually a veiled ultimatum and that you're about to nail them. On the other hand, if you just green-light an attack there'll likely be casualties and you'll spend the rest of your life wondering if you might have gotten the takers to give up without any bloodshed.

Then too there was the Judas factor. The betrayal. Potter was promising Handy one thing and delivering something very different. Possibly—likely—the man's death. However evil Handy was, he and the negotiator were partners of sorts, and betraying him was something Potter would also have to live with for a long, long time.

"No," the agent said slowly, "no surrender pitch. He'll hear it as an ultimatum and figure we're planning an assault. Then we'll never get him out."

"What happened here?" D'Angelo pointed at the burned portion of the command van.

"Tell you about it later," Potter responded.

Inside the van D'Angelo, Potter, LeBow, and Budd looked over the architectural plans of the building and the terrain and SatSurv maps. "This is where the hostages are," Potter explained. "That was current as of an hour ago. And as far as we know the gas bomb is still rigged."

LeBow searched for his description of the device and read it aloud.

"And you're confident you'll get one more out?" the tactical agent asked.

"We're buying her for fifty thousand."

"The girl should be able to tell us if the trap's still set," D'Angelo said.

"I don't think it matters," Potter said, looking at Angie, who nodded her agreement. "Bomb or no bomb, he'll nail the hostages. If he's got any time at all, one or two seconds, he'll shoot them or pitch a grenade in."

"Grenade?" D'Angelo frowned. "Have a list of his weaponry?"

LeBow had already printed one out. The HRT commander read through it.

"He's got an MP-5? With scope and suppressor?" He shook his head in dismay.

There was a knocking on the side of the van and a young HRT officer stepped into the doorway. "Sir, we've completed initial reconnaissance."

"Go ahead." D'Angelo nodded at the map.

"This door here is wood with steel facing. Looks like it's rigged already with cutting charges."

D'Angelo looked at Potter.

"Some enthusiastic state troopers. That's how he got the Heckler & Koch."

D'Angelo nodded wryly, brushing his flamboyant mustache.

The trooper continued, "There's another door on the south side, much thinner wood. There's a loading dock in the back, here, by the river. The door's open far enough to get a tunnel rat under if they strip. Couple of the smaller guys. Next to it's a smaller door, reinforced steel, rusted shut. There's a runoff pipe here, a twenty-four-incher, barred with a steel grille. Second-floor windows are all barred with three-eighths-inch rods. These three windows here aren't visible from the HTs' position. The roof is covered with five-sixteenths-inch steel plates and the elevator shaft is sealed. The shaft access door's metal and I estimate bang-to-bullets of twenty to thirty seconds if we go in that way."

"Long time."

"Yessir. If we do four-man entry on the two doors, covering fire from a window, and two men in from the loading dock, I estimate we could engage and secure in eight to twelve seconds."

"Thanks, Tommy," D'Angelo said to his trooper. To Potter he added, "Not bad if it weren't for the trap." He asked Potter, "How Stockholmed is he?"

"Hardly at all," Angie offered. "He claims the more he knows somebody the more inclined he is to kill them."

D'Angelo's mustache received another stroke. "They good shots?"

Potter said, "Let's just say they're cool under fire."

"That's better'n being a good shot."

"And they've killed cops," Budd said.

"Both in firefights and as execution," Potter offered.

"Okay," D'Angelo said slowly. "My feeling is we can't do an entry. Not with the risk of the gas bomb and grenades. And his frame of mind."

"Have him walk to the chopper?" Potter asked. "It's right there." He tapped the map.

D'Angelo gazed at the portion of the map showing the field and nodded. "Think so. We'll pull everybody back out of sight, let the takers and hostages walk through the woods here."

Angie interrupted. "Handy'll pick his own route, don't you think, Arthur?"

"You're right. He'll want to be in charge of that. And it probably won't be the straightest one."

D'Angelo and Potter marked off four likely routes to get from the slaughterhouse to the chopper. LeBow drew them on the map. D'Angelo said, "I'll set up snipers in the trees here and here and here. Put the ground men in deep camouflage along all four routes. When the takers go by, the snipers'll acquire. Then we'll stun the whole group with smokeless. The agents on the ground'll grab the hostages and pull 'em down. The snipers'll take out the HTs if they show any threat. That sound okay to you?"

Potter was staring down at the map.

A moment passed.

"Arthur?"

"Yes, it sounds good, Frank. Very good."

D'Angelo stepped outside to brief his agents.

Potter looked at Melanie's picture and then sat down once more, staring out the window.

"Waiting is the hardest, Charlie. Worse than anything."

"I can see that."

"And this is what you'd call your express barricade," Tobe offered, eyes on his dials and screens. " 'S'only been about eleven hours. That's nothing."

Suddenly someone burst through the open doorway so quickly every law enforcer inside the van except Potter reached for weapons.

Roland Marks stood in the doorway. "Agent Potter," he said coldly. "Do I understand you're going to take him down?"

Potter looked past him at a tree bending in the wind. The breeze had picked up remarkably. It would bolster the lie about the river being too choppy to land a helicopter.

"Yes, we are."

"Well, I was just speaking to your comrade Agent D'Angelo. He shared with me a disturbing fact."

Potter couldn't believe Marks. In the space of a few hours he'd nearly screwed up the negotiations twice and almost lost his life in the process. And here he was on the offensive again. The agent was a few seconds away from arresting him just to get the pushy man out of his life.

Potter lifted an eyebrow.

"That there's a fifty-fifty chance one of the hostages will die."

Potter had assessed it at sixty-forty in the hostages' favor. But Marian had always chided him for being an incurable optimist. The agent rose slowly and stepped through the burnt doorway, motioning the attorney general after him. He took a tape cassette from his pocket, held it up prominently then put it back. Marks's eyes gave a flicker.

"Was there anything else you wanted to say?" Potter asked.

Marks's face suddenly softened but just for a moment, as if he recognized an apology forming in his throat and shot it dead. He said, "I don't want those girls hurt."

"I don't either."

"For God's sake, put him in a chopper, have him release the hostages. When he lands the Canadians can come down upon him like the proverbial Assyrians."

"Oh, but he has no intention of going to Canada," Potter said impatiently.

"I thought . . . But that special clearance you boys put together . . ."

"Handy doesn't believe a word of that. And even if he did he knows we'd put a second transponder in the chopper. His plans are to head straight to Busch Stadium. Or wherever his TV tells him there's a big game tonight."

"What?"

"Or maybe a parking lot at the University of Missouri just as evening classes are letting out. Or McCormick Place. He'll land someplace where there'll be a huge crowd around. There's no way we can take him in a scenario like that. A hundred people could be killed."

Understanding dawned in Marks's eyes. And whether he saw those lives jeopardized, or his career, or perhaps was seeing nothing more than the hopeless plight of his own poor daughter, he nodded. "Of course. Sure, he's the sort who'd do just that. You're right."

Potter chose to read the concession as an apology and decided to let him be.

Tobe pushed his head out of the doorway. "Arthur, I just got a phone call. It's that Kansas State detective Charlie told us about. Sharon Foster. She's on the line."

Potter had doubts that Foster could help them. Introducing a new negotiator in a barricade can have unpredictable results. But one thing Potter had decided might be helpful was her gender. His impression of Handy was that he was threatened by men—the very fact that he'd gone to ground with ten female hostages suggested that he might listen to a woman without his defenses raised.

Inside the van Potter leaned against the wall as he

spoke. "Detective Foster? This is Arthur Potter. What's your ETA?"

The woman said that she was proceeding under sirens and lights and should be at the incident site by ten-thirty, ten-forty. The voice was young and matter-of-fact and extremely calm, though she was probably doing a hundred miles an hour.

"Look forward to it," Potter said, a little gruffly, and hung up.

"Good luck," Marks said. He hesitated, as if thinking of something else he might say. He settled for "God save those girls" and left the van.

"DEA's on the way," Tobe announced. "They've got the cash. Coming in by confiscated turbo helicopter. They get the best toys, those pricks."

"Hey," Budd said, "they're bringing a hundred thousand, right?"

Potter nodded.

"Where're we gonna keep the fifty that we don't give him? That's a lot of cash to store."

Potter held his finger to his lips. "We'll split it, Charlie, you and me."

Budd blinked in shock.

At last Potter winked.

The captain laughed hard, as did Angie and Frances.

Tobe and LeBow were more restrained. Those who knew Arthur Potter understood that he rarely made jokes. He tended to do so only when he was at his most nervous.

10:01 P.M.

The killing room had become cold as a freezer.

Beverly and Emily huddled against Melanie as they all watched Mrs. Harstrawn lying ten feet away: eyes open, breathing, but otherwise dead as Bear, who still blocked the entrance to the room and whose body was sending three long fingers of black blood reaching slowly toward them.

Beverly, air rasping into her lungs, as if she'd never breathe again, could not take her eyes off the streams.

Something was going on in the other room. Melanie couldn't see clearly but it seemed that Brutus and Stoat were packing up—guns and bullets and the tiny TV set. They were walking through the large room, looking around. Why? It was as if they felt sentimental about the place.

Maybe they were going to give up. . . .

Then she thought, No way. They're going to get into that helicopter, drag us along with them, and escape. We'll live this same nightmare over and over and over again. Fly to someplace else. There'll be other hostages, other deaths. More dark rooms.

Melanie found her hand once more at her hair, uneasily entwining a finger in the strands, which were now damp and filthy. No "shine" now. No light. No hope. She lowered her hand.

Brutus strode into the room and gazed at Mrs. Harstrawn, looking down at her creased brow. He had that slight smile on his face, the smile Melanie had come to recognize and to hate. He pulled Beverly after him.

"She's going home. Going home." Brutus pushed her out of the door of the killing room. He turned back, pulled a knife from his pocket, opened it, and cut the wire that had run to the canister of gasoline. He tied Melanie's hands behind her back and then her feet. Emily's too.

Brutus laughed. "Tying your hands up—that's like gagging you too. How 'bout that?"

Then he was gone, leaving the three remaining hostages.

All right, she thought. The twins had done it; they would too. They'd get out by following the scent of the river. Melanie turned around, her back toward Emily's, offered her bound hands. The little girl understood and struggled with the knots. But it was useless; Emily admired long fingernails but had none of her own.

Try harder, come on!

Suddenly Melanie shivered as Emily's fingers dug deep into her wrists. She cringed as the little girl's hands

tugged once desperately at her fingers then suddenly disappeared. Someone had the girl, was dragging her away!

What's going on?

Frowning, Melanie twisted around.

Bear!

His face bubbling with blood and twisting in rage, he
pulled Emily to the wall. He shoved her against the tile.
She fell, stunned. Melanie opened her mouth to scream
but Bear lunged forward, stuffing a filthy rag into her
mouth and clamping his bloody hand on her shoulder.

Melanie fell backward. Bear's huge face dropped down
onto her breast and kissed her, wet and bloody. She felt
the moisture through her blouse. His blurry eyes looked
over her body as she tried to spit the rag from her mouth.
He pulled a knife from his pocket. He opened it with a
bloody hand and his teeth.

She tried to squirm away but he continued to clutch her
breast. He rose up on one elbow and rolled off her. She
kicked hard but her bound feet rose only an inch or two. A
stream of blood poured from his slacks, where it had been
pooling for the past hour, and covered her legs with the
cold, thick liquid.

Melanie, sobbing in terror, tried to push away from
him, but he gripped the cloth over her breasts with a desperate strength. He threw his leg over her calves, pinning
her to the ground as more blood cascaded over her.

Please, help me. Somebody. De l'Epée. . . .

Somebody! Please—

Oh, no. . . . She shivered in horror. Not this. Please, no.

He tugged her skirt above her waist with his knife hand.
Yanked down her black tights. The knife started up along
her thigh to her pink cotton panties.

No! She tried to struggle away, her ears roaring from
the effort. But there was no escape. His huge bulk lay
upon her and dripped his heavy blood onto her legs. The
blade touched her mound, cut through one seam of the
underwear. Through the sparse hair between her legs
she felt the cold steel and recoiled.

A hideous grin on his face, he looked at her with icy
disks of eyes. The metal sliced the other side of the
panties. They fell away.

Her vision grew dim. Don't faint! Don't lose your sight too!

Pinned to the ground by his weight. Afraid to move anyway; the knife hovered an inch above her pink cleft, the faint hair, the pale skin.

With his free hand Bear reached down to his crotch and unzipped. He coughed, spraying more blood upon her, spattering her chest and neck. As he reached in his pants the knife dipped and she groaned, nearly gagging on the rag, as the cold metal slipped in between her legs.

Then the blade rose again as he guided his huge, glistening penis out. She struggled away from him but he let go of himself and once more grabbed her breast, holding her still.

He rubbed against her leg, blood pouring off his twitching organ and running onto her bare thigh. He pressed against her skin once, twice, and then shifted his weight to move further along her body.

And then . . .

Then . . .

Nothing.

She was breathing faster than she believed possible, her chest trembling. Bear was frozen, eyes inches from hers, one hand on her chest, the other holding the blade, point down, poised between her legs, millimeters from her flesh.

She spit the rag from her mouth, smelled his putrid stink, the rich, rusty smell of blood. Sucked in air.

Felt the cold knife twitch against her skin once, twice, and then it went still.

It took a full minute before she realized that he was dead.

Melanie fought down the nausea, sure that she'd be sick. But then slowly the sensation passed. Her legs were numb; his bulk had cut off her circulation. She planted her bound hands firmly on the concrete beneath her and pushed. A huge effort. But the blood was slick, like fresh enamel, and she managed to slide several inches away from him. Try again. Then once more. Soon her legs were almost out from under him.

One more time . . .

Her feet popped out and came to rest exactly where he held the knife. Tensing her stomach muscles, she lifted her feet slightly and began sawing the wire against the steel blade of the knife.

She glanced toward the doorway. No sign of Brutus or Stoat. Her stomach muscles screamed as she sawed against the wire.

Finally . . . snap. It gave way. Melanie climbed to her feet. She kicked Bear's left hand once, then again. The blade fell to the ground. She kicked it to Emily. Gestured for her to pick it up. The little girl sat up, crying silently. She looked at the knife, which was resting in a pool of blood, and shook her head no. Melanie responded with a fierce nod. Emily closed her eyes, turned, and groped in the slick red pool for the weapon. Finally she gripped it, wincing, and held the blade up. Melanie turned and began rubbing the wire binding her wrists against the blade. A few minutes later she felt the strands break. She grabbed the knife and then cut Emily's wire as well.

Melanie stole to the doorway. Brutus and Stoat were at the windows, looking away from the killing room. Beverly was standing by the door and Melanie could see a trooper approaching with an attaché case. So they were exchanging the girl for something. With luck, they'd be busy for some minutes—long enough for Melanie and the others to get to the dock.

Melanie bent over Mrs. Harstrawn, who was now soaked in Bear's blood. The woman stared at the ceiling.

"Come on," Melanie signed. "Get up."

The teacher didn't move.

"Now!" Melanie signed emphatically.

Then the woman signed words Melanie had never seen before in ASL. "Kill me."

"Get up!"

"Can't. You go."

"Come on." Melanie's hands stabbed the air. *"No time!"* She slapped the woman, tried to pull her to her feet; the teacher was dead weight.

Melanie grimaced in disgust. "Come on. Or I'll have to leave you!"

The teacher shook her head and closed her eyes. Melanie

put the knife, still open, into the pocket of her skirt and, pulling Emily by the hand, slipped out of the doorway. They stepped into the door leading to the back of the slaughterhouse and vanished through the dim corridors.

Lou Handy looked at the cash, a surprisingly small pile for that much money, and said, "We should've thought of this before. Every little bit helps."

Wilcox looked out the window. "How many snipers you think they got on us?"

"Oh . . . lessee . . . 'bout a hundred. And with us nailing that trooper of theirs, they've probably got one'r two ready to shoot away and pretend they didn't hear the order not to."

"I always thought you'd be a good sniper, Lou."

"Me? Naw, I'm too, you know, impatient. I knew some of 'em in the service. You know what you do mosta the time? You gotta lie on your belly for a couple, three days 'fore you can make one shot. Not move a muscle. What's the fun of that?"

He flashed back to his days in the military. They seemed both easier and harder than life on the run, and very similar to life in prison.

"The shooting'd be fun, though."

"I'll give you that. . . . Oh, fucking hell!"

He'd glanced at the back of the slaughterhouse and saw bloody footprints leading out of the room where the girls had been.

"Shit," Wilcox spat out.

Lou Handy was a man driven by positive forces, he truly believed. He rarely lost his temper and, yes, he was a murderer but when he killed he killed for expediency but hardly ever from rage.

Yet, a few times in his life, a fierce anger bubbled up from his soul and he became the cruelest man on earth. Unstoppably cruel.

"That cunt," he whispered, his voice cracking. "That cocksucking cunt."

They ran to the doorway, where the bloody prints disappeared.

Handy said, "Stay here."

"Lou—"

"Stay the fuck here!" Handy raged. "I'm gonna fix her clock like I shoulda done a long time ago." He plunged into the murky bowels of the slaughterhouse, the knife in his hand, held low, with the blade up, as he'd been taught not in the army but on the streets of Minneapolis.

10:27 P.M.

Sight is a miracle and it's the foremost of our senses. But we are as often informed by the adjunct perception, sound.

The sight of a river tells us what it is but the sound of water also can explain its character: placid or deadly or dying itself. For Melanie Charrol, deprived of this sense, smell had taken over. River rapids were airy and electric. Still water smelled stale. Here the Arkansas River smelled ominous—pungent and deep and decaying, as if it were the grave of many bottom feeders.

Still, it said, Come to me, come to me, I'm your way out.

Melanie followed its call unerringly. Through the maze of the deserted slaughterhouse she led the little girl in the hopeless Laura Ashley dress. The floorboards were rotting through in many places, but the bare bulbs from the main portion of the slaughterhouse were so bright that even back here enough light filtered into these reaches to illuminate their path. Occasionally she paused, lifted her nose, and breathed the air to make certain they were headed in the right direction. Then she'd turn once more toward the river, spinning around and looking behind her when the panic got to be too much.

Smell has not replaced sound as our primitive warning system.

But Brutus and Stoat didn't seem to have noticed the escape yet.

The teacher and student continued through the increas-

ing gloom, pausing often and feeling their way along. The
thin shafts of light were Melanie's only salvation, and
now she glanced up at them. The upper part of the walls
had rotted away and it was from there that the faint heav-
enly glow filled the murky underworld sky of this part of
the slaughterhouse.

Then there it was, in front of them! A narrow door below a sign that said *Dock*. Melanie tightened her grip on
Emily's hand and tugged the little girl along behind her.
They pushed through the door and found a large loading-
dock area. It was mostly empty but there were some oil
drums that looked like they might still float. But the large
door opening onto the outside was raised only a foot or
so—high enough for them to crawl under but not high
enough to push out one of the drums.

They walked to it and slipped outside.

Freedom, she thought, breathing the intoxicating air.

She laughed to herself at the irony—here she was re-
joicing at being Outside, tearfully thankful for escaping
from the horrible Inside. Motion startled her; she saw a
boat not far offshore. Two officers in it. Somehow, they'd
already spotted the girls and were now rowing toward the
dock.

Melanie turned Emily around, signed, "Wait here for
them. Stay down, hide behind that post."

Emily shook her head. "But aren't you—"

"I'm going back. I can't leave her."

"Please." The little girl's tears streaked down her face.
The wind tossed her hair around her head. "She didn't
want to come."

"Go."

"Come with me. God wants you to. He told me He
does."

Melanie smiled, embraced the little girl, and stepped
back. Looked over her tattered, filthy dress. "Next week,
we have date. Shopping."

Emily wiped tears and walked to the edge of the dock.
The policemen were very close, one smiling at the girl,
the other scanning the building with a short black shotgun
pointed toward the black windows above their heads.

Melanie glanced at them, waved, then slipped back beneath the loading-dock door. Once inside, she took Bear's knife from the pocket of her bloody skirt and started back into the slaughterhouse, instinctively following the same route she'd taken to arrive here.

Her neck hairs stirred suddenly and she felt a wave of the sixth sense that some deaf people claim they possess. When she looked, yes, yes, there he was—Brutus, about fifty feet away, crouching, making his way from one piece of machinery to another. In his hand he too held a short knife.

She shivered in terror and ducked behind a stack of employee lockers. She thought of climbing into one but remembered that he'd hear any sound she made. Then the sixth sense came back, pelting her neck. Melanie realized, though, that this wasn't anything supernatural at all; it was the vibration of Brutus's voice, calling to Stoat.

What was he saying?

A moment later, she learned. The lights went out and she was plunged into blackness.

She dropped to the ground, paralyzed with terror. Deaf, and now blind. She curled into a ball for a moment, praying she'd faint, the terror was so great. She realized she'd dropped the knife. She patted the ground but soon gave up on it; she knew that Brutus would have heard the sound of the weapon falling and was probably making his way toward her right now. He could be kicking aside everything in his way and she'd never know, while Melanie herself had to crawl carefully over the ground, picking her way silently over bits of metal and wood, machinery and tools.

I have to—

No!

She felt something on her shoulder.

She turned in panic, lashing out with her palm.

But it was just a wire dangling from the ceiling.

Where is he? There? Or there?

Be. Quiet. It's the only thing that'll save you.

Then a reassuring thought: He can hear, yes, but he can't see any better than I can.

Want to hear a joke, Susan? What's worse off than a bird that can't hear?

A fox that can't see.

Eight gray birds, sitting in dark . . .

If I'm absolutely silent he'll never know where I am.

The remarkable internal compass that the otherwise unjust son of a bitch Fate gave Melanie tells her that she's headed in the right direction, back toward the killing room. And by God she *will* carry Donna Harstrawn on her shoulders if she has to.

Slowly. One foot before the other.

Silent. Absolutely silent.

Going to be easier than he'd thought.

Lou Handy was at his worst and he knew it—still fired up with bitterness, aching for a payback, but thinking coolly now. This was when he killed and tortured and enjoyed it the most. He'd followed the bloody footsteps to the loading dock, where, he'd assumed, both of the little shits had gotten out. But then as he was about to start back he'd heard something—a clink of metal, a scrape. And he'd looked down the corridor and seen her, Melanie, the mouse bitch freak of nature, making her way back to the main room of the slaughterhouse.

He'd moved closer and what was that he'd heard?

A *squish, squish* sound.

Her footsteps. Bloody footsteps. Good old Bonner, leaking and gross to the very end, had bled all over her shoes. With every step Melanie took she was broadcasting exactly where she was. So he'd called to Wilcox to shut the lights out.

It was wild how dark the place was. Pitch. Couldn't see your hand. At first he was real careful about making sounds. Then he thought, Why, you fuck, she can't hear you! And he hurried after her, pausing every few minutes to listen for the sound of the wet squish.

There it is.

Beautiful, honey.

Closing in.

Listen. . . .

Squish.

Can't be more than thirty feet away. Look, here we go. There she is. He saw a ghostly form in front of him, walking back toward the main room of the plant.

Squish, squish.

He walked closer to her. He knocked a table over but her footsteps just kept rollin' along. She didn't hear a fucking thing. Closing the distance now, fifteen feet . . . ten. Five.

Right behind her.

The way he'd been behind Rudy, smelled the man's Vitalis, seen the oak dust on his shirt and the bulge in the back pocket that was a wallet filled with what it shouldn't've been filled with. "You fucker," Handy'd screamed to his brother, not seeing red, like the expression, but seeing black fire, seeing nothing but his rage. Rudy had sneered, kept on walking. And the gun in Handy's fist began firing. A little gun, a .22, loaded with long, not even a long-rifle, slugs. Which left little red dots on the neck and his brother doing the fucking scary little dance before he fell to the floor and died.

Handy raged again at Art Potter for bringing up the thought of Rudy today, like he was planting the memory in Handy's soul the way a pebble got pushed into your palm in a prison yard fight. Raged at Potter and at fat, dead Bonner and at Melanie, the fucking spooked mouse bitch.

Two feet behind her, watching her timid steps.

She didn't have a clue. . . .

This was fucking great, walking in step with her. There were so many possibilities. . . .

Hello, Miss Mouse. . . .

But he picked the simplest. He leaned close and licked the back of her neck.

He thought she'd break her back she leapt away from him so fast, twisting sideways and falling into a stack of rusted sheet metal. His hand closed on her hair and he dragged her after him, twisting and stumbling.

"Yo, Shep, put those lights back on!"

A moment later the room filled with dim light and Handy could make out the doorway to the main part of the slaughterhouse. Melanie struggled to pry his hands from her hair but he had a good grip and she could beat till kingdom come and he'd never let her go.

"You're making strange little peeps. I don't like it. Shut up! Shut the fuck up!" He slapped her in the face. He didn't think she got what he was saying but in any case she shut up. He dragged her through the cascading water, through the aisles of junk.

Straight to a decapitation guillotine.

It was basically a huge piece of butcher block, carved out with an indentation for the pig's or steer's chest. On the top was mounted a frame holding a triangular blade, operated by a long rubber-covered handle. A big fucking paper cutter.

Wilcox watched. He asked, "You really gonna . . . ?"

"What about it?" Handy screamed.

"It's just we're so close to getting out, man."

Handy ignored him, grabbed a piece of wire from the floor, and wrapped it around Melanie's right wrist. Twisted the tourniquet tight. She struggled, hit him in the shoulder with her left fist. "Fucking freak," he muttered, and slugged her hard in the back. She dropped to the floor, where she curled into a ball, moaning, staring in horror at her hand turning blue.

Handy lit his Bic lighter and ran it slowly over the blade of the guillotine. She shook her head violently, eyes huge. "Should've thought about it before you turned on me." He scooped her up from the floor and slammed her against the guillotine.

Sobbing, slapping at him, the mouse bitch tried to struggle away. He figured the pain in her right hand, now deep purple from the wire, was close to unbearable. Handy shoved her groin against the guillotine and pushed her forward, facedown, extending her right arm under the blade. He kicked her legs out from underneath her. She lost all leverage and dangled, helpless, from the machine. Handy easily pinioned her hand in the cutting groove.

He hesitated a moment and looked down at her face, listening to the gasping sound that rose from her throat. "God, I hate that fucking sound you people make. Hold her, Shep."

Wilcox hesitated, stepped forward, and took her arm in

both of his hands. "Don't think I want to watch this," he said uneasily, and looked away.

"I do," Handy muttered. Unable to resist the urge, he lowered his head close to her face, inhaled her scent, rubbing his cheek against her tears. Stroked her hair.

Then his hands rose to the lever. He worked it back and forth, loosening it up, dropping the blade to her flesh, lifting it again. It rose to its full height. He took the rubber handle in both hands.

The phone rang.

Handy looked at it.

A pause. Wilcox released Melanie's hand, stepped away from the guillotine.

Shit. Handy debated.

"Answer it."

" 'Lo?" Wilcox asked into the receiver. Then listened. He shrugged and glanced at Handy, who paused. "Yo, homes, it's for you."

"Tell Potter to go to hell."

"It ain't Potter. It's a girl. And I'll tell you, sounds like she's some fox."

10:58 P.M.

Potter sat at the window, looking through his Leica binoculars, while behind him young, fierce Detective Sharon Foster, who'd pulled her cruiser hell-for-leather into the forward staging area ten minutes before, was pacing nervously and swearing like a sailor at Louis Handy.

"The fuck you say, Lou," she snarled. Like many female line officers Foster had that resolute, humorless grit that her pert blond ponytail and pretty face couldn't belie.

"Been a while, you bitch. You a detective now?"

"Yep. I got promoted." She bent down and squinted through the command van's window at the slaughterhouse, her head inches from Potter's. "What the hell've you done with *your* life, Lou? Aside from screwing it up royal?"

"Hey, I'm right proud of my accomplishments." From the speaker came the cold chuckle Potter recognized so well.

"I always knew you were one grade-A fuckup. They could write a book about you."

Potter recognized exactly what Foster was doing. It wasn't his way. He preferred to be more easygoing, Will Rogersish. Tough when he needed to be, but he avoided jousting, which could easily escalate into emotional skirmishes. Arthur Potter hadn't bantered with Marian and he didn't banter with his friends. But sometimes with certain takers—usually brash, overconfident criminals—this young woman's style worked: the barbs, the give-and-take.

Potter continued to stare at the slaughterhouse, trying desperately to get a look at Melanie. The last of the students, Emily, had been picked up by Stillwell's deputies in the skiff behind the building. Through Frances the little girl had explained that Melanie had gotten her out and then gone back for Mrs. Harstrawn. But that had been nearly twenty minutes ago and no one had seen the last two hostages escape. Potter assumed Handy had found her. He was desperate to know if she was all right but would never interrupt a negotiator at work.

"You're an asshole, Lou," Foster continued. "You may get away in that chopper but they're going to catch you. Canada? They'll extradite your ass so fast it'll make your head spin."

"They gotta find me first."

"You think they wear red jackets and Smokey the Bear hats and chase down muggers with whistles? You've killed, Lou—hostages and cops. There isn't a law enforcer in the world gonna stop till they get you."

LeBow and Potter exchanged glances. Potter was growing uneasy. She was pushing him a lot. Potter frowned but she either missed or ignored the expression, above criticism from an older man—and a Feebie at that. He was also feeling the thorns of jealousy. It'd taken him hours to build up a rapport with Handy; Potter was Stockholmed through and through. And here was this new kid on the

block, this blond chippy, stealing away his good friend
and comrade.

Potter nodded discreetly at the computer. LeBow
caught his meaning and went on line to the National Law
Enforcement Personnel Database. A moment later he
turned the screen for Potter to read. Sharon Foster only
looked young and inexperienced; she was in fact thirty-
four and had an impressive record as a hostage negotiator.
In thirty barricade situations she'd managed clean surrenders in twenty-four. The others had gone hot—HRT assaults had been required—but they'd been EDs. When
emotionally disturbed takers are involved, negotiated solutions work only ten percent of the time.

"I like Art better," Handy said. "He don't give me any
shit."

"That's my Lou, always looking for the easy way."

"Fuck you," Handy barked.

"Something I've been thinking about, Lou," she added
coyly. "I'm wondering if you're really going to Canada."

Now Potter glanced at D'Angelo. The tactical plan required that Handy and Wilcox trek through the woods to
the helicopter. If Foster made him think they hadn't believed him, Handy would suspect a trap and stay holed up.

Potter stood up, shaking his head. Foster glanced but
ignored him. LeBow and Angie were shocked at the dis-
respect. Potter sat down again, more embarrassed than hurt.

"Sure, I'm going to Canada. I've got myself a special
priority. I've talked to the fucking FAA myself."

As if he hadn't spoken, her southern-accented voice
rasped, "You're a cop killer, Lou. You touch down anywhere in these United States, with or without hostages,
you're dead meat. Every cop in the country knows your
face. Wilcox's too. And believe me, they'll shoot first and
read rights to your bleeding body. And I promise you,
Lou, any ambulance carrying you to a prison hospital's
gonna take its own sweet fucking time gettin' you there."

Potter had heard enough of her hardball tactics. He was
sure she'd push Handy right back into his hole. He
reached for her shoulder. But he stopped when he heard
Handy say, "Nobody can catch me. I'm the worst thing
you'll ever come across. I'm cold death."

It wasn't Handy's words that gave Potter pause but the tone of his voice. He sounded like a scared child. Almost pathetic. However unorthodox her style, Foster had touched something in Handy.

She turned to him. "Can I make a surrender offer?"

LeBow, Budd, and D'Angelo all looked at Potter.

What was in Handy's mind? he wondered. A sudden awareness of the hopelessness of the situation? Maybe a reporter had managed to broadcast that federal Hostage Rescue had arrived and surrounded the slaughterhouse, and Handy had heard it on his television.

Or maybe he'd simply gotten tired.

It happened. In an instant the energy dissipates. HTs ready to come out with guns blazing will just sit on the floor when HRT kicks in the door and look at the approaching agents without the energy to lift their hands over their heads.

Yet there was another possibility, one that Potter hated to consider. Which was that this young woman was simply better than he was. That she'd breezed in, assessed Handy, and then pegged him right. Again the jealousy tore at him. *What should I do?*

He thought suddenly of Melanie. What would be most likely to save her?

Potter nodded to the young detective. "Sure. Go ahead."

"Lou, what'll it take to make you come out?"

Potter thought: *Lemme fuck you.*

"Can I fuck you?"

"You'd have to ask my husband and he'd say no."

A pause.

"There's nothing I want but freedom. And I got that."

"Do you?" Foster asked softly.

Another pause. Longer than the first.

Potter speculated. *Fuck, yeah. And nobody's taking it away from me.*

But Handy said, in effect, just the opposite. "I don't . . . I don't want to die."

"Nobody wants to shoot you, Lou."

"Everybody wants to shoot me. And I go back, the judge'll give me the needle."

"We can talk about that." Her voice was gentle, almost motherly.

Potter stared at the yellow square of light. Somewhere in his heart he was beginning to believe that he'd made some very serious mistakes tonight. Mistakes that had cost lives.

Foster turned to the agent. "Who can guarantee the state won't seek the death penalty?"

Potter told her that Roland Marks was nearby, sent Budd to find him. A moment later Marks climbed into the van and Foster explained to him what Handy wanted.

"He'll surrender?" The assistant attorney general's cold eyes were on Potter, who felt all the censure and scorn he'd fired at Marks earlier that day flow right back at himself. For the first time today Potter found he couldn't hold Marks's eye.

"I think I can get him to," Foster said.

"Yes indeed. I'll guarantee whatever he wants. Put a big red seal on it. Ribbons too. I can't get an existing-sentence reduction—"

"No. I'm sure he understands that."

"But I'll guarantee we don't go sticking those little needles in his arm."

"Lou. The state assistant attorney general is here. He's guaranteeing that they won't go after the death penalty if you surrender."

"Yeah?" There was a pause, the sound of a hand over the receiver. Then: "Same for my boy Shep here?"

Foster frowned. LeBow turned his computer to her and she read about Wilcox. She looked at the AG, who nodded.

"Sure, Lou. Both of you. And the other guy with you?"

Potter thought: *Son of a bitch had himself an accident.*

Handy laughed. "Had a accident."

Foster lifted an inquiring eyebrow to Potter, who said, "Believed dead."

"Okay, you and Wilcox," the blond detective said, "you got a deal."

The same deal that Potter, through Charlie Budd, had offered him. Why was Handy accepting it now? A moment later he found out.

"Hold up, you frigid bitch. That's not all."

"I love it when you talk dirty, Lou."

"I also want a guarantee to stay outta Callana. I killed that guard there. I go back and they'll pound me to death for sure. No more federal time."

Foster looked once more at Potter, who nodded to Tobe. "Call Justice," he whispered. "Dick Allen."

The deputy attorney general in Washington.

"Lou," Foster said, "We're checking on it now."

Potter again anticipated: *I'm still horny. Let's fuck.*

Handy's voice brightened and the old devil was back. "Come sit on my cock while we're waiting."

"I would, Lou, but I don't know where it's been."

"In my Jockeys for way too long."

"Just keep it there for a while longer then."

Potter was patched through to Allen, who listened and agreed reluctantly that if Handy was willing to surrender he could serve his state time first. Allen would also waive the federal charges for the escape though not for the murder of the guard. The practical effect of this was that Handy wouldn't have to surrender to any federal jailers until about fifty years after he'd died of old age.

Foster relayed this to Handy. There was a long pause. A moment later Handy's voice said, "Okay, we'll do it."

Foster looked at Potter with a cocked eyebrow. He nodded numbly, dumbfounded.

"But I gotta see it in writing," Handy said.

"Okay, Lou. We can arrange that."

Potter was already writing the terms out longhand. He handed the sheet to Henry LeBow to type and print out.

"So, that's it," LeBow said, eyes on his blue screen. "Score one for the good guys."

Laughter broke out. Potter's face burned as he watched the elation on the faces of Budd and the other federal agents. He smiled too but he understood—as did no one else on the threat management team—that he had both won and lost. And he knew that it was not his strength or courage or intelligence that had failed him but his judgment.

Which is the worst defeat a man can suffer.

"Here we go," LeBow said, offering the printout to Potter. He and Marks signed the document and Stevie Oates made one last run to the slaughterhouse. When he returned he wore a perplexed expression and carried a bottle of Corona beer, which Handy had given him.

"Agent Potter?" Sharon Foster had apparently been calling his name several times. He looked up. "Would you like to coordinate the surrender?"

He stared at her for a moment and nodded. "Yes, of course. Tobe, call Dean Stillwell. Ask him to please come in here."

Tobe made the call. Unfazed, LeBow continued to type in information on the incident log. Detective Sharon Foster glanced at Potter with a look that he took to be one of sympathy; it was patronizing and hurt far more than a snide smile of triumph would have. As he looked at her he felt suddenly very old—as if everything he'd known and done in his life, every way he looked at things, every word he'd said to strangers and to friends was, in an instant, outmoded and invalid.

If not an outright lie.

He was in camouflage gear so no one saw the lean man lying in a stand of starkly white birch not far from the command van.

His hands clasped the night-vision binoculars, sweat dotting his palms copiously.

Dan Tremain had been frozen in this position for an hour, during which time a helicopter had come and gone, the federal HRT had arrived and assembled nearby, and a squad car had streaked up to the van, bearing a young policewoman.

Tremain had taken in the news, which was spreading like fire in a wheat field from trooper to trooper, that Handy had decided to give it up in exchange for an agreement not to seek the death penalty.

But for Dan Tremain this wasn't acceptable.

His trooper, young Joey Wilson, and that poor girl this afternoon had not died so that Lou Handy might live long enough to kill again, certainly to gloat and relive the perverse joy at the carnage he'd caused throughout his pointless life.

Sacrifice was sometimes necessary. And who better than a soldier to give up his life in the name of justice?

"Surrender in ten minutes," a voice called from behind him. Tremain could not possibly have said whether it was the voice of a trooper or that of an angel dipping low from God's own heaven to make this announcement. In any event he nodded and rose to his feet. He stood tall, wiped the tears from his face, adjusted his uniform, brushed his hair with his fingers. Never one to preen, Tremain had decided it was important that he look strong and resolute and proud when he ended his career in the dramatic fashion he had planned.

11:18 P.M.

Surrender is the most critical stage of a barricade.

More lives are lost in surrenders than during any other phase of hostage situations except assaults. And this one would be particularly tricky, Potter knew, because the essence of surrender was Handy's nemesis—giving up control.

Again his natural impatience prodded him to get things over with, to get Handy into custody. But he had to fight this urge. He was running the surrender by the book and had assembled the threat management team before him in the van.

The first thing he did was shake Dean Stillwell's hand. "Dean, I'm putting Frank and the Bureau's HRT in charge of containment and tactical matters now. You've done a fine job. It's just that Frank and I've done this in the past a number of times."

"No problem at all, Arthur. I'm honored you let me help." To Potter's embarrassment Stillwell snapped a salute, which the agent reluctantly returned.

Budd, LeBow, Tobe, and D'Angelo all hunched over the terrain maps and diagram of the slaughterhouse as Potter went through the procedure. Angie, who had no tactical experience and could offer little assistance to

D'Angelo and the HRT, was escorting Emily and Beverly
to the Days Inn. Intense, young Detective Sharon Foster
was outside smoking—very real Camels. Frances was in
the van, waiting patiently.

"Everybody's going to be wired up and half-nuts," Potter said. "Our people *and* the takers. We're all tired and
there's going to be a lot of carelessness. So we have to
choreograph every step." He fell silent and was looking
out the window at the square yellow eyes of the building.

"Arthur?" LeBow said.

He meant, Time's awasting.

"Yes, sure."

They bent over the map and he began to give commands. It seemed to him that he'd lost his voice completely and he was surprised to find that the men who
stood before him nodded gravely as if listening to words
that he himself hardly heard at all.

Twenty minutes later, as Potter lay in a stand of fragrant
grass and hit the speed-dial button, it occurred to him that
something was very wrong. That Handy was laying a trap.

He thought of Budd's words earlier in the day, about
Handy's planning something clever and flamboyant—a
breakout maybe, a run for it.

A gut feel. Listen to it. He's usually right.

And now the feeling was undeniable.

The click of an answered phone.

"Lou." Potter began what was probably their last conversation via throw phone.

"Whatsa game plan, Art?"

"Just want to go over a few ground rules." Potter was
fifty yards from the slaughterhouse entrance. Frank
D'Angelo and Charlie Budd were beside him. LeBow and
Tobe remained in the command van. "Is the older woman
conscious? The teacher?"

"Zonked out. Told you, Art. She had a bad night. Bonner's—well, *was* a big fella. I'm talking in all ways."

Potter found his voice quavering as he asked, "And the
other teacher?"

"The blond one? The little mouse?" There was a pause
and Handy offered his famous chuckle. "Why you so

interested in her, Art? Seem to recall you asked about her a couple times."

"I want to know how our last hostages are."

"Sure you do." Handy laughed again. "Well, she's probably had better nights herself."

"How do you mean, Lou?" he asked casually. What terrible retribution had he exacted?

"She's too young for an old fart like you, Art."

Damn it, Potter thought, furious. Handy was reading him too clearly. The agent forced himself to put her out of his mind and returned mentally to Chapter 9 of his handbook, entitled "The Surrender Phase." Potter and D'Angelo had decided to send in the tunnel rats—point men—under the loading-dock door to secure the interior and guard the hostages then have the takers come out through the front.

"All right, Lou," Potter continued. "When I tell you to I'd like you to put your weapons down and just step outside, with your arms out to your side. Not on your head."

"Like Christ on the cross."

The wind had grown much worse, bending saplings and stands of sedge and bluestem, Queen Anne's lace, sending up clouds of dust. It would play hell with the snipers' shooting.

"Tell me the truth. Is Bonner dead or wounded?"

Potter had visited Beverly, the poor asthmatic, in one of the hospital tents and learned that the big man indeed had been shot. But the girl explained that she'd done her best to avoid looking at him. She couldn't say for certain if he was still alive.

"Tired of talking, Art. Me and Shep're gonna chat for a few minutes then we'll give it up. Hey, Art?"

"Yes, Lou?"

"I want you out front. Right where I can see you. It's the only way I'm coming out."

I'll do it, Potter thought instinctively. Anything you want.

"I'll be there, Lou."

"Right out front."

"You've got it." A pause. "Now, Lou, I want to tell you exactly—"

"Goodbye, Art. It's been fun."

Click.

Potter found himself gripping the phone long after Handy's voice was replaced by the rush of static. From nowhere the thought formed: The man's bent on suicide. The hopelessness of the situation: the impossibility of escaping, the relentless pursuit, an unbearable prison term awaiting him. He's going out in a flash.

Ostrella, my beloved. . . .

It would be the ultimate control.

D'Angelo broke into the reverie, saying, "We'll assume Bonner's alive and armed until we get a confirmation."

Potter nodded, pressed disconnect, put the phone in his pocket. "Choreograph it carefully, Frank. I think he may go down shooting."

"You think?" Budd whispered, as if Handy had a Big Ear on them.

"A hunch is all. But plan accordingly."

D'Angelo nodded. He got on the horn and doubled the number of snipers in the trees, moved up some explosives experts to the initial takedown team. When they were in place he asked, "Should we move in, Arthur?"

Potter nodded to him. D'Angelo spoke into his microphone and four HRT troopers slipped along the front of the slaughterhouse. Two paused at open windows and the others disappeared into the shadows on either side of the door. The ones by the window had mesh bomb blankets over their shoulders.

Then the HRT commander called the two point men inside the building. He listened for a moment then repeated the report to Potter: "Two hostages, apparently alive, lying on the ground in the room you indicated. Injured but extent unknown. Bonner appears to be dead." The unemotional voice grew troubled. "Man, there's blood everywhere."

Whose? Potter wondered.

"Are Handy and Wilcox armed?"

"No weapons in their hands but they're wearing bulky shirts. Could be hidden."

Injured but extent unknown.

Potter said to D'Angelo, "They had tools. Might've

brought tape with them too and taped weapons under their shirts."

The HRT commander nodded.

Blood everywhere . . .

Sharon Foster joined the men on the hillock. She'd put on bulky body armor.

How was this going to end? Potter wondered. He listened to the mournful sound of the wind. He felt a desperate urge to talk to Handy once more. Pressed the speed-dial button on the phone he carried.

A dozen rings, two dozen. No answer.

D'Angelo and LeBow were looking at him. He hung up.

Inside the slaughterhouse, the lights went out. Budd stiffened; Potter motioned him to relax. HTs often doused lights upon leaving, afraid to present a silhouette target even though they were giving up.

The crescent moon had moved fifty degrees through the windy sky. Often there's a sense of familiarity, even a perverse comfort, that a negotiator finds in the setting in which he's spent hours or days. Tonight, though, as he gazed at the black and red brick, all Potter could think of was Handy's phrase "Cold death."

The door opened slowly, stuck halfway, then opened further.

No movement.

What will it be? he wondered. Good or bad? Peaceful or violent?

Ah, my beautiful Ostrella.

During surrenders, he'd seen it all: Terrorists falling to the ground, crying like babies. Unarmed criminals streaking for freedom. Hidden guns. The young Syrian woman who walked slowly from an Israeli consulate, arms properly outstretched, and smiled sweetly at him just before the grenades in her bra blew herself and three HRT agents to pieces.

Be forewarned.

For only the third or fourth time in his career Arthur Potter lifted his weapon from his belt holster, high on his padded hip, and awkwardly pulled the automatic's slide, chambering a round. He replaced the gun, not clicking on the safety.

"Why isn't anything happening?" Budd whispered in irritation.

Potter stifled a sudden, inexplicable urge to laugh hysterically.

"Art?" Handy's voice floated from inside the slaughter-house, a soft, ragged sound on the wind.

"Yes?" Potter called through the megaphone.

"Where the fuck are you? I don't see you."

Potter looked at Budd. "Here's where I earn my pay-check." He rose unsteadily, polished his glasses on the lapel of his sports coat. Sharon Foster asked if he was sure he wanted to do this. He glanced at her then walked awk-wardly down the hill and stepped over an ancient split-rail fence. He paused about thirty yards from the front of the slaughterhouse.

"Here I am, Lou. Come on out."

And there they were.

Handy first. Then Wilcox.

The first thing he noticed was that their arms were at the backs of their heads.

It's all right, Ostrella. Come out however you want. Come home. You'll be okay.

"Lou, stretch your arms out!"

"Hey, take it easy, Art," Handy called. "Don't give yourself a fucking heart attack." Blinking against the powerful glare of the blinding lights. Amused, looking around.

"Lou, you've got a dozen snipers aiming at you—"

"Just a dozen? Shit! Thought I was worth more than that."

"Put your arms out or they'll shoot."

Handy stopped walking. Looked over at Wilcox. They broke into smiles.

Potter's hand went to the butt of his pistol.

Slowly the prisoners' arms extended.

"I look like a fucking ballerina, Art."

"You're doing fine, Lou."

"Easy for you to say."

Potter called, "Move in separate directions about ten feet, then lie facedown on the ground."

They walked away from the slaughterhouse, farther

than ordered but then dropped to their knees and went prone. The two HRT agents by the door kept their H&Ks trained on the fugitives' backs and stayed clear of the doorway just in case Bonner wasn't in fact dead or there'd been other takers inside that even the hostages hadn't known about.

The two agents hovering by the windows climbed inside, followed by two more, who ran from the shadows and sped through the door. The beams of the powerful flashlights attached to their guns whipped throughout the slaughterhouse.

They'd been briefed about the incendiary device Handy'd rigged and they'd be moving very slowly, looking for tripwires. Potter believed he'd never been so anxious in his life. He expected the interior of the slaughterhouse to blossom into orange flame at any instant.

Outside, two more HRT agents had moved up, covering the two beside the door, who now advanced on Handy and Wilcox.

Did the men have armed grenades on them?

Hidden knives?

It wasn't until they'd been cuffed and patted down that Arthur Potter realized the barricade was over. He'd escaped, alive and unhurt.

And had once again read Handy wrong.

Potter returned to Budd, D'Angelo, and Foster. Told the HRT commander to radio the agents taking the two convicts into custody with orders on how to handle them. Potter remembered that Wilcox was the cowboy in the group, more impulsive than the others. He'd ordered him shackled around the waist as well as cuffed but told them nct to do so with Handy. Potter knew Lou would be more willing to cooperate if he retained at least a little control.

Other agents appeared silently and covered the two men. They pulled them to their feet and frisked them again, more carefully, then quickly led them into a gully and hurried them away from the slaughterhouse.

Then the lights went on inside.

A long, long moment of silence, though it was probably just seconds.

Where *is* she?

"Go ahead," D'Angelo said into his mike. He listened for a minute then said to Potter, "It's secure. No other takers. No traps. There was something rigged in the room but it's been dismantled."

The others rose to their feet too and watched Handy's progress as he approached up the gully.

"And the hostages?" Potter asked urgently.

D'Angelo listened. He said aloud, "Bonner's dead."

Yes, yes, *yes?*

"And they found two female hostages. One, white, late thirties. Conscious but incoherent."

For chrissake, what about—

"Second one, white, age mid-twenties. Also conscious." D'Angelo winced. "Seriously hurt, he says."

No. Oh, my God.

"What?" Potter cried. "What happened to her?" The negotiator lifted his own radio and cut into the channel. "How is she? The younger woman?"

The HRT agent inside said, "Handy must've really done a number on her, sir."

"How *bad*?" Potter said furiously. Budd and D'Angelo stared at him. Handy was approaching, two agents on either side. Potter found he couldn't look at him.

The agent inside said into the radio, "Well, sir, she doesn't look that badly hurt but the thing is he must've beat the hell out of her. She can't hear a word we're saying."

The surrender had happened so fast he'd forgotten to tell the tactical agents Melanie was deaf.

D'Angelo said something to him and so did Charlie Budd but Potter didn't hear, so loud was his manic, hysterical laughter. Sharon Foster and nearby troopers looked at him uneasily. Potter supposed, without caring, that he sounded like the crazy old man that he was.

"Lou."

"Art, you don't look nothing like what I thought. You *do* have to lose a few pounds."

Handy stood behind the van, hands cuffed behind him. Sharon Foster was nearby, looking over the prisoners. When Handy glanced at her body, grinning, she stared

back contemptuously. Potter knew that after a hard negotiation, particularly one in which there'd been a killing,
you felt an urge to insult or belittle your enemy. Potter
controlled it himself but she was younger and more emotional. She sneered at Handy, walked away. The convict
laughed and turned back to Potter.

"Your picture doesn't do you justice," the negotiator
said to him.

"Fuckers never do."

As always, after a surrender, the hostage taker appeared
minuscule compared with the image in Potter's mind.
Handy's features were hard and compact, his face lean
and lined and pale. He knew Handy's height and weight
but still he was surprised at how diminished he seemed.

Potter scanned the crowd for Melanie. He didn't see
her. Troopers, firemen, medics, and Stillwell's now-
disbanded containment force were milling about outside
the slaughterhouse. The car and the school bus and the
processing plant itself were of course crime scenes and
since by agreement this was technically now a state operation Budd had formally arrested Handy and Wilcox and
was trying to preserve the site for the forensic teams.

Where is she?

There was a brief incident when Potter arrested Handy
on federal charges. Handy's eyes went cold. "What the
fuck is this?"

"I'm just preserving our rights," Potter said. SAC Henderson explained that it was a mere technicality, and
Roland Marks too confirmed that everyone would adhere
to the written agreement, though Potter had a bad moment
when he thought Marks was going to take a swing at the
convict. The assistant AG muttered, "Fucking child
killer," and stormed off. Handy laughed at his receding
back.

Shep Wilcox, grinning, looked around, disappointed, it
seemed, there were no reporters present.

The older teacher, Donna Harstrawn, was brought out
on a gurney. Potter went to her and walked alongside the
medics. He looked at one of the techs, eyebrow raised.
"She'll be okay," the young man whispered. "Physically,
I mean."

"Your husband and children are at the Days Inn," he told her.

"It was . . ." she began, and fell silent. Shook her head. "I can't see anyone now. Please. No . . . I don't ever . . ." Her words dissolved, incoherent.

Potter squeezed her arm and stopped walking, watched them carry her up the hill to the waiting ambulance.

He turned back to the slaughterhouse just as Melanie Charrol was being escorted out. Her blond hair in disarray. She too—like Handy—seemed smaller than Potter expected. He started forward but paused. Melanie hadn't seen him; she was walking quickly, her eyes on Donna Harstrawn. Her clothes were dark—gray skirt, black stockings, burgundy blouse—but it seemed to Potter that they were saturated with blood.

"What's all that blood on her?" he asked one of the HRT agents who'd been inside.

"Not hers," came the response. "Bonner's probably. Man bled out like a gutted twelve-point buck. You want to debrief her?"

He hesitated.

"Later," he said. But in his mind the word was more of a question and the answer was unknown.

Detective Sharon Foster strode up to Potter and shook his hand.

" 'Night, Agent Potter."

"Thanks for everything," he said evenly.

"Piece of cake." She jabbed a blunt finger at him. "Hey, great job with that surrender. Smooth as silk." Then wheeled and returned to her squad car, leaving Potter standing alone. His face burned like that of a rookie dressed down by a tough training sergeant.

Angie Scapello returned momentarily from the Days Inn to collect her bags and say goodbye to Potter and the others. She still had some work ahead of her at the motel, where she would debrief the hostages further and make sure they and their families had the names of therapists who specialized in post-traumatic stress syndrome.

Budd and D'Angelo hitched a ride with Angie to the rear staging area. Potter and two troopers escorted the takers back to the van. Squad cars waited nearby to take them to the state police troop HQ ten miles away.

"Had yourself a fire, looks like," Handy said, looking over the black scorch marks. "You ain't gonna blame that on me, I hope?"

As he gazed at the convict Potter was aware of a man approaching from the shadows of a gully. He paid little mind since there were dozens of troopers milling about. But there was something purposeful about the man's stride, too quick and direct for him to be passing through the crowd casually. He was heading directly for Potter.

"Weapon!" Potter cried as Dan Tremain, twenty feet away, began to lift the gun.

Wilcox and the trooper holding him dove to the ground, as did the second escort trooper, leaving only Handy and Potter standing. Within easy pistol range.

Handy, smiling, turned to face Tremain. Potter drew his own gun, pointed it at the HRU commander, and stepped in front of Handy.

"No, Captain," the agent said firmly.

"Get out of the way, Potter."

"You're already in enough trouble."

The gun in Tremain's hand exploded. Potter felt the bullet snap past his head. He heard Handy laughing.

"Get out of the way!"

"Do it," Handy whispered in Potter's ear. "Pull the trigger. Waste the fucker."

"Shut up!" the agent barked. Around them four or five troopers had pulled their sidearms and were sighting on Tremain. No one knew what to do.

Or wanted to do what they knew they should.

"He's mine," Tremain said.

"It's legal," Handy whispered. "Kill him, Art. You want to anyway. You *know* you do."

"Quiet!" Potter shouted. And yet suddenly he understood that Handy was right. He *did* want to. And what's more, he felt that he had permission—to kill the man who'd nearly burnt his Melanie to death.

"Do it," Handy urged. "You're dying to."

"This'll bring you nothing but grief, Dan," Potter said

slowly, ignoring his prisoner. "You don't want to do this."

"There you go, Art. Telling people what they want to do. I'll tell you what *you* want to do. You want to shoot the prick. Man almost got your girlfriend killed. She is your gal, isn't she, Art? Mel-a-nie?"

"Shut your damn mouth!"

"Do it, Art. Shoot him!"

Tremain fired again. Potter cringed as the bullet streaked past his face and dug a chunk out of the slaughterhouse.

The captain steadied the gun, seeking a target.

And Arthur Potter spread his arms, sheltering the man who was his prisoner. And—yes, Charlie, who was his friend.

"Do something bad," Handy whispered in a smooth, reassuring voice. "Just step aside a inch or two. Let him kill me. Or you shoot him."

Potter turned. "Will you—?"

Several FBI agents had drawn guns and were shouting for Tremain to drop his weapon. The state troopers were silently rooting for the HRU commander.

Potter thought: Handy *had* almost killed Melanie.

Just step aside a few inches.

And Tremain had nearly killed her too.

Shoot. Go ahead.

Handy whispered, "He'd had his way, Art, your girlfriend'd have third-degree burns over most of her body now. Her hair and tits all burned up. Even you wouldn't want to fuck somebody like—"

Potter spun, his fist lashing out. It drove into Handy's jaw. The prisoner reeled back and landed on the ground. Tremain, now only ten feet away, aimed once more at the man's chest.

"Drop the gun," Potter commanded, spinning around and stepping forward. "Drop it, Dan. Your life isn't over with yet. But it will be if you pull that trigger. Think about your family." He remembered the ring he'd seen on Tremain's finger. He said softly, "God doesn't want to waste you over somebody as worthless as Handy."

The pistol wavered, dropped to the ground.

Without looking at Potter or Handy again, Tremain

walked over to Charlie Budd and held his hands out for the cuffs. Budd looked over his fellow officer, seemed about to say something but chose to remain silent.

As he scrambled to his feet Handy said, "You missed a good bet, Art. Not many people have the chance to waste somebody and—"

Potter had him by the hair, and the pistol's muzzle drove up under Handy's stubbled jaw.

"Not a single word."

Handy reared back, breathing hard. He looked away first, truly scared. But only for a moment. Then he laughed. "You're a real piece of work, Art. Yessir. Let's get it over with. Book me, Dano."

MIDNIGHT

Arthur Potter was alone.

He looked at his hands and saw they were quivering. Until the incident with Tremain they'd been rock solid. He took an imaginary Valium but it had no effect. He realized after a moment that his unease wasn't so much the aftermath of the showdown after all as an overwhelming sense of disappointment. He'd wanted to talk to Handy. Find out more about him, what made him tick.

Why had he really killed Susan? What had he been thinking? What had happened in that room, the killing room?

And what does he think about me?

It was like watching the troopers escort a part of himself away. He gazed at the back of Handy's head, his shaggy hair. The man looked sideways, a hyena grin on his face. Potter caught a glimpse of an acute angle of jawbone.

Be forewarned.

He remembered his pistol. Unchambered the round and replaced it in the clip then holstered the gun. When he looked up again, the two squad cars bearing Wilcox and

Handy were gone. At the moment it seemed like the perverse camaraderie between negotiator and taker would never fade. Part of him was heartsick to see the man go.

Potter considered the work left to be done. There'd be an IR-1002 to write up. There'd be a debriefing tonight via phone with the operations director in the District and a live debriefing with the Admiral himself after the man had read the incident report. Potter ought to start preparing the presentation now. The Director liked his briefings to be as short as news bites, and real-life incidents rarely had the courtesy to line up so willingly. Potter had stopped into Peter Henderson's press conference but answered only a few questions before heading out the door, leaving the SAC to take as much credit and apportion as much blame as he wished; Potter didn't care.

He'd also have to figure out how to deal with the aborted assault by the state HRU. Potter knew that Tremain never would have tried what he did without sanction from above—possibly even the governor's. But if that were the case, the chief executive of the state would already have distanced himself from the commander. He might even be planning a subtle offensive maneuver of his own—like the public crucifixion of one Arthur Potter. The agent would have to prepare a defense for that.

And the other question—should he stay here for a few days? Return to Chicago? Return to the District?

He stood not far from the scorched van, abandoned by the crowds of departing officers, waiting to see Melanie. He gazed at the slaughterhouse, wondering what he would say to her. He saw Officer Frances Whiting leaning against her car, looking as exhausted as he felt. He approached her.

"Have time to give me a lesson?" he asked.

"You bet."

Ten minutes later they walked together to the hospital tent.

Inside, Melanie Charrol sat on a low examining table. A medic had bandaged her neck and shoulders. Perhaps to help him she'd twisted her hair into a sloppy French braid.

Potter stepped toward her and—as he'd told himself, had *ordered* himself, not to do—he spoke straight to the medic applying some Betadine to her leg, rather than to Melanie herself. "Is she all right?"

Melanie nodded. She stared at him with an intense smile. The only time her eyes flicked away from his was when he spoke and she glanced at his lips.

"It's not her blood," the medic said.

"It's Bear's?" Potter asked.

Melanie was laughing as she nodded. The smile remained on her face but he noticed that her eyes were hollow. The medic gave her a pill, which she took, then she drank down two glasses of water. The young man said, "I'll leave you alone for a few minutes."

As he left, Frances stepped inside. The two women exchanged fast, abrupt signs. Frances said, "She's asking about the other girls. I'm giving her a rundown."

Melanie turned back to Potter and was staring at him. He met her gaze. The young woman was still unnerved but—despite the bandages and blood—as beautiful as he'd expected. Incredible blue-gray eyes.

He lifted his hands to sign to her what Frances had just taught him and his usually prodigious memory failed him completely. He shook his head at his lapse. Melanie cocked her head.

Potter held up a finger. Wait. He lifted his hands again and froze once more. Then Frances gestured and he remembered. "I'm Arthur Potter," he signed. "It's a pleasure to meet you."

"No, you are Charles Michel de l'Epée," Frances translated Melanie's signing.

"I'm not *that* old." He was speaking now, smiling. "Officer Whiting here said he was born in the eighteenth century. How are you feeling?"

She understood without a translation. Melanie waved at her clothes and gave a mock frown then signed. Frances translated, "My skirt and blouse have had it. Couldn't you have gotten us out just a little earlier?"

"The movie-of-the-week people expect cliffhanger endings."

And as with Handy he felt overwhelmed; there were a

thousand things to ask her. None of which found their way from his mind to his voicebox.

He stepped even closer to her. Neither moved for a moment.

Potter thought of another sentence in ASL—words that Frances had taught him earlier in the evening. "You're very brave," he signed.

Melanie looked pleased at this. Frances watched her sign but then the officer frowned and shook her head. Melanie repeated her words. To Potter, Frances said, "I don't understand what she means. What she said was, 'If you hadn't been with me I couldn't have done it.' "

But *he* understood.

He heard a chug of engine and turned to see a harvester. As he watched the ungainly vehicle he believed for a moment it was driving hordes of insects before it. Then he realized he was watching husks and dust thrown skyward by the thresher blades.

"They'll do that all night," Frances translated.

Potter looked at Melanie.

She continued, "Moisture's critical. When conditions're right they run like nobody's business. They have to."

"How do you know that?"

"She says she's a farm girl."

She looked straight into his eyes. He tried to believe that Marian had gazed at him thus so he could root this sensation in sentiment or nostalgia and have done with it. But he couldn't. The look, like the feeling it engendered, like this young woman herself, was an original.

Potter recalled the final phrase that Frances had taught him. He hesitated then impulsively signed the words. As he did it seemed to him that he felt the hand shapes with absolute clarity, as if only his hands could express what he wanted to say.

"I want to see you again," Potter signed. "Maybe tomorrow?"

She paused for an endless moment then nodded yes, smiled.

She reached out suddenly toward him and closed her hands on his arm. He pressed a bandaged hand against her shoulder. They stood in this ambiguous embrace for a moment then he lifted his fingers to her hair and touched the back of her head. She lowered her head and he his lips, nearly touching them to the thick blond plait. But suddenly he smelled the musky scent of her scalp, her sweat, latent perfume, blood. The smells of lovers coupling. And he could not kiss her.

How young she is! And as he thought that, in one instant, his desire to embrace her vanished and his old man's fantasy—never articulated, hardly formed—blew away like the chaff shot from the thresher he'd been staring at.

He knew he had to leave.

Knew he'd never see her again.

He stepped back suddenly and she looked at him, momentarily perplexed.

"I have to go talk to the U.S. attorney," he said abruptly.

Melanie nodded and offered her hand. He mistook it for a signing gesture. He stared down, waiting. Then she extended it further and took his fingers warmly. They both laughed at the misunderstanding. Suddenly she pulled him forward, kissed his cheek.

He walked to the door, stopped, turned. " 'Be forewarned.' That's what you said to me, isn't it?"

Melanie nodded, her eyes hollow once again. Hollow and forlorn. Frances translated her response: "I wanted you to know how dangerous he was. I wanted you to be careful."

Then she smiled and signed some more. Potter laughed when he heard the translation. "You owe me a new skirt and blouse. And I expect to be repaid. You better not forget. I'm Deaf with an attitude. Poor you."

Potter wandered back to the van, thanked Tobe Geller and Henry LeBow, who were taking commercial flights back to their respective homes. A squad car whisked them away. He shook Dean Stillwell's hand once more and felt a ridiculous urge to give him a present of some sort, a ribbon or a medal or a federal agent decoder ring. The sheriff brushed aside his mop of hair and had the presence of mind to order his men—federal and state alike—to walk carefully, reminding them that they were, after all, at a crime scene and evidence still needed to be gathered.

Potter stood beneath one of the halogen lights, looking out at the stark slaughterhouse.

"Night, sir," a voice drawled from behind him.

He turned to Stevie Oates. The negotiator shook his hand. "Couldn't have done it without you, Stevie."

The boy did better dodging bullets than fielding compliments. He looked down at the ground. "Yeah, well, you know."

"A word of advice."

"What's that, sir?"

"Don't volunteer so damn much."

"Yessir." The trooper grinned. "I'll keep that in mind."

Then Potter found Charlie Budd and asked him for a lift to the airport.

"You're not going to hang around for a while?" asked the young captain.

"No, I should go."

They climbed into Budd's unmarked car and sped away. Potter caught a last glimpse of the slaughterhouse; in the stark spotlights the dull red-and-white structure gave the appearance of bloody, exposed bone. He shuddered and turned away.

Halfway to the airport Budd said, "I appreciate the chance you gave me."

"You were good enough to confess something to me, Charlie—"

"After I almost fixed your clock."

"—so I better confess something to you."

The captain rubbed his tawny hair and left it looking like he'd been to the Dean Stillwell hair salon. He meant, Go ahead, I can take it.

"I kept you with me as an assistant 'cause I needed to show everybody that this was a federal operation and state took second place. I was putting you on a leash. You're a smart man and I guess you figured that out."

"Yup. Didn't seem you really needed a high-priced gofer like me. Ordering Fritos and beer and helicopters. It was one of the things made me put that tape recorder in my pocket. But the way you talked to me, treated me, was one of the things that made me take it out."

"Well, you've got a right to be good and mad. But I just wanted to say you did a lot better than I expected. You were really part of the team. Handling that session by yourself—you were a natural. I'd have you negotiate with me any time."

"Oh, brother, not for any money. Tell you what, Arthur—I'll run 'em to ground and you get 'em out of their holes."

Potter laughed. "Fair enough, Charlie."

They drove in silence through the miles and miles of wheat. The windswept grain was alive in the moonlight, like the silken coat of an animal eager to run. "I've got a feeling," Budd said slowly, "you're thinking you made a mistake tonight."

Potter said nothing, watching the bug eyes of the threshers.

"You're thinking that if you'd come up with what that Detective Foster did you could've got 'em out sooner. Maybe even saved that girl's life, and Joey Wilson's."

"It did cross my mind," Potter said after a minute. *Oh, how we hate to be pegged and explained. What's so compelling about the idea that our selves are mysteries to everyone but us? I let* you *in on the secrets, Marian. But only you. It's an aspect of love, I think, and reasonable enough there. But how queasy it makes us feel when strangers have the eye to see us so unfurled.*

"But you kept 'em alive through three or four deadlines," Budd continued.

"That girl though, Susan . . ."

"But he shot her before you even started negotiating. There was nothing you could've said to save her. Besides, Handy had plenty of chances to ask for what Sharon offered him, and he never did. Not once."

This was true. But if Arthur Potter knew anything about his profession it was that the negotiator was the closest thing to God in a barricade and that every death fell on his shoulders and his only. What he'd learned—and what had saved his heart over the years—was that some of those deaths simply weigh less than others.

They drove another three miles and Potter realized he'd

grown hypnotized, staring at the moon-white wheat. Budd
was talking to him once again. The subject was domestic,
the man's wife and his daughters.

Potter looked away from the streaming grain and listened to what the captain was telling him.

In the tiny jet Arthur Potter slipped two sticks of
Wrigley's into his mouth and waved goodbye to Charlie
Budd, who was waving back, though the interior of the
plane was very dim and Potter doubted that the captain
saw him.

Then he sank down into the spongy beige seat of the
Grumman Gulfstream. He thought of the flask of Irish
whisky in his briefcase but found himself decidedly not in
the mood.

How 'bout that, Marian? No nightcap for me and I'm
off-duty. What do you say about that?

He saw a phone on a console nearby and thought he
should call his cousin Linden and tell her not to wait up
for him. Maybe he'd wait until they were airborne. He'd
ask to speak to Sean; the boy would be thrilled to know
that Uncle Arthur was talking to him from twenty thousand feet in the air. He gazed absently out the window at
the constellations of colored lights marking runways and
taxiways. Potter took from his pocket the still-damp note
Melanie had written him. Read it. Then he crumpled the
paper, stuffed it into the pocket of the seat in front of him.

The jets whined powerfully and with a sudden burst of
thrust he found the plane not racing down the runway at
all but streaking straight into the sky, almost from a dead
stop, like a spaceship headed to Mars.

They rose up and up, aiming for the moon, which was
an eerie sickle in the hazy sky. The plane pointed itself at
the black disk surrounded by the white crescent. Unchar-
acteristically poetic, Potter thought of this image: the icy
thumb and index finger of a witch, reaching for a pinch of
nightshade.

The negotiator closed his eyes and sat back in the soft seat.

Just as he did, the Grumman banked fiercely. So sharp
was the maneuver that Arthur Potter knew suddenly he
was about to die. He considered this fact very calmly. A

wing or an engine had fallen off. A bolt holding together the whole airplane had finally fatigued. His eyes sprang open and—yes, yes!—he believed he saw his wife's face clearly in the white glow surrounding the moon as it scythed past. He understood that what had joined the two of them, himself and Marian, for all these years joined them still, just as powerfully, and she was pulling him after her in death.

He closed his eyes again. And felt utterly at peace.

But no, he was not destined to die just yet.

For as the plane completed its acute turn and headed back toward the airport, dropping the landing gear and flaps, sliding down down down to the flat Kansas landscape once more, Potter clutched the telephone to his ear, listening to SAC Peter Henderson tell him in a shaking, grim voice how the real Detective Sharon Foster had been found dead and half-naked not far from her house a half-hour ago and how it was now suspected that the woman who'd impersonated her at the barricade had been Lou Handy's girlfriend.

The four troopers who'd been escorting Handy and Wilcox were dead, as was Wilcox himself—all killed in a violent shootout five miles from the slaughterhouse.

And as for Handy and the woman—they were gone without a trace.

IV

A MAIDEN'S
GRAVE

1:01 A.M.

As they drove through the fields beneath the faint moon the couple in the Nissan reflected on the evening at their daughter's home in Enid, which had been exactly as unpleasant as they'd expected.

When they spoke, however, they spoke not about the children's shabby trailer, the unwashed baby grandson, their stringy-haired son-in-law's disappearing act into the trash-filled backyard to sneak Jack Daniel's. No, they talked only about the weather and unusual road signs they happened to pass.

"We'll get rain this fall. Floodin'."

"Might."

"Something 'bout the trout in Minnesota. I read that."

"Trout?"

"Bad rains I'm talking. Stuckey's's only five miles. Look there. You wanta stop?"

Harriet, their daughter, had made a dinner that could be described only as inedible—woefully overdone and over-salted. And the husband had found what he was sure was some cigarette ash in the succotash. Now they were both starving.

"Might do that. For coffee only. Lookit that wind— whooee! Hope you shut the windows at home. Maybe a piece of pie."

"I did."

"You forgot last time," the wife reminded shrilly.

"Don't want to lose the lamp again. You know what three-way bulbs cost."

"Well," the husband said. "What's going on here?"

"How's that?"

"I'm being stopped. A police car."

"Pull over!"

"I'm doing it," he said testily. "No point in leaving skid marks. I'm doing it."

"What'd you do?"

"I didn't do *nothing*. I was fifty-seven in a fifty-five zone and that's not a crime in anybody's book."

"Well, pull off the road."

"I'm pulling. Will you just settle? There, happy?"

"Hey, look," the wife offered with astonishment, "there's a lady officer driving!"

"They have 'em now. You know that. You watch *Cops*. Should I get out or are they going to come up here?"

"Maybe," the wife said, "you oughta go to them. Make the effort. That way if they're right on the borderline of giving you a ticket they might not."

"That's a thought. But I still don't know what I done." And, smiling like a Kiwanian on Pancake Day, the husband climbed out of the Nissan and walked back to the squad car, fishing his wallet out of his pocket.

As Lou Handy drove the cruiser deep into the wheat field, cutting a swath in the tall grain, he was lost in the memory of another field—the one that morning, near the intersection where the Cadillac had broadsided them.

He remembered the gray sky overhead. The feel of the bony knife in his hand. The woman's powdery face, black wrinkles in her makeup, dots of her blood spattering her as he drove the knife downward into her soft body. The look in her eyes, hopelessness and sorrow. Her weird scream, choking, grunting. An animal's sounds.

She'd died the same way that the couple in the Nissan just had, the couple now lying in the trunk of the cruiser he was driving. Hell, they had to die, both of the couples. They'd had something *he* needed. Their cars. The Cadillac and the Nissan. This afternoon Hank and Ruth'd smashed the fuck out of his Chevy. And tonight, well, he and Pris *couldn't* keep driving in a stolen squad car. It was impossible. He needed a new car. He *had* to have one.

And when Lou Handy collected what he was owed, when he'd scratched that itch, he was the most contented man on earth.

Tonight he parked the cruiser, which stunk of cordite and blood, in the field, fifty yards from the road. It'd be found by tomorrow morning but that was okay. In a few hours he and Pris'd be out of the state and flying over the Texas-Mexico border, a hundred feet in the air, on their way to San Hidalgo.

Whoa, hold on tight. . . . Damn, the wind was fierce, buffeting the car and sending the stalks of wheat slapping into the windshield with a clatter like birdshot.

Handy climbed out and trotted back to the road, where Pris sat in the driver's seat of the Nissan. She'd ditched the trooper's uniform and was wearing a sweater and jeans and Handy wanted more than anything else at the moment to tug those Levi's down, them and the cheap nylon panties she always wore, and fuck her right on top of the hood of the tinny Jap car. Holding her ponytail in his right hand the way he liked to do.

But he jumped in the passenger's seat and motioned for her to get going. She pitched her cigarette out the window and gunned the engine. The car shot away off the shoulder, hung a tight U, and sped up to sixty.

Heading back in the direction they'd just come from. North.

It seemed crazy, sure. But Handy prided himself on being as off-the-wall nuts as a man could be and still get on in this life. In reality their destination made sense, though—because where they were going was the last place anyone would think to look for them.

Anyway, he thought, fuck it whether it's crazy or not. His mind was made up. He had business back there. Lou Handy was owed.

The Heiligenstadt Testament, written in 1802 by Beethoven to his brothers, chronicles his despair at his progressive deafness, which a decade and a half later became total.

Melanie Charrol knew this, for Beethoven not only was her spiritual mentor and role model but was a frequent visitor to her music room, where he, not surprisingly, could hear as well as she could. They had had many fascinating conversations about music theory and composition. They both lamented the trend away from melody and harmony in modern composition. She called it "medicinal music"—a phrase Ludwig heartily approved of.

She now sat in the living room of her house, breathing deeply, thinking of the great composer and wondering if she was drunk.

At the bar in the motel in Crow Ridge she'd poured down two brandies in the company of Officer Frances Whiting and some of the parents of the hostages. Frances had gotten in touch with Melanie's parents in St. Louis and told them she was fine. They would return immediately after Danny's operation tomorrow and stop by Hebron for a visit—news that for some reason upset Melanie. Did she want them to stop by or not? She had another brandy in lieu of deciding.

Then Melanie had gone to say goodbye to the girls and their parents.

The twins had been asleep, Kielle was awake but snubbing her royally—though if Melanie knew anything about children it was that their moods are fickle as the weather; tomorrow or the next day the little girl would drop by Melanie's cubicle at school and sprawl out upon the immaculate desktop to show off her latest X-Men comic or Power Rangers card. Emily was, of course, in an absurdly frilly and feminine nightgown, fast asleep. Shannon, Beverly, and Jocylyn were the centerpiece of the action. At the moment, coddled and the center of loving attention, they were cheerful and defiant and she could see from their gestures that they were recalling aspects of the evening in detail that Melanie herself could not bear. They had even dubbed themselves "the Crow Ridge Ten" and were talking about having T-shirts printed up. Reality would hit home later, when everyone began to feel Susan's absence. But for now, why not? Besides, whatever misgivings she'd shared with de l'Epée about the politics of Deafness, the members of its community were nothing if not resilient.

Melanie said goodnight to everyone, refusing a dozen offers to spend the night. Never before had she signed "No, thank you" as often as she had this evening.

Now, in her home, all the windows were locked, all the doors. She burned some incense, had another brandy—blackberry, her grandmother's cure for cramps—and was sitting in her leather armchair, thinking of de l'Epée . . . well, Arthur Potter. Rubbing the indentation on her right wrist from the wire Brutus had bound it with. She had her Koss headset clamped over her ears and had Beethoven's Fourth Piano Concerto cranked up so loud the volume was redlined. It was a remarkable piece of music. Composed during what music historians call Beethoven's "second period," the one that produced the *Eroica*, when he was aware of, and tormented by, his hearing loss but before he had gone completely deaf.

As she listened to the concerto now she wondered if it had been written by Beethoven in anticipation of future years when the deafness would be worse, if he'd built in certain chords and dynamics so that a deaf old man might still make out at least the soul of the piece—for though there were passages she could not hear at all (as faint and delicate as smoke, she imagined) the passion of the music came from its emphatic low notes, two hands crashing down on the bass keys, the theme spiraling downward like a hawk falling on prey, the orchestra's timpani and low-pitched strings churning out what for her was the hopeful spirit of the concerto. A sensation of galloping.

She could imagine, through vibration and notes and sight-reading the score, most of the concerto. She thought now, as she always did, that she'd give her soul to be able to actually hear the entire piece.

Just once before she died.

It was during the second movement that she glanced outside and saw a car slow suddenly as it passed her house. She thought this was odd because the street in front was little traveled. It was a dead end and she knew everyone who lived on the block and what kind of cars they drove. This one she didn't recognize.

She pulled off the headset and walked to the window. She could see that the car, with two people inside, had parked in front of the Albertsons' house. This was curious too because she was sure the family was away for the week. She squinted at the car. The two people—she couldn't see them clearly, just silhouettes—got out and walked through the Albertsons' gate, disappearing behind the tall hedge that bordered the couple's property, directly across from her house. Then Melanie remembered that the family had several cats. Probably friends were feeding the animals while the couple was away. Returning to her couch, she sat down and pulled on the headset once more.

Yes, yes . . .

The music, what she could hear of it, as limited as the sound was to her, was an incredible comfort. More than the brandy, more than the companionship of the parents of her students, more than thoughts about the inexplicable and inexplicably appealing Arthur Potter; it lifted her away, magically, from the horror of this windy day in July.

Melanie closed her eyes.

1:20 A.M.

Captain Charlie Budd had aged considerably in the last twelve hours.

Potter studied him in the adulterating fluorescent light of the cramped office of the sheriff of Crow Ridge, which was located in a strip mall off the business loop. Budd no longer appeared young and was easily a decade past callow. And like all of them here tonight, his face showed the patina of disgust.

And uncertainty too. For they had no idea if they'd been betrayed and if so by whom. Budd and Potter sat across the desk from Dean Stillwell, who leaned into the phone, nodding gravely. He handed the receiver to Budd.

Tobe and Henry LeBow had just arrived in a mad race from the airport. LeBow's computers were already booted up; they seemed like an extension of his body. Angie's DomTran jet had hung a U-turn somewhere over Nashville and she was due back in Crow Ridge in a half-hour.

"All right," Budd said, hanging up. "Here're the details. They aren't pretty."

The two squad cars carrying Handy and Wilcox had left the slaughterhouse and headed south to the Troop C headquarters in Clements, about ten miles south. Between Crow Ridge and the state facility the lead car, driven by the woman who was presumably Priscilla Gunder, braked so suddenly it left twenty-foot skid marks and sent the second car, behind it, off the road. Apparently the woman pulled her pistol and shot the trooper beside her and the one in the backseat, killing them instantly.

The crime scene investigators speculated that Wilcox, in the second car, had undone his cuffs with the key that Gunder had slipped him and grabbed the gun of the trooper sitting beside him. But because he'd been double-shackled, according to Potter's surrender instructions, it had taken him longer to escape than planned. He'd shot the officer beside him but the driver leapt from the car and fired one shot into Wilcox before Handy, or his girlfriend, shot him in the back.

"Wilcox wasn't killed outright," Budd continued, brushing his hair, as being in Stillwell's presence made you want to do. "He climbed out and crawled to the first squad car. Somebody—they think it was Handy—finished him with a single shot to the forehead."

In his mind Potter heard: *You kill when people don't do what they're supposed to. You kill the weak because they'll drag you down. What's wrong with that?*

"What about Detective Foster?" Potter asked.

"She was found beside a stolen car about a mile from her house. Her husband said she left the place about ten minutes after she got the call about the barricade. They think the Gunder woman flagged her down near the highway, took her uniform, killed her, and stole her cruiser. Prelim forensics show some of the prints were Gunder's."

"What else, Charlie? Tell us." For Potter saw the look on his face.

Budd hesitated. "After the real Sharon Foster had stripped down to her underwear Handy's girlfriend gagged and handcuffed her. Then she used a knife. She didn't have to. But she did. It wasn't too pleasant what she did. It took her a while to die."

"And then she drove to the barricade site," Potter spat out angrily, "and waltzed out with him."

"Where'd they head?" LeBow asked. "Still going south?"

"Nobody's got a clue," Budd said.

"They're in a cruiser," Stillwell said. "Shouldn't be hard to find."

"We've got choppers out looking," Budd offered. "Six of them."

"Oh, he's already switched cars," Potter muttered. "Concentrate on any report of car theft in south-central Kansas. Anything at all."

Tobe said, "The engine block of the cruiser'll retain heat for about three hours. Do the choppers have infrared cameras?"

Budd said, "Three of them do."

LeBow mused, "What route'd put them the furthest away in that time? He must know we'd be on to them pretty soon."

In the otherwise drab, functional office five brilliant, red plants sat on a credenza, the healthiest-looking plant life Potter had ever seen indoors. Stillwell was hovering beside a wall map of the four-county area. "He could cut over to 35—that's the turnpike, take him northeast. Or 81'd take him to I-70."

"How 'bout," Budd asked, "81 all the way into Nebraska, cut over to 29?"

"Yep," Stillwell continued. " 'S'long drive, but it'd take him up to Winnipeg. Eventually."

"Was that Canada thing all smoke screen?" Tobe wondered.

"I don't know," Potter said, feeling that he'd stumbled into a chess game with a man who might be a grand master or who might not even know the movement of the pieces. He stood and stretched, which was tough in the cramped quarters. "The only way we're going to find him, short of luck, is to figure out how the hell he did it. Henry? What was the chronology?"

LeBow punched buttons. He recited, "At nine thirty-three p.m. Captain Budd said he'd received a call from his division commander about a woman detective who'd gotten Handy to surrender several years ago. She was located in McPherson, Kansas. The commander wondered if he should send the woman to the barricade site. Captain Budd conferred with Agent Potter and the decision was made to ask this detective to come to the site.

"At nine forty-nine p.m. a woman representing herself as Detective Sharon Foster called from her cruiser and reported that she would be at the barricade site by ten-thirty or ten-forty.

"At ten forty-five a woman representing herself to be Detective Sharon Foster, wearing a Kansas State Police uniform, arrived at the barricade and commenced negotiations with subject Handy."

"Charlie," Potter asked, "who was the commander?"

"Ted Franklin over at Troop B." He already had the phone in his hand and was dialing the number.

"Commander Franklin please . . . it's an emergency. . . . Ted? It's Charlie Budd. . . . Nope, no news. I'm going to put you on the squawk box." There was a click and static filled the room. "Ted, I've got half the FBI here. Agent Arthur Potter in charge."

"Hey, gentlemen," came Franklin's electronic greeting.

"Evening, Commander," Potter said. "We're trying to track down what happened here. You remember who called you about Sharon Foster this evening?"

"I've been racking my brain, sir, trying to remember. Some trooper or another. I frankly wasn't listening to who he was as much as what he had to say."

"A 'he,' you say?"

"Yessir. Was a man."

"He told you about Detective Foster?"

"That's right."

"Did you know her beforehand?"

"I knew about her. She was an up-and-comer. Good negotiating record."

Potter asked, "Then you called her after this trooper called."

"No, I called Charlie first down in Crow Ridge to see if it'd be all right with you folks. Then I called her."

"So," Stillwell said, "somebody intercepted your call to her and got to Detective Foster's just as she was leaving."

"But how?" Budd asked. "Her husband said she left ten minutes after she got the call. How could Handy's girl-friend've got there in time?"

"Tobe?" Potter asked. "Any way to check for taps?"

"Commander Franklin," Tobe asked, "is your office swept for bugs?"

A chuckle. "Nope. Not the kind you're talking about."

Tobe said to Potter, "We could sweep it, see if there are any. But it'd only tell us yea or nay. There's no way to tell who got the transmission and when."

But no, Potter was thinking. Budd was right. There was simply no time for Priscilla Gunder to get to Foster's house after the phone call from Franklin.

LeBow spoke for all of them. "This just doesn't sound like a tap situation. Besides, who'd know to put the bug in Commander Franklin's office anyway?"

Stillwell said, "Sounds like this was all planned out ahead of time."

Potter agreed. "The trooper who called you, Commander Franklin, wasn't a trooper at all. He was Handy's accomplice. And the girlfriend was probably waiting outside Detective Foster's house all along, while he—whoever *he* is—made the phone call to you."

"That means somebody'd have to know about the real Sharon Foster in the first place," Budd said. "That Handy'd surrendered to her. Who'd know about her?"

There was silence for a moment as the roomful of clever men thought of clever ways to learn about past police negotiations—through the news, computer databases, sources within the department.

LeBow and Budd were tied for first. "Handy!"

Potter had just arrived there himself. He nodded. "Who'd know better than Handy himself? Let's think back. He's trapped in the slaughterhouse. He suspects he isn't going to get his helicopter or that if he does we're going to track him to the ends of the earth—with or without his M-4 clearance—and so he gets word to his accomplice about Foster. The accomplice calls the girlfriend and they plan out the rescue. But Handy couldn't have called on the throw phone. We'd have heard it." Potter closed his eyes and thought back over the evening's events. "Tobe, those scrambled transmissions you were wondering about . . . We thought they were Tremain and the Kansas HRU. Could they have been something else?"

The young man tugged at his pierced earlobe then dug several computer disks from a plastic envelope. He handed them to LeBow, who put one in his laptop. Tobe leaned over and pushed keys. On the screen played a stilted, slow-moving graphic representation of two sine waves, overlapping each other.

"There are two!" he announced, his scientist's eyes glowing at the discovery. "Two different frequencies." He looked up. "Both law-enforcement assigned. And retrosignal scrambled."

"Are they both Tremain's?" Potter wondered aloud.

Ted Franklin asked what the frequencies were.

"Four hundred thirty-seven megahertz and four hundred eighty point four," Tobe responded.

"No," Ted Franklin answered. "The first one is assigned to HRU. The second isn't a state police signal. I don't know whose it is."

"So Handy had another phone in the slaughterhouse?" Potter asked.

"Not a phone," Tobe said. "It'd be a radio. And four eighty is often reserved for federal operations, Arthur."

"Is that right?" Potter considered this, then said, "But a radio wasn't found at the site, was it?"

Budd dug through a black attaché case. He found the sheet that listed the inventory of evidence found at the crime scene and the initial chain of custody. "No radio."

"Could've hidden it, I suppose. There'd be a million nooks and crannies in a place like that." Potter considered something. "Is there any way to trace the transmissions?"

"Not now. You have to triangulate on a real-time

signal." Tobe said this as if Potter had asked if it could snow in July.

"Commander Franklin," the agent asked, "you got a phone call, right? From this supposed trooper? It wasn't a radio transmission?"

"A landline, right. And it wasn't patched in from a radio either. You can always tell."

Potter paused and examined one of the flowers. Was it a begonia? A fuchsia? Marian had gardened. "So Handy radioed Mr. X, who then called Commander Franklin. Then X called Handy's girlfriend and gave her the go-ahead to intercept Sharon Foster. Tobe?"

The young agent's eyes flashed with understanding. He snapped his fingers and sat up. "You got it, Arthur," he responded to the request that Potter was about to make. "Pen register of all incoming calls to your office, Commander Franklin. You object to that?"

"Hell, no. I want this boy as much as you do."

"You have a direct line?" Tobe asked.

"I do, yes, but half of my calls come in from the switchboard. And when I pick up I don't know where it's coming in from."

"We'll do them all," Tobe said patiently, undaunted.

Who's Handy's accomplice? Potter wondered.

Tobe asked, "Henry? A warrant request, please."

LeBow printed one out on Stillwell's NEC and handed it to Potter then called up on his screen the *Federal Judiciary Directory*. Potter placed a call to a judge who sat on the district court of Kansas. He explained about the request. At home at this hour, the judge agreed to sign the warrant on the basis of the evidence Potter presented; he'd been watching CNN and knew all about the incident.

As a member of the bars of D.C. and Illinois, Potter signed the warrant request. Tobe faxed it to the judge, who signed and returned it immediately. LeBow then scrolled through Standard & Poor's *Corporation Directory* and found the name of the chief general counsel of Midwestern Bell. They served the warrant via fax to the lawyer at home. One phone conversation and five minutes later the requested files were dumped ingloriously into LeBow's computer.

"Okay, Commander Franklin," LeBow said, scrolling through his screen, "it looks like we have seventy-seven calls coming into your HQ today, thirty-six into your private line."

Potter said, "You're a busy man."

"Heh. The family can attest to that."

Potter asked when the call about Foster came in.

"About nine-thirty."

Potter said, "Make it a twenty-minute window."

Keys tapped.

"We're down to about sixteen total," LeBow said. "That's getting workable."

"If Handy had a radio," Budd said, "what'd the range of that thing be?"

"Good question, Charlie," Tobe said. "That'll narrow things down even more. If it's standard law-enforcement issue I'd guess three miles. Our Mr. X would have to've been pretty close to the barricade."

Potter lowered his head to the screen. "I don't know these towns, other than Crow Ridge, and there's no listing of any calls from there to you, Commander. Charlie, take a look. Tell us what's nearby."

"Hysford's about seventeen miles. Billings, nowhere near."

"That's the missus," volunteered Commander Franklin.

"How 'bout this? A three-minute call from Towsend to your office at nine twenty-six. Was that about how long you talked to the trooper, Commander Franklin?"

"About, yessir."

"Where's Towsend?"

"Borders Crow Ridge," Budd said. "Good-sized town."

"Can you get us an address?" Budd asked Tobe.

The downloaded files from the phone company didn't include addresses but a single call to Midwestern Bell's computer center pinpointed a pay phone.

"Route 236 and Roosevelt Highway."

"It's the main intersection," Stillwell said, discouraged. "Restaurants, hotels, gas stations. And that highway's a feeder for two interstates. Could've been anybody and he could've been on his way to anywhere."

Potter's eyes were on the five red plants. His head rose

suddenly and he reached for the telephone. But it was a curious gesture—he stopped suddenly and seemed momentarily flustered, as if he'd committed some grievous social faux pas at a formal dinner party. His hand slipped off the receiver.

"Henry, Tobe, come with me. You too, Charlie. Dean, will you stay here and man the fort?"

"You bet, sir."

"Where are we going?" Charlie asked.

"To talk to somebody who knows Handy better than we do."

2:00 A.M.

He wondered how they'd announce their presence.

There was a button on the jamb of the front door, just like any other. Potter looked at Budd, who shrugged and pushed it.

"I thought I heard something inside. A doorbell. Why's that?"

Potter had heard something too. But he'd also noticed a red light flash inside, through a lace curtain.

There was no response.

Where was she?

Potter found himself about to call, "Melanie?" And when he realized that would be futile, he lifted his fist to knock. He shook his head at that gesture too and lowered his hand. Seeing the lights inside a lifeless house, he felt a stab of uneasiness and he pulled his jacket away from his hip, where the Glock sat. LeBow noticed the gesture but said nothing.

"Wait here," Potter told the three men.

He walked slowly along the dark porch of the Victorian house, looking in the windows of the place. Suddenly he stopped, seeing shoeless feet, legs sprawled on a couch, motionless.

Alarmed now, in a panic, he hurriedly completed his

circuit of the porch. But he couldn't get any view of her—only her unmoving legs. He rapped loudly on the glass, shouted her name.

Nothing.

She should be able to feel the vibration, he thought. And there was the red flashing light—the "doorbell"—above the entryway, flashing in her clear view.

"Melanie!"

He drew his pistol. Tried the window. It was locked.

Do it.

His elbow crashed into the glass and sent a shower of shards onto the parquet floor. He reached in, unlocked the window, and started through. He froze when he saw the figure—Melanie herself, sitting up, terrified, staring at the intruder coming through her window. She blinked away the sleep and gasped.

Potter held up his hands to her, as if surrendering, an expression of horror on his own face at the thought of how he must have frightened her. Still, he was more perplexed than anything else: Why on earth, he wondered, would she be wearing stereo headphones?

Melanie Charrol opened the door and motioned her visitors inside.

The first thing that Arthur Potter saw was a large watercolor of a violin, surrounded by surreal quarter- and half-notes in rainbow colors.

"Sorry about the window," he said slowly. "You can deduct it from your taxes."

She smiled.

"Evening, ma'am," Charlie Budd said. And Potter introduced her to Tobe Geller and Henry LeBow. She looked out the door at the car parked two doors down, the two people standing behind a hedge, looking at the house.

He saw her face. He said to her, "They're ours."

Melanie frowned. He explained, "Two troopers. I sent them here earlier tonight to keep an eye on you."

She shook her head, asking, Why?

Potter hesitated. "Let's go inside."

With flashing lights, a Hebron PD squad car pulled up. Angeline Scapello, looking exhausted though no longer soot-smudged, climbed out and hurried up the stairs. She nodded to everyone, and like her fellow threat management team members she wasn't smiling.

Melanie's house had a homey air about it. Thick drapes. In the air, incense. Spicy. Old prints, many of them of classical composers, hung on the walls, which were covered with striped paper, forest green and gold. The largest print was of Beethoven. The room was full of antique tables, beautiful Art Nouveau vases. He thought with some embarrassment of his own Georgetown apartment, a shabby place. He'd stopped decorating it thirteen years ago.

Melanie was wearing blue jeans, a black cashmere sweater. Her hair was no longer in the awkward braid but hung loose. The bruises and cuts on her face and hands were quite prominent, as were the chestnut Betadine stains. Potter turned to her, tried to think of words that required exaggerated lip movements. "Lou Handy's escaped."

She didn't understand at first. When he repeated it her eyes went wide with horror. She started to sign then stopped in frustration and grabbed the stack of paper.

LeBow touched her arm. "Can you type?" He mimicked keyboarding.

She nodded. He opened his two computers, booted them into word-processing programs, hooked up a serial port cable, and set the units side by side. He sat at one, Melanie at the other.

Where did he go? she typed.

We don't know, that's why we came to see you.

Melanie nodded slowly. *Did he kill anyone escaping?* She could touch-type and she kept her eyes on Potter as she asked this.

He nodded. *Wilcox—the one you called Stoat—was killed. Troopers too.*

Again she nodded, frowning, thinking over the implications of this.

Potter typed, *I have to ask you to do something you're not going to want to do.*

She looked at his message, wrote: *I've already been through the worst.* Her hands danced over the keys invisibly, not a single mistake.

God compensates.

I want you to go back to the slaughterhouse. In your mind.

Her fingers hovered over the keyboard. She wrote nothing but merely nodded.

We don't understand certain things about the barricade. If you can help us to I think we can figure out where he's gone.

"Henry," Potter called, rising and pacing. LeBow and Tobe caught each other's eyes. "Call up his profile and the chronology. What do we know about him?"

LeBow began to read but Potter said, "No, let's just speculate."

"He's a clever boy," Budd offered. "He comes across like a hick but he's got some smarts."

Potter added, *He plays the dummy but that's largely an act, I think.*

Melanie typed, *Amoral.*

Yes.

Dangerous, Budd offered.

Let's go beyond that.

He's evil, she wrote. *Evil personified.*

But what kind of evil?

Silence for a moment. Angie typed, *Cold death.*

Potter nodded and spoke aloud, "Right. Lou Handy's cold evil. Not passionate evil. Let's keep that in mind."

Angie continued, *Not a sadist. Then he'd be passionate. He feels nothing for the pain he causes. If he needs pain or death to get his way, he'll cause pain or death. Like blinding the hostages—simply another tool for him.*

Potter leaned forward and typed, *So, he's calculating.*

"And?" Budd prompted.

Potter shook his head. *Yes, he's calculating, but you're right, Charlie, what does that* mean?

The men stopped speaking while Melanie's fingers danced over the keyboard. Potter walked around her and stood close as she typed. His hand brushed her shoulder and it seemed to him that she leaned into his fingers. She wrote: *Everything he does has a purpose. He's one of those few people who isn't driven by life; he drives it.*

Angie typed, *Control, control, control.*

Potter found his hand was resting on Melanie's shoulder. She lowered her cheek to it. Maybe it just was an accident as her head turned. Maybe not.

"Control and purpose," Potter said. "Yes, that's it. Type this out so she can see it, Henry. Everything he's done today has a purpose. Even if it seemed random. Killing Susan—it was to make clear that he was serious. He demanded a helicopter that seated eight but he had no problem giving away most of the hostages. Why? To keep us busy. To stretch out the time to give his accomplice and girlfriend a chance to set up the real Sharon Foster. He brought with him a TV, a scrambled radio, and guns."

Angie leaned forward to type, *So what is his purpose?*

"Well, escaping," Budd laughed. "What else would it be?" He leaned forward and two-finger typed, *To escape.*

No!! Melanie typed.

"Right!" Potter shouted, and pointed at her, nodding. "Escape wasn't his priority at all. How could it've been? He virtually let himself get trapped. There was only one trooper on his tail after the accident with the Cadillac. The three of them could've ambushed him, taken his car, and escaped. Why would anybody let themselves get trapped?"

"Hell," Budd said, "a spooked rabbit'll run right into a fox's den not even thinking." He dutifully hunted-and-pecked this in.

But he does think, Melanie wrote. *We can't forget that. And he isn't spooked.*

Not spooked at all, Angie offered. *Remember the voice stress analysis.*

Potter nodded to Melanie, smiling and gripping her shoulder once more. *Calm as ordering a cup of coffee at 7-Eleven.*

Melanie typed, *I called him Brutus. But he's really like a ferret.*

Budd continued, *Well, if he's a ferret, then he'd go to ground only if he knew he wasn't trapped at all. If he had an escape route.*

Melanie typed, *When he first walked into the slaughterhouse Bear said that there was no way out. And Brutus said, "It doesn't matter. It doesn't matter at all."*

Potter nodded, mused, "He could've run, but no, he risked taking a detour to the slaughterhouse and getting trapped. But it wasn't that great a risk at all because he knew he could get out. He had guns and he had a radio to call his accomplice and work out some escape plan. Maybe he'd already thought up substituting his girlfriend for Foster." He typed, *Melanie, tell us exactly what happened when they picked you up.*

She typed, *We found the wreck. He was killing those people. In no hurry.*

He was confident?

Very. He took his own sweet time, Melanie typed, grim-faced.

Potter unfurled a map. *What route did you drive?*

I don't know roads, Melanie wrote. *Past a radio station, a farm with lots of cows.* She frowned for a moment then traced the route on the map. *Maybe this.*

The prison's south of the slaughterhouse ninety or so miles, Potter typed. *The three of them drove north to here, had the accident with the Cadillac here, took the van and drove all the way around here. . . .* He traced a route that had Handy driving well past the slaughterhouse then doubling back.

Melanie typed, *No. We drove straight to the slaughterhouse. That was one thing I thought funny. He seemed to know where it was.*

But if he went straight there, Potter typed, *when did you pass the airport?*

We didn't, she explained.

So he knew about it ahead of time. When he was asking me for the helicopter he knew there was an airport just two or three miles up the road. How did he know?

Budd typed, *He'd already arranged to fly out of there.*

But, LeBow typed as fast as he could speak the words, *if it was just a few miles up the road, and if there was an airplane or helicopter waiting for him, why go to the slaughterhouse at all?*

"Why?" Potter muttered. "Henry, tell me what we know. Let's start with what he had with him."

You're carrying a key, a magic sword, five stones, and a raven in a cage.

He went into the slaughterhouse with hostages, the guns, a can of gasoline, ammunition, a TV, the radio, a set of tools—

"The tools, yes," Potter said, as LeBow typed. He turned to Melanie. "Did you see him use them?"

No, Melanie answered. *But I was in killing room for most of time. Toward end I remembered them walking around looking at the machinery and fixtures. I thought they were taking a nostalgic look at the place, maybe they were looking for something, though.*

Potter snapped his fingers. "Dean told us something similar."

LeBow scanned through the incident chronology. He read, " 'Seven-fifty-six p.m. Sheriff Stillwell reported that a trooper under his command observed Handy and Wilcox searching the factory, testing doors and fixtures. Reason unknown.' "

"Okay. Good. Let's put the tools on hold for a minute. Those are the things he had with him when he went in. What did we *give* him?"

"Just the food and the beer," Budd said. "Oh, and the money."

"The money!" Potter cried. "Money he didn't ask for in the first place."

Angie typed, *And he never tried to bargain up the fifty thousand. Why not?*

There's only one reason a man doesn't want money, LeBow typed. *He's got more than he needs.*

Potter was nodding excitedly. *There's money hidden in the building. It was part of his plan all along—to stop at the slaughterhouse and pick it up.*

That's why he had the tools—to get the cash out from where it was hidden, Budd managed to type. Potter nodded.

"Where did it come from?" Tobe wondered.

"He's a bank robber," Budd said wryly. "That's one possibility."

"Henry," Potter said, "jump into Lexis/Nexis and let's read about that most recent robbery of his. The arson."

In five minutes LeBow was on-line with Mead Data. He read newspaper accounts and summarized, "Handy was

found with twenty thousand stolen from the Farmers &
Merchants heist in Wichita."

"Had he ever burned anything before that?"

LeBow scrolled through the news accounts and his own
sixteen-page profile of Louis J. Handy. "No prior arson."

Then why the fire? Potter typed.

He always has a purpose, Angie reminded.

Melanie nodded emphatically then shivered and closed
her eyes. Potter wondered what terrible memory had in-
truded into her thoughts. The agent and Budd looked at each
other, four eyebrows arched. Then: "Yep, Charlie. That's
right." Potter reached down to the keyboard. *He wasn't
there to rob that bank at all. He was there to burn it down.*

LeBow was reading the profile. "And he shot his accomplice in the back when they'd been trapped by the
troopers. Maybe so no one would find out what he was really doing there."

But why did he do it? Budd typed.

Someone hired him? Potter asked the question. LeBow
nodded. "Of course."

"And whoever did," Potter said, "was paying him a ton
of money. A lot more than fifty thousand. That's why he
didn't think to ask for cash from us. He was already a rich
man. Henry, get into the Corporation Trust database and
get me the corporate documents on the bank."

The intelligence officer went off-line with Mead and
was soon scrolling through the articles of incorporation,
bylaws, and securities filings of the bank. "Closely held,
so it's limited public information. But we do know that
the directors are also the officers. Here we go: Clifton
Burbank, Stanley L. Poole, Cynthia G. Grolsch, Herman
Gallagher. The ZIP codes are close together. All near Wichita. Burbank and Gallagher live in the city proper.
Poole lives in Augusta. Ms. Grolsch is in Derby."

Potter recognized none of the names but any one of
them could have some connection to Handy. As could,
say, an embezzling teller, a former employee who'd been
fired, the spurned lover of one of the directors. But Arthur
Potter would much rather have too many possibilities than
none at all. "Charlie, what hotels are near that pay phone
where Mr. X called Ted Franklin? In Towsend."

"Hell, there's a bunch. Four or five at least. Holiday Inn, a Ramada, I think a Hilton and some local one. Towsend Motor Lodge. Maybe another one or two."

Potter told Tobe to start calling. "Find out if any of those directors were registered in the hotels today or if anybody from any of those towns was registered."

In five minutes they had an answer. Tobe snapped his fingers. Everyone, except Melanie, looked at him. "Somebody registered from Derby, Kansas. Same as Cynthia Grolsch."

"Too much of a coincidence," Potter muttered, taking the phone. He identified himself, spoke to the clerk for a few moments. Finally he shook his head grimly, asked, "And what room?" He jotted down *Holiday Inn. Rm. 611* on a pad. To the clerk he said, "No. And don't mention this call." He hung up, tapped the pad. "May be our Judas. Let's go have a talk with 'em, Charlie."

Melanie glanced at the pad of paper. Her face went still. *Who? Who is it?* Her eyes flared. She stood up abruptly, pulled a leather jacket from a hook.

"Let them handle it," Angie said.

Melanie looked back to Potter, her eyes flaring. She typed, *Who is it?*

"Please." Potter took her by the shoulders. "I don't want anything to happen to you."

Slowly she nodded, pulled off the jacket, slung it over her shoulder. She looked like an aviatrix from the thirties.

Potter said, "Henry, Angie, and Tobe stay here. Handy knows about Melanie. He might come back." He said to her, "I'll be back soon." Then he hurried to the door. "Come on, Charlie."

After they'd gone Melanie smiled at the agents who remained. She typed *Tea? Coffee?*

"Not for me," Tobe said.

"No, thank you. Want to play solitaire?" LeBow booted up the game.

She shook her head. *I'm going to take a shower. Long day.*

"Gotcha."

Melanie disappeared and a few minutes later they heard the sound of running water from a bathroom.

Angie began working on her incident report while Tobe called up Doom II on his laptop and started to play. Fifteen minutes later he'd been blown apart by aliens. He stood up and stretched. He looked over Henry LeBow's shoulder, made a suggestion about the red queen, which was not received very generously at all, and then paced in the living room. He glanced at the sideboard, where he'd left the keys to the government pool car. They were gone. He wandered to the front of the house and glanced outside at the empty street. Why, he wondered, would Potter and Budd have taken two separate cars to the Holiday Inn?

But his blood lust was insatiable and he stopped worrying about such a trivial matter as he returned to his computer and prepared to blast his way out of the fortress of Doom.

2:35 A.M.

It had been Hawaiian Night at the Holiday Inn.

Steel guitar still pumped through the PA and limp plastic leis hung around the night clerks' necks.

Agent Arthur Potter and Captain Charles Budd walked between two fake palms and took the elevator up to the sixth floor.

For a change Budd was the law enforcer looking perfectly confident; it was Potter who was ill-at-ease. The last kick-in the agent had been involved in was the arrest of a perp who happened to be wearing a turquoise Edwardian suit and silver floral polyester shirt, which carbon-dated the bust to around 1977.

He remembered that he wasn't supposed to stand in front of the door. What else? He was reassured to glance at Budd, who had a shiny black leather cuffcase on his belt. Potter himself had never cuffed a real suspect—only volunteers at the live-fire hostage rescue drills on the Quantico back lot. "I'll defer to you on this one, Charlie."

Budd raised surprised eyebrows. "Well, sure, Arthur."

"But I'll back you up."

"Oh. Good."

Both men pulled their weapons from the hip holsters. Potter chambered a round again—twice in one night and three years from the last barricade in which a bullet had rested in his gun's receiver and meant business.

At room 611 they stopped, exchanged glances. The negotiator nodded.

Budd knocked, a friendly tap. Shave and a haircut.

"Yeah?" the gruff voice called. "Hello? Who's there?"

"It's Charlie Budd. Can you open up for a minute? Just found something interesting."

"Charlie? What's going on?"

The chain fell, a deadbolt clicked, and when Roland Marks opened the door he found himself staring into the muzzles of two identical automatic pistols: one steady, one shaking, and both safeties off.

"Cynthia's a director of the S&L, yes. It's a nominal position. I'm really the one who calls the shots. We kept it in her maiden name. She's not guilty of anything."

The assistant attorney general could protest all he wanted but it would be up to the grand and petit juries to decide his wife's fate.

No raillery. Marks was now playing straight man. His eyes were red and damp and Potter, feeling nothing but contempt, had no trouble holding his gaze.

The AG had been read his rights. It was all over and he knew it. So he decided to cooperate. His statement was being taken down by the very same tape recorder he'd slipped Budd earlier in the evening.

"And what exactly were you doing at the savings and loan?" Potter asked.

"Making bad loans to myself. Well, to fictional people and companies. Writing them off and keeping the money." He shrugged as if to say, Isn't it obvious?

Marks, the prosecutor specializing in white-collar crime, had learned well from his suspects: he'd bled the Wichita institution's stockholders, and the public, for close to five million dollars—much of it spent already, it seemed. "I thought with the turnaround in the real estate market," he continued, "some of the bank's legitimate investments would pay off and we could cover up the shortfall. But when I went over the books I saw we just weren't going to make it."

The Resolution Trust Corporation, the government agency taking over failed banking institutions, was about to come in and seize the place.

"So you hired Lou Handy to burn it down," Budd said. "Destroy all the records."

"How did you know him?" the agent asked.

Budd beat Marks to it. "You prosecuted Handy five years ago, wasn't it? The convenience-store heist—the barricade Sharon Foster talked him out of."

. The assistant attorney general nodded. "Oh, yes, I remembered him. Who wouldn't? Smart son of a bitch. He took the stand in his own defense and nearly ran circles around me. Had to do some digging to find him for the S&L job, you can bet. Checked with his parole officer, some of my contacts on the street. Offered him two hundred thousand to torch the place as part of a robbery. Only he got caught. So I had no choice—I had to cut a deal with him. I'd help him escape, otherwise he'd blow the whistle on me. That cost me another three hundred thousand."

"How'd you get him out? Callana's maximum-security."

"Paid two guards their annual salaries in cash to do it."

"Was one of them the guard Handy killed?"

Marks nodded.

"Saved some money there, didn't you?" Charlie Budd asked bitterly.

"You left a car for him with the guns, the scrambled radio, and the TV in it," Potter continued. "And the tools to get the money out of the slaughterhouse where you'd hidden it for him."

"Well, hell, we couldn't exactly leave the money in the car. Too risky. So I sealed it up in this old steam pipe behind the front window."

Potter asked, "What were the escape plans going to be?"

"Originally, I'd arranged for a private plane to fly him and his buddies out of Crow Ridge, from that little airport up the road. But he never made it. He had the accident—with the Cadillac—and lost about a half-hour."

"Why did he take the girls?"

"He needed them. With the delay he knew he didn't have time to get the money *and* make it to the airport—with the cops right on his tail. But he wasn't going to leave without the cash. Lou figured with the hostages inside and me working to get him out, it didn't matter how many cops were at the slaughterhouse. He'd get out sooner or later. He radioed me from inside and I agreed to convince the FBI to give him a helicopter. That didn't work but by then I remembered Sharon Foster's negotiation with Handy a few years ago. I found out where she was stationed now and called Pris Gunder—his girlfriend—and told her to drive over to Foster's house. Then I pretended I was a trooper and called Ted Franklin at state police."

Potter asked, "So your heart-rending offer to give yourself up for the girls . . . that was all an act."

"I *did* want them out. I didn't want anyone to die. Of course not!"

Of course, Potter thought cynically. "Where's Handy now?"

"I have no idea. Once he got out of the barricade that was it. I'd done everything I'd agreed. I told him he was on his own."

Potter shook his head. Budd asked coldly, "Tell me, Marks, how's it feel to've murdered those troopers?"

"No! He promised me he wouldn't kill anyone! His girlfriend was just going to handcuff Foster. He—"

"And the other troopers? The escort?"

Marks stared at the captain for a minute and when no credible lie came to mind whispered, "It wasn't supposed to work out like this. It *wasn't.*"

"Call for some baby-sitters," Potter said. But before Budd could, his phone buzzed.

"Hello?" He listened for a moment. His eyes went wide. "Where? Okay, we're moving."

Potter cocked an eyebrow.

"They found the other squad car, the one Handy and his girlfriend were in. He's going south, looks like. Toward Oklahoma. The cruiser was twenty miles past the booking center. There was a couple in the trunk. Dead. Handy and his girlfriend must've stolen their wheels. No ID on them so we don't have a make or tag yet." Budd stepped close to the assistant AG. The captain growled, "The only good news is that Handy was in a hurry. They died fast."

Marks grunted in pain as Budd spun him around and shoved him hard into the wall. Potter did nothing to interfere. Budd tied the attorney's hands together with plastic wrist restraints then cuffed his right wrist to the bed frame.

"It's too tight," Marks whined.

Budd threw him down on the bed. "Let's go, Arthur. He's got a hell of a lead on us. Brother, he could be nearly to Texas by now."

She was surrounded by the Outside.

And yet it wasn't as hard as she'd thought.

Oh, she supposed the driver had honked furiously at her when she crossed the center line a moment ago. But, all things considered, she was doing fine. Melanie Charrol had never in her life driven a car. Many deaf people did, of course, even if they weren't supposed to, but Melanie had always been too afraid. Her fear wasn't that she'd be in an accident. Rather, she was terrified that she'd do something wrong and be embarrassed. Maybe get in the wrong lane. Stop too far away from a red light or too close. People would gather around the car and laugh at her.

But now she was cruising down Route 677 like a pro. She didn't have musician's ears any longer but she had musician's hands, sensitive and strong. And those fingers learned quickly not to overcompensate on the wheel and she sped straight toward her destination.

Lou Handy had had a purpose; well, so did she.

Bad is simple and good is complicated. And the simple always wins. That's what everything comes down to in the end. Simple always wins ... that's just nature and you know what kind of trouble people get into ignoring nature.

Through the night, forty miles an hour, fifty, sixty.

She glanced down at the dashboard. Many of the dials and knobs made no sense to her. But she recognized the radio. She turned switches until it lit up: 103.4. Eyes flicking up and down, she figured out which was the volume and pushed the button until the line in the LED indicator was all the way at full. She heard nothing at first but then she turned up the bass level and she heard thumps and occasionally the sliding sound of tones and notes. The low register, Beethoven's register. That portion of her hearing had never deserted her completely.

Maybe his Ninth Symphony was playing, the soaring, inspiring "Ode to Joy." This seemed too coincidental, considering her mission at the moment, and 103.4 was probably rap or heavy metal. But it sent a powerful, irresistible beat through her chest. That was enough for her.

There!

She braked the car to a screeching stop in the deserted parking lot of the hardware supply store. The windows held just the assortment of goods she'd been looking for.

The brick sailed tidily through the glass and if it set off an alarm, which it probably did, she couldn't hear it so she felt no particular pressure to hurry. Melanie leaned forward and selected what seemed to be the sharpest knife in the display, a ten-inch butcher, Chicago Cutlery. She returned leisurely to the driver's seat, dropped the long blade on the seat next to her, then put the car in gear and sped away.

As she forced the engine to speed the car up to seventy through the huge gusts of silent wind, Melanie thought of Susan Phillips. Who would soon be sleeping forever in a grave as silent as her life had been.

A Maiden's Grave . . .

Oh, Susan, Susan . . . I'm not you. I can't be you and I won't even ask you to forgive me for that, though I would have once. After today I know I can't listen to imaginary music for the rest of my life. I know if you were alive now you'd hate me for this. But I want to *hear* words, I want to *hear* streams of snazzy consonants and vowels, I want to *hear* my music.

You were Deaf of Deaf, Susan. That made you strong, even if it killed you. I've been safe because I'm weak. But I can't be weak anymore. I'm an Other and that's just the way it is.

And Melanie realizes now, with a shock, why she could

understand that son of a bitch Brutus so well. Because she *is* like him. She feels exactly what he feels.

Oh, I want to hurt, I want to pay them all back: Fate, taking my music away from me. My father, scheming to keep it away. Brutus and the man who hired him, kidnaping us, toying with us, hurting us, every one of us—the students, Mrs. Harstrawn, that poor trooper. And of course Susan.

The car raced through the night, one of her elegant hands on the steering wheel, one caressing the sensuous wooden handle of the knife.

Amazing grace, how sweet the sound . . .

The wind buffeted the car fiercely and, overhead, black strips of clouds raced through the cold sky at a thousand miles an hour.

That saved a wretch like me.
I once was lost but now I'm found.
Was blind, but now I see.

Melanie dropped the knife back onto the seat and gripped the wheel in both hands, listening to the powerful bass beat resonate in her chest. She supposed the wind howled like a mad wolf but of course that was something she couldn't know for sure.
So you'll be home then.
Never.

They were three miles outside of Crow Ridge, speeding south, when Budd sat up straight, making his perfect posture that much better. His head snapped toward Potter.
"Arthur!"
The FBI agent cringed. "Of course. Oh, hell!"
The car skidded to a stop on the highway, ending up perpendicular to the roadway and blocking both lanes.
"Where is it, Charlie? *Where?*"
"A half-mile that way," Budd cried, pointing to the right. "That intersection we just passed. It's a shortcut. It'll take us right there."

Arthur Potter, otherwise the irritatingly prudent driver, took the turn at speed and, on the verge of an irrigation ditch, managed to control his mad, tire-smoking skid.

"Oh, brother," Budd muttered, though it wasn't Potter's insane driving but his own stupidity he was lamenting. "I can't believe I didn't think of it before."

Potter was furious with himself too. He realized exactly where Handy was. Not going south at all but heading directly back to his money. All the other evidence had been removed from the slaughterhouse by the police. But Crime Scene had never gotten the scrambled radio—or the cash. They were still there, hidden. Hundreds of thousands of dollars.

As he drove, hunched over the wheel, Potter asked Budd to call Tobe at Melanie's house. When the connection was completed he took the phone from the captain.

"Where's Frank and HRT?" the agent asked.

"Hold on," Tobe responded. "I'll find out." A moment later he came back on. "They're about to touch down in Virginia."

Potter sighed. "Damn. Okay, call Ted Franklin and Dean Stillwell, have them send some men to the slaughterhouse. Handy's on his way. If he's not there already. But it's vital not to spook him. This might be our only chance to nail him. I want them to roll in without lights and sirens and park at least a half-mile away on side roads. Remember to tell him Handy's armed and extremely dangerous. Tell him we're going to be inside. Charlie and me."

"Where are you now?"

"Hold on." Potter asked Budd, who gave him their whereabouts. Into the phone he said, "Charlie says, Hitchcock Road, just off Route 345. About two minutes away."

A pause.

"Charlie Budd's with you?" Tobe asked uncertainly.

"Well, sure. You saw him leave with me."

"But you took both cars."

"No. We just took mine."

Another pause. "Hold on, Arthur."

Uneasy, Potter said to Budd, "Something's going on there. At Melanie's."

Come on, Tobe. Talk to me.

A moment later the young agent came on. "She's gone, Arthur. Melanie. She left the shower running and took the other car."

A chill ran through him. Potter said, "She's going to the Holiday Inn to kill Marks."

"What?" Budd cried.

"She doesn't know his name. But she knows the room number. She saw what I wrote down."

"And I left him trussed up there without a guard. I forgot to call."

Potter remembered the look in her eyes, the cold fire. He asked Tobe, "Did she take a weapon? Was there one in the car?"

Tobe called something to LeBow.

"No, we've both got ours. Nothing in the car."

"Well, get some troopers over to the hotel fast." He had an image of her madly going for Marks despite the troopers. If she had a gun or knife they'd kill her instantly.

"Okay, Arthur," Tobe said. "We're on it."

Just then the sulky landscape took on a familiar tone— déjà vu from a recurring nightmare. A moment later the slaughterhouse loomed ahead of them. The battlefield was littered with coffee cups and tread marks—from squad cars, not the swales of covered wagons. The field was deserted. Potter folded up the phone and handed it back to Budd. He cut the engine and coasted silently the last fifty feet.

"What about Melanie?" Budd whispered.

There was no time to think about her. The agent lifted his finger to his lips and gestured toward the door. The two men stepped outside into the fierce wind.

They were walking through the gully down which Stevie Oates had carried Shannon and Kielle like bags of wheat.

"Through the front door?" Budd whispered.

Potter nodded yes. It was wide open; they could enter without having to risk squeaky hinges. Besides, the windows were five feet off the ground. Budd might make the climb but Potter, already exhausted and breathing heavily, knew that he wouldn't be able to.

They remained motionless for some minutes but there

was no sign of Handy. No cars in sight, no headlights approaching, no flashlights. And no sound except that of the extraordinary wind.

Potter nodded toward the front door.

They crouched and hurried between hillocks up to the front of the slaughterhouse, the red-and-white brick, blood and bone. They paused beside the spot where the body of Tremain's trooper had been dumped.

The pipe by the window, Potter remembered. Filled with half a million dollars, the bait drawing Handy back to us.

They paused on either side of the door.

This isn't me, Potter thought suddenly. This isn't what I was meant to do. I'm a man of words, not a soldier. It's not that I'm afraid. But I'm out of my depth.

Not afraid, not afraid . . .

Though he was.

Why? Because, he supposes, for the first time in years, there is someone else in his life. Somehow, existence has become somewhat more precious to him in the past twelve hours. Yes, I want to talk to her, to Melanie. I want to tell her things, I want to hear how her day went. And, yes, yes, I want to take her hand and climb the stairs after dinner, feel the heat of her breath on my ear, feel the motion of her body beneath me. I want that! I . . .

Budd tapped his shoulder. Potter nodded and, guns before them, they stepped inside the slaughterhouse.

Like a cave.

Darkness everywhere. The wind roared through the holes and ill-fitting joints of the old place so loudly that the men could hear virtually nothing else. They stepped instinctively behind a large metal structure, some kind of housing. And waited. Gradually Potter's eyes became accustomed to the inky darkness. He could just make out two slightly lighter squares of the windows on the other side of the door. Beside the closest one was a stubby pipe about two feet in diameter, rising in an L shape from the floor like a vent on a ship. Potter pointed to it and Budd squinted, nodding.

As they made their way forward, like blind men, Potter understood what Melanie had gone through here. The wind stole his hearing, the darkness his vision. And the cold was dulling his sense of touch and smell.

They paused, Potter feeling panic stream down his spine like ice water. Once he gasped as Budd lifted his hand alarmingly and dropped into a crouch. Potter too had seen the leveraging shadow but it turned out to be merely a piece of sheet metal bending in the breeze.

Then they were five yards from the pipe. Potter stopped, looked around slowly. Heard nothing other than the wind. Turned back.

They started forward but Budd was tapping his shoulder. The captain whispered, "Don't slip. Something's spilled there. Oil, looks like."

Potter too looked underfoot. There were large dots of silvery liquid—more like mercury than water or oil—at the base of the pipe. He bent down, reached forward with a finger.

He touched cold metal.

Not oil.

Steel nuts.

The end plate was off the pipe.

Handy had been here al—

The gunshot came from no more than ten feet away. An ear-shattering bang, ringing painfully off the tile and metal and exposed wet brick.

Potter and Budd spun around.

Nothing, blackness. The faint motion of shadow as clouds obscured the moon.

Then the choked sound of Charlie Budd whispering, "I'm sorry, Arthur."

"What?"

"I'm . . . I'm sorry. I'm hit."

The shot had been fired into his back. He fell to his knees and Potter saw the ragged exit wound low in his belly. Budd keeled over onto the floor.

The agent started forward instinctively. Careful, he reminded himself, turning toward where the gunshot had come from. Guard yourself first.

The piece of pipe caught Potter squarely on the shoulder, knocking the wind out of him. He dropped hard to the ground and felt the sinewy hand yank his pistol from his grip.

"You alone? You two?" Handy's voice was a whisper.

Potter couldn't speak. Handy twisted his arm up behind his back, bent a little finger brutally. The pain surged through Potter's hand into his jaw and head. "Yes, yes. Just the two of us."

Handy grunted as he rolled Potter over and bound his hands before him with thin wire, the strands cutting into his flesh.

"There's no way you're going to—" Potter began.

Then a blurring motion, as Handy was slammed sideways into the pipe where the money'd been hidden. With a hollow ringing sound, the side of his head connected with the metal.

Charlie Budd, face dripping sweat as copious as the blood he shed, drew back his fist once more and slammed it into Handy's kidney. The convict wheezed with pain and pitched forward.

As Potter struggled futilely to get to his feet, Budd groped in the dark for his service automatic. He felt himself starting to black out and lurched sideways. Recovered slightly then staggered into a large cube of stained butcher block.

Handy leapt at him, growling in fury, throwing his arms around Budd's neck, pulling him down to the floor. The convict had been hurt, yes, but he still had his strength; Budd's was draining rapidly from his body.

"Oh, brother," Budd coughed. "I can't—"

Handy took Budd by the hair. "Come on, sport. Only round one."

"Go to hell," the trooper whispered.

"There's a boy." Handy got his arms around Budd and pulled him to his feet. "Ain't heard the bell. Come on. Fans're waiting."

The trooper, bleeding badly, eyes unfocused, pulled away and began flailing at Handy's lean face. One blow struck with surprising force and the convict jerked back in surprise. But after the initial burst of pain dissipated, Handy laughed. "Come on," he taunted. "Sugar Ray, come on. . . ." When Budd connected a final time Handy

moved in close and rained a half-dozen blows into his
face. Budd dropped to his knees.

"Hey, down for the count."

"Leave him . . . alone," Potter called.

Handy pulled the gun from his belt.

"No!" the agent cried.

"Arthur . . ."

To Potter, Handy said, "He's lucky I'm doing it this
way. I had more time, wouldn't be painless. Nosir."

"Listen to me," Potter began desperately.

"Shhh," Handy whispered.

The wind swelled, a mournful wail.

The three gunshots were fast and were soon replaced by
the sound of Potter's voice crying, "Oh, Charlie, no, no,
no. . . ."

3:00 A.M.

Through the murky chutes, where the condemned longhorns had walked, between rectangular boulders of
butcher block, beneath a thousand rusting meat hooks,
clanging like bells . . .

And all the while the wind screamed around them,
hooting through crevices and broken windows like a
steam whistle on a tug.

Potter's wrists stung from the wire. He thought of
Melanie's hands. Of her perfect nails. He thought of her hair,
spun honey. He wished fervently that he'd kissed her earlier
in the evening. With his tongue he pushed a tooth, loosened
in his fall, from its precarious perch and spit it out. His
mouth filled and he spit again; blood spurted to the floor.

"You poor fuck," Handy said with great satisfaction in
his voice. "You just didn't get it, did you, Art? You just
didn't fucking get it."

Ahead of them, some illumination. It wasn't light so
much as a vague lessening of the darkness. From outside,
faint starlight and the sliver of moon.

"You didn't have to kill him," the agent found himself saying.

"This way. Go there." Handy pushed him into a moldy corridor. "You been in this line of work how long, Art?"

Potter didn't answer.

"Probably twenty, twenty-five years, I'd guess. An' I'll bet mosta that's been doing what you did today—talking to assholes like me." Handy was a small man but his grip was ferocious. Potter's fingers tingled as he felt the circulation cut off.

They passed through a dozen rooms, black and stinking—the bloody dream of Messrs. Stoltz and Webber.

Handy pushed Potter through a back doorway. Then they were outside, rocking against the blast of wind.

"Whoa, bumpy ride tonight." Handy tugged Potter toward a grove of trees. He saw the outline of a car. Engine blocks take three hours to cool. If he'd had an infrared viewer they'd have seen it.

And Charlie Budd would still be alive. . . .

"Twenty-five years," Handy shouted over the wind. "You always been on the other side of the police line. The safe side. You ever think what it'd be like being a hostage yourself? Wouldn't that be a fuckin' *experience?* Come on, Art, hustle. I want you to meet Pris. She's a ball buster, she is.

"Yessir, that's what you're gonna be—a hostage. You know, people don't experience stuff. Most people've never shot anybody. Most people've never walked into a bank and pulled a gun. Most people've never looked at a girl and not said a fucking word but just stared and stared while she cried like a swatted pup and then started taking off her clothes. 'Cause she figured that's what you want her to do.

"And most people've never been up close when somebody dies. I mean, touching 'em when it happens. When the last cell of somebody's body stops swimming around. I done all that. You don't even come close to feeling stuff like that. Like I've felt. *That's* experience, Art.

"You tried to stop me. You shouldn't've done that. I'm going to kill you, you probably know that. But not for a while. I'm taking you with us. And there ain't nothing you can say to stop me. You can't offer me a six-pack, you can't offer me a M-the-fuck-4 priority to Canada. When we're safe and away then the only thing I want is you dead. And if we don't get safe and away, then I want you dead too."

Handy suddenly quivered with fury, grabbed Potter by the lapels. "You shouldn'ta tried to stop me!"

There was a crinkling sound in Potter's jacket pocket. Handy smiled. "What've we got here?"

No! Potter thought, twisting away. But Handy reached inside the sports coat and lifted the photo from the pocket.

"What's'is?"

The picture of Melanie Charrol. The one that had been pinned up on the bulletin board in the van.

"Your girlfriend, huh, Art?"

"There's nowhere in the world," Potter said, "you'll be safe."

Handy ignored him. "We'll be away for a while, Pris and me. But I'm gonna hold on to this snapshot here. We'll come back and visit her. Melanie, she's a pistol. She got me down on my back, knocked the wind clean outta me. Did this—see these scratches? And she pitched that little girl out the door 'fore I could say boo. And got that other one, the pretty little one Sonny had his eye on, got her out too. Oh, Melanie'll get her payback." As if revealing trade secrets Handy added, "A man can't let anybody walk on him. Especially a woman. May be a month, may be two months. She'll find Pris and me in her bed waiting for her. And she can't even scream for help."

"You'd be nuts to come back here. Every cop in the state knows your face."

Handy was angry again. "I'm owed! I am fucking owed!" He shoved the photo into his pocket and dragged Potter after him.

They were headed for the airport—*"Bumpy ride tonight."* They'd kill him as soon as they were safe. Maybe drop him from the airplane, three thousand feet over a wheat field.

"There she is now, Pris." Handy nodded at the Nissan, parked in a grove of trees. "She's quite a gal, Art. I was shot one time, got hit in the side, and the same shit trooper got me'd drawn down on Pris. She had her piece in her

hand but he could've nailed her 'fore she could lift it
even. What happens but, cool as ice, she unbuttons her
blouse, smiling all the time? Yessir, yessir. He wanted to
shoot her, that man did! But he couldn't bring himself to.
Soon as he glanced down at her titties she lifted her Glock
and took him out, pow, pow, pow. Three in the chest.
Then walked over and put one in the head in case he was
in armor. You think your girlfriend'd be that cool? Oh,
I'll betcha not, Art."

Handy stopped, pulled Potter to a halt and then looked
around, head up, sniffing the air, frowning. Melanie had
called him Brutus and given the other two the names of
creatures but the agent knew Handy was more animal-like
than either Wilcox or Bonner.

Handy's eyes turned toward the car.

Potter could see the open driver's door and the woman inside, who'd impersonated Sharon Foster, gazing out the
windshield. Her blond hair was pulled back in the same
ponytail as before. But she'd changed clothes. No longer in
uniform, she was now wearing pants and a dark turtleneck.

"Pris?" Handy whispered.

She didn't respond.

"Pris?" Louder. "Prissy?" Rising on the wind.

Handy shoved Potter to the ground. The agent fell and
rolled helplessly on the grass then watched as Handy ran
to the driver's seat and cradled his girlfriend.

The convict howled in horror and rage.

Potter squinted. No, not a turtleneck, not a garment at
all. The slit in the woman's throat extended from one
jugular vein to another and the dark sweater was half the
blood in her body streaming down over her shoulders and
arms and breasts. Her sole plea for help had been to lift a
bloody hand to the windshield and gesture madly, leaving
a fingerpainting of her terror on the dirty glass.

"No, no, no!" Handy cradled her, rocking frantically
back and forth.

Potter rolled to his side and tried to scrabble away. He
got only three feet then heard the snap of brush and rush
of feet. A boot slammed into his ribs. Potter dropped to
the ground, lifting his bound hands to his face. "You did
this! You snuck up on her! You did this, you fuck!"

Potter curled up, tried to ward off the vicious kicks.

Handy backed up and lifted the pistol.

Potter closed his eyes and lowered his hands.

He tried to picture Marian but she wouldn't come to mind. No, only Melanie was in his thoughts as, for the second time tonight, he prepared to die.

Arthur Potter was suddenly aware of the wind around him. Howling, hissing, it rose and formed words. But they were words not of this earth: eerie syllables rising deep from within some banshee mimicking the language of pitiful humans. He couldn't make out the content at first, a phrase repeated manically, spoken in pure loathing and fury. Then the scream coalesced, and as Handy whirled around Potter heard the malformed words over and over, "I hate you I hate you I hate you. . . ."

The knife plunged deep into Handy's shoulder and he cried in agony as Melanie Charrol's strong hands pulled the long blade from his flesh and drove it again into him—into his right arm. The gun dropped to the ground. Potter rolled forward and scooped it up.

Handy swung a fist at her face but she leapt back easily, still holding the knife in front of her. Handy dropped to his knees, eyes closed, gripping his arm, from which blood poured and poured, spiraling down his right finger, extended like God's in the Sistine Chapel.

Potter struggled to his feet and walked around Handy, stopped beside Melanie. She looked at his hands and untied the wire binding them. The young woman was quivering fiercely. So she too had made the same deduction about Handy that he and Budd had—that he'd be returning here for his money. She hadn't gone after Marks at all.

"Go ahead, do it," Handy snarled to Potter, as if he were the long-suffering victim of tonight's events.

Feeling the weight of the Glock in his fingers, Potter glanced down at Handy's creased, hating face. The agent said nothing, did nothing.

Have you ever done anything bad?

Then suddenly Arthur Potter understood how different he truly was from Handy and had always been. During the barricades the agent was like an actor—he became someone else for a short while, became someone he distrusted, feared, even loathed. But this talent was mercifully balanced by his uncanny ability to relinquish the role, to return.

And so it was Melanie Charrol who stepped forward and drove the long knife deep between Handy's ribs, all the way to the bloody handle.

The thin man choked, coughed blood, and fell backwards, shivering. Slowly she drew the knife out.

Potter took the weapon from her, wiped the handle on his sports coat, dropped it on the ground. He stood back, watching Melanie crouch beside Handy, who was trembling as the last of life fled his wiry body. She crouched over him, her head down, her eyes on him. In the dimness of the night Potter couldn't see her expression clearly though he detected what he believed was a faint smile on her face, one of curiosity.

And he sensed something else. In her posture, in the tilt of her head near his, it seemed as if she were inhaling the man's pain like spiced incense wafting through her house.

Lou Handy's mouth moved. A wet sound rose, a rattle, but so soft that Arthur Potter was nearly as deaf to it as Melanie would be. When the man quivered violently once, then again, and was finally still, Potter helped her to her feet.

His arm around her shoulders, they walked through the night while around them saplings and sedge and buffalo grass whipped from side to side in the sinewy wind. Fifty yards up the road they came to the government car Melanie had commandeered for the drive here from Hebron.

She turned to him, zipping up her battered brown leather jacket.

He gripped her shoulders, felt the wind slap her hair against his hand. A dozen things he might have said to her came to mind. He wanted to ask if she was all right, ask what she was feeling, tell her what he intended to explain to the troopers, tell her how many times he thought about her during the barricade.

But he said nothing. The moon had slipped behind a lesion of black cloud and the field was very dark; she couldn't, he told himself, see his lips anyway. Potter suddenly pulled her to him and kissed her on the mouth, quickly, ready to step away at the least hesitation. But he felt none and held her tightly to him, dropping his face to the cool, fragrant skin of her neck. They remained in this embrace for a long moment. When he stepped back the moon was out once again and there was pale white light on both their faces. But still he remained silent and merely guided her into the driver's seat of the car.

Melanie started the engine and, glancing back, she lifted her hands off the wheel and gestured to him in sign language.

Why would she do that? he wondered. What could she be saying?

Before he could tell her to wait, to write out the words, she put the car in gear and drove to the dirt road, rocking slowly over the uneven field. The car made an abrupt turn and disappeared behind a row of trees. The brake lights flashed once and then she was gone.

He trudged back to the bloody Nissan. Here, he smudged all the fingerprints but his own and then rearranged the bloody knife, the guns, and the two bodies until the crime scene told a credible, if dishonest, story.

"But what exactly is a lie, Charlie? The truth's a pretty slippery thing. Are any words ever one hundred percent honest?"

He was surveying his handiwork when, suddenly, it occurred to him what Melanie had said a few moments before. The words were among the few in his own paltry vocabulary of sign language, words he in fact had signed to her earlier in the evening. "I want to see you again." Was this right? He lifted his hands and repeated the sentence to himself. Awkwardly at first, then smooth as a pro. Yes, he believed that was it.

Arthur Potter saw a car approaching in the distance. Turning his collar against the relentless stream of wind, he sat down on the rocky ground to wait.